BUDDHA IN REDFACE

BUDDHA IN REDFACE

Eduardo Duran Ph.D.

Writers Club Press
New York Lincoln Shanghai

Buddha in Redface

Writers Club Press
an imprint of iUniverse, Inc.

For information address:
iUniverse
2021 Pine Lake Road, Suite 100
Lincoln, NE 68512
www.iuniverse.com

ISBN: 0-595-13898-5

Printed in the United States of America

*When iron birds fly in the sky
and when the iron horse moves across the land,
the Buddha will be in the land of the Redface.*

Prophesied by Padmasambava, Indian Holy Man who introduced
Buddhism into Tibet, circa 700 A.D.

Contents

Acknowledgments

A process such as the one that allowed for the "Buddha in Redface" to emerge is one that necessitates appropriate thanksgiving offerings to the dreamtime itself and then to the people who are in the dream. My heartfelt thanks go to the Old Apache Woman who brought the dream story to me. My gratitude to my original teacher cannot be put into words, and in the language of the dream I leave this as a silent space that can only be understood in that space where silence is aware of itself and the emptiness from which all things emerge.

I want to thank my wife, Bonnie, who gave me the greatest gift one can give anyone in a given lifetime—that is, the gift of the Dharma. It is this gift that provided the thread that was used to weave Aboriginal Dharma with the Dharma of the historical Buddha.

These writing projects are not possible unless there is someone who believes in the process unfolding and is willing to become the midwife who makes the needed adjustments to facilitate the birth of the story. Well into the project the dream dreamed Karen Villanueva. A publicist and agent, Karen has had incredible faith in the story and the desire to get the story to readers. She has been instrumental in the editing process, and without her, the book would not have become the polished work that it is within the present dream.

Karen acquired the services of two wordsmiths, otherwise known as editors. Lisa D'Angelo edited the first version of the third edition, transforming my ramblings into coherent English. Author Margaret Tessler, another warrior of the written word, was enormously helpful during the final editing stage. She proved to be a thorough and gifted line editor, ensuring that the storytelling was as complete, precise, and fluid as the dream would allow without losing the intent or spirit of the story. I am truly grateful for their time, talent, and dedication.

An offering of thanks would not be complete without mentioning the spirit of Coyote, who continues to guide the process through some rough spiritual terrain. Many lessons that appear as obstacles are gifts from Coyote that must be recognized as such. In that process the Howl of Coyote has brought many helpers in the form of Power Dreamers, Dream Sorcerers, and other assorted technicians of the Sacred. Much gratitude to my Native Spiritual leaders Richard Movescamp, Marilyn Youngbird, Daniel Freeland, Kenny Begay, and many others. I also want to thank my Dharma teachers, Joseph Goldstein, Ralph Steele, and many others with whom I have sat for many days in the quest for liberation from the world of illusion. Jim Willems has given me the gift of realizing "Metta," or loving kindness, as a "heart-moment" instead of a concept.

Eduardo Duran

Introduction

*A*s I walk away from the ceremonial field and gravesite, I know that I have been part of something extraordinary. I had been allowed to witness some timeless mysteries that at times threatened what I knew as sanity. I have been privileged to have had a great, and until now, unknown teacher. All of these memories will forever be imprinted in my heart with the powerful images of a man with his powerful simplicity whose insights were lightning bolts to the heart. Olfactory imprints of cedar smoke mixed with fresh earth will remain etched in my soul; smells distinct to his humble home with its earthen floors, a home simply designed for the purpose of meditation and prayer. All that remains is clarity gained through the powerful and paradoxical words of the Buddha in Redface.

The wisdom that was imparted through Tarrence's teachings continues to illuminate issues that presently arise in our world. Recent scandals of sexual abuse in the Catholic Church can be understood through the words that were expressed to me by this humble teacher many years ago. Teachings on the desecration of female energy also shed light on events that have shaken the planet and on the ongoing "terrorism" that continues to threaten life itself through an undifferentiated male psychology.

"There has always been a dream. Everything is still the dream. All that we call creation and Creator is the dream. The dream continues to dream us and to dream itself. Before anyone or anything was, there was a dream, and this dream continued to dream itself until the chaos within the dream became aware of itself. Once the awareness knew that it was, there was a perspective for other aspects of the dream to comprehend itself. One of the emerging dream energies, or 'complexes,' that came from the chaos of the dream and still remains in the dream as a way for the dream to recognize itself, is called 'human beings.' Human beings required a way to have perspective and reference, and because of that, another energy emerged from the dream, and this is known today as 'time.' It is from the two energies of dream and time that the third was given birth to, and that third one is known as the 'dreamtime.' Dreamtime is also known as 'mind,' which is by nature luminescent and pure. And the dreamtime mind is reflected by the emptiness of awareness."

This is how Tarrence talked and thought. These were some of the first words I recall from my earliest contacts with my friend and teacher. Presently Tarrence has returned to the dream, and on occasion he reconnects with the dreamtime so we can visit and continue our discussions. I hope the story that follows gives some insight into some very ancient processes. At the same time, I hope these events illuminate the importance of our actions and thoughts in the timeless karmic strings of awareness that interconnects all awareness.

This story has been in process for many years. Recently a series of events that had their beginnings in a dream made it clear that I had to write the story, although I have not been a storyteller per se. In the dream, an old Apache woman handed me a golden fountain pen. It doesn't take a Freudian or Jungian analyst to figure out the meaning of the dream. I realized I had to write something.

Shortly after that, I told the dream to my friend Harvey. He called me to his house the next day and handed me a small box. In the box was a beautiful fountain pen, thus making the dream materialize in the physical plane. On the card he wrote, "I told her to give you this one, and she wanted that one. The old woman and I finally agreed on this one." Now I knew I had something to write.

I had no outline or story. I wrote a paragraph one morning just to let the old woman in the dream know I was willing to do what I was assigned. It all happened quickly. A sentence was written on the computer for which there was no explanation. The sentence became a paragraph, the paragraph a page, and then another, until finally this story was written.

As for the Manhattan project, all I can say is that this part of the story is true in the dream and also the physical realm. The land on which the bomb was built belonged to my grandfather. Grandpa was expelled at gunpoint from the land when the Manhattan project took over. We have never been compensated for the land, although we have documents signed by Theodore Roosevelt attesting to the ownership of the land forevermore by our family.

Our family has tried to litigate for compensation to no avail. Los Alamos National Laboratory continues to operate on the land, and the spiritual process discussed in this story still continues here. Our story has never been allowed to see the light of day by either the mainstream media and other avenues that might be sensitive to what occurred to a poor family in the 1930s.

Imagine that military people with guns invade your house, kill all your livestock, then tell you to leave. This is what happened to my father and his family when the scientists—referred to as sorcerers in this story—decided that his land was the place to build the destructive fire gourd known as the atomic bomb.

Attempts at getting justice and compensation for our land have not been successful. Senator Domenici of New Mexico has expressed his opinion that there are no legitimate complaints by any of the people who were dispossessed from the Los Alamos area during the time of the Manhattan Project. It is through this kind of insensitivity that the oppression of poor people in this country continues and the voice of the powerless becomes fainter with each passing day. That faint voice will always remain a scream of lamentation to the ears of the Creator, who will dispense ultimate karmic justice.

In this story, there are some areas which may seem beyond the realm of magical realism. There are psychologists who believe in a parallel process in all of life's events and who believe that nothing happens in a vacuum. I believe there are processes that move in an area just underneath the breath of what we perceive to be reality, and these realms are constantly in movement with our physical movements. The spiritual processes that I delineate in this story are as real as the historical events that are part of our daily reality.

We all have to live with the threat and fear of complete devastation of our planet through nuclear contamination or outright holocaust. How can we not think that something with this much potential for evil does not have its roots in some type of evil intent? It is this evil intent and the ramifications thereof that are explored in this story. The story also gives us a way out of these actions laden with evil intent through some teachings of the Buddha, as seen through the eyes of a Native American holy man. Fortunately, through these insights, there is a glimmer of hope that the evil intent can actually be returned into the realm of the Sacred and back to God. As my relatives—the Navajo people—say at the end of each prayer,

"May the Sacred be restored in Beauty. May the Sacred be restored in Beauty. May the Sacred be restored in Beauty. May the Sacred be restored in Beauty…."

Dreamtime

$\mathcal{T}$ arrence was a simple man who lived in the mountains of Northern New Mexico. He was one of the so-called "detribalized Natives" who are scattered through that area. This means that he is an Aboriginal person who does not belong to an official tribe, due to the colonization process in the area.

I was working as a therapist in another state and would consult in the mountains of New Mexico periodically. A couple of people who worked with me at the clinic kept mentioning this person named Tarrence. As far as I knew, he was probably someone in need of psychological help, and he could find help without me. At one point, I simply asked, "Who is Tarrence, and what business do I have with him or does he have with me?"

The reply was confusing: "He goes up to the mountains in his wheel chair and sees. He's been asking about you and what you're doing."

At the time, I was working in a clinic that served Native people. Tarrence was from this community. Since not much of my western training was showing any effectiveness with the patients I was seeing, and since the people I worked with valued dreams, I started utilizing a crude form of dream-analysis therapy.

I felt this would be a good therapeutic intervention in the community, and therefore my time wouldn't be totally wasted with my attempts to implement cognitive behavioral strategies that were unwelcome and made no sense to the people I was working with. It seemed the only time I was able to engage people from this community in any type of treatment was when we worked on dream material. It was in this manner that other interventions were then welcomed and made possible. Without the dream as the vehicle, there was no intervention with individuals, or with the community for that matter.

One day when I was working in the dream community, since this is the best way to describe the place, all my afternoon appointments were canceled. Amy, one of the clinic's client transporters, let me know this would be a good time to go visit Tarrence. Little did I know that my afternoon cancellations were not accidental. Tarrence and Amy had premeditated the meeting.

I got into Amy's truck, and we proceeded to drive up a dirt road that had never been worked on. This path had become a road only because people drove on it repeatedly. There were holes in it that would swallow a small car in one bite if the driver were not aware of how to avoid them. The holes in the road would surprise you when you were well into your travel, unless you had memorized the road from childhood.

It was an ordinary day. It wasn't hot or cold. The wind wasn't blowing; there were just a few clouds moving across the sky. This was the type of day that, if one wasn't aware, many of the remarkable qualities hidden in the daylight itself could be missed and therefore forgotten.

Going up the gnarly road, we came to an old house. It appeared abandoned and unkempt. The mud plaster was almost non-existent, and the bare adobe walls were worn from the weathering the house had been exposed to over a long time. Actually, the adobe from this house looked older than the adobe I had seen at some of the ruins like Chaco Canyon. At the time, I thought that perhaps it was just a lesser-quality adobe that didn't weather as well as the stuff I had seen at Chaco or Aztec.

In retrospect, I understand this was my way of making sense of what was becoming an anxiety-producing trip to see this person of whom I knew nothing. I wondered why I was feeling this type of concern, since I had seen hundreds of people in treatment. This would just be another intake evaluation, and then back to work and life as it had been.

I got out of the truck and noticed that most of the windows on the house were broken or tattered. Yellowing drapes followed the movement of the after-noon breeze and exposed themselves outside the windows. Pine needles were everywhere, and though there was a thick layer, for some inexplicable reason I could see each pine needle individually, with clear precision. The moment dis-appeared and I went on seeing in the usual manner.

The steps to the house were broken, and I crossed the porch carefully. I soon realized I was pretty much on my own; Amy was purposely staying out of the way. I interpreted this as a therapeutic confidentiality issue.

I looked around at the surroundings—mostly pine trees and scrub. The quiet was of a different quality. I had always thought quiet was simply an absence of sound. For the first time in my life I felt as if quiet had its own life, and I had the eerie feeling that silence was its own entity, with an awareness and consciousness. I was aware of the silence being aware of me.

Amy motioned for me to go in. I guess I was expecting to ring a doorbell or to make my presence known in some other way. I stepped inside and discovered there was no one in the room. Now what? I thought to myself. I can't just go looking in someone else's house without a proper invitation.

Furnishings were non-existent, and the dirt floors hadn't been swept in some time. A few old clothes were hanging on nails on the wall, but these hadn't been touched in years, or so it appeared. As I moved into the house, the smell of cedar burning was distinct, and I recalled that cedar is used for prayer purposes by many of the Aboriginal people of the area. Amy was nowhere to be seen, so I decided to go into the next and only other room in the house, which was to the left of where I stood. The cedar smoke started to quiet my mind and my anxiety.

My gaze moved to the left, where I saw an old bed with old bedding, the kind of bedding that was already musty and yellowing when it was obtained from a second-hand store or as a gift from some well-meaning missionary trying to help the Indians. I noticed an assortment of books on psychology and religious studies, as well as several books on Buddhism, on a chair next to the bed. *Discourses of the Buddha* was one of those remarkable books, and it seemed worn from use.

In the middle of the bed was what appeared to be no more than a skeleton with some skin on its bones. Coming out of the skeleton were assorted tubes attached to bags. Yellowish body fluids dripped into the bags. I made eye contact with the face and was greeted by a big smile.

Upon meeting my gaze, he said, "Don't worry, there are other realities," then proceeded to introduce himself as Tarrence. I saw that he was severely paralyzed, and with what little movement he could make, he pushed a twisted hand in my direction so that I could shake it. I was a bit surprised and overwhelmed. What was this day developing into?

My attempts at making conversation were useless and full of meaningless psychobabble, since I was still under the impression that I had been brought here to do some sort of psychological assessment.

Tarrence asked me at one point, "Have you ever seen the colors?"

Of course I had no clue what he was referring to. In my mind, I took this as "intake assessment data" that was starting to lean toward a diagnosis of a thought disorder. I merely responded, "No, I haven't seen the colors."

Tarrence pressed it further. "Do you want me to show them to you?"

For some reason, this question was very troubling, and I found myself experiencing what I can best describe as the beginnings of a panic attack in my stomach.

"Not today," I replied. I wanted to just leave and never come back. I figured I could give my assessment in writing and be done with this whole experience, then let some medical person medicate Tarrence so that he could be more in touch with what my profession calls "reality." I managed to stay present. Tarrence, sensing my discomfort, made light talk.

He went on for a while. "You see, I've been here for over thirty years. I was in an accident and became paralyzed. During all this time, I've read all kinds of things, and I spend a lot of time watching my mind or meditating. Twice a year they take me up the mountain where I sit and see. Things have not gone well for my community for quite some time. There is much of what you might call unhealthy living, and there is a lot of drinking of alcohol, and recently, a lot of drug abuse.

"My grandparents were involved in healing work, but they were some of the last ones who took on that sort of life. As you know, it's a very difficult life, and healing work leaves nothing for yourself. You can't be too selfish and live in that way. I've heard about you and some of the work you're trying to do in this community. I hear that you work with dreams also?"

At this point, I didn't realize this was really an assessment of me, and not the other way around. Later I found out that Tarrence's people had been using dream interpretation as a key traditional healing method for at least seven thousand years or so, according to the anthropological literature. The main reason for his concern was that dreams could be used not only for healing but also for a more sinister reason. His community had a history in which sorcery was performed in the dreamtime, causing sickness and death to targeted people. Therefore, his question was more than rhetorical.

I answered, "Yes, that's one of the approaches that seems to work when I'm with some of the patients in this area. They seem to become more open and warm up to the process when I ask them if they're dreaming anything."

Tarrence asked very seriously, "Where did you learn to do this?"

I was getting more comfortable, since we were covering what was more my area.

"I've taken a couple of courses in my program, and I've studied Freud and Jung and how they approach the whole subject."

Tarrence, a bit more relaxed, asked, "Where do you get the power to do this, and do you dream?"

This caught me off guard. I quickly resorted to my training where disclosure has its place in practice but has to be clinically warranted. Therefore I chose to go around the question and gave the stupidest response that western therapists have in their bag of tricks.

"Why do you ask?"

He smiled and said, "Just a curiosity. Don't mind my nosiness."

"It's all right."

"Could I ask you a silly question?" Tarrence asked.

"Why, of course; anything."

"What were you doing this morning when you ate your breakfast?"

"What? Are you serious?"

"I wouldn't ask if I really didn't want to know."

"I guess I was eating breakfast, listening to the radio, reading the paper, and planning the day."

"In other words, you weren't eating breakfast—your mind was kind of wandering," he said with a smile.

"I guess...now that you mention it. What else can one do while eating breakfast?"

"Be aware that you're eating breakfast," he said kindly, with a crooked smile.

Some of the muscles in his face must have weakened, I thought. What in the hell is this guy talking about? I was wondering if perhaps he had a serious thought disorder, with some underlying organic or brain-disorder components complicating the clinical picture.

Amy appeared in the room to let me know it was time to leave. I was a bit puzzled since there had been so much energy expended in bringing me here, and now in just a few minutes, it was time to leave. Amy, being clever, made some excuse about how she had to transport some people to the clinic and needed to get back soon.

Tarrence smiled and said, "Come back so I can show you the colors—and next time you put on your shoes, take notice of what you are doing."

"We'll see. It's been nice meeting you."

We left the house and said nothing on the way back into town. Amy seemed to be at peace with what was going on, and I tried to maintain a professional demeanor, thinking I was involved in a difficult assessment, but that was all. I also thought it would be wise to get a consultation on the case from a friend and colleague. In this manner, the case would progress, and I would stay away from common errors that are made in these so-called cross-cultural situations.

My profession at that time was beginning to be very concerned with such things, and I wanted to make sure the ethics of the case remained aboveboard. My feelings of ambiguity were to become part of the ongoing process. On one hand, I had my western training. On the other, there was an unconscious blood inheritance of an awareness, one that did not rely on linearity as its root metaphor.

2

Visit with Dr. Jones

$\mathcal{L}$ater that evening, I called my friend and associate Carl Jones to set up a time to talk about some of the cases I was encountering in my work with the Indigenous folks.

"Hello," he said.

"Yeah, Carl, when can we go and suck up some cappuccinos and talk about cases, theory, and the like. We haven't done this in a bit, and I need to run down some stuff to you."

"Hey, how about tomorrow? I've got an hour before lunch, and we can sit for a while and catch up. I miss these meetings myself. We should do this more often."

"OK, catch you at the Latte' Hey coffee shop."

"Sounds like a plan, my man." Carl tried to show his cultural sensitivity to me by using what he thought was Black slang, and it bothered me a bit when he did this. It seemed incongruous with who he was—an aspiring yuppie and "wannabe" great psychiatrist.

Tuesday morning arrived. I'd had some disturbing dreams the night before, although I couldn't remember all of the content. I thought this might be some material for the conversation later in the day.

I met with two clients at the office before setting off for the Latte' Hey. As I was driving, I realized that working with White clients is qualitatively different from working with Native clients, but I couldn't quite get clarity as to what this might be. More stuff for the meeting with Carl, I thought.

Carl was a cognitive behavioral psychiatrist who thought if a person had a mental-health problem, it had to do with brain chemistry, or that the problem could be solved with cognitive strategies, or both. He did a lot of research and wrote endless journal articles on the topic. He was born somewhere in the Midwest and hadn't seen a person of color until he went to graduate school. All of his developmental milestones were accomplished within a very Euro-phalo-centric world, and he was thoroughly convinced that this was the only way of life. Carl believed that as soon as the whole world subscribed to his truth, then peace and some sort of utopian society would emerge.

He tried his best to take on what he thought was an "ethnic" appearance, complete with ponytail, jeans, and boots. Somehow he never managed to pull off the look. If someone was fooled for an instant by Carl's appearance, one word out of his mouth was enough to dispel any notion that he was anything but Midwest middle-class folk with little or no contact with different cultures or religious viewpoints.

His family tree included several relatives who had been missionaries in Africa and South America. Ingrained into his family psyche was the belief that the only truth for everyone was the one espoused by the Judeo-Christian tradition. These roots went deep in Carl's psyche, and although he tried to appear open-minded, he didn't have much tolerance for differences in people or opinions.

I must admit that through the educational process, I had bought into many of the ideas Carl sold. Although I'd achieved a very different set of developmental milestones, I liked the precision of the western logical "positivist" model that took care of the ambiguities I had learned during my developmental years.

After all, what is so wrong with wanting to see, feel, weigh, and quantify everything? By definition, things were not anything unless you could do this quantification exercise. As for other things or notions that involved a more intuitive or transpersonal cognition, well, that was for people like Tarrence and my grandparents, who really didn't understand the real world. At least that's what I thought at this time.

I arrived at the Latte' Hey coffee shop, named after a popular Navajo greeting, "Ya-te-hey," meaning "hello," that had become part of the regional slang. At the door were some regulars—homeless people selling underground newspapers or just asking for change. I usually ignored them and what they said as I walked by.

I made my way past several small tables occupied by people deep into all types of interdisciplinary discussions that ranged from rocket science to herbal and massage therapies. New Mexico had really changed since I was growing up, and the aging New Agers were thriving and getting many converts from the congregations of mainstream academic and technical circles.

The tables were covered with books and backpacks, as well as empty coffee mugs, foaming cappuccinos, and all sorts of extravagant pastries. I saw Carl in the corner already sucking the foam off his drink.

"My man," he said as soon as he saw me, and I shuddered at his saying this in public. I made a mental note to bring up the subject with him someday.

"Carl, how's things?" I said, and noticed that he'd taken the liberty of ordering my breakfast.

What a presumptuous asshole. Not only does he know what's the best way to think for all of humanity, he even knows what I want for breakfast, I thought—a little guiltily since he had ordered exactly what I wanted.

"What's going on, my man? Looks like you lost your best friend or something," Carl said.

"Oh, nothing really. Some of the work I've been doing in the mountains has been bothering me. I think I could use a consultation."

Carl's face lit up. He loved knowing things and talking about it. I could see that he wanted to set this straight for me, and he'd enjoy doing so.

"Let's have it," he said. "There's nothing that can't be solved using reality-based cognitive behavioral psychology, my man. All the way from my main man Skinner to the rest of the lineage up to now, we've figured out how to deal with all of it. Know what I'm sayin'?"

My God, he's getting worse, I thought. He really needs to stop consulting with the adolescent drug-treatment program; he just doesn't fit into that world.

"Carl," I started, "I've been having some interesting experiences in my work up in the mountains. A lot of our therapeutic techniques are just not getting through with the patients. Also, I've been having some weird and disturbing dreams."

"Of course they'll work. These will work with anyone and everyone. It must be a matter of approach. And dreams, you say? Hey, my man, you are joking, aren't you! You can't possibly be serious about dreams and stuff that's not rational or quantifiable. Remember what my main man Dave Hume said: 'If you can't weigh it or measure it, burn it.' Know what I'm sayin'?"

"Yes, I know, but this is bothering me—and that's an objective reality. I can measure my subjective units of distress if I want to, right?"

"Shit, you are serious about this. Sorry, man, I see. So, let's see what you got, where these cognitions are coming from, and how you can make sense of the cognitive storyline. You know that's the best way to approach this."

"Of course, you're right on this. You see, most of the patients I'm seeing up in the mountains are Native people or people with Native roots. They see the world differently, and my putting everything in a cognitive context is just not making sense to them. We must be ethical, after all, and deliver culturally sensitive treatments, eh? Oh, and another thing. I met this old guy, Tarrence, and this has been especially bothersome. He's also in my dreams now."

"Slow down, my man. Say one thing at a time. We need to dissect this stuff with the precision of the science in which we've been trained. Let's take the treatment strategy thing first. And yeah, yeah, I hear you on the cultural sensitivity stuff, but we can't be going in there with our hands tied when we know what works. We need to maybe put another wrapping on the truth so that it's a tastier morsel."

Carl took a huge bite of his muffin, causing crumbs to spread all over his beard. He then sucked on his cappuccino, and milk foam began building on top of the earlier crusty milk foam on his mustache. He looked like a wild man.

I was going to reply, but Carl interrupted me. "I know you have roots in that area, and you have grandparents or ancestors who thought differently, but you have learned the truth, and they can do the same. It's a matter of staying with what you know is right. What greater sensitivity could one have than to give the gift of Socratic thought to folks who are stuck in pre-enlightenment thinking? Now that's not only sensitive, it's our human duty to save the leftover pagans of the world…. Well, you know what I mean."

Having many relatives in the area where I was working, I didn't feel right about what Carl was saying. Although I was getting agitated, I knew Carl didn't mean any harm with his demeaning statements. I wondered, though, if push came to shove, how he would really respond. I decided to keep talking, since I needed to vent about some of the work situation.

"Carl, you've heard that there might be other ways of seeing the world, other epistemologies, as you call them. Some of these might actually be legitimate ways of conceptualizing the world. After all, the western worldview is about to end life as we know it. This can't be a good thing, can it? I know that all this cognitive behavioral stuff is good and helps people. Still, I can't help but wonder if imposing it, whether by force or by trickery, wouldn't cause more harm than good. There's research on this, you know. After all, wasn't this the whole colonizing approach that brought so much destruction in the first place?"

Carl almost choked on his muffin and had to drink some coffee quickly so he could respond. "Now you are losing it, my man. No one, especially not me, is trying to colonize anyone. You're sounding like one of those ignorant radicals that have a cause for everything. We are scientists and we are objective! We don't have the luxury to entertain this mealy-mouth, bleeding-heart shit!"

His eyes and face were red; some internal psychic button had been pushed. I wondered why would he get so upset over such an unthreatening discussion as ours if he were so sure of the truth. Could it be that he wasn't as sure of himself as he appeared?

"Calm down, Carl, you're starting to attract attention. I'm not saying you're wrong in what you believe. As scientists we have to keep an open mind, and as social scientists we must keep all of our so-called science within the context of history."

Again, Carl couldn't contain himself. "'*So-called*' science? And what's this fuckin' '*context of history*' shit? You need to think about what you're saying. What the hell does history have to do with scientific objectivity? Our science is based on numbers and data, not some pie-in-the-sky, historical, tired Marxist shit. Look at where all that got the rest of the world."

"Come on, Carl, you're smart enough to know that all this data and objectivity is a setup in order to keep the fat cats getting fatter—and keep the poor, especially the poor coloreds, in the toilet," I retorted.

"Not you, too, with the colored shit now. Why does everything have to come to that? We're scholars, man, and to reduce everything to race issues is a cheap shot. It's a 'Catch Twenty-Two,' cuz at this point, no matter what I say will be wrong. We need to stay objective and stay with what we know science has proven to be true," Carl said in a voice that was becoming more insecure.

"All right, relax," I said calmly. "We can't leave anything uncovered though. At any rate, I came here to talk about clinical issues and kind of get some of your scientific objectivity with the work I'm doing up in the mountains. Also, this Tarrence fellow…. I keep thinking about him. I don't even know why. He's a nice enough person, but I can't help but wonder who he really is. What and how does he think, and all that."

"OK, sorry I lost it. It should be interesting to see what happens in this cross-cultural work," Carl muttered.

I was in a deeper thought process as I said, "You know, Carl, I have close ancestors who lived up in those mountains. My dad was raised up there, and my grandparents used to own the land where the bomb was built."

"What bomb?"

"What bomb, you ask! There's only one bomb, man. The one that can destroy all life: the atomic bomb."

"Are you shittin' me? Come on, get real. Why are you joking like this?" Carl asked in disbelief.

"No joke. When Oppenheimer and the rest of his homies came out in the Thirties to scout out the place for the bomb, they chose my grandpa's land. One day the army came, killed all his animals, gave him a couple hundred bucks, and said get the hell out. Because of national security and such, there was no recourse except leave or get shot along with all the cows and horses. It's pretty interesting that I'm working up there now, huh? It's almost like a synchronistic thing or something."

"Oh, please don't even bring up that Jungian stuff. You know all that Jungian psychology shit is based on total non-science and borders on some kind of occultist religion. I mean Jung himself was nuts most of his life, and his work is total unscientific unsubstantiated bullshit. Most of those analysts walk around in a half-psychotic state most of the time," Carl responded with new-found energy.

Anytime Carl's perfectly created scientific cosmology was in the least threatened, he became very agitated and defensive. It was as if he really didn't totally buy into it himself, and his views were fragile enough that he was afraid to have them shatter right in front of him.

I was open to these other ways of seeing how the human psyche worked and had already begun to read a lot of Jung's writings. I was being secretive about it so colleagues like Carl wouldn't think badly of me. I realized that the work I'd been doing was not going to be enough to deal with the needs of the mountain community, and I was trying to learn as much about psychology that came from a non-linear paradigm as possible. My grandparents believed in a different cosmology, although I had been socialized through the educational process to attempt to understand everything via the rationalism of western science.

"Well, Carl, any words of wisdom before I head back up there? What would you say to someone like Tarrence? Would you try to convince him that his way of seeing the world might need a tune-up, or what? What about the community people who look up to him? What is the transference going to be like for me? These are all things I worry about, and I'm isolated, and there's no literature to consult," I related in a voice that indicated "let's finish our coffee and go."

"Just don't forget the tools of objectivity that you've spent most of your life learning. Don't get sucked into some occultist, primitive psychological hole that might threaten your standing in the professional community. Keep good notes, and let's talk frequently. I'm interested in everything that's going on there."

"OK, thanks for the talk. I'll be calling you sooner than later, I think…. By the way, how do you put on your shoes?"

"What in the hell…. Are you serious?" he muttered.

"Yeah, that Tarrence guy asked me to watch how I do it and also asked how I eat breakfast."

"My man, I think you might be dealing with a very disturbed person. He might need some major tranquilizers. Sounds like word salad or very loose associations at best," Carl said confidently.

"Well, I'll do more assessing and let you know," I said as I got up to leave.

"Be cool, my man, and just remember who your homies are," Carl said, as he regressed and tried to get back to being something he wasn't. His attempts at playing the part were embarrassing, as usual.

3

Reflections

*I*t would be a few days before I went back up to the mountain community to see patients. In the meantime, I'd be seeing other patients in a private-practice setting in the city and doing hospital work as well. Already I was realizing that the work I did in the city and the work I did in the mountains were as different as the settings themselves. The problems, interventions, and the air itself were so different—and yet I had only one set of tools to deal with both sets of issues.

How could the rationally oriented therapies of the west have a healing effect to a group of people who didn't necessarily think this way? What are the ethical issues involved in forcing western therapies down the throats of people who were already suffering from problems that were a result of the loss of most of their life-world, and the subsequent replacement by a life-world which still made no sense to them?

I remembered my childhood and the way of life my grandparents had. It was a simpler lifestyle; things in the world were viewed differently and in a more intuitive manner, although the life that they led was still far removed from the manner in which *their* grandparents had lived. Somewhere in the previous generations there must have been a point in time where the harmonious relationship with the life-world was broken and the relationship became more antagonistic.

These were my thoughts now, as I tried to make sense of what was going on with my work. I was trying to find a technique, method, or theoretical approach that would fit the task like a template; then I could just go in there and help solve problems and see the results. The training I had required this type of approach. At least I could use Carl as a sounding board, and even his immature tantrums were tolerable simply to have some dialogue on the matter.

The night before I went back to the mountains, I was a bit anxious, and I had a dream. In the dream, there was a huge and overbearing doctor in a white coat. He was treating an Indian patient whose size was tiny in comparison. I woke up with the clear images in my mind, and wondered exactly what this dream meant. Could it be that the western medical model might indeed be what is needed here? I knew that the dream was important to the process I was involved in, but didn't let it take too much of my energy at this point.

I was sure of what Carl would say about the dream. Although he claimed that dreams were useless, he would assume the dream was deifying the western medical model over the "primitive" or "pagan" model of healing.

The whole notion of eating breakfast and putting my shoes on kept bothering me. I really didn't think Tarrence was schizophrenic; on the other hand, he didn't make much sense. Probably some regional cultural joke he's playing on me. That was the best I could come up with for the time being.

Tuesday morning I made my way up to the community. On the side of the road, I saw a large eagle that was struggling and appeared either sick or injured. Its feathers were in bad shape, and there was dirt all over it. I had never seen an eagle outside a cage before, therefore I thought this was an important sighting that could mean something, although I still had no idea what.

4

Patient Chavez

During the first day back in the mountains, I realized that many of the presenting problems began to resemble each other. There was a tremendous amount of grief in the people I was seeing. I gathered this information about their angst from short sessions, since the patients didn't really have trust in the process, or in me.

I need to mention that the people in this community came from different tribes, and many of the tribes were very small. Some of the tribes that used to exist even two generations ago had since ceased to be. Due to the colonization process, many of the people who used to live in this area were victims of genocide, either through direct military means or through eradication of culture. Some of the smaller tribes had a few remnants of the Aboriginal traditional ways that used to be. Some had none. Much of the spiritual belief system had been eradicated and replaced with the daily practice of alcohol or some other spiritual substitute.

An older woman was referred to me, although it wasn't clear why. When I first saw Ms. Chavez, she was friendly and didn't appear to have the depressive and addictive symptoms I was seeing so frequently. She carried herself in a respectful manner, and the introductions went smoothly. I also noticed she was carrying a small book that looked like a diary of some sort.

"Well, Ms. Chavez, what brings you to the mental health clinic? Are you experiencing some problems?"

"No, not really. I know that I need to talk to you because I saw myself talking to you in a dream."

Now this was a new one on me. I thought that transference between patient and doctor took some time to develop, and then dreams and fantasies would follow. I had never seen this woman before, and she was already dreaming about me. I wasn't prepared to respond to this.

"Really? Was it me or someone in my position that you saw in the dream?" I questioned, hoping it was a general dream that I could make sense out of.

"It was you," she answered firmly.

I needed to buy some time. My next approach was to get away from this particular topic and proceed with background information. I decided to let her know a little of how dreams were useful in therapy—at least what little information I had from my training, which was practically none.

"I see that dreams are important to you. It's useful to write dreams down in a journal so that you can have a continuity of them."

She took the diary in one hand, brought it close to me, and said, "I've been doing that for years. I'm a dreamer, and dreams have been the way we used to do what you call therapy for many generations."

I felt very outclassed and was wondering why this old woman even came to see me—besides the fact that she saw me in a dream. What to do now? Of course: Proceed with intake questions, which I could stretch out for the rest of the session.

Why was I feeling so uncomfortable? I tried to think about how Carl in his rational approach would solve this. Rationality would help my thought process but not the deep anxiety that was developing in the pit of my stomach. My mind jumped to Jung and his notion of psychological contamination. Was I in fact taking on some deep anxiety that she was feeling? She didn't appear anxious, nor did she report any anxiety. My mind raced to Tarrence for some reason, and this only served to deepen my concern.

"I can see that dreams are of significance to you," was my attempt at a weak interpretation that might slow this process down enough so that I could get back in control of the session.

"They are, and they have been to my people for many generations. From the beginning, you might say. By the way, did you dream of me?" she responded in a friendly and kind manner.

I really didn't know what to say. I didn't want to ruin the beginnings of a therapeutic relationship by having no idea of what to tell her. However nothing I could say that came from my training would suffice. This woman wasn't being contrary or resistant. Her questions were genuine, and her dreams appeared to be a very ordinary part of her life.

I decided that honesty was the best policy. Simple honesty would in no way compromise my professional standing with the woman, and it would give me time to study the topics that she presented.

"No, not yet," I replied.

"Oh, well, maybe you will soon. I'm sure that you're the right person I need to talk to, otherwise I wouldn't have seen you in the dream. I guess I'll leave now and come back to see you another time," she said, as she got up with the use of a cane.

I had never had a first session in which I didn't do an appropriate intake. Nor had I had a session that ended in this manner, in which the patient had so much control over the process.

"I'll be glad to see you again," I said.

"Maybe by then you will have had a dream about me.

"You never know," was my weak comeback.

"You will, don't worry. This isn't so mysterious. We're all part of the awareness called the dreamtime. We're just bits of illusion scattered in the dreamtime, not realizing that all we are is part of the dream. You see, there is an eye of awareness in which all else becomes aware of it. All of this is empty, yet there is knowing. It works the way it's supposed to."

I was left bewildered and confused. What is this dreamtime business and the awareness? She sounds a bit like Tarrence. Is there some sort of community joke being carried out systematically? And what the hell was that eye of the awareness stuff?

I enjoyed the thought of seeing Carl's reaction. He would go nuts coming up with a logical solution to this situation. Having gone through the Carl-consultation-scenario in my mind, I realized I needed real help on this case and on many of the cases I was seeing.

Someone had referred me to a therapist in another town who was trained in Jungian dream work. This would be at least a straw to hold on to. I found her card in the corner drawer of the desk. "Dr. Beerli, depth therapy and dream work" was written in cursive. Different kind of name, I thought, but I would have to give her a call soon.

Most of that day went on with patients coming in for a quick consult on children's behavior problems or with alcohol and drug-addiction problems. Most of the interventions I did were problem-solving, although most of the patients insisted on telling me at least one dream. For the most part, I would listen to the dream and offer some obvious advice, and this seemed to suffice for the time being.

An interesting feeling prevailed most of the afternoon—the feeling was that I wanted, or needed, to go see Tarrence. Why this feeling persisted was beyond me, but I made time to go see him the next morning. I had the secretary block off two hours with lunch right after, and I thought at least I would enjoy the ride and the time to contemplate the surroundings and get to know this man a little more.

He seemed to know a lot about the people here, and since he was a natural historian, who knows what else he knew? Keep an open mind and just see what happens, I said to myself, although I felt some apprehension at the idea of going to see Tarrence all by myself. Where the apprehension was coming from was a mystery to me, but as they teach in graduate school, "There is no growth without at least a little anxiety."

5

Second Visit With Tarrence

*T*oward the middle of the following day, I got into my truck, Ruby, and went to visit Tarrence. I really didn't have any expectations. A mixture of curiosity and an underlying hope that he would help make sense of the work I was attempting, such as the work with Ms. Chavez and her dreams, prompted the visit.

The day was warm, and the early morning rain had left a distinct smell in the air. The mingled scents of earth, pine, and cedar seemed unique to this particular place. As I drove from the paved road to the dirt road, the stillness had a profound presence of its own. I wondered if stillness might not be a real consciousness. A strange thought or feeling was emerging in my mind. Is the stillness aware of me? It definitely appears to be that way. What's going on with this? This makes no rational sense, and stillness is just the absence of things going on. How can this be any more than that?

Carl would definitely think this was a bizarre notion and would admonish me that I'm losing touch with my training and objectivity. Nevertheless this is happening, and as a scientist, shouldn't I take note of the internal events? After all, this is what we ask patients to do all the time. I became caught up in this internal dialogue and almost missed the turnoff from the dirt road to the unkempt road that led to Tarrence's place.

I had to slow down now, since the road was treacherous and the morning rain had left it extra slippery and slick. Later I wondered if this was not some sort of parallel process that reflected my own personal journey at that time. Much later I became certain it was. Slowing down allowed me to see the drops of rain hanging on to the pine needles and waiting for the right moment to let go. "How does the raindrop know when it's time to let go?" I asked myself out loud.

Somewhere in the forest, a woodpecker was at work, and I wondered how it could vibrate its head so fast and not sustain some type of brain injury.

As I attempted to accelerate, the back of the truck fishtailed, and I realized that the slow speed had to be maintained; trying to hurry up would only bring an element of danger to the situation.

I thought about what to say about eating breakfast and putting my shoes on. Nothing I came up with made sense. Maybe it was one of those Japanese Zen exercises—like the sound of one hand clapping. It had to be something like that. That is, if he's serious and not just being funny; or maybe he does have a thought disorder. In that case, I guess meds would keep him from further nonsense, stuff that might be harmful to him anyway.

At last I could see the house in the distance. What a simple house and way to live. Wonder what it would be like to never leave this place and be stuck here most of your life? My thoughts wandered. It would have to be very depressing, and maybe this is what I needed to get Tarrence to realize. A dash of Prozac or Zoloft, he'd be as good as new, and he'd be able to maximize his life's options, I decided.

The curious part of my visit is that I came because I wanted to see him. This wasn't a professional visit. This was something I had never done in my career. After all, this would disturb the therapeutic transference and wouldn't be in keeping with the demeanor of the profession. That thought passed through my mind as a quick flash of insight. For the time being, I would consider this an interesting exercise and let it go at that. I did not attend to the sense of urgency I felt about visiting Tarrence. Realizing there was urgency would have been more than my mind, which was under logical positivistic socialization, could handle at this time.

I arrived at the house and saw that everything was quiet; it appeared that no one was around. As I approached the door, I tried to make noise on the wooden steps to alert Tarrence that I was coming. I knocked on his door, then came in and went to his room.

Tarrence was in a half-sitting position, wearing a cheap pair of WalMart reading glasses and holding one of the books on Buddhism. He looked up and gave me a crooked smile. I was certain it was lopsided due to the paralysis or some brain problem rather than just the way he smiled.

"Hello. How are you?" Tarrence started the conversation. "Been expecting you, and I'm glad you're finally here. Hope the drive was nice for you."

I wondered how he could be expecting me. Perhaps Amy had alerted him since she knew the entire goings-on of the clinic.

"I've been fine. Working and trying to be of some help with the people here. I notice you're reading about Buddhism. There's a lot to that way of thinking." I was trying to be observant.

"There is a lot and there is not much. It's all in a way of seeing. You know? It's a matter of seeing and not looking. What the Buddha said in his teachings is the same as the teachings of our people. I just find it interesting to see the parallels," Tarrence said casually.

I realized I was meeting with a very intelligent and extraordinary man. I was a bit ashamed at the assumptions I had made about him. I became aware that I had stereotyped him simply because of where he lived and because he was so poor. In addition, the fact that he had been in that bed for over thirty years influenced my impressions. My training had taught me to think in a manner that wasn't respectful to the person but merely allowed me to think in terms of diagnostic categories and pathology. My mind had been trained to travel down a path in which sickness was the main issue of interest when being with people like Tarrence.

"So are you a Buddhist?" I asked. "I see that you're reading the discourses of the Buddha. What little I know about that has been very reassuring."

"No, I wouldn't say I was or am a Buddhist. Saying you are Buddhist would in itself show that you don't understand the teaching. See, being anything is not being a Buddhist, because in thinking you are anything, then you're attached to that idea or mind state. There is no essence to being a Buddhist. But some people would say that I am, in principle, although his teachings and the teachings of our people are very similar," Tarrence reiterated.

"Really?"

"Yes.... Lying here in this bed has allowed me to practice unhampered for over thirty years. The mind can achieve great concentration when it lies in a very still body like the one I'm using now. It's through concentration—that is, the right concentration—that the heart opens with love and compassion. Of course, there are hindrances that need to be reckoned with."

"Right concentration? What hindrances? I didn't know there was a wrong concentration."

"Yes, there is. For instance, you can concentrate on the hindrances of the mind and that would be wrong—or let's say unskillful—concentration, and it would lead to everything but an open heart. Hindrances are those states of mind that get in the way of having an open heart: desire, aversion, laziness, excited mind, anger, jealousy, and greed. These hindrances actually take up the space, if there were space of the actual concentration and still mind.

"Of course it's all empty, but for the sake of discussion, I say it like this," Tarrence continued. "These are the aspects of the mind that lead to a sense of self when you get attached to them. There is a sequence to all this, and it starts with the senses and perception. Once you perceive, then the door opens to pleasure or pain, attachment and clinging. Clinging only leads to a new birth of empty ego that dies as soon as it arises, and so on. I'm sure you probably already know all this. After all, you're very highly educated."

"Not really. My education has been pretty narrow, and these things you talk about I have only surface knowledge of."

"That you know of. All of the knowledge of countless lifetimes is there when you open your heart."

"If you say so. What was that about breakfast and the shoes anyway?"

With great laughter, Tarrence answered, "Those are ways that you can still your mind and get concentration. That is, by being in the moment and being aware of what you're doing. Most people never taste their breakfast or even know how they chew and swallow. It's important to be present in what you're doing," Tarrence said in a manner that indicated his personal knowledge of this.

Listening to Tarrence, I realized I was outclassed in the topic we were discussing. My interest perked up, and I wanted to be here with him at this moment. My anxiety was gone. This poor, paralyzed man had so much depth, and I had only been thinking of diagnosing him. All of my training was prefaced on finding pathology. The way I saw people was through diagnostic categories, and while I'd been searching for a label, here was a man who was simply a human being. My mind began to question much of what I'd been doing.

"I would like to hear more about that sometime, if you don't mind," I said.

"Oh, yes, I guess we could do that. I see that you continue to work with the folks here. How is that going?"

"To tell you the truth, not so well. I've been getting some patients who require care in a way that I'm not used to. I saw this elderly woman who asked me if I was dreaming about her, and I had no idea how to respond to that," I said, not realizing that I really didn't want to divulge too much about my work. I wondered immediately why I had revealed this information and felt slightly panicky. It didn't help when Tarrence just burst out laughing in a manner I thought inappropriate.

"Dreaming—that is our way. Everything comes from the dream. All of our medicine comes from the dream. All teachings, the Buddha, God, all are the dream. Our relatives from the north call this the 'eye of the awareness.' Our Tibetan cousins call this 'big mind' or 'the awareness.' That's what she's talking about. It's the awareness, the emptiness, that's the mirror for the natural luminescence of the mind. She wants to know if you know about the dreamtime," Tarrence said slowly, glancing at me sideways and giving me his crooked smile.

"I know a little about dreams and psychology, but this dreamtime business I'm not too sure about," I answered hesitantly.

"It all leads to the same place. There is only one place that is in balance and harmony within the dream. This is a place of complete concentration. The Buddha calls it Samadhi. By the way, when I say 'the Buddha,' I don't mean the man—he has nothing to do with a personal existence. The Buddha is a place of freedom from all the crazy mind states that we get into. This freedom has always been, and has been here with our people.

"You might even say there has always been a Buddha in Redface," Tarrence added with a slight giggle in a voice that still held strong conviction and understanding.

Tarrence's last statement gave me a slight shiver, yet created a tranquil assuredness. *Buddha in Redface*, what a concept, I thought. Images began to stir in my psyche. It makes sense that the Buddha is a construct and not a person, therefore it is everyone at anytime, just as my limited reading in the area had taught me. I was sure Tarrence would have something to say at the notion that I saw this as a concept, but I had no idea how else to frame what he was alluding to. In essence, he was saying that these spiritual ideas are collective, if I recalled my *Jungian 101*. Therefore, Buddha in Redface was a logical idea. This made me feel I was on track understanding what he was saying. I still didn't have much of a clue to this dreamtime stuff that he alluded to.

"I sort of see what you're saying about the Redface Buddha. It has to do with the awareness and not the man," I said, trying to show my understanding.

"Yes, yes…. Not the man. Although there has to be the man too, since the man was," Tarrence replied, again with the giggle and side-glance.

I thought Tarrence was playing mind games with me. He said one thing in one breath, then changed to another. Not only that, he appeared to be enjoying this game at my expense. Resentment stirred, and I began to think I didn't need this type of roundabout discussion. After all, I came here for a purpose. I wanted to learn a little about how the people here used dreams in a traditional healing method, and all I was getting was this far-off-track discussion on the Buddha and whatnot.

"This is going somewhere, although somewhere is really nowhere, so don't worry about it," Tarrence said, as if reading my thoughts.

"Oh, I have no doubt. But what I really came here for in the first place was to discuss how dreams are used in traditional healing."

"That's what we've been talking about." Tarrence was still smiling.

"I'll take your word for it. I guess I'm a little more structured about these things, and I thought it would be more like a case conference where everything is outlined in a logical manner," I said, thinking at this point I could use some of Carl's rational consultation.

"One thing at a time. Can't rush into things. Things have a way of working their own way, in their own time. All of nature does this, and we're part of nature, right? Just trust that you're doing what you're doing for a purpose that was decided even before you came into this dream in this lifetime. It's all there," Tarrence said in a fatherly voice.

"Thank you for saying so, although I really don't get much of what you're saying."

"Maybe not with your head. Your heart understands this already. It might give you some anxiety, but this is just the head struggling to keep control over something that it cannot control. In your own dreams, and in the work you're doing here, this will reveal itself.

"Patience is also important. It's like the leaves on the aspen tree. They open when their nature tells them to open. Any interference with this will only result in the destruction of the leaf—this is an insult on life. So, allow the nature of mind to take its course. Your task is to be there and be aware as it happens.

"Now I can tell you a bit about some of the dream history of our people," Tarrence continued in a low sad voice.

"I appreciate this. Also, I am thankful for your time," I politely stated.

"There has always been a dream. Everything is still the dream. That which we call creation and Creator is the dream. The dream continues to dream us and to dream itself. Before anyone or anything, there was a dream; and this continued to dream itself until the chaos within the dream became aware of itself. Once the awareness knew that it was there, there was a perspective for other aspects of the dream to comprehend itself.

"One of the emerging dream energies, or as you call them, 'complexes,' that came from the chaos of the dream and still remains in the dream, and that the dream recognizes itself, is called 'human beings.' Human beings required a further way to have perspective and reference, and because of that, another energy emerged from the dream, and this is known today as 'time.' It is from the two energies of dream and time that the third was given birth to, and that third one is known as the 'dreamtime.'

"Of course, this was in the beginning, but we must have awareness of the essence of what you're talking about when you discuss your patients here and now. The history of our particular people is also of importance. There was a time when we were all in harmony with the dreamtime, and all was done in balance with the dream. Something happened a long time ago that had a profound effect on this relationship. It happened not too far from here, and this will be something we can discuss or experience more directly at another time. For now it will suffice to say that things are not in balance, as you well know from some of the work you've been doing here."

As Tarrence was talking, I could feel myself becoming very relaxed, and I began to have images as in a dream, although I was fully awake. Tarrence continued to talk, and I was no longer aware of his voice or words. Instead, I was *seeing* what he was saying. I saw myself in a cave, and Tarrence was there pointing out some things. In the pictograph, I saw that there was a circle of people, and in the center was one person of obvious importance. The people in the circle had arrows flying toward the person in the center. It was some sort of execution. Then I could hear Tarrence's voice again.

"That's how it happened. We forgot that we were part of the dreamtime. Many of the dream healers began to think that the dream was a part of them and not the other way around. At this point, they began to be hurtful in the dream. They started using power in an exploitive manner in order to gain material wealth and favors. They started using the wrong type of concentration; they started to rely on their sense of self, which doesn't exist in the first place.

"From the sense of self, their concentration focused on selfish motives, and in their ignorance they caused a lot of suffering. So the people had only one choice and that was to send them back into the dreamtime, or death, as some would say. In this way, they could continue to learn and develop so they would stop operating from their own egos.

"Actually, that's one of the reasons I wanted to see you," he continued. "When I heard that people were telling you their dreams, I became concerned that you might be one of these dream healers who uses dreams to hurt people. Then I saw that you still didn't have conscious awareness of what was going on, and I wanted to be of help. You see, not knowing things is even more dangerous than using the worst kind of sorcery in a conscious way."

"So you're saying that they killed the healers, shamans, or whatever they were called, because they started to use their therapies in a destructive way?"

"You catch on quick. You see, all healers have this potential. You cannot be a true healer if you don't have access to the other side of power, which is evil, which is basically ignorance. This ignorance is usually interpreted as evil. There really is no evil in the original awareness of the dreamtime. You must be aware of these things. Otherwise, you're just half a healer, and that's pretty useless. Might as well be a college professor and just spout off stuff without really having an impact on healing what has been ailing our people for generations." Tarrence said this in a manner that indicated he wasn't going to say a lot more today.

"You know, when you were talking a while ago, I kind of saw what you were saying," I said.

"That's because you allowed your heart to see, and the heart doesn't see in words or language. Images, feelings, and realizations make up the heart and are still very much a part of the dreamtime."

By now I sensed that conversations with Tarrence were somewhat like a dual-track experience. His words conveyed a lot of meaning and information. But from the beginning, there was always another level of communication, as is common in all interactions, which is the non-verbal. Tarrence's non-verbal communication conveyed more than his limited body language since he was paralyzed. Tarrence operated so often in what is known as the transpersonal, that he had become a master of communicating in this manner.

The only association I have of someone doing this in a purely western sense would be Milton Erickson, the famous hypnotist who was in actuality a shaman, who as chance would have it was also paralyzed. His method has been categorized as hypnosis. With both of these masters, there's something more subtle and mysterious than just another hypnosis trick. Somehow, they connect with the spirit of the person they're relating to, and the interaction loses the subject-object relation that is the common in western thought. Instead of subject-object or me-you relationship, there is simply a relation-ship and a oneness.

This occurred when talking with Tarrence. It was as if he was in my mind and I could be in his. His openness and total lack of fear were amazing. On another occasion when I asked him why he wasn't afraid of being so open, he simply said, "Why not? If there is no one there to get hurt, there is no one there to protect…. So just let it go."

I stood up. "I should be going. I have a lot to think about and to see how this applies to what I'm doing. Thanks."

"Don't think too much, and come back. It's good to talk to you and visit with an old relative," he said.

As I left, I couldn't help but think that he made that last remark about "old relative" just to get me to think what he meant. It worked, and my mind was full of thoughts as I started back down the old road toward the main road.

Man, do I have a lot to talk to Carl about. He'll flip, so I'll have to go easy, I thought to myself. Also, I recalled Dr. Beerli, who came recommended for understanding things from a more transpersonal point of reference.

I'll talk to her first, my thoughts continued. What was that hypnologic thing he did while he was talking? It was as if I were dreaming. Am I losing my mind here or what? This is interesting, but not something to mess with. That's how people have psychotic breakdowns, and there's no way I can afford to have one of those. This is getting out of hand. I need some ego boundaries.

What's the worst thing that could happen? If I lost my mind, that is. No, you can't even contemplate that. What would Tarrence say to this idea? Probably he would smile and say, "Let it go." My God, how can I do that? If I let it go, then I won't know anything; that is, I'll be psychotic.... I need to stop this before it gets out of hand.

6

Consultation with Dr. Jones

*W*hen I got home that evening, there was a message on my answering machine from Carl.

"My man, been thinking of you and what you're doing. Hope you aren't letting all that mumbo-jumbo stuff get the best of you. Let's have coffee and talk. I'm curious as to how the work is going up in the mountains. Let me know if eight a.m. tomorrow is OK. On second thought, let me know if it's not OK. Be seeing you at the Latte' Hey, my man, and we can suck up some sweet cappuccinos. Know what I'm sayin'?"

Carl's tone aggravated me even more than usual this evening. Still, I needed to talk to him, and even though he was frustrating, he was handy, so I decided to go. I felt at this time of ambivalence in my life that Carl would keep me within striking distance of the rational life-world.

That evening I had a dream. In the dream was an old man holding a luminescent spherical object in his hand. He held out the object to me and said, "Whatever you do, don't drop it."

As he was handing it to me, it slipped through my fingers. When the object hit the floor, it came apart and became several smaller luminescent objects. I woke up with a clear memory of the dream and felt as if I had been there with the old man in the dream. I couldn't recall such vivid dreaming in my whole life. Probably brain chemistry acting out from the dinner I had, I thought to myself, yet feeling it was more than just random brain biochemistry.

It was an early fall morning, and the leaves were just starting to turn different colors. As I saw the aspen leaves outside, I thought of the time when Tarrence asked me about seeing the colors. Maybe these were the colors he was referring to. If that were the case, why did I react with such anxiety back then?

Oh well, time to head for my coffee chat with "the great Dr. Jones, who's a legend in his own mind," I thought with a bit of guilt for being judgmental.

Traffic was light in the gray morning, and the crisp air made for a remarkable feeling of life in transition, which is one of the ways that I thought of autumn. I had no idea where this transitional feeling came from, but it was one that I remember always having. Thoughts were random, and my grandparents came to mind. I wondered how life must have been for them in a world that was truly in transition. They went through a big autumn as their way of life was undergoing a major change.

Inside the Latte' Hey were the usual Bohemian folks, deep in thought or discussion, with their bundle of books on the table. They appeared to be exactly the same people who were there when I visited two weeks ago. Don't these people ever go anywhere else? Is this all they have? I thought idly.

I was looking around for Carl when I heard his voice from behind, yelling, "My man, wassup? Here, I got us a table by the window so we can see life unfold in the streets as we talk. So how's it going? How's work? Are the Natives friendly?"

"Yes, Carl, the Natives are very friendly." My disgust was evident in my tone.

"Oh, I didn't mean anything by it. Just trying to liven up the day. You look so serious, that's all. I guess that wasn't a nice thing to say. I take it back." Carl retorted.

"No biggie, just that there's too much of that going on in the world. Innocent slips of the tongue that don't mean anything hurt a lot of folks. It's OK. I got some interesting stuff to run by you."

"That's what we're here for," Carl said as the coffee and pastries arrived at our table. "Ah, yes. Nothing like a hot mocha first thing in the morning," he continued as he leered at group of young brown women sitting in the middle of the room. "Don't get crazy; I'm just being a guy."

"Yeah, yeah, don't worry. Hey, you got to get a load of this guy Tarrence. He is deep."

"You mean the one you kinda started talking about before? Don't tell me you're treating him successfully with cognitive behavioral therapy! I knew it. You came through, my man," Carl said as he greedily sucked up the foam on his special mocha drink.

"Actually, no."

"What?" Carl stopped his foam-sucking abruptly.

"Well, I went to see him, and he's not a patient. He is a very wise elder in the community and knows a lot about the history of the people. Also knows a lot about dreams."

"Oh, man. Come on. Dreams, you say? You know that is just pure unadulterated bullshit, man. Dreams? It's random biochemistry in the brain, and you know it. That is not even a moot point any more. It's been proven in the lab.

Moreover, there is no reason to even go there. As for this wise old guy, how do you know he's not really a characterological disorder? Or a borderline psychotic? Come on, my man." Carl pleaded with an energy that was curious, as if he were trying to convert me to something.

"Carl, I'm with you. Why do you think I'm talking to you now? I need some of your scientific objectivity. It's hard being up there on your own with no one to bounce cases off of. Also, this Tarrence guy can really get under your skin quick. He's so kind and unassuming. Guess what? He was reading discourses of the Buddha. He also had all kinds of books on Freud, Jung, and even *Science and Human Behavior* by Skinner," I said defensively.

"Well, the last book is OK, but Jung? Pleeeeze. Now you're getting into that New Age crap again. The Buddha? Religion? The poison of the masses? We need to set you straight, and quick," Carl blurted out.

"You know, Carl, Tarrence reminds me a lot of Milton Erickson—"

Carl cut me off. "Fuck me. Erickson, the hypnotist? The one who brought stage magic into the therapeutic office? Now that is way fucked, dude. Erickson, the one in the wheelchair, the one who only wore purple shirts? Shit. Now I am genuinely upset. But what else do you know about this Tarrence guy?"

"Carl, he has a deep understanding of things. He ran this line by me on dreams and the dreamtime that was truly out of this world. The guy talks like a quantum physicist at times. He has a deep knowledge of phenomena like space and time. I'm sure he does. I don't know how I know. I just do."

"Now you're losing your scientific objectivity. You know you are, as much as you know you're sitting there. All you know is what you can quantify. The sooner you come to grips with that, the better. If you can't weigh it or measure it, like my man Hume says, burn it."

I wondered if I should tell him of the experience I had while talking to Tarrence and actually seeing what he was saying. Then I thought, no, this would be too much, and it would serve no purpose. I could already guess his response to this, and there was no need to subject it to his closed mind. I was feeling protective of Tarrence, although I didn't know why. I also knew that I needed to consult with someone else—someone who might have at least a *half*-open mind, in order for me to be able to adequately address the work that I was involved in.

"Come on, Carl. You're just having Cartesian anxiety," I said triumphantly, using a new term I had picked up while reading some newly acquired post-colonial literature.

"What? What the fuck...over? What are you talking about? I know that is not in the Diagnostic Manual," Carl threw back.

"It's just one of those things, 'my man'! You know, when the paradigm shifts from all that Cartesian subject-object shit, it's going to give the Newtonian left-over-science kids all kinds of stomach cramps, cuz they're going to know then that in reality their science-god is dead. Then what? You've got to wake up. Quantum ideas are now. Newton is dead. And psychology with its wannabe science. Shit. All that is, is physics envy,"

As soon as I'd said it, I was surprised and wondered, where did that come from? I realized that the place where my training had brought me wasn't adequate, and I needed to find new ways of knowing and understanding.

"Now that's it. That pisses me off. Maybe we shouldn't talk about this anymore. Ah, who gives a shit? We're just passing the time," Carl said uncertainly.

"Carl, someone gave me a referral. They said there's a Dr. Beerli up north somewhere who has written extensively on dreams and has a practice based on dream work. She studied with Jung himself, and I'm going to give her a call."

In a calm sad voice Carl replied, "Yeah, do what you have to. I heard of her. She's nothing but a modern-day witch with a license to practice. I'll be curious to see what she says."

"This is really bothering you for some reason, huh? Carl, I've never seen you get this upset about work-related stuff. What's going on besides this?"

"Nothing really. It just bothers me to see you start throwing out your training and your talents to pursue some off-the-wall psychological construct that's not substantiated by any research. That is what we do, and I hate to see you go off the beaten path looking for your roots, or whatever this whole exercise is about."

"So that's what you think I'm doing? I have roots, Carl, and I don't have to look for them. They are right here, and the people in those mountains are part of my roots. Where are your roots?" I asked without even thinking.

"Now that's a cheap shot. I'm a red-blooded American, and that's all the roots I need," Carl retorted.

"There's no such thing as American, Carl. That's just an invention some guys came up with to fill in a gap or to create a construct, as you call it. With the history of this country being what it is, I wouldn't make that my only root. After all, America is a creation that occurred off the theft of Indian land and Black slave labor." I surprised myself at what I was saying and was also curious to see where the conversation was leading.

"Now that's it. I'm tired of this liberal shit that tries to put guilt trips on those who had nothing to do with killing Indians or owning slaves. That is pure unadulterated bullshit, and you know it."

"We can't look at today out of the context of history. Come on, you're smart enough to know that you enjoy a lot of privilege just because of who you are and because of the history that brought you to this day. You stand on your historical roots, Carl, and it would do you and your work a lot of good to begin to understand this. As a matter of fact, the whole profession needs to take a serious look at the part that it has played in providing tools of social control, especially for people of color. It's not accidental that all of what we learn in graduate school is carefully gleaned by the industrial complex to ensure that people are controlled in a manner that will be profitable for America."

"Shit, how did we go into that? Let's just finish our coffee and enjoy the day. I don't like what I'm hearing. Maybe you need to get into therapy to deal with some of your obvious anger. It's not good that you're still practicing and seeing clients when you're so obviously biased. Your over-identification with Indian culture is clouding your judgment, my man. Do something before it's too late," Carl said semi-threateningly.

"I am doing something. I intend to call Dr. Beerli for a consult since she seems to know something about all this."

"Shit. I'm being serious, man. You need to see someone like Dr. Smith, who not only has extensive experience in cognitive behavioral work, but also has a good background in anthropology. That's the ticket. Here I'll give you her number—do call her."

"Thanks for the number. It's getting a bit late. We should get going," I said as I took the card.

As I was driving toward the office in town, I wondered if a rift of some sort was happening between Carl and me. We weren't close friends, and most of our interactions stemmed around work-related issues. He had taken an interest in me when I finished training, and at the time the interest was innocent enough.

What I couldn't understand was his missionary zeal at insuring that I was part of the new wave in mental-health-care delivery. There had to be more to it, and I wondered if I'd pushed some personal buttons with my new work. Oh well, I thought, he'll either get over it or he'll just leave me alone—or else we can keep arguing. Arguing is not such a bad thing; we can at least vent, and maybe one or both of us will get another perspective. My thoughts were interrupted as my cell phone started ringing.

"Hello, this is Dr. Beerli," a thick German accent said on the other side of the line.

"Yes, Dr. Beerli. I've been thinking about calling you." I wondered what was going on, and how and why was she calling *me*.

"I heard that you were doing some interesting work up in the mountains, and I would like to meet you and talk about it, if you don't mind."

"I would like to do that." My mind was racing and wondering if things were not out of my control. How did she know to call me just at this time? Maybe

Carl is right in his approach—no tricky stuff, and everything measurable. This coincidence was a bit much, but it had to be just that. We set up a time for the next day, since her voice conveyed a sense of urgency about our visit.

7

Dr. Beerli

Dr. Beerli had trained at the Jung institute in Zurich and had actually worked under the supervision of Carl Jung himself. Not only that, but some of the inside circles of the Jungian world suspected she had actually helped to analyze Jung himself in his later years. In addition to all the training she had in analytic psychology, she had also been in intensive training in India under the guidance of Sai Baba, a modern teacher held in great respect throughout the world.

I realized she had the perfect background for my present situation. She was well-trained in western treatment and had extensive knowledge of things that were not from a totally cognitive root metaphor. Why should Carl think the way he did about her? Professional jealousy is all I could come up with. Any other possibilities were difficult for me to entertain at this time.

The next day I got up early and finished some paperwork before embarking on the trip north to visit Dr. Beerli. I got into the truck, got onto the two-lane highway, and proceeded on my journey. Northern New Mexico is spectacular during all seasons since the view extends for great distances, and peaks of the various mountains are visible. To the left I could see the Sangre de Cristo Mountains; to the right I could see the Pecos; and way in the distance, the Truchas Peaks.

Los Alamos is in the Sangre de Cristo mountains. I wondered how it must have been for my grandparents, great-grandparents, and so on, when they lived there.

Why were they called Sangre de Cristo: "Blood of Christ"? What possible connection could these mountains have with the blood? Maybe some old Spaniard had just run out of names. No, they usually had some reason or other for naming things. What did the ancient ones call these mountains? We might never know, unless there's a way to ask the ancient ones, and they are all gone.

Maybe Tarrence would know—seems like he knows a little bit of everything. Guess he would, being laid up in that bed for so long. Wonder what that's like? To just lie there by yourself day after day.... That must be difficult, especially in the beginning. Who is this Tarrence anyway, and why do I spend so much time thinking about what he's thinking? My mind wandered all over the place.

As I neared the village in the mountains north of Santa Fe, my awareness of the present came back. Black clouds were looming over the peaks. These clouds were very peculiar. In my travels, this was the only place I had ever seen any like them. They were the kinds of clouds that are at least ten stories high, and they looked like floating cliffs.

Looking off into the distance to the right, I noticed that one of these floating cliffs had become a waterfall, and rain was pouring on another part of the mountain. The image made me see how the ancient ones must have realized there was an actual entity that caused the rain, since the water falling from the floating cliff in the sky was falling with such purpose and precision. I could see the blue of the mountains in the distance, and as I got closer, I saw their color change into blue, gray, green, and brown hues.

I had the instructions to Dr. Beerli's house on a piece of paper. I turned off onto a dirt road that seemed headed into the heart of the mountain. A few miles up the road, I came to a smaller ungraded road that was her driveway. As I turned onto this road, I had the same experience I had while going to Tarrence's place. I felt I was able to see the individual pine needles on the trees and on the ground with clear precision. As soon as I noticed this shift in seeing, my perception changed. It went back to the usual way of not perceiving much except the gross interplay of light and shadow, which is the way most people see the world.

I did wonder what this was, but dismissed it right away as I caught sight of the house nestled on the side of a mountain. Smoke was emerging from the chimney, and there were dogs on the front porch. Since the dogs appeared friendly, I decided to get out instead of honking as was customary in these parts where people had dogs as early warning systems.

On the door was a sign indicating that this was the office of Dr. Beerli. I rang the doorbell, and shortly thereafter the door opened slowly and deliberately. Standing in front of me was a short older woman with very penetrating eyes. Her hair was cut short in a simple yet attractive style.

"Good morning, I am Dr. Beerli," she said in a very thick German accent. "You may call me 'Beerli.' Please do come in; I have been expecting you. I hope that you didn't have any problems finding the place."

"Oh, no. The drive was quite inspiring, and there was a lot to see. I'm glad that you did make time to see me."

"Of course I would. I have heard some good things about the work you are doing up in the mountains. I'm glad to see that someone is doing something besides the dreary stuff that our profession is being mandated to do by the insurance companies. You dream, yes?"

"Dream? Of course. Everyone does," I replied. Dreaming, dreamtime, all juxtaposed with cognitive behavioral and Jungian stuff. I was trying to get a sense of this woman. She was friendly, yet there was a fierce determined look in her eye. That look was tempered at the same time with the appearance of compassion. She kind of reminded me of what I thought I saw in Tarrence. Also, before this moment, I thought that fierceness and compassion were mutually exclusive. "Interesting," was all I could come up with as far as an immediate assessment.

"Would you like some coffee or something to drink?" Beerli asked.

"Not right now, thank you. I really came up to talk about some clinical things. I guess it's a consult that I need. I've been talking to a friend, but he has no understanding of some of the clinical issues involved in this situation. Also, he has little knowledge of some of the cultural ramifications of working with patients such as mine."

I was trying to sound expert and official, although to this day I don't know why. Beerli just listened with her beady eyes looking at me, or through me, and with a half-grin that resembled the way Tarrence looked at me.

"When you start doing this kind of work with the psyche, it can become personally dangerous," Beerli said in a stern voice. "You are dealing not just with individual patients. What's involved is the psyche of the whole community and the whole history of suffering that has brought the community to the issues you see today."

"Dangerous? How's that? Exactly what are you talking about? Maybe you're referring to transference issues in the relationship such as Freud wrote about." I realized that this consult and the ones with Carl were already as different as night and day. This was not following any type of logical sequence, and we were just starting.

"It's dangerous in that there is a contagion that occurs psychologically, very much in the same way that physical illness is passed on at times. Jung refers to this in his work, and I have seen it many times. The only sure way of staying on top of this is to get a feel for what your dreams are telling you of the situation. Are you dreaming anything?"

I felt as if I were a patient myself. This is not the way I was trained as far as doing consultations with colleagues. Now she wanted to get inside my head and know if I'm dreaming. Carl would never ask this, nor would he care if I were dreaming or not. What is it these days with dreams? I guess I can tell her the dream about the old man and the sphere. That's safe enough, I thought to myself.

"I have had some dreams, and the one that stands out is one in which an old man is holding a sphere…." I recounted the dream to her.

"My God! This is a very serious dream. It is telling you that if you don't handle the situation correctly, you might have some psychological splitting. It is critical that you are very careful in your present work," she said in a concerned voice.

"Slow down. What are you saying? I'm just doing a few days of work in this community, and no one is saying anything about splitting anything. I feel pretty intact, except for a bit of anxiety about this talk about dreams and this old man named Tarrence."

"The anxiety is a mild symptom and could get worse. It is important that you realize this is very real. The work you are involved with has more than one parallel process occurring. You are Native American yourself, no?"

I nodded, and she went on. "This fact means that your psyche is close to this situation, therefore you are more prone to be affected by what is going on collectively. Sorry, I use Jung's terms assuming everyone knows what they mean. What I'm saying is, the total psyche of the Native community has a level of commonality since it has been impacted in similar manner—much like a layer of psyche that has specific cultural memories and ways of being in the world.

"You see," she continued, "we have our personal psyche with all the familiar images and memories, and this is what Freud dealt with. Then there is an ethnic or racial layer of psyche, and of course this is where the collective memories of the tribe reside. Finally, there is the collective psyche, and this is where all of human experience, knowledge, and potential are. You could say that this is the place of the dreamtime connection. This is where all of humanity is tied together to the common dream out of which we emerged."

I realized she was saying some of the basic stuff that Tarrence had said about the dreamtime. This whole notion of emergence out of this place of singularity was new and interesting to me. Still, she didn't know Tarrence, or so I thought at the time. So how could she be thinking on exactly the same page as he, if she hasn't even met the guy? What's going on here? my mind questioned.

I figured I might as well ask. "So Beerli, you sound remarkably like Tarrence when you talk about dreams and this dreamtime, yet you've never met him. I don't think there's much written on this, so how could it be?"

Laughing, she replied, "I just told you. There are different layers, although layers are not the correct image of psyche. It's more of a blob of mercury that is intertwined within itself. The dreamtime would be the larger blob of mercury of which our psyches are just a part. Since we are part of it, we are it. Imagine a sealed bottle of ocean water floating on the ocean. It is the ocean, but the boundary of the bottle might allow the water inside to think it exists by itself and of itself. This is egotistical, yes?"

"OK, I kind of see what you're getting at. I really don't know a whole lot about this part of the field. In school we don't get much training in this area." I had begun to feel more comfortable and braver, and I was very curious as to her relationship with Jung. So I asked, "I hear that you knew Jung. I even heard a rumor that you analyzed some of his dreams toward the end of his life."

Again she laughed. "Yes, I knew him." She did not answer the second part of my question.

"Well, did you? Analyze him, I mean?" I persisted.

In a full-blown girlish giggle, Beerli said, "Of course you know that would be confidential, no?"

"I guess it would. I've read that he had a premonition of his death. He had a dream of himself sitting in a yoga or meditative posture, and he knew from this that his life would be over. I find that interesting."

"Ah, yes. He saw himself sitting in a position similar to the Buddha. You might call it Buddha in White Face."

At this remark, I knew there had to be a conspiracy. What is this with the different colors of the Buddha's face? I thought to myself. Why am I even concerned? Carl's right. This is too much to contend with, and behavioral psychology is where it's at. It's precise, predictable, and has none of this incomprehensible crap. I'm sure if I talked to enough people, there would also be a Buddha in Black Face, and there was the original one in Yellow Face. So what?

I replied, "Interesting, White Face, umm."

Beerli went on, "Of course there are also the other faces of the Buddha. The Buddha has a red, a black, and—as you know—a yellow face. There is even one with a female face. I guess this goes along with what I was talking about a while ago. The different ethnic masks of the psyche as they all connect to the dreamtime."

"So you're saying Jung was a Buddha?"

"Heavens, no. And of course, yes. We are all Buddha and have Buddha nature. As you know, Buddha simply refers to one who is awake—awakened from the illusion. There is no physical Buddha per se, just bottles of water floating out in the ocean. The ocean would be the overall Buddha nature, which is also interconnected with the dreamtime—where all awareness is and where awareness is aware of itself.

"The bottle itself might be symbolic of the illusion that we exist separately—that is, the water inside the bottle might feel special, but there is only a fine veil that separates it from its true nature—the ocean itself. Furthermore, you could say that the bottle is water soluble and will soon dissolve; then the water inside the bottle will be at one with the water in the whole ocean—back to the source," Beerli said with deep attention. Her eyes were getting even more penetrating as our conversation progressed.

"So what do you suggest in the meantime, for those like me who don't know all this stuff?"

"Just continue to work and observe your dreams. They know all you need to know. Also, keep talking to this man Tarrence and to me if you wish. I am interested in the psyche of this area, and that would be my payback for the consultations. Also, in this area of dreams, you might want to read Jungian psychology and Buddhism. I'll let you borrow my *Middle Discourses of the Buddha* so you can get a start."

Beerli reached toward a bookshelf, then brought down a huge book for me. "Don't read every word, unless you have a lot of time. As you see, this is massive."

Right, I thought. When am I going to find time to read all this? I have two practices going, plus a life. I'll just skim and get the highlights. It's interesting though, and I am meeting some people you don't just run into everyday.

I got up to leave. "Well, Dr. Beerli, it has been a pleasure meeting you. I really hope we get to talk again. This dreamtime stuff is very interesting, and I appreciate your willingness to share knowledge in this area."

"Of course. Anytime. It's not easy to find people who are immersed in this work and are willing to spend time learning about the nature of the psyche and its relationship to the dreamtime."

8

Driving Reflections

$\mathcal{A}$s I left Beerli's house and headed back in the opposite direction, my thoughts continued to percolate. Why am I all of a sudden in the middle of all this dreamtime? What is the meaning of it, and what does it have to do with the work I trained to do for so many years? How come in the training program there never was anything said about the dreamtime and all of this interconnectedness—and this Buddha business.

I'm as interested as the next guy in comparative religions, but the way these two talk, it's as if this has immediate relevance to the now, as I understand what they're saying. Maybe this has something to do with my grandparents and where they come from. After all, they do come from that same area, and for all I know, they might have even known Tarrence....

The way this is turning out, I would bet on this, the fact that they knew each other. So, is this some sort of conspiracy to bring me back to my ancestral roots or what? I didn't go into all this debt to become a professional, simply to go on some "Kunta-Kinte-find-your-roots" type of head-trip. I need boundaries, I need to keep perspective, and I don't need to get sucked into this psychic abyss that's pulling me in.

The rain shower had cleared, and the earth had that peculiar smell that it has in this area after a storm. I thought this smell must have been one of the earliest earth memories, and one of the original perceptions that all creatures have had. I immediately wondered why I had this thought. After all, the smells are just part of the chemistry that occurs when it rains. These particles stimulate the smelling senses; then the brain interprets the smell. That's really the end of the story. At least that's what Carl would say. Carl, yes, I need to keep talking to him. No matter how aggravating he is, he can help me stay objective with all this stuff, I thought.

My mind drifted to the experience I had on the previous visit with Tarrence and what I had seen in that hypnogogic state. The meaning of the image where the person was being executed had some sort of fascination, and I wanted to understand more of it. Why did the shaman have to be executed? What type of violation would incur such a sanction? The worst that the profession would do these days is to publicly embarrass a provider.

There must have been more to it than that. It was my understanding that there were no more shamans left in this community, and I wondered if that could mean they had all undergone the sanctioning treatment. That would definitely have a lot of meaning.

All of a sudden an owl came right at my windshield. I swerved in an effort to miss it, but the impact was unavoidable. That brought me back with an adrenaline surge and took my mind off what might have become of the healers and shamans.

That night I had a dream. In it I could see myself working with Ms. Chavez, and I saw there was a fire in the office. The fire was not out of control, and we were putting something in it. Later in the dream I was talking with Tarrence. As we were talking, I saw an owl staring at me through the window. The owl resembled the one I had encountered the previous day. There was a chilling feeling to the stare, and he was trying to convey some sort of warning, although I didn't know what. Tarrence was giving me that usual crooked smile of his and didn't appear concerned.

When I woke up, I was worried about the dreams. Not so much about the content, but about the fact that I had had these dreams. I knew that Ms. Chavez was going to ask me if I dreamed of her, and what could I tell her? Professional clinical boundaries discouraged getting close to patients, and I knew Freud would turn over in his grave if he knew I was contemplating telling a patient one of my dreams.

What to do? There were no clear protocols for this in western therapeutic practices. What little I knew of Jung made it easier, because he took risks and paid the price of being ostracized by the profession. I decided that, just to be on the safe side, I would get a phone consult from Carl before I headed up to the mountains, since today I knew there was an appointment with Ms. Chavez. This was nerve-racking; I was wishing I had just stayed with my work in private practice, where things were simpler and there were answers to all the situations encountered.

After getting dressed and having breakfast, I called Carl, and as I was dialing, I was thinking he was going to shit his pants and rave like a crazy man!

"Hello, this is Dr. Jones," Carl answered.

I couldn't resist the impulse to act out and disarm him from his cool street-wannabe style and said, "Wassup, my man?"

"Who's this? Is this you? Boy, I didn't recognize your voice at first. Yeah, wassup, and what it is and all that. You OK? It's unusual for you to call first thing in the morning."

"Yeah, things are OK. Just need to ask you something before I head up to work. Remember I was telling you about one of the patients asking if I had dreamed anything about her? Well, I did have a dream with her in it, and I know she's going to ask me again. I don't know if I can lie to her or give her the usual psychobabble about boundaries, because she's old and not like most patients. I don't know if this makes sense or not."

"What in the fuck are you saying? I can't believe you even have to ask me this. You know you have to remain a blank screen. You're getting close to blowing it, my man. I know there's all this cultural stuff that's of concern, but what is right is right. Of course you can't tell her your dream—and just for the record, I said it. Just in case you're ever brought before a board or something, I gave you a sound consult on this.

"Come on. Keep your objectivity. You're a scientist trained in the highest methodologies and strategies. Don't get sucked in by some mystical mumbo jumbo. I know that you're a descendant of those people, but don't let that cloud your objectivity.

"By the way," he continued, "I did some checking of my own on my background. Found out I am one-sixty-fourth Cherokee. So see, my man, we's blood here, so we got to watch out for each other. Know what I'm sayin'? Seriously, watch your boundaries, and don't let that little old grandma make you think there's anything else going on. And whatever you do, stay away from that old guy you saw up there. I think he's sucking you into his psychotic process. So just do what you've been trained to do. OK, my man? It'll be all right as long as you be cool," Carl pontificated.

"Well, thanks for the consult. So, you're an Aboriginal person, eh? Who'd've ever thought?"

"See, it's time you stop treating me like I'm some sort of colonizing White man who can't be sensitive to these types of issues. We should do breakfast soon, maybe next week, so we can talk about how it's going for you up there. Maybe sometime I can come up with you and help you diagnose and medicate Tarrence."

"Yeah, I suppose that might be an idea. Well, thanks for the insights, and I'll be seeing you. Later," I said, and hung up.

9

Work Day

I made my way up the main highway and turned off at the frontage road that soon became a dirt road on the way to the mountain clinic. Couldn't help but think of the dreams I had with the owl and how in the dream it resembled the one in real life. Wish-fulfillment or anxiety is probably it. At least that's what Freud would make of all this. After all, he invented all this dream stuff, so he should know.

However, what about Ms. Chavez and the dream I had of her? I wondered. I guess I'll just keep my objectivity and boundaries. I really don't know how to do this dream stuff—and especially not in this setting with these folks. They live in a dream world, yet the world around them seems to be falling apart in despair with all the social problems that have been going on for generations.

Driving up this road had become pretty routine, and I had never really noticed the beauty of the rock formations before. There were deep orange and red colors that had many contours, and the shadows were black in the areas where the early morning sun still hadn't shed its light. The shadows seemed to be hiding some special events or possibilities that needed the darkness in order not to be disturbed.

As the sun made its way across the sky, it illuminated these shadows and created others, as the rock formations continued the interplay of light and shadow. This process seemed to have a life of its own, and I was surprised that I had never seen this over the years. Maybe this is what it means when they say that everything is alive, I thought. All of the constant changing was something I had never realized, and in my mind things were solid and constant across time.

My journey up the mountain continued with more of the same thoughts and realizations. I had some apprehension about the day's clinical activities, and especially what to say to Ms. Chavez. My thoughts also turned to planning another visit to see Tarrence and Beerli. Life as I had known it was changing for me. New ideas and energy seemed to be emerging from unknown places in my psyche. This must be how it works with the rock formations and the illumination of shadows, I thought. I wonder, though, if the rocks know they are being illuminated. Who knows? Why is this important?

I arrived at the clinic. The building was old and made of adobe manufactured by some New Age company that prided itself in benefiting the environment. My office was a small space at the end of the hall, opposite the rooms where the physician and nurse practitioner saw patients for their medical concerns. All of the professional providers were Caucasian, while Native people, who came from this area or other parts of the country, held the lower para-professional positions.

As a consultant, I was able to come and go more freely. In addition, it kept me from having to get involved in community politics and feuds, some of which spanned at least three generations. I was the first psychologist to work in this community. This allowed for the community and me to invent my role, and allowed for more creativity than some of the others working there had.

After all, how much leeway could a medical practitioner have in diagnosing a physical problem? Matters of the mind were another thing altogether, especially when the Aboriginal healing factor was included in the equation. In actuality, the Aboriginal healing factor affected the physical aspects of the person, except that not all of the practitioners were open to any ideas except those generated from the western medical model.

During that day, I saw several people who were suffering from addictive disorders. There appeared to be many of these disorders in this community. The patients discussed the difficulty they were having in becoming free of addictions. I listened and offered some behavioral interventions and referrals to the local twelve-step programs, which appeared not to be having much of an effect on the patients.

I knew these programs were not effective, because most of the people I referred there had already been to them and still couldn't deal with their severe addictions. Many were in the second and third generation of addiction and saw little hope in view of so many deaths in the community, which were directly tied to addiction disorders.

That afternoon I had an appointment with Ms. Chavez. I was still a bit nervous about the dream and still ambivalent about how much I should disclose, if anything. My guess was that she would have other things to talk about and all this dream stuff would just evaporate. Otherwise, the focus should remain on her and leave me out of it. Ms. Chavez was early, and she appeared to be in a pleasant mood when I went to greet her.

"Good afternoon, Ms. Chavez, I hope your week is going well."

"Oh, yes, thank you, and I hope things are well with you. I've been thinking about today, and I'm glad we get to talk some."

"Have a seat and make yourself comfortable, Ms. Chavez."

"Again, thank you for your kindness to an old woman."

I was wondering how to start the session. I could see she was holding her dream journal, and I could feel a little trepidation at the thought of going in that direction. I really didn't want to go there.

Ms. Chavez had no such apprehension, and she had a mind of her own. She started the session by saying, "I did have some dreams last week. Of course, I always do. There is one that bothers me a bit though, and I would like to know what you think of it."

"Of course. I'm sure I mentioned to you that I'm not an interpreter of dreams, and my knowledge isn't very deep in this area. I'm sure we can find some meaning in it for you though."

"Well, the dream that I want to talk about is…. I mean, the dream took place in this office with you and me sitting just like this. There was a fire in the middle of the room here, and I was putting my baskets into the fire. I couldn't help myself. I know that I would never do that, since those baskets are sacred and there are many stories in each one of them. So that's the dream." She sat back and gave me a look that seemed to imply "well, what do you think of that?"

I really tried to hold on to my sense of blank-screen professionalism. She had had the exact same dream I had a couple of nights ago. As soon as she said she was putting baskets into the fire, I remembered distinctly that the objects being put into the fire in my dream were also baskets.

Now what? I thought. I bet they were the exact same baskets too. Man, I'm in over my head. What to do now? I've got to say something, and whatever I say is going to determine the therapeutic alliance and could determine if her neurosis gets better or worse. What would Freud say? Of course. He'd put it back on her and ask what she thinks this means. Yeah, yeah, this is about transference. Jung? I don't know what the hell he would say. Probably some crazy stuff. Shit! Beerli? There's no one to ask!

My mind went through these thoughts in the space of two seconds. In order to get more time to think about this, I replied, "That's an interesting dream, Ms. Chavez. Do you have any associations?" After saying that, I felt really stupid. How condescending that must have felt to this old woman who was being sincere in her quest for understanding and healing.

"Not really. If I had all that, then I guess I wouldn't have had to come to you with the dream in the first place, huh? I really need you to tell me what this means. Especially since I have had the dream several times—except that this time you were in it, of course."

My thoughts raced again over some of the things I had read on dreams. Recurring dreams are important. The fact that I had the same dream as hers must mean something. Let's see.... Somewhere in his crazy writings, Jung talks about psychological contagion; that is, the psyche of two people having a relationship that is a sort of transference counter-transference kind of thing.

Bet Beerli would know what to say. Tarrence would too. Shit, where are these people when you need them? I want to say something right now; I can't wait for a consult. Let's see, cognitive behavioral stuff.... No, that won't even touch this, and it would just insult her even further. I need a theory now. These were the loose associations that took place in about five seconds.

I was getting visibly anxious. I could feel sweat forming on my forehead, and I knew she could see this. Before any more thinking could go on, I blurted out, "I had the same dream." I immediately felt both relief and an overwhelming damning feeling, as if I had betrayed all of my training and all of the teachings of all the fathers of western psychology.

I can't believe I said that, I thought. However it's the truth, and I couldn't help it if I had the dream. I'm just being honest about the counter-transference stuff. Carl will literally freak out—that is, if I tell him. He might even take me before an ethics committee and get me into supervision. Oh, it'll be OK; you haven't done anything wrong here, I told myself.

Ms. Chavez gave a smile and replied, "So you did dream about me. I knew that you could do this; my dreams have always told me the truth, and when they told me to see you, I knew that you were also a dreamer."

Her obvious relief was confusing to me. She acted as if I had done a wonderful intervention, and I felt I had really done the opposite. Why should she be so happy just because I dreamed about her and had a similar dream? These were questions that would require both intensive study and conversations with people who knew about this dreamtime business. And what is this stuff about me being a dreamer? Everyone is a dreamer. Studies definitely support that, my mind rambled.

"Well, I guess we're all dreamers," I said.

"Not really. I agree that everyone has dreams. Even animals have dreams. But not everyone is a dreamer."

"I guess I don't see the difference," I replied weakly. I didn't want to have her start helping me, since she was the one who came for help, or at least that appeared to be her initial reason for coming.

"The main difference is that dreamers are those who can move into the dreamtime and keep an awareness that they have been there and then get understanding. This can happen only after many lifetimes of practice. Eventually, everyone will become a dreamer."

Again my mind wandered. Here's this dreamtime business again. And these Buddhist ideas? What's with this "lifetimes of practice"? I thought that was all Asian stuff.

"So you also believe in reincarnation, huh?" I asked.

"What's to believe? That's just the way things are," she replied with simple assuredness.

"It's interesting to see that similar beliefs are held by people in different parts of the world. A man named Carl Jung called that the collective unconscious and explained it by saying that somehow we are all interconnected," I lectured as if I knew what I was saying.

"Collective unconscious is just another way of saying the dreamtime," she said. "I have heard of this Jung person. He actually came and visited some of the Pueblos up north during the Thirties. I've heard that he is also a dreamer."

"He was a dreamer. He died some years ago."

"He is, still. You see, once you become a dreamer, you will always be a dreamer, and you will always be alive in the dreamtime. I guess not everybody knows this," she said gently.

"I appreciate your kindness in telling me these things. I guess I don't know much about this dreamtime business."

"You know all there is to know. You just don't know that you know," she replied and got up to leave.

"We still have some time left," I said.

"I know, but we did what we needed to do today. We'll talk about the dream itself next time," she said in a manner that let me know she knew I needed some time to reflect and study.

"Well, thank you, Ms. Chavez, and I hope to see you soon."

"Maybe see you in the dreamtime again, huh?" she said with a sheepish smile.

"Maybe," I replied, and she was gone.

After Ms. Chavez left, I sat in my office for a while. I wondered if there might have been an ethical infraction in my telling her my dream. I know it's all right to disclose to clients, but this might be a bit much. After some pondering, I decided I was being a bit too particular about this, and that there was no ethical infraction, but there might be a blurring of the therapeutic boundaries. How could it be otherwise? After all, I had shared some very private information with this patient. Perhaps this is a way that hasn't been studied in western psychology, I thought. This might be something that needs to be explored further through research.

Once I had settled in my mind that things were going to work out with Ms. Chavez, I went out to the waiting area. It was about two o'clock in the afternoon, and Amy was there, waiting to speak with me. Amy always seemed so serious; she rarely laughed or smiled, even if everyone else was laughing at some funny story or joke. Because of her serious nature, it was difficult to know if there was a pressing matter, or if she just wanted to catch up on some patient scheduling.

"Good afternoon, Amy," I said.

"Hello. I noticed that you have some time late this afternoon, and Tarrence wants to see you."

"About anything in particular?" The moment I said it, I realized the question didn't make any sense. There couldn't be anything specific with this man. His whole life consisted of what appeared to me inaccurate generalizations tied together by an even more general construct—that is, this thing he called the dreamtime. I knew that if I went, it would go into the evening, and I really wasn't planning to stay late, but then I realized that a visit with Tarrence might shed some light into this dreaming I'd been doing.

"OK, I guess I can go see him. I just have to see a couple more people and tidy up some charting, and then we can go up there. I guess you're coming too?"

"No, I just came to let you know he wants to see you. I just came back from his place."

"Is everything all right? Is Tarrence doing OK?" I asked.

"He's always all right. Even when the doctors say that he's very sick, he doesn't believe that he is. He says it's just the body that isn't feeling good…and something about watching the sickness. You know how he talks. It's hard sometimes to know what he's really saying."

"That's a relief—I mean, I thought I was the only one who didn't understand him. Guess I was thinking that he spoke in some special dialect that only people from here were privy to."

"Oh, no. Everybody knows that Tarrence is a special person and has special knowledge. Some understand him better than others do. Like the woman you just saw. She understands him, and he seems to understand her."

I felt there was some kind of conspiracy between Tarrence and Ms. Chavez. So these two talk to each other and actually understand each other, eh? I said to myself. What's to keep them from making me the fool in some kind of prank? Easy now, you don't want to start slipping into some paranoid place.

"Yes, they both seem to talk about similar things. I guess this dream stuff is, or was, pretty important around here, huh?" I asked.

"Some of the old people tell stories of how the dream was and still is the medicine. Not too many left who know about these things, and the ones who are left don't like to talk about it. Guess they're kind of afraid of it."

"Afraid? Why would anyone be afraid of such a natural thing? After all, everyone dreams," I replied feebly.

"I really don't have too much time, and your next patient is here. However, some time ago the shamans in this area and other areas were involved in a dream war. A lot of people were hurt, and some of the families still suffer from the pain that was inflicted by these evil dreamers—guess you might call it witchcraft or bad medicine. Well, gotta go."

With that, she left.

I stood there for a few seconds trying to analyze what she had just said. My mind also went to the images I had seen with Tarrence a few weeks ago and how the image showed the killing of a shaman. That is a pretty rough sanction for ethical violations—and talk about negative transference. What's going on with that? Why would anyone hurt their community when there's already a lot of pain? Who were these evil dreamers?

Man, there's a lot to learn, I thought as I turned my attention to the next patient, a man suffering from chronic alcoholism, as were so many of my patients here. I must admit I was less than present in my next two sessions and felt a little guilty about this. My mind kept drifting toward Tarrence, Ms. Chavez, and evil dreamers.

I thought I should ask Tarrence about this when I saw him later. I felt that perhaps I should be more proactive, ask specific questions, and get some specific answers. I actually started looking forward to seeing him. I was really feeling left alone by my profession and also very insecure about what I was getting myself into—even though intuitively this felt right.

10

Cave of the Evil Dreamers

It was late in the afternoon, and dusk was beginning to make a move to take over the rest of the day. Dusk energy was present, and I had never experienced it as a living entity before. This took my memories back to childhood. Some of the old people would make offerings to the dawn and to the dusk. At the time, I thought these old people were trapped by some old superstition. This moment was the first time I understood what the offerings were for. I nodded toward the dusk and had the eerie sensation that the dusk also acknowledged my greeting.

This is beginning to be a habit, I thought. Every time I'm on my way to see Tarrence, I get some insight into this old Indian stuff. What's up with this anyway? Maybe it's just the collective unconscious making itself known, just like Jung theorized. So there doesn't have to be any more to it than that.

I got into my truck and turned toward Tarrence's place. Driving at dusk was interesting, mostly because I hadn't taken this road in the evening before. Probably just the Hawthorne effect, I mused. All it takes is a change in the environment, and people change their habits. It was interesting simply because it was different and nothing else.

I could see the sun make its descent through the pine trees, and I had the feeling that death was in the air. I didn't know what death felt like, but the feeling of dread, or ending, was very present, and I could only interpret this as death itself.

"Just another thought," I said to myself, actually saying the words out loud, which surprised me since I wasn't in the habit of talking to myself. The oncoming darkness required me to hear my own voice, and in this manner, I didn't have to feel so alone. I turned on the radio to get someone else's voice in the truck, but the radio reception was very poor due to the terrain.

I made my way up the dirt road, and when I'd gone about two-thirds of the way, I saw a white pickup truck parked on the side of the road facing me, about two hundred yards away. I couldn't see if there was anyone in it, and I turned on my headlights to get a better look. The other truck then turned on its lights.

Guess there's someone up ahead. Wonder who that could be? I thought.

I continued toward the vehicle with a sense of apprehension. I had grown up watching movies of how people met with foul play in these types of situations and were never seen or heard from again. When I came close to the vehicle, I noticed that Tarrence was sitting in the passenger seat. He gave me that same crooked smile he always did. The man driving was one of the local people, and he merely nodded. I pulled off the road, got out of my vehicle, and went to the passenger side of the pickup.

"Hello, Tarrence. I'm surprised to see you here. I was coming up to see you. Is everything OK?"

"It's always OK. Just thought I'd meet you here. I want to show you something. You can follow us or jump in the back—the roads aren't very smooth around here."

"I'll follow you." I thought I'd keep some sense of control if I drove my own truck. "Where are we going? Is it far?"

"Not far. We're going to this place you need to see."

With that, Tarrence motioned to his driver to get moving, and I ran to my truck, then followed them up a non-existing road.

It was getting darker, and I was wondering what kind of stupid idea this was. I should know better than to follow these two strangers into the night. At least Amy knew where I was. She's probably in on it, and no one will ever hear from me again, I thought, while my mind played endless scenarios.

After about forty minutes of this driving into the darkness, they stopped by what appeared to be a wall of rock protruding from the mountain. The nameless driver proceeded to get the wheelchair out of the back and make it operable. The driver placed Tarrence's arms around his neck, then placed his own arms around Tarrence's waist. Then in one smooth motion, he picked Tarrence up and put him in the chair. I could see that they had done this procedure before.

"OK. We're here," Tarrence said as the driver took out a tobacco pouch and put some tobacco in Tarrence's twisted hand. Tarrence said a few words in the dialect that was spoken here, and in a spastic motion scattered the tobacco around.

"Yes, we are here," I said. "Where is here?"

"A historical place," the driver answered in a tone that showed his displeasure. I took it to mean he didn't want me to be there.

"I always like to see historical places. Old Indian historical places, especially. My grandpa used to show me some stuff when I was little. Actually not very far from where we are, I think. I just never appreciated it. Guess it was too common then. I remember he showed me some paintings and carvings on rocks. Said that our ancient relatives put these here in order to talk to their descendants," I said, and immediately felt self-conscious at talking too much and at trying to be part of the group here. I knew that since my family had left these parts a long time ago, we really were not considered to be part of the people.

"This is all true. I know about your family, and this is part of that knowing. We should go in now," Tarrence said, smiling.

"Go in where?" Due to the darkness, I couldn't see the opening on the side of the rock that led into the cave.

"Just follow us," said the quiet man pushing the wheel chair.

We walked on a smooth stone pathway that appeared worn from many people walking on it. I finally saw the opening to the cave and followed the two inside. I couldn't help but wonder why I was here, why this had to be right now, and what was so important about this place anyway? Nevertheless, I followed. The quiet man lit a white gas lantern, which illuminated the place in a remarkable fashion.

My eyes took a few seconds to focus. Right away I was amazed at what I saw. All around me, painted and carved in stone, was the same image I had seen when I had the hypnotic experience in Tarrence's house a few weeks ago. I could see the image of an obviously important figure surrounded by other figures. The ones in the circle were executing the person at the center as arrows were flying toward him.

I was in a state of semi-shock, and anxiety was welling at an enormous rate. I couldn't believe this was the exact image I had seen before, and the thought that I might be losing my mind was emerging. I knew that all I had to do was let go of my reality, and I would no longer know anything. I struggled to remain with the experience and looked over at Tarrence.

"Relax. Don't get so worked up. This is all very normal. It's part of the dreamtime. You're worried because this doesn't make sense to your intellectual mind, and you're afraid of losing it. It's OK to lose your intellectual mind once in a while," Tarrence said, laughing loudly.

"Normal to you maybe…. What's going on? Why are we here?" I said as I started to return to my senses.

"We are here because we need to be here. There's a lot you need to learn, and this is a good starting point. You see, there are profound and ancient reasons why we're in the difficulty that we're presently in. This needs to be brought out into the open. Otherwise it will be hard to heal the people and continue into the future. I know that you've been asking about dreaming and dreams, and it's best to start in the beginning and nip it in the bud, as they say."

"Nip what in the bud?"

"That guy in the middle of the circle being killed—how do you think he got there in the first place?"

"He did something bad or inappropriate."

"You could say that. It started before he did the bad or inappropriate thing, as you call it. Actually, the bad thing is just the tip of the iceberg. You see, when the shaman obtained power, it was power received directly from the awareness of the dreamtime. Power is just power though, and it needs to be tempered with wisdom and loving compassion.

"Many of these shamans were fine initially, but they isolated themselves because of who they were. The community usually reinforced this by keeping away from them except when they needed help. Without a mirror to see themselves, it was easy for their ego and sense of self-importance to get the best of them. You see, the only true way to be a great shaman is to have the loving compassion that only comes with a diminished sense of self. Otherwise you're just some ignorant guy with power. Anyone can have power—a criminal with a gun has power."

He motioned to the Quiet One, who was building a fire, to hand him something. The Quiet One opened a little leather pouch and poured some green powder into Tarrence's hand. Tarrence bent his head down, licked some of the powder, and was in a prayerful mood. He then extended his hand out to me and motioned me to do the same.

My mind went through all the questions one can imagine in this situation. What is this? What will it do? Is it legal? I wondered all this and more.

"Don't worry so much. It's medicine, and it's only to calm down your monkey mind. If your mind is calm, you will be able to see what is there. Pretty simple really," Tarrence said.

"OK." I leaned over to lick some of the powder. It was the bitterest taste I had ever experienced. So much so that my body quivered as in a convulsion as I swallowed this medicine. I looked up. Tarrence was singing a chant in a soft voice, and his image in the firelight gave him a surreal appearance. He sang for a while, and I sat there not knowing what to expect.

As I felt myself calming down, I was becoming aware of more things than I was used to. I could see all the creases in our clothes, as well as every rock and shadow in the cave. The painting on the cave wall had amazing detail. The interesting part of this perceiving is that it did not take extra effort, and I didn't have to spend time examining things to see the details. All of the details were there just for the seeing. My hearing was also very sharp, and it took no special effort.

"How are you?" Tarrence asked in a kind voice.

"Good. I'm calmer, and I can see clearly."

Laughing, he said, "So many people never stop their minds long enough to even realize they are breathing. That's all we really know is going on in any instant, and most folks even miss that. Stopping the mind brings clarity. Just like putting a glass of juice that is all shaken up on the table. Eventually it settles, and then you can see through it. It's clear then.

"Our relatives across the water call this Samadhi—it means that there is pure concentration, and it's part of the nature of the mind. Although once you do have concentration, it's important not to get attached to that either, since it's just another mind state."

"I can see a little of what you're saying. I am very aware of my breathing right now. I didn't realize the breath did so many different and interesting things," I said.

"It's through the process of being aware of the breath that you can cultivate concentration. Through learning how to use your concentration, you can have your heart open. Many of the healers only dealt with the power side of the equation. Their concentration focused on power, and power is very useless without discriminating wisdom.

"Those people up in the picture—the one in the middle lost his ability to see clearly. His ego became attached to the power he had, and he started using his power to gratify his own egotistical needs in using the dreamtime. He hurt some people, especially young women. He felt he could use his power to have sex with them. When he was denied these favors, he would hurt the family through his power within the dreamtime. People died because of his attachment to power and his lack of compassion—pure ignorance is all it is really," Tarrence explained.

"How long ago did all this happen? Were these the same people who are here now?"

"Long time ago and also a short time ago. It's still happening. It happens in your profession even. This place has been called 'the cave of evil dreamers' by some of the locals. They don't realize there is no such thing as an evil dream. All dreams just are. Our intent arising from our ego makes the dream evil or good."

I looked at him. He was sitting very straight, his twisted hands on his lap, his eyes half-closed. At that moment he looked exactly like many of the pictures and statues I had seen of different Buddhas. He appeared to be very tranquil, and he felt like love—at least that's the only way I could describe the feeling. Tarrence felt to me like he wanted nothing or required nothing from me, and he was totally compassionate and giving. He was giving of himself and his knowledge to me for what remained an unknown reason at this time.

As I continued to look at him, I realized there was a sphere forming right in his twisted hands. It was luminescent, and it was of different colors. I could see black, red, yellow, and white. The top half of the sphere was surrounded by blue; the bottom half by green. They were the sharpest and most luminescent colors I had ever seen. Somehow I remained calm and just noticed the sphere. Maybe these are the colors he mentioned on our first meeting, I thought.

"Don't get too attached to this experience," Tarrence said. "It's just a part of nature that is always there. This merely represents the cosmos as known by your ego. All the colors of people surrounded by blue sky and green earth. These colors also can be used by the ego for purposes that can cause a lot of suffering. As if there isn't enough suffering already."

At this moment I felt a familiarity with the colors. I also felt a familiar presence from the picture in the cave, as if I knew these people. Also, I felt as if I had been around this all my life. I looked at the picture of the shaman who was being executed. His eyes looked strangely familiar.

"We're to the point where I have to tell you the purpose of our meeting here," Tarrence said in a somber yet peaceful voice. "Understand that it's all in a good way, and no attachment should be made by what I will tell. It is true, and this will help you to do what you need to do with the purpose that has been given to you in the dreamtime. And don't worry; I will help you."

"What?" was all I could say. I felt my mind stir with apprehension and curiosity before it settled back to its quiet place.

"You see the one in the middle? The shaman? Well, he's your great-great-grandfather. He lived many generations ago—seven, then seven more. You're his descendant. He worked in the dreamtime, just like you do. It's important that you understand him so that you won't go the same way he did."

"You're serious? Like a blood relative, or just a professional relationship, or what?" was the silly response from me.

"Blood."

I realized what this meant, and I lost some of the composure I had been enjoying for the past hour or so. I felt ashamed, guilty, and angry; and it made no sense that I was feeling this. My rational mind thought that I hadn't done anything wrong, therefore there shouldn't be a problem with this last bit of information. The fact that one of my ancestors was depicted as a shaman who had to be executed was frightening and fascinating at the same time.

"What does this mean for me? Why do I even need to know this?"

"Because of who you are and what you're doing. The fact that you work in the type of field that you do means that you are practicing some of the old ways. You think that because you're a psychologist, this is all you do. Anyone who works with people's minds and spirits is working in the same area as the old shamans used to—it's just that it's coated with more layers of dishonesty and tricks these days. In the old days, everyone knew who was who. You come here, people tell you their dreams, and you start dreaming about the people. What do you expect me to think?" Tarrence said, still sitting, still looking like a Buddha.

"What dreams did I have? Unless you're talking about the one I had last week with Ms—" The sudden recollection of confidentiality didn't allow me to finish the name.

"Chavez," Tarrence finished for me.

"How do you know about that? Did she tell you?"

"No…. Remember, I was in the dream too. How could I not know if I was in the dream? The owl at the window concerned me, and that's when I decided to bring you here."

"Owl? You know about the owl? Why is that meaningful?"

"Owls are sacred creatures. Some of the old people used them for flight in the darkness and to accomplish some of the ego desires, therefore some of them are still used that way. The one you killed on the road was coming your way, and you saw its spirit in the dream. Someone in the dreamtime is being used to get you to act on your ego impulses, so that the people here remain spiritually oppressed by the spirits of alcohol and other drugs. I have a feeling that your ancestor there is still trying to carry on in his ignorant ways through you.

"You see, he was one of the most powerful types of dreamers who had achieved very high levels of concentration. His type of healer was known as an "Owl Dreamer." Owls have the ability to see in the darkness and are gifted in seeing the dream. They have special abilities that can be harnessed through the effort of concentration on the part of the shaman. You could do this if you wanted to."

"What spirit of alcohol? What are you saying?"

"That's for another time. We need to focus on the here and now, and what we are here for."

"OK, so tell me. I want to know whatever it is I need to know."

"Your ancestor there in the picture was a great healer and had the gift of flight into the dreamtime even when he was awake. He could move in the darkness with the help of Owl spirit power he attained in a dream. He helped a lot of people. At some point he forgot that the power was not coming from his ego, and he identified with it—this is very tricky and dangerous.

"The people started honoring him, seeing him as a great healer, and after years of this—it's a subtle process, you know—well, he started believing it. I guess you would say he took on the fantasies and projections of the community and made them his own and forgot that he was merely a vessel. As things would have it in spiritual matters, a female spirit usually hooks a man's ego, since she is the one who tries to bring attention to his egotistical ways. However, when a man's female spirit tries to get his attention, he almost always misunderstands this as a physical sexual need. You follow?"

"I think I do. In my field we call this transference, and Freud talked about how this can be a trap in therapy. It's been the ruin of many people in our field."

"See. It goes after healers, because healers must integrate their opposite male or female, as the case may be. Everyone has to do this, but healers have to really get on task and get this inner relationship taken care of."

I recalled that I had read something in Jung's works about all this integration of male and female spiritual or psychological energy. I seemed to remember that he used the Latin names of Anima for the female counterpart of the male, and Animus for the male counterpart of the female.

Pretty sophisticated stuff, I thought. I wonder where Tarrence picked all this up. I don't think he's read all of Jung, especially not this esoteric stuff on anima and animus. Then I felt a sense of shame for stereotyping this old gentleman. I decided I needed to talk to Dr. Beerli as soon as possible to run all this by her, since Carl would be out of the question. Carl would definitely have me involuntarily committed if I were to tell him any of the events of this day.

Then I was back in the moment with Tarrence and the Quiet One, as I chose to name him, since he didn't volunteer to tell me his name. I realized this was a conscious choice on his part.

"I know that in White psychology there are some ideas that refer to these energies in the healing or therapeutic situation. There appear to be some parallels—" I started to explain, but Tarrence interrupted me.

"Yes, Jung talked about it. Unfortunately, he did not belong to a tribe in which he could be in a sacred circle when he was learning about this. That's why he got into difficulty with it."

"What kind of difficulty?"

"Of course you must know with all your education and all. I'm sure you've read of some of his exploits with Toni Wolfe—the Wolf Lady. Interesting that he was attracted to the Wolf Spirit. He didn't realize this, so he got attracted to the lady instead. You see, my relative Carl Jung did not have a circle of dreamers to help him get clarity. He did well on his own though. A good prophet, this Jung.

"We exchanged ideas when he came through here back in the Thirties. Not with me personally, but some of the dreamers in this area spent time in the dream with him. He actually visited this very cave and sat right where you are sitting. You see, he was one of the old power dreamers also, and he needed to come back and retrace some past lifetime steps, you might say—it's all connected together in the dream."

"I've heard something about that, but I don't know the details."

"Details are the same as with the—I mean, your great-grandfather and many others who have lost their power through physical sex, since they misunderstand the meaning of the union with God."

"You seem to know a lot about this."

"Let me tell you a bit more. When power comes to the shaman, it's a spiritual gift. The problem starts because the spirit of the shaman is in a physical body. All we have are our senses of perception to tell us what is going on with the rest of us. Usually the senses are directly linked with the ego. The relationship of the shaman with God is so intense and so intimate that the senses can only interpret this one way—well, there can be other ways, but most people, and especially men, have difficulty understanding relationship in a way that is not sexual. Men are wired that way, you might say. Then their sexual energy becomes intensified, because this is directly from the Creator and the dreamtime within the Creator.

"Since the dreamtime is linked closely with the man's spirit, which is feminine, the man wants to have intimacy with his female spirit. However the problem is that the ego, instead of seeing this as a spiritual event and going inward, projects this outward, and this lands on a female person. Unfortunately, for many healers this intimacy is projected onto the patient they are seeing, because she is in the healing circle with him during the healing process.

"It isn't just healers per se. Anyone with a spiritual task is open season for this energy. In the past, all types of spiritual leaders and priests have been blindsided by their own inner search for God. At this point, the healer and the patient are very close to the Creator's healing energy that seeks to unite the patient with the Creator. Then, when the ego becomes drunk with power and the shaman thinks it's *his* power, he is open to being possessed by his own power, which becomes sorcery if acted out. This is the sorcery that has been unleashed on all peoples for many generations, and it is why there is so much sickness in the world," Tarrence explained in a sad tone.

"You mean to say that because shamans and therapists lose their boundaries, this is why there are so many problems in the world? Seems it should just be kept between the parties in question."

"No. When you deal with medicine, you deal with all the people. I think you would call it the collective psyche. I'm not saying that the shaman starts off as a bad person. All he wants is a union with his spirit, which is part of the Dreamtime Creator process. In essence, he wants to unite—and this is interpreted by his ego as sexual—that is, he wants to have sex or integrate with his inner female.

"That's why in many of our creation stories, there is always a component of incest, and usually poor Coyote gets blamed for this. I'm sure you're familiar with the story of Quetzalcoatl and how he was tricked into incest with his sister by his brother Tetzcatlipoca, the smoking mirror. There is lack of clarity if the mirror is smoky. And even now, when you look up in the sky, you see the heart of Quetzalcoatl as Venus, the morning star, in the sky—because of course he had to immerse himself in the fire after he became aware of what he had done while drunk. That's another part of the story—drinking, that is."

"So you mean that the shaman wants to have sex or connection with his internal female, which is really his spirit and actually is God in some way. Kind of like having sex with God?"

Somberly, Tarrence pondered my question, and I knew he wanted to answer this in a manner that conveyed the meaning I was asking for. He then replied, "Yes, the shaman wants to fuck God, I guess you would say. But he's too ignorant to know this, so instead he wants to fuck the patient." Tarrence's words bordered on anger. It was like both a pronouncement and a hopeful plea. His use of profanity was also done in order to get my attention and convey the impression he needed to make.

"This is where the healing energy becomes distorted and has deep implications in the dreamtime," Tarrence continued. "It's a violation of karmic rules in that energy is placed in the wrong direction and a whole process is set in motion that must complete itself—usually with a lot of sacrifice. It's really quite simple—cause and effect; the conditions are set in motion for immense suffering."

I sat quietly and stared at the picture on the cave wall. If he had only known all this, maybe the shaman wouldn't have had to die that way. What could have led him down the wrong path? There has to be an answer to this. These healers must have been good at one time. Maybe the colonization process brought this on?

"Yes and no," Tarrence replied without my asking the question aloud. "You see, when the missionaries, the black coats, first came here, they believed that only their way of communing with God was right and all else was wrong. They openly said, and still say, that our way of relating with the dreamtime is of the devil. But you see, the devil exists only in their projection, which means that they are also ignorant of their female side and of their relationship with their spirit.

"I think that responsibility lies on both sides—between the shaman and the missionaries," Tarrence continued, "because if the shaman had had the insight, he would not have accepted their projection and would not have become possessed by the fantasy. But most shamans were already pretty full of themselves, and they were easy targets for the missionaries' shadow projection that possessed them very quickly. And unfortunately the projection was a demonic one."

"So it does tie together. The colonization and the subsequent abuse of power by the shaman?" I asked.

"Oh yes, but we can't blame the White man. You see, the power sorcery went beyond incest with patients. When things became really bad for our people because of the destruction that was going on…." Suddenly Tarrence fell silent. A few minutes passed.

Finally he began speaking again. "That's when the worst offense was committed in the dreamtime. Shamans from all the six directions got together in a spot not too far from here and decided to deal with the Spaniards in a spiritual manner to get rid of them. There were shamans from all over—Europe, Africa, Asia, and Australia—who met in the dreamtime to try to fix what they felt needed immediate attention. Of course it's only human to act desperately in a desperate situation.

"These shamans—there were women shamans also—decided to put their power of intent into a focused beam, you might call it. They focused this beam into and through the dreamtime onto the other side of it, trying to reverse what was going on. Instead, they activated something they had no power over. This was a power that was very destructive, and once unleashed they couldn't retrieve it. Too late. Pandora's box, I think they call it."

"I guess this makes sense. What does it have to do with us? Why is it important that I know all this?"

"Blood—remember? Also, land—earth—which is also blood, since blood comes from the earth. In the blood is the map, the blueprint of the original dream. God is the spiritual essence of blood, and therefore blood is not tied to space and time. I don't mean just physical blood; I'm talking about the original and absolute awareness. You'll understand more as your road progresses."

"Now you lost me. Not that I was following all that you said up to now."

"In four days."

"What? Four days? What in four days?"

"We have to come back in four days and complete the dream."

"What dream? This is real. Just when I thought I was starting to get something." I felt irritated.

"It's all a dream. Our relatives across the water, the Kalahari, have a saying, 'There is always a dream dreaming us,'" Tarrence said, as the Quiet One moved toward the wheelchair and started to wheel Tarrence out. Tarrence glanced at me and said, "Be back on the evening four days from now. It's important."

"OK, but I sure wish I knew what's going on," I said as the Quiet One smiled at me.

When I went outside the cave, I was surprised to discover it was morning. I didn't realize we had been there all night. It seemed like only a couple of hours or so. All around us were enormous cliffs of red and orange stone formations. In those formations were many caves that appeared to have been communities at some distant time. I noticed many ceremonial pits lined up in a design of some sort.

I decided to climb higher and look at the landscape. When I got up to high ground, I noticed that the ceremonial pits were lined up and crossed at the middle, with mounds and other pits surrounding the crossed ones. A plus sign or a cross within a circle, I observed to myself.

I got into my truck and made my way home, following the track to the main dirt road. What an evening, was my only thought.

After a short time on the road, I noticed the sun emerge over one of the cliffs. As I focused back on the road, out of the corner of my eye, I saw what resembled a flash of lightning at the spot where the sun was emerging. I looked directly at the spot and realized that the first ray of light had made its way to me. Never in my life had I seen the sun emerge in such a fashion, and I decided I would ask Tarrence about it next time I saw him. While driving and thinking, I decided all this required some processing.

Beerli, I thought as I picked up my cell phone and called her number.

"Hello, this is Dr. Beerli."

"Sorry to call you this early. I'd like to see you at your earliest convenience."

"All right. I can see you tomorrow afternoon."

"Thanks. I'll pick up something to eat."

"That would be lovely."

"OK, see you then."

"OK, and bye," Beerli said as she hung up.

The rest of the day I caught up on paperwork at the clinic and did a couple of group sessions for people who were mandated by the court to receive treatment for alcoholism. I did the usual cognitive behavioral stuff. One patient insisted on telling a dream instead of dealing with his behavioral problem. In the dream, he saw a bottle of Tequila that was still sealed, and he described how he saw fire inside the bottle. I gave him a simple explanation about how the dream meant he needed to stop drinking, but I didn't feel this was enough, and he was polite enough to pretend that it was. After that, I went home and went to bed.

During the night, I had a dream that was disturbing and hard to understand. I saw a hypodermic needle and syringe. The syringe was full of a black substance that I recognized as the essence of evil. I was supposed to inject the substance into myself. When I woke up, I was ill at ease since the dream was so real. I was grateful that I was going to see Beerli that afternoon, although I didn't know why. Perhaps I saw her as the connecting voice of sanity for my psyche. She could interpret the realms of the psyche and the spiritual stuff that I was becoming involved in—at least that was my hope. I already have transference toward this woman, and I hardly know her, I thought. She's not even my therapist. This is getting too weird, and none of the rules are being observed. Where is all this going?

11

Second Visit With Dr. Beerli

*O*nce I finished with charting work and meeting with patients on the ward at the hospital, I got on my way to see Beerli. I drove through town, and when I saw the Latte' Hey, I decided to have a double mocha. I felt I deserved some sort of a treat after the events of the last couple of days and nights. Parking wasn't a problem at this time of the day, and I parked up front.

As I went in the door and got in line, I heard as if in a dream, "My man, wassup?" The last thing I needed right now was to talk to Carl, but I was ambushed. I would have to at least be polite. With my drink and pastry in hand, I made my way to his table.

"How's it going, Carl?"

"Whoa…why so serious? Life is too short—know what I'm sayin'?"

"I know, so how's things with you. Amazing to run into you here and all."

"Guess you might call it a synchronicity or one of those Jungian déjà vu trips, huh?" Carl said in a somewhat condescending tone.

"You never know, Carl. They say there's a reason for everything. I'll be damned if I can figure out any of them."

"How's things going up in Indian country? How was the visit with Beerli? She is something, if I do say so myself. Met her only once, and she sure gave me the willies. Reminds me of some sort of witch or something."

"Things are going well. Interesting, I guess you would say. As for Beerli, I found her to have a lot of insight. As for your projection of seeing her as a witch…well, I don't know where that comes from."

"Just talking. Don't mean anything by it. What's this projection shit? Don't tell me you're selling out to the primitive side with just one visit to her. See, she does have some sort of power. You see her one time, and you start sounding like her."

"Oh, ease up," I said, half under my breath. "I just have a lot on my mind. In fact, I was headed up to see Beerli right now. I just stopped to get me a mocha."

"Again? You just saw her last week. What can you possibly need to talk about again this soon? Anything I can help with? You know I'm willing to help any way I can. You do seem a bit down—depressed. I'm worried about you; I can get you some Prozac. Nothing wrong with a little psychotropic medicine to get you over the rough spots, you know. No disgrace in it," Carl offered.

"I am not depressed. I'm simply in a pensive mode. A lot is going on with my work, and there's no paradigm or theoretical construct that I know of that can be of help to me right now. That's why I am going to see Beerli—to start making some sense of the things that have transpired in the last few days. Right now I'm not at liberty to discuss any of it." I hoped he would just let it go at that.

"Oh, come on. The theory is there. What more do you need? You're a social scientist. You have the seven-step scientific method. Just let it work for you, that's all," Carl rambled.

"Carl, do you know anything about Buddhism? That old man I was telling you about kind of inspired me to read up on it. So I've been doing that in my spare time. Some of what the Buddha says sounds remarkably similar to cognitive psychology."

"Bullshit. What can that old mystic in India sitting under some tree come up with that would be close to our scientific understanding? Now I know you need meds, and maybe something a wee bit stronger than an antidepressant."

"Keep an open mind, 'my man.' Don't close yourself within a Cartesian boundary. There's more than what your brain chemistry can produce regarding insight and realization," I came back with my weak understanding of my new knowledge.

"Well, my mind is open. It's open for scientific proof. It's either there or it isn't. Right now you're just talking without any empirical data. Simply put, just anecdotal data—not good enough, my man. You need statistical significance, as you know," Carl said with a smile.

"You know, been thinking about this scientific shit. Most studies in our discipline are based on forty subjects, mostly college-freshmen level. Even at that, we admit that there's error in our process. Aboriginal science has had thousands of years of trials and thousands of real people involved, so who has the anecdotal data? On the other hand, is it just that western colonial science, which took over for the medieval church, still prevails? You might be some sort of missionary, the way you talk," I said, not really wanting to engage this much.

"Now that's uncalled for. You know that's not where I'm coming from. That is really a cheap shot."

"No, it isn't, Carl. As social scientists we must take into account the historical context. Otherwise, by expounding our truth to the world that might have another truth, we're no better than the colonizing missionaries. After all, our science is merely the secularization of the Judeo-Christian myth. Read your Foucault. He has it all down for you."

"I hope you know what you're doing. This is too much, and right now I don't have time for this shit. I guess you have to be going too."

"Yes, that's true. Carl, you really should read some of the postcolonial social-science literature. I think it would do wonders for your Cartesian Anxiety. That's the type of anxiety that's not amenable to psychotropics. Take care, and I didn't mean to piss you off. So chill," I said as I extended my hand to him.

"All right, I'll chill." He shook my hand.

I bought a few groceries and filled Ruby with gas. Since it looked like there would be rainstorms, I made sure the four-wheel-drive function was working as I started up the highway. Some huge thunderclouds were already pouring on the nearby mountains. It was raining so hard that the peaks of the mountains, which are usually visible even on quarter-moon nights, were totally blacked out. An occasional bolt of lightning was a clear reminder that the power being unleashed was unlike any available to human beings. The earth began to give its fresh-rain smell, and the afternoon felt calm even as it was charged with the potential of the rainstorm.

Traffic was almost non-existent as I made my way to the turn-off that led up to Beerli's home and therapy office. I made remarkably good time, or so it seemed—perhaps due to my being preoccupied with all the thoughts that kept spinning in my mind.

I rang the doorbell, and Beerli opened the door with a smile.

"Good afternoon. It's good to see you again," she said.

"Yes, it's good to see you too. How have you been? I brought some bread and cheese for a snack while we talk."

"Oh, thank you. You're too kind. Come in and have a seat," she said as she led me to her office.

The last time I visited, I hadn't seen her office. It was remarkable. She had two sand trays, and the walls were covered with shelves. On the shelves were at least a thousand toys that were used in some sort of projective therapeutic technique that I wasn't trained in.

"You have quite a collection," I said. "Obviously you're not a cognitive behavioral therapist."

"Not entirely, although there are uses for cognitive methods at times. I work mostly with people who want to do depth work and find out where their life as a spiritual journey is leading. Some people prefer to work on the everyday problems without connecting them to the overall bigger picture, and that's fine; they prefer to work on the rental property and not their real home, you might say," she replied with a smile. "I refer them to cognitive behavioral therapists who don't mind the dishonesty of the managed-care system where healing is handled by insurance executives. This is true sorcery."

"Dishonesty? That's quite a statement."

"Not really. They make no bones about the fact that they're in it for the money. Healing has nothing to do with most modern therapeutic systems. Then they wonder why the world is going to hell in a handbasket."

"I'm beginning to agree with you. I have some things I need to discuss. First, I need to ask what your consulting fee is. I really don't want to presume that I get to consult with you for free."

"The bread and cheese will do. Don't worry about it. I also enjoy discussing the psyche with colleagues, although that is becoming less and less possible. Most of my colleagues think my work is not mainstream enough, and the fact that I work with dreams is considered close to craziness."

"Well, thanks. There's been a series of events since I last talked to you. These events are not the types of things that I've been trained to handle, and at least one of my colleagues has suggested medication for me." I recounted all the events of the past two weeks. These included the dream I had at the same time as Ms. Chavez, the Tarrence visit of the past two days, and the dream of the hypodermic needle full of evil.

"Very interesting. You are obviously on an individuation journey that includes some of, or at least one of, your ancestors. The most recent dream is of great importance as I see it. There is evil energy in your lineage. This evil has been available to you; obviously Tarrence spotted it, and he took you into the cave so that you could have conscious contact with that presence. The hypodermic injection, as I see it, is an inoculation against the lineage of evil that you have inherited. Therefore I see it as a positive dream in which you are being protected, and it's probably this man Tarrence who is instigating this protection for you. Otherwise I'm afraid you might have been following the footsteps of your great-grandpa, and you would have had the same ending in one way or another. In a way, you're part of his healing since you're a part of him."

"It's making some sense. Kind of like what it says in the Bible about the father's sins being visited on the children up to several generations. I still don't quite understand what my role is in all this. I just want to be a simple psychologist with a simple life like the rest of my colleagues. I really don't want to mess with these forces—I'm starting to believe they're quite powerful. I've had glimpses into the power."

"Yes. Power on one hand—but like Tarrence told you, this is not the real power anyway. The true power is in the act of love and compassion. I think it's wonderful how he categorized it—the idea of a criminal having power also, and how this power without wisdom is merely a crime."

"What about dreaming about patients and their dreaming the same dream on the same night?"

"This is quite natural. Should be happening all the time. Jung called this part of the contagion that happens in the therapeutic process. Your psyche is closely aligned with the patient, and both of you appear in the same part of the dreamtime at the same time. Jung's essay on synchronicity is a good explanation of this. There is no accident to any of this, nor is it mere coincidence. It's all part of the nature of mind itself. It does what it does. We make a big deal of it. You don't see the trees making a big deal when their leaves turn green, do you?"

"Guess you have a point, although I can only pretend to start to understand this. I found Tarrence's explanation of transference a bit archaic or a bit bizarre—the notion of sex with God a bit on the blasphemous side."

"Not at all. I can see that Tarrence would get along wonderfully with Jung. He's talking about archetypal energies and not about ego energy. He's referring to the 'absolute' versus the 'relative' world that most people live in. You must differentiate between the two. Tarrence appears to be talking in mythological metaphor, and you appear to be stuck in some sort of Sunday-School understanding of the relationship between masculine and feminine forces that are at the same time part of God—the dreamtime. You must read Jung's Volume Fourteen—the title says it all: *Mysterium Coniunctionis*, the mysterious conjunction that is precisely what Tarrence is speaking about and what the healing relationship is about also."

"So you mean to tell me that Tarrence knows all this Jungian stuff? How would he know such esoteric teachings?"

"They're more common than you think. These are collective truths, and they don't belong to Jung or Tarrence. These are truths that occur in the dreamtime," Beerli replied with assurance.

I realized there wasn't much difference between the way she conceptualized the psyche and the way Tarrence did. There was an uncanny similarity between the two. Almost as if they had been plotting all this.

"The experience in the cave, the medicine he gave me, and my concentration are all things I won't soon forget," I said.

"It appears that he's teaching you to be more present. Being in the moment is the most fundamental teaching of most spiritual practices. The Buddha basically gave us all of the understanding we need in order to make this a practice.

Why do you think Christ went and fasted forty days in the desert? He was meditating and clearing his mind. Usually it takes time in meditation practice to hone your concentration. It appears that Tarrence has you on a crash course for some reason. Apparently he believes that you must achieve Samadhi rather quickly, and I'm sure he has his reasons."

"That word—'Sam-adi-yah.' He used the exact word. What's going on here? Do you know this guy? It seems to be too neatly packaged—hate to say it—like some sort of conspiracy."

"Of course it's a conspiracy.... What do you think the word means? The word *conspiracy* means to breathe with someone or be intimate in the breath or spirit. Anyone who is doing spiritual practice is part of the breathing-with. By the way, it would do you a great deal of good to learn how to breathe properly and to pay more attention to the breath."

"Why is that?"

"Because that is all you really know. Without it you die, and it's something that is always there. From what you told me, Tarrence has great ability to rest on the nature of his mind by focusing on his breath. He's giving you a great gift by teaching you what he obviously wants to. This is very good karma that you have a teacher like him."

"Teacher? I didn't ask him to be my teacher. I just go and visit sometimes and talk.... I guess you have a point though. I'm learning a lot from the old guy."

"'When the student is ready, the teacher will appear.' It's an old Buddhist saying."

"Well, I don't really know what else he's going to teach me. He wants me back at that cave in three days. Says this will complete the ceremony and he wants to tell me more, probably about my great-great-grandfather. He must have been a character. You should have seen his eyes.... In the cave painting, you can see a strange energy emanating from those eyes, even as he's about to die. In a way, I'm a bit ashamed of all this. I mean, who wants to have some evil sorcerer as part of their lineage?"

"He wasn't evil. He became confused because of the power he had. You see, power doesn't come wrapped in wisdom and compassion. The only way to attain wisdom and compassion is through effort and practice. The shaman usually attains power directly from the Creator or Dreamtime—unless there's someone who can guide that power. There have been few who have been able to work with it. For the most part, their egos became drunk with this power, and then the ego split them up through their inappropriate actions, while disguising themselves as healers. Happens a lot in our profession, you know, except that we don't kill our bad therapists," she said with a half-grin.

"That would leave us with just a few of them, or so it seems," I filled in.

"The split between the ego and the unconscious leaves the ego pretty much on its own. Ego nature—it is part of nature after all for the ego to identify itself with the unconscious," Beerli continued. "Then it has the same demise as Icarus did when his wings of wax melted and he crashed after trying to fly to the sun. No one starts out bad or inflated; it's a byproduct of not paying attention and losing concentration. Once concentration is out, then the ego falls prey to any seduction that comes its way. Power is the main seduction for healers. In my later years, I have come to believe that the ego is basically the shadow side of nature—what else could it be?"

"Is this sort of what happened to Jung? I hear stories of how he fell for his patients and was overwhelmed by his sexual acting out. Is there any truth to this?" I asked. I could see that the question made her uncomfortable, but Beerli was not one who shied from the truth.

"Of course it's not something that's hidden. What happened between Jung and Toni Wolfe, who was a patient of his at one time, is common knowledge. There are similarities in what we're talking about. Jung was a shaman by classic definition. In other words, his power came directly from the collective unconscious or the dreamtime—therefore there were no defined boundaries from within the mental health profession to deal with this type of doctor.

"Since no boundaries were established, his ego set its own boundaries, and they included acting out the shadow part of his relationship to his inner femininity, or as he called it, his anima. Since he didn't have a conscious relationship to his anima, he then projected her onto Toni and united with her. It ties in with the whole sex-with-God idea we talked about earlier and what Tarrence was referring to. No matter how we justify what he did, it still has to fall under the shadow side of healing, which in the end is simple sorcery. It seems Jung and your great-great-grandpa had something in common—they both were seduced into sorcery," Dr. Beerli said in a very serious tone.

"That's kind of a strong word, isn't it? I mean, it has serious connotations."

"You see, healers, because of what they do, are held to a higher standard. Healers stand in the middle of life and death. Therefore their work involves being in a sacred realm. When they act out their shadow, and we all have one, then the act takes place within ceremony—ceremony of healing. If it's not in keeping with healing, then its opposite must be true.

"This same sorcery is being acted out at the collective level presently," she continued. "Most healing, as is being practiced in the western world, is an acting-out to make profit and not for healing. Since the acting-out is happening under the guise of healing, then the shadow is acted out in the healing ceremony and the whole thing becomes sorcery. This sorcery then infects the rest of the society, and there are countless illnesses of soul and body that are the result of this. I'm sure this is some of the concern Tarrence has expressed for you, and you are fortunate that you have someone to keep an eye on your ego as it starts to inflate. I'm sure Tarrence will know what to do. The dream with the owl indicates that they are already looking for you, and he is there watching."

"This is pretty amazing stuff. I grew up hearing stories of witches and the like, but I thought the stories were just to keep us kids from acting out. I didn't realize this stuff is real and is still part of the human picture here in the present, for Pete's sake. This sounds like a fairytale, but somehow I believe at least some of it. I just don't know where to go from here or what to do with all this."

"Don't worry about what to do. You're on a path that will give you what you need next. Make sure that you go see Tarrence on the fourth day as he asked. I'm sure he has more teaching and more guidance that needs to be handed to you."

"I will definitely do that. I never thought I'd be taking time for this sort of thing. I really want to thank you for your teachings on these issues. It helps to have the western vehicle to allow for understanding some of this surreal stuff.

"I guess I'll leave now," I said as I started to get up.

"It's been nice talking," she said. "It's good to see that someone else is doing this work. It would be nice to see Tarrence again some time. Have a nice drive back."

After leaving her house, I recalled her last remark and realized that she did know Tarrence, or it could be some more dreamtime way of expressing relationship. Recalling all of Beerli's words had a calming effect as I drove back in the rain. And somehow hearing her explain the events using western concepts was validating. Perhaps I felt as if some of the spiritual energies that I had heard about ever since childhood really were a part of ongoing life on this planet. No wonder the Native people all over the hemisphere still continue doing ceremonies that help to appease these forces, I thought. The ceremonies started taking on a new meaning. Until now, I'd thought that many of the ceremonies practiced by the folks in the area were merely for tourists and social interaction. After last week's events, I was sure there was more to the ceremony than I had envisioned.

I stopped at a service station and bought some tobacco. Not really knowing what to do, I took pinches of tobacco and offered it to the six cardinal points as I had seen my grandparents do. The act of doing this felt real, and I had awareness that someone was aware that I had given the offering. Thank God, Carl didn't see or hear any of this, I thought with a half-smile.

Interesting that my grandpa, Jung, and others are part of the picture of the dreamtime. Amazing that they have all known each other—I guess for a long time if not forever. Do they come back from time to time? Looks like this rein-carnation stuff might have some reality to it. Who is Tarrence in all this? How come he's not an evil dreamer? Was he at one time, and now he's back to fix things?

Many questions, and no answers. Who is that Quiet One anyway? There's a lot going on, and I have no clue why I'm even involved in all this. Hope some insight comes quickly. Otherwise I might just have to go on an extended vacation until all this blows over…. Yeah, right, as if I could really leave now, my mind meandered.

Other thoughts went to the next event Tarrence had mentioned. The idea of a ceremony of some sort to bring balance was fascinating but still didn't make sense within the logic of the science that I was supposed to be practicing. Somewhere in the distance, I heard a howl as I made the last turn toward the regular highway. The howl felt piercing and personal, although I dismissed it after a few seconds.

Time to get home and just rest, I decided.

12

Fourth Day in the Cave

*D*uring the next day and a half or so, I focused on my patients at the office and the hospital. Whenever I had a break between seeing patients, my mind would drift back to the ongoing events in my "other life." I felt I was actually leading two lives. I felt there were things that could be out in the open in one of my life-world settings and not the other, and vice versa. After all, there would be judgments and at best a diagnosis from one of the life settings, and misunderstanding from the other.

My task in all this was very cloudy to me. The events in the Indian world were very interesting, and even seductive in a way, but there were moments when I longed for the simple life I had just a few weeks ago. Things were in place then—I knew where to go every day, my work was straightforward, and there were no intrusions into my psyche by owls or Tarrence. What's wrong with that? I asked myself.

I had my secretary block off the next three days, since I didn't know what to expect from the four-day event Tarrence wanted to see accomplished. After the last experience, I wanted to make sure that I allowed enough time to decompress, or to just "chill," as the expression went these days.

It's a strange thought to have an ancestor who was a sorcerer. What was he like? I wonder what he thought about at times of leisure? He couldn't have been bad all the time. Did he have a wife? Must have, otherwise there wouldn't be descendants. Wonder how he treated his children.... Did he play with them? How did he pray? Did he know when he started to slip into the shadow? How did he feel when he hurt someone? Maybe someone hurt him, and he was doing this out of some narcissistic need to avenge an injury he'd suffered. Perhaps he suffered from shame and guilt; after all he was just a human being. I wondered how his power came to him. Did he carry objects like feathers, medicine, and the like? How does Tarrence know so much about him?

My mind went over these and many more questions. I was a bit afraid that I was becoming obsessed with this person. Something in me was realizing that I really did know this man. I wonder if Tarrence knows his name, I mused.

That evening was quiet, and I had a dream. In the dream I found myself sitting in the cave. Tarrence, the Quiet One, and my ancestor were there, all sitting in the lotus position. They motioned me to join them. As I sat around the fire with them, they remained silent. The only words spoken were from Tarrence, who would say "Watch your breath" every two minutes or so. Every time he spoke, my awareness would remain fixed on my breath for a few seconds, but then my mind would wander, and thoughts of all types would flood my consciousness. Then he would say "Watch your breath" again. At one point in the dream, Tarrence said, "You must become silent in your mind. The silence must become so profound that you will be able to hear a sparrow take a drink of water, even if he's over the next mountain."

When I woke up, I was interested in the dream, but it didn't make much sense. Why would I have a dream with such interesting characters and then just have to sit there and watch my breath? I could do that anywhere without the cast of people present. I really wanted to talk to my great-great-grandfather and ask all types of questions. I guessed this wasn't the time for that. I didn't know if it would ever be the time for that.

The truck was ready for the trip, and I set off early that afternoon. This would give me ample time to find the place and maybe even stop and eat something before I got there. I dreaded the thought of having to take more of the bitter herb, so I felt if I had something in my stomach, it wouldn't be so difficult to take if it was offered.

My senses noticed that the air was very crisp after all the rain, and there were weeds growing everywhere on the side of the road and in the hills. It was a steep grade up to the plateau and to the community where I worked, so I kept the truck in third gear most of the way. I was in no hurry, and this gave me an opportunity to look around at all the formations that appeared more interesting and intricate every time I came up here. Why didn't I see all this before? I wondered. I'm sure all this was here the whole time. Maybe that's what they mean when they say to stop and smell the roses.

I made my way to a little café in the town and went in. I sat at a booth by myself and had just ordered when Ms. Chavez walked in. After saying hello, she sat down opposite me. Of course my thoughts ran amok thinking of patient boundaries and so on. How would I tell this old lady that she couldn't sit there?

I guess it won't harm anything, I told myself. She's just being friendly, and she obviously doesn't care if people notice that she's talking to me. So much for confidentiality. Carl would shit if he saw this. Cultural sensitivity, that's what this is—if anyone says anything, that's what I'll tell them. A whole scenario and story were created and solved in a few seconds of thought time.

"You seem to have a lot on your mind," Ms. Chavez stated.

"Oh…well, some, not that much really…a few things though." I stumbled over my words.

"You really should slow down. It's not good to be thinking all the time. Just be; listen to your breath; it will help quiet you down."

I can't believe this, I thought. Don't tell me she's been in my dreams again. How would she know about this breath stuff?

"I keep hearing about the breath," I said. "Why is that so important?"

"That's really all you know; the rest is just your coyote mind making up stuff that isn't real."

"Coyote mind?"

"Yes, you know—coyotes are always looking for some mischief to get into and are constantly creating something out of nothing. They actually created everything we know in our coyote mind. I think you might call it illusion. It's like a movie—looks real enough, but it's just a bunch of pictures projected onto a screen. It's only through the emptiness of awareness that we can even know what is so-called real."

"Is everything that way? Even solid stuff?" I asked, just to see what she would say.

"Everything is essentially empty. It's all a movie coming in and out of the dreamtime. Even the dream itself is nothingness; this realization is one of the last ones you'll get before you dissolve. Then it won't matter because you'll be in that nothingness that is beyond the dreamtime. All that will be left is love and compassion without an ego to mess things up."

I wondered if everyone around here—or at least some of the older people— was involved in some sort of New Age amateur Buddhist cult or something. She was talking in a manner that I thought out of character for her. Then with Tarrence saying similar things—it had to be a conspiracy.

"So we're not having this conversation right now?" I asked skeptically.

"We're involved in the illusion of having a conversation, but there's no essential solidity to that. One way of understanding would be to know that conversation is happening and awareness is aware of it. More of a 'conversationing' than conversation." She paused. "I know you have to be somewhere soon, so we can't sit here all day. Tarrence is on his way already."

"Are you and Tarrence close? Must be, if you know where he's going at any given time—or is this another dreamtime thing again?"

"Yes" she answered sharply.

"I really don't know why I'm even getting involved in all this. I was doing OK without all these complications in my life."

"You chose this before you came into the present dream. It's something that has to be done in order to help more than just yourself. We've been watching you for a long time, and Tarrence doesn't have much time to help you do this. It was all decided in the dreamtime. Of course, there is no time there, but if there were, it would be a long time that this has been in process. It's really important that you learn to focus on the breath; this will allow your mind to quiet down. Your mind must become quiet and silent. So much so that you will be able to hear a sparrow take a drink from across the mountains."

I was almost surprised when she said this, but by now I was beginning to expect these coincidences. Especially if they had anything to do with the dreamtime.

"I keep hearing about the breath. In my line of work, we also use breathing techniques for relaxation—guess relaxation is quieting the mind. Seems like some of the work I've been doing in what we call cognitive psychology has similar principles. We work with people so they can change their thoughts so they can change their lives," I rambled.

"It's all the same—has to be—all comes from the same place…."

"Dreamtime," we both said at the same time.

"Now you're getting it," she replied. As she started to get up, I had a sudden flash of insight, or what I thought was insight, into the dream she had told me some time ago. I thought the baskets on fire in the therapy setting might be speaking to the fact that the culture was transforming and purifying through fire. I had no idea where this thought came from, but I decided to risk asking, even though we were in a restaurant.

"Ms. Chavez, the dream you had about the baskets on fire, well, I have a thought on that."

She sat back down and looked directly into my eyes. "Yes, I was wondering if you had forgotten."

"I guess I had till just now. My thought is that the dream might be speaking to the transforming of culture. In other words, things that worked in the past or were used in the past might need a new direction. Since baskets are symbolic of many things that are part of traditional culture, perhaps there will be a new birth—kind of like the phoenix arising from the ashes. Since the dream took place in a therapy setting, it must have something to do with the transformation of traditional religion or spirituality, something to that effect."

"I think this is a good interpretation. Spirituality needs to change from what it has been. I'm not saying it's been bad—just that there have been a lot of spiritual abuses over the past, because so much of the spiritual practice has been coming from the ego. The transformation needs to happen, and ego needs to give way to love and compassion. If we can't do this, then we're doomed, and we'll have to start all over again, just like we've done four times already. That is, if we get another chance."

"I've heard a little about that. Actually, I think Tarrence is very concerned over this."

"Yes, he is. That's why it's important that you work with him and listen to his teachings. I have to go now, and you do too before it gets too much later," she said as she proceeded to get up again.

"Good talking to you."

"Yes…and remember to watch the breath." She walked away.

As I finished eating, I felt at ease, and from time to time my awareness would go to my breath. I didn't feel anything in particular happening, so I thought this must be some curious traditional Aboriginal relaxation technique that resembled those from cognitive behavioral psychology, and therefore, what could be the harm? Relaxation, after all, is a great stress-reduction method, and it's well known how stress correlates with most sickness and ailments in society today.

Now this is something that Carl would get into. *The Comparison of Aboriginal and Cognitive Methods of Relaxation Therapy* would be the name of the journal article. Why not? Maybe Carl isn't so far off base after all. Could be just the metaphors that are being used. Except what would he call the dream-time? Is there a comparable metaphor in psychology for this? It would require some thought, but I'm sure there's a way to bridge all this. After all, we all come from the same dream…. This last thought surprised me since I recognized that I was starting to buy into this dreamtime stuff.

I filled Ruby with gas and made my way toward the cave. There would be enough daylight for me to find the road, so I felt the travel would be a peaceful experience. I didn't like getting lost or being late for anything.

Dark thunderclouds lingered over the mountains, and the high mountain sun was intense, although the air itself wasn't warm. I made my way toward the road trail that led to the cave and shifted into four-wheel drive in order to have more traction. Once I was halfway up the mountain, I could see the canyon with all the cave dwellings, and for the first time in my life, I saw a bald eagle sitting on a dried-up piñon tree. Seeing the eagle gave me the distinct impression that the eagle was also seeing me, and there was a strange feeling to this relationship. As I got closer, the eagle took to flight, and I was surprised to notice that in its talons was a rattlesnake that was still alive and writhing in its attempt to hold onto life. It was an amazing sight as the eagle flew right over my truck, and I could see that the snake was bleeding and didn't stand a chance of not becoming dinner for the bird. The sight of the bird and the snake is an image that will not soon lose its impact. It was more than an image—it felt as if some necessary process was taking place.

As I drove up the trail, I noticed fresh tire marks. This could only mean that Tarrence and the Quiet One were already there. Who is this quiet guy anyway? Why is he so quiet?

From a distance I could finally see their truck and the face of the cliff where the cave was. I approached the cave, and as I did I heard the hooting of an owl. My senses had me turn left, and there, on a nearby juniper tree, sat an owl similar to the one I had seen in the dream a few days ago. This gave me a chill, and anxiety emerged. Then I remembered Ms. Chavez reminding me to stay with the breath. I started to relax, and calmness returned. Hey, this stuff works, I thought. I've been telling patients this for years, and I should have been doing it myself all along.

I got out of the truck and started walking to the cave. The Quiet One was there waiting, and he handed me a bag with tobacco in it. He let me know through body language that I should leave tobacco in the six directions. I took the tobacco and offered it around. Then he led me into the cave.

There was a fire going, and Tarrence was in his wheelchair. He was sitting with his twisted hands on top of each other in the same position and with the same Buddha face as the previous time. When I approached, I noticed that his face was painted red. In the firelight, this gave him what would have been an eerie appearance except for the kindness he projected through his half-open eyes.

"It's for your protection in the dreamtime," Tarrence said without being asked.

"Oh…. OK…. You mean the red face, I guess?"

"Yes. It's important to mind our manners in the dreamtime. The energies honor what we do in ceremony as we enter different aspects of the dreamtime," Tarrence said, as the Quiet One approached me and put some red paint under my eyes and on my cheeks. He also had paint on his cheeks.

There were two piles of dirt mixed with sage and placed as cushions around the fire. The Quiet One pointed me toward one and motioned me to sit on it. He sat on the other one and crossed his legs. I did the same.

By now Tarrence was singing a chant, and things were very tranquil in the cave. I could see the eyes on the painting and remembered the dream I had the night before, where my ancestor actually joined us in a similar setting.

After Tarrence had sung for a while, he stopped. The Quiet One gave him some of the green powder, took some for himself, and passed it to me. I took a small lick of the powder from my palm. Tarrence smiled at me and said, "Take some; don't be afraid. Relate to it, talk to it. It wants to help you, but you have to ask."

So I took a bit more, and Tarrence said something in his Native language to the Quiet One, who approached me, took my hand, and poured a huge mound of the powder on my hand. Tarrence smiled again and motioned me to take the whole amount. It was a struggle to take that much of any kind of powder, especially this very bitter stuff. After a few minutes, I managed to eat all of it, and I was already feeling very calm.

"Breathe," Tarrence said. I looked at him and could see that his face was luminescent red and full of peace and compassion.

"Through a quiet mind—this is the only way to heal what needs to be healed," Tarrence began. "If the mind is full of thoughts, ideas, theories, and distractions, then this is what feeds the ego and sense of self. It is the sense of self that is the cause of the witchery that has happened for so long. By quieting the mind of all thoughts, there remains only clarity. In clarity there is no temptation for power, tricks, or negative actions. In this way we can proceed and feel that the task will be one of compassion and love. Our task has nothing to do with fixing, revenge, or resisting evil forces that emerge out of the natural events coming from the ego. This place of ego is where our medicine took a turn in the wrong direction and the witchery began. This witchery has bigger implications than you can imagine, and we're going to talk about it tonight."

"I'm here to learn and help the best way I can," I said, as I felt my mind beginning to settle. My body also began to feel very heavy and rooted to the ground, as if I couldn't be moved.

"The more your mind clears, the more your body will clear also. They are really one and the same."

"Is that how it is for you too?" I asked without contemplating my words. I started to feel guilty for asking, but my mind recognized the guilt and settled again.

"Yes. I know you're asking because of the way you see my body. My body carries a lot of the energy that has been used in a negative way in the dreamtime. There's a price for everything. It's part of natural law, or cause and effect. I can't be any other way."

"It doesn't seem quite fair. After all, you didn't do anything wrong to anyone.... Or—"

Tarrence interrupted. "It was the spirit of alcohol that has been set in motion by some of the evil energy released by some of the egotistical shamans."

"You've said that a couple of times now. I mean, 'the spirit of alcohol.' I don't get your meaning."

"It's a spirit that was unleashed through the ignorance of people like your grandpa there," he said, looking at the picture on the side of the cave. I was aware that in this quiet and tranquil place we could be so honest with each other. What we said to each other was true, and because of this, there were no attachments and negative guilt feelings. It was as if the sense of self and ego were set aside, and not much could be said to get me upset. This was remarkable because outside of this context I could be easily upset.

"I will say more on that later. Now we need to focus on what we're here for," Tarrence finished. Tarrence and the Quiet One sang four songs, and the songs seemed familiar to me, although I had never heard them before. I was feeling very quiet and settled and, for some reason, very aware of my breathing. It was as if my whole awareness was focused on the act of breathing. I was aware of the intricacies of breathing, and I was following the breath from its coming in to its going out. Somehow this was all I needed to do at this time, and at a certain point I became aware that Tarrence and the Quiet One were breathing in synchronization with me. I realized we were not separate but part of a greater whole.

Tarrence broke the silence. "A long time ago, several of the most powerful dreamer shamans got together to try to solve some of the problems they saw. It all started when some of the dreamers from the New World felt that the survival of the Indian world was at stake. This is when the same kinds of horrible things done in the Holocaust were also being perpetrated here on this very land. The dreamers up to this point had some problems with their egos, like I was telling you before. They were using power in a way that it was not supposed to be used.

"After millions were killed in Mexico during the first few years of the conquest, there were dreamers who met in the dreamtime to try to stop this. Unfortunately, because of the devastation that was occurring, these dreamer shamans were in a rage, and in the center of their being, they wanted revenge against those who were doing this. It makes sense that they would—but, you see, the problem is that rage and anger can only act in service of the ego. Once the ego gets involved, then there is the problem of the negative side of power— guess they call it witchcraft. You follow?"

"I'm starting to. And I can understand how someone would do anything to save his people from genocide. I can't really see why this would be so wrong— drastic events sometimes require drastic steps."

"Yes and no. You see, you can't enact spiritual power just to stop your suffering in the moment. Spiritual power needs to be used in a manner that is within the karmic rules of the dreamtime. You can't use ill-will and sickness to try to solve problems of ill-will and sickness. The laws of karma are such that anything and everything you do will come full circle back to you; this you can count on even if you don't believe anything else I say."

"You mean as in the Buddhist sense?"

"I mean as in the laws of everything that arises in the dreamtime having a cause and effect. Guess you can call it Buddhist—but even the Buddha became a Buddha because of the laws of karma. If he didn't have the right causes to become awakened, he wouldn't have."

"So today we're reaping some of that karma. Is that what you're saying?"

"Yes. Some of the lesser dreamers went into the dream and recruited some of the more powerful dreamers with good arguments about survival and so on. Some of the leading Aztec dreamers then called a meeting in the dreamtime of other shaman dreamers, or Thunder Dreamers, as they are known at times. The meeting required that they meet in a place of natural power on our mother earth—she has places like that, you know. One of the ancestors of your grandpa was there and suggested a place not too far from here, since it's a place of deep and incomprehensible power with an easy access to the dreamtime. So, they decided to materialize themselves for the meeting at this place. You'll see it soon enough."

"This is starting to sound a lot like science fiction. Materializing? Sounds like *Star Trek*; I'm sure you've seen it."

"It was a lot like that. Then what happened is that some of the shaman dreamers from all over the world became aware of the doings, since they also had access to the dreamtime and wanted to be of assistance. So, in a certain moment, they all convened and formed a circle: men and women, shaman and thunder dreamers—also owl dreamers.

"As you can imagine, the air must have been crackling with energy from all of the medicine power that these people carried. Some of the thunder dreamers were no longer in a physical body, as a direct result of being killed by Cortez and his gang of witches—so you can see, it wasn't hard for resentment to arise. Even the dreamers from Europe were very disappointed in their spiritual leaders who came here in the guise of missionaries, but with the purpose of taking material wealth at any cost for the church. Some of the thunder dreamers, mostly women from Ireland, were not too happy with the church because it had also caused a lot of suffering and genocide of their people. Well, you're a shrink, you figure it out."

"I can see that there was so much pain and shame underneath all the trauma. Actually, there is a name for it. It's called intergenerational post-traumatic-stress disorder, and it has profound effects even across generations."

"Yes.... This pain, this soul-wound, brings on so much shame. It's the shame that causes people to react, get angry, and lash out with anything they have—including the medicine." Tarrence paused, a tear rolling down his cheek. It felt as if he was taking on the suffering of generations in that very moment, and somehow I could feel that his heart was so full of pain it could explode.

"All these thunder dreamers in the same place with so much pain in their souls—men and women together with power," he continued. "It's not hard to put it together: The need for healing of the internal spirit or wounded soul, which is your opposite, was projected by some of them onto each other. That is, some of the men were attracted to the women, and vice versa. In the middle of the meeting was Tetzcatlipoca, the smoking mirror, up to his job of confusing the ego, just as he had done with his brother Quetzalcoatl. The reason I mention this again is because if even the Gods can be seduced by incest, then how much more easily are pitiful humans open to this?

"Once Tetzcatlipoca clouded the minds of some of the dreamers, it opened the door for rage propelled by shame to be released. I'm not saying that Tetzcatlipoca was bad or anything like that; it's just what the energy of the smoking mirror is—not good or bad, it just is. Tetzcatlipoca is the cloudy smoke that you can see through and get the first insight into the luminescent nature of your mind. Some folks would never see this if it weren't for Tetzcatlipoca. You have to remember that without Tetzcatlipoca, Quetzalcoatl would not have become the morning star.

"By the way, it was at the moment the morning star rose that the Buddha became fully awake…. Interesting stuff, eh? It has to do with the intention of the dreamer, which way the energy will be enacted. Right there in the meeting, several of the dreamers openly planned to get revenge in the dreamtime for what was being done to the people, so they were on the path of enacting dreamtime karma. Dreamtime karma follows the same rules of cause and effect, except that there are larger implications because it can involve a greater amount of cosmic cause and effect."

After saying this, Tarrence closed his eyes and sang four more songs. It was as if the songs provided a boundary for our meeting. While he was singing, it seemed there was nothing that could bother the container in which we were present. His red face was still luminescent in the fire that was being fed by the Quiet One.

My mind was quiet, and I still had clarity about what I was being taught by Tarrence. It made perfect sense, and there was no doubt in my mind that this is how it happened. The fact that in my lineage there was some connection to all this also became just a fact. The sense of shame and wondering that I had originally felt at the information about my great-great-grandfather was no longer there. There was an idea of being able to do something in the moment that would generate a different effect. I felt there was a power present that would be able to change the karma that was ongoing for so long. I didn't know what that might be, but I had a feeling that Tarrence might have a notion of what could be done.

After more singing, Tarrence sat in silence for about an hour. This was a very quiet time, and I was very aware of everything that was going on in my body and in the cave. It was as if I *was* the cave as well as all of the participants in the ceremony.

At around midnight by my calculations, there was noise at the entrance of the cave. I looked up to see Ms. Chavez entering with a bucket and a ladle in her hand. She sat in the circle and placed the bucket of water in front of her.

After a few moments, Tarrence spoke. "Fire, Water, Air, and Earth—now all of the elements are present in their pure form. Ms. Chavez will be offering a prayer with the water, and then we will drink some."

The Quiet One went over to Ms. Chavez, who was sitting in a very erect and meditative posture. He took some of the paint powder, and after wetting it, he commenced to paint the face of Ms. Chavez. Seeing her sitting opposite Tarrence was an incredible sight as the fire illuminated their faces. I sensed that the female energy in Tarrence was being materialized in her body, and the masculine energy in her was being materialized in Tarrence.

The Quiet One spoke. "Buddha in Red Face…. Buddha in Red Female Face. There must be a balance present. Otherwise the balance will manifest itself in the shadow. When it manifests in shadow, then it creates suffering, because anything unknown is ignorance, and ignorance is the source of most suffering."

Then Ms. Chavez prayed for quite a while. She included all manner of people, plants, animals, minerals, earth, and universe in her prayer. The prayer was powerful and from the heart.

Toward the end, she mentioned my journey and me, and prayed that I would receive the wisdom and help I needed to accomplish the task ahead of me. I had no idea what journey or task she was referring to. Then she took some of the water and poured it on the ground in front of her. Then she passed the bucket toward Tarrence and lifted the ladle to his lips. After he drank, the Quiet One drank, and then the water was passed to me. I drank some, and the bucket went back to Ms. Chavez.

Ms. Chavez spoke as the water was being passed around. "It's important that you remain mindful of the elements. These elements are the essence of all that is, all that can be known, until they finally dissolve. For now, be mindful that the earth and water elements are manifested in your body, the air element in your breath, and the fire element in all that makes you move, think, and be mindful."

"Now that the balance is present in this circle, it's time for the next phase. We're going to go outside and leave you here," Tarrence said, looking toward me. "It's time to restore the circle, the circle that was broken so long ago by the dreamers who met to restore order through power without wisdom, without awareness. It was that power released in the dreamtime that has caused so much suffering to countless people all over the world for many generations. Because of karma and blood connection, you have an opportunity to heal your ancestor in the dreamtime. By your healing him, he will be able to intercede with the other dreamers, and the ceremony they enacted might have some seeds of positive karma that can still be realized in the present. In a way, they will undo what they set in motion at that time of desperation."

The Quiet One got up, went to the wheelchair, and started wheeling Tarrence out. Ms. Chavez got up and started to follow quietly, whispering prayers as she went toward the entrance. I had no idea what was going on, but I decided to go along with it. After all, there had been a lot of effort expended in the activities so far, and I wanted to honor what I felt was a sincere effort, on the part of all the participants, to right something they felt was made wrong a long time ago. I tried to believe in what was going on, and I decided that whatever I experienced would be real. The rest, well, a bunch of theories that might not have a basis in reality.

After everyone had left, I was alone in the cave with the fire and the wood left there by the Quiet One. During the first few moments, I wondered what exactly was going on. Somehow in the past few days, I had developed trust in the process and in Tarrence. I knew he wouldn't do anything to hurt me and that he was much invested in healing what he saw as a very old wound in people. He had explained how not only the victim's soul becomes wounded: "The one perpetrating the wounding also wounds himself when he acts in an ignorant fashion."

It was interesting that Tarrence stayed away from the word "evil" and used the word "ignorance" in its place. "There is no evil ultimately, only delusion and ignorance which in actuality help us into learning about the essence of the dreamtime," he'd said on one occasion. These thoughts were comforting as I was sitting here in this cave with an ancestor on the wall being executed for his delusion and ignorance. It felt as if I were part of an unfolding film.

Things became very still within me. Body sensations came and went. I just sat there, and on occasion, I would put a little more wood on the fire. After a few hours the wood was diminishing, and I wondered if I was going to be in complete darkness.

"Not yet. Here's more wood," I heard the Quiet One's voice say.

"Oh, thanks."

I noticed the dog that came in with him. "Sure looks like a coyote," I remarked.

"No such thing. Even the ones that are called coyotes are not coyotes. They are merely coyoteing, or are in the act of being such. Just like you; you are not a human. You're just humaning. When the conditions arise for coyoteing to happen, then coyote arises and vanishes in the same instant. There is really nothing about the event to cling onto; it's all a rising and falling phenomena. All is empty. See?"

"I guess. Do you know what's going on here? I'm getting pretty thirsty and hungry."

"You'll probably get thirstier and hungrier. You'll be here for a while. It must be so."

"Must be so? Why?"

"The mind is a tricky thing. In order to settle it, we must have the power of concentration. Concentration isn't that easy to acquire since we don't have practice at it. Therefore, what is done in many of our ceremonies is a way to concentrate the mind on one object. You see, the followers of the Buddha know this, and they concentrate on the breath. That is good, and it works. You haven't had the time to do this, so Tarrence is putting you into a crash course, you might say.

"Once you get very thirsty and very hungry, your attention will be totally focused on these two mental functions—that's all they are, you know. Then, after a while, you'll be completely focused on thirst. That means you won't be able to think about anything else but the thirst. What this will do is concentrate the mind on one thing. If you remain calm and watch out for fear, anger, and other thoughts that might try to move you from calmness, then you will be totally concentrated and resting in the nature of your own mind. You will have to be especially mindful of the hindrances, like wanting, not wanting, sleepiness, or excitement. The most important thing is that you know this is happening when it happens. Mindfulness helps to balance the energy of the concentration so you don't just drift off in some sort of bliss or dreamlike place," explained the Quiet One.

I was amazed at his knowledge. Who was this Quiet One who finally spoke? I wondered. I felt it best left unasked, since he didn't volunteer to say who he was or what his function here was.

"Sounds as if everyone around here has a similar understanding of these things and the way they relate to the dreamtime."

"Not everyone. Some of us have been studying and training our minds for some time now. It's really the way things were a long time ago. Our communities had ways and ceremonies that would focus the mind and bring clarity. Unfortunately not all concentration is necessarily good, and you can develop a strong concentrated mind around ignorance," he said, tilting his head toward the picture on the wall.

"Well, gotta go now. Keep alert. Don't fall asleep. If it gets dark, it's OK. See you sometime…maybe," he said with a half-grin that sent a chill up my spine. The dog with him was also grinning in a coyote-like manner.

Yeah, part of the dreamtime I suppose, I thought to myself. His leaving in this manner brought a new level of alertness to the situation and was due in part to my being afraid.

Hours went by. I didn't realize it at the time, but two days had elapsed since I had entered the cave. The woodpile was getting thin, and I was using the wood sparingly because I didn't want it to be completely dark. My awareness was aware of fear of the dark. Especially sitting in the dark with old Great-Grandpa-Evil-Shaman staring in the darkness at me.

I had gone through the headache portion of the fast without too much of a problem, but the lack of food was causing my mind to become weaker. Water was starting to become the most constant thought in my mind. Most people rarely appreciate thirst since they don't ever experience it. It starts to slowly overwhelm the psyche and become a torment that no other thought can compete with. All that remains is thirst. Even the fact that there was an "I" was taking a back seat; there was thirst, and thirst alone.

Thirst had a life of its own, it seemed. Thirst became my personality and who I was at that point in time—by now the morning of the third day. Water became sacred. and the thought of a drop of water looked like a shiny jewel sprinkled in space. This went on for hours. As I sat there, I just experienced the thirst and was grateful for the comments the Quiet One had made the last time I saw him. It gave the experience meaning, and I could see that my mind was focused. Slowly, fear, anger, doubt, and other emotions and thoughts disappeared. Sitting with thirst became very peaceful. Then thirst also started to wane, and all that was left was empty space—and silence.

Silence is another thing that isn't well appreciated in most settings. This was the type of silence that had a presence. The silence became more alive as the last embers of fire extinguished and there was dark and silence. This type of silence is very fragile at first, and one must sit with it as with a new friend and not make any sudden moves in the mind; otherwise the silence retreats.

I was aware that I could somehow still see in the darkness; it was another type of perceiving. All of my explanations of the experience would fall short of what really happened. I was aware of all my surroundings, and it wasn't so much that I was aware; it was as if awareness itself was being aware and somehow I was a part of it. What Tarrence said about the dreamtime in the beginning of this story is the best explanation I have on this experience.

13

Awareness Travel in the Dreamtime

*I*t's been years since the experiences that I recount in this story took place. These occurrences were life-transforming and, at the same time, although interesting, not fully understood. The mystery remains, especially to the mind that is seeking a rational and logical explanation of what happened. One thing is certain: These things happened and continue to happen. There is a dreamtime that is everything, and in that dreamtime all is possible—even the telling of the things that I have already mentioned. The events that transpired during those days of fasting require an open heart, and there is no need to either believe or disbelieve. The dream simply is, and it doesn't depend on validation.

Some folks need labels for these types of realities. Some would say it's in the genre of magical realism, or simply categorize it as science fiction. It's true that the story is told in fiction format. Ultimately, though, fiction emerges from the same place that everything else does. That is, the mind is simply a spark or a psychological complex in the dreamtime.

These realities are the ones that are still being lived by many Aboriginal peoples of the world. Due to the colonization process, these realities have been deemed less valid through a process of hegemony that has been unequaled in human existence over the past five-hundred years.

It was in reaction to the genocide and hegemony that some of the events recounted in this story took place many generations ago. Desperation stemming from what had already happened in Mexico and South America and the clear insight of what lay ahead in the future prompted these masters of the dreamtime, known as shamans, to enact energy that they themselves did not properly understand.

Lack of understanding then unleashed energy that still plagues the minds of most people with worry and unrest. It isn't until the source is understood that the solutions to the problems can be made manifest. For instance, if there's a lake that you want drained and you keep pumping water out without cutting off the underground source of water, you aren't making good use of your time. It's in the spirit of trying to understand the source that I tell this story. I'm not saying that all the answers are here. I'm simply offering a direction toward an area of possibilities that have been completely ignored so far.

As I sat in the cave with the awareness, or as the awareness was there being aware of what was going on in the cave that night, my psyche was transforming. There was no "I," but for the sake of simplicity, I will continue to use the "I" as a point of reference.

I looked in front of me and saw someone sitting there. His head was hanging down, so I couldn't recognize him. I knew it wasn't Tarrence, the Quiet One, or Ms. Chavez; yet there was an uncanny familiarity about this person. I didn't say anything at first, and when the conversation started, it wasn't verbal, as we know verbal. Instead, communication was within the awareness and was more to the point and precise. It was the type of communication that happens without language symbols—more of a knowing deeply the things in themselves rather than using signs and symbols to describe events or things.

"Welcome to the dreamtime," were the first words conveyed by the person, who was still hiding his face.

"Thank you for being here with me," I said. "It's been a while since I've seen anyone. Did you walk in? I didn't notice how you got here. Must have been a lapse in my awareness."

"I didn't walk in, not in the usual way. I just happened here. It's possible to do this once you're in dreamtime awareness. I guess you might say there is no space and time in the dreamtime. With some practice, you'll understand what I'm talking about."

"Are we going somewhere, or are we going to do something? I know Tarrence has a purpose for all this, and it's not entirely clear to me yet. You must be part of this whole thing that is happening."

"Yes, to all of your questions. The first few times I delved into the dreamtime awareness, it was difficult to let go of the mind that clings to experiencing space and time. With practice, it's possible. Tarrence—he never changes. He has somehow managed to gain the wisdom that has allowed him to remain free of wanting or clinging to anything. He has been that way for a long time. His concentration has been focused in the area of love and compassion. It was that way for all of us at one point. Then we lost track of the understanding that is awareness itself, and we gave in to ignorance," he said in a soft sad tone.

"Who is all this 'we'? I don't exactly follow what you're saying."

"Remember when Tarrence was telling you about how the dreamers had a meeting to try to change the way things were going on in the world? Terrible things had happened. Over five-million relatives had been killed in Mexico. Thunder dreamers could see that the same thing was going to happen toward the north and in other places where people were still practicing the ways of the dreamtime awareness. So we thought we had to intervene. I guess that's what you would call it nowadays. What had happened in Mexico caused some to lose their focus. Their concentration was fueled by sadness, desire, aversion, shame, doubt, and anger. Even the Gods Quetzalcoatl and Tetzcatlipoca ceased to give comfort, or so it seemed. The female Goddesses were nowhere to be found. All were simply blinded by grief. If you knew who these dreamers were—well, you wouldn't want their concentration fueled by anger directed at you. They could generate a lot of power with the focus of their minds. Concentration can be used for love and compassion—or for anger."

"So you're talking about the meeting that happened—at least Tarrence alluded to this. Somehow power was unleashed that got out of control. What does that have to do with me? I mean, aside from the fact that I'm a descendent of one of those dreamers who seemed to have lost the path."

I turned my attention to the picture on the wall. I was trying to direct my companion's attention to my ancestor being executed in the ancient mural. But when my gaze focused on the mural, I noticed that my ancestor was no longer in it, and the center of the circle was empty. This was disconcerting since I was sure of what I had seen earlier.

"So he's not there anymore? Where do you think he is?" my companion asked, lifting his face. To my amazement, this person who had joined me looked exactly like the person who had been on the wall painting. I was shocked out of being in the awareness for a few moments.

He felt this and said, "Keep breathing. Watch the breath. Move back to awareness softly. Come back to the silence. What's happening is just part of nature—the nature of mind." The words were so reassuring and comforting that I was able to return to awareness and to being awareness itself.

"Are you the one in the picture?"

"Yes, no, yes…. The answer is all of the possibilities. You will see with your heart who I am. For now, yes, I am the one in the picture. Good to see you, Great-Great-Grandson. I've been watching you from the dreamtime even before you came into this space-time part of the dreamtime. I'm glad to finally be able to do something about things that happened a long time ago in the relative reality of earth. The actions taken in this reality have had profound implications in the dreamtime, and it's time to heal the effects of ignorance."

"I'll do what I can. I am just a psychologist who kind of stumbled onto all this dreamtime business."

"That's what you think. That's your self-doubt keeping you from achieving the level of concentration you deserve to have. Your doubt will change in its own time and through its own nature," he replied in a kind voice that perplexed me a bit.

As the conversation was happening, my moments of disbelief would cause me to lose touch with the awareness, which was being aware of itself, and I would be back into my own mind. Then moments later I would be back in the dreamtime awareness. It was as if I was homing into something very delicate, and any slight mind-noise would distract me from the awareness.

"There is something that you need to know first," he said. "There are layers upon layers of dreaming, and then there is the absolute awareness that is within and without those layers of awareness."

As he spoke, I felt awareness expanding to encompass everything. Awareness then became aware that there were two rattlesnakes present in the cave. Through the precision of awareness, I was able to see the snakes in their minutest detail. Instead of scales, they were covered with the most beautiful tiny feathers, and the colors were profound. I couldn't believe what I was seeing; my mind drifted back to an ego state, and I thought of the plumed serpent and the meaning of the animal. "This is something else. The only story I know about this is the one about Quetzalcoatl—Jesus Christ!"

As soon as the words "Jesus Christ" came out, the rattlesnakes answered in unison, "Yes, is there something you want to say?"

"Ah, no, yes…. Is this for real? What is this? Is this one of those dreams? Is this really happening? Is it my imagination? Am I losing it?" was all I could come up with.

"Yes, to all of your questions," they answered.

"So you are Quetzalcoatl? And you also answered that you are Jesus Christ. This is something I can't understand."

"You can understand…and you will."

"I'll take your word for it. Are you going to explain?"

"Yes." They began to teach in a voice that was awareness itself and had no shades of doubt. "In the beginning of the dreamtime, we were there with the awareness that is aware of everything, including itself. All of the people who emerged out of the dreamtime needed a way to remain part of the awareness, and in their finite minds, they lost the ability to concentrate and focus their energy on awareness. The world that their small awareness became aware of became very distracting, since their awareness was just a part of that world—and nature pays attention to itself. That's when the absolute awareness allowed us to emerge, in order to teach concentration and awareness to people.

"You see, by this time people had lost the ability to think with an expanded heart, since their minds became trapped in their brains. Initially, the brain was placed there just for sense information. It was never intended to be the place where awareness resides. But the brain, being part of nature, became self-absorbed and took all the sense information available and made it appear to be real. It was only real to itself, and since the brain can only be aware of itself, then all that existed was this world of the brain. It became very seductive to the human awareness that had at one time been part of the absolute awareness.

"People thought this was how things are, and for many thousands of years, this illusion or trick played on them by this brain energy has caused profound suffering. Our task was to help people realize the trick or illusion and find their place in the absolute dreamtime once again."

"Why were humans allowed to do this in the first place?" I asked. "If they were part of the absolute awareness, why were they allowed to create their illusion and suffering?"

"Right at this moment, all we can say is, that's none of your business. First things first. We need to tell you how things happened. I'm sure you already know this from all the stories that abound in all of the religions that the illusions of the brain have created. Even though most religions are complete illusion and merely give the brain awareness of something to cling to, it doesn't mean there aren't traces left of the absolute awareness in that illusion. You still interested?"

"Very interested," I said, hoping to finally get some answers to life questions that I had been pondering. At that moment, awareness was aware of two other rattlesnakes. One was engulfed in luminescent white light. The other one appeared as a reflection in a gray hazy mirror.

"And just who are you two?" I asked, undistracted. By now my awareness was completely still, silent, and empty. What I knew as my awareness was not my awareness; it was simply awareness being in its own awareness.

"We are who we are. I guess you want to know specifically who we are, as in human brain history of sensory illusion?" they asked.

"At least to have a context for understanding, just in case I might have to explain this to someone who's not in the absolute awareness."

"Very well. All of us are related. We are part of the absolute, and our purpose is basically the same as the feathered relatives here. We are part of the same family. The luminescent one you would know as Lucifer, the devil, or as evil. The mirrored one—same idea. He/she was known as Tetzcatlipoca—the smoking mirror. I'm sure you know some of the story that has seeped into the dreamtime of illusion. 'It all has a purpose,' they say, through the language of awareness that is not removed at all from what is, through cognitive processes, usual human language.

"The best way to do this would be through what you would call a panel discussion. This way it will keep its meaning when you relate the story to those who don't have a concentrated mind. This is important in order for you to understand some of the things that will be explained to you later by that gentleman over there."

Great-Great-Grandpa was still sitting in a perfect lotus position in the circle. He was neither man nor woman per se. He was human awareness resting in absolute awareness. Interesting notion of genderlessness, I noted.

The feathered snakes started speaking. The one called Quetzalcoatl spoke to the one called Jesus Christ. "We were allowed to join the awareness of illusion in order to try to shake the illusion back into the absolute. We made our way into the dreamtime of illusion and lived among the human illusion and suffering that was created by the nature of the sense awareness that was available to humans. We came and told the simple truth, of how to re-enter into awareness. Humans, through their sense perceptions, made us into beings that would fit the hierarchy of their illusion. Instead of relating and being one with us, they removed themselves and promoted us to gods.

"Once they make you a god, there is no more relationship possible. The only way of relating is through an even greater layer of illusion, as if it were possible. The only ones who could relate to this new invention of the senses called 'gods' were special people who were initiated into the mysterious realms. You would know them as priests and other religious zealots who mostly pretended to have special power in order for them to immerse themselves even further into the illusion of things and possessions, both physical and spiritual.

"And the result now is that humans are totally out of touch with awareness itself...all except a few who persevered and broke through the illusion that the senses had created. These people were called Buddhas—awakened ones. It was apparent in the title they gave these enlightened ones that most people knew they were asleep with illusion, yet they did nothing about their own awakening. Pretty astonishing when you take it all into perspective."

I was impressed by the relationship between the one called Quetzalcoatl to the one called Jesus Christ, as well as the relationship they all had to one other, as if they were one being reflected by the same awareness.

"It's amazing what the illusion of the senses produced. But then again, that's what material stuff will produce, simply an awareness of self in a manner that is separate from all other awareness and even a greater awareness to the absolute," said the rattlesnake called Jesus Christ.

"What is really remarkable is that they made the very image of who we came in as to be evil. What was that with the snake in the Garden of Eden? Here we try to bring awareness, and they call it evil and make sure that no one even thinks of moving toward awareness and lack of separateness. That was a really good trick.... One of those two must have been playing a joke," Quetzalcoatl said, pointing toward the luminescent one and Tetzcatlipoca.

"It was only a joke, but I guess jokes that would be funny lose the humor if the absolute dreamtime is taken seriously in the brain-illusion world that human beings created," said the luminescent one called Satan.

"Yes, my little brother, it's especially sad because of the amount of suffering this type of ignorance brings," replied the snake called Jesus Christ.

"And what about the big stink they made about the incest that I tricked you into, big brother with all your feathers," retorted the one called Tetzcatlipoca to Quetzalcoatl. "They're still making something out of it. Didn't they realize you were just having a relationship with your female side of the dreamtime—that this would be a lesson for them to be able to unite themselves once and for all with the absolute awareness? All they could think of is that you screwed your sister, and in their ignorance, they created much suffering by their acting out sexually with their close relatives."

Jesus Christ then said, "The saddest thing they did, though, is when they divided the absolute awareness according to how they divided their brain illusion, to where they came from on the earth. The ones who professed to be the chosen people on one side of the world came up with an illusion that taught that only their knowledge of the awareness was valid, and all those who didn't believe in this way must die or go and burn forever. That is beyond ignorance—and they did it on our behalf, or so they say. They didn't have the courage to take the responsibility for their own brain illusion."

"It was heartbreaking to see the extent of ignorance of the ones who had placed themselves in the representing awareness," Quetzalcoatl said. "The sun-priests, and their lack of heart...how could they, even in such ignorance, justify the killing of innocent ones simply because they thought their brain illusion about the awareness and dreamtime was truer than the belief held by the ones living here on the place called Turtle Island? This is really the illusion inflating itself to the point that it starts to imagine itself as the awareness.

"And speaking of heart," he continued. "how could they have been so ignorant as to imagine that the awareness wanted actual physical hearts in order to stay in balance with them? In their illusion, they mistook an open heart of wisdom, compassion, and love to mean taking out actual hearts from people and sending them up to the sun. How could they not have known that all they had to do is relax the heart with love. And this love would then become part of the awareness that was already there, and through this act, the sun would then warm them all with wisdom and compassion. What pride the illusion created in order to trick them into more suffering without an end in sight. They would even remark that my heart was up in the sky as the morning star, and still they didn't understand. The pride the illusion created was the thing that most blocked their path to a heart of love and one with the awareness."

Satan immediately responded, "I know where this is headed. Pride, original sin, inflation of the ego to the point that it identifies with the awareness itself. I had my task, and that task was given by the awareness. It's true that I was to confuse their minds with illusion and ignorance. This was all part of a process that would trick them into realization of illusion. The way they took to the illusion, though, surprised even me. There was a point in time where it actually became boring to me because the illusion developed a life of its own and I became very unnecessary. Amazingly enough, the masters of the illusion continued to place blame on me for continuing to do this trickery and being the cause of suffering. In reality, it was their ignorance that continued to grow and feed on itself in an ever-perpetrated wheel of suffering. Any attempt by someone who was awake to intervene was dealt with in the harshest and most ignorant way. Guess you would know about that." Satan looked toward Jesus Christ.

"Yes. All attempts by us to bring an end to suffering were met with even more ignorance," Jesus Christ said.

"What about Quetzalcoatl and how he had to throw himself in the fire because of his having a relationship with his soul, his female-sister side?" Tetzcatlipoca said. "All I did is give him the spirit of alcohol to reduce some of the inhibitions he had acquired from being around the human beings in the first place. Once he had the thought of committing a taboo, all that was left for him was purification by fire—couldn't have been much fun even for someone who was still within the awareness of the dreamtime. I'm here with my cousin from across the ocean, Satan. All we did is provide the vehicle for awareness and liberation. We did this through trickery. After all, when someone is so completely stuck in the illusion of the senses, he can only realize the illusion through some sort of shock or major trick of the senses. They even created stories about tricksters and such to continue within the illusion—talk about clinging.

"The ultimate illusion was through the priests they called scientists. Now these folks took the brain illusion to new levels and created a circle that was beyond ignorance. They call me and my cousin evil, yet all we were doing was helping. What they came up with was actual evil, in that it created so much suffering. All my cousin and I did was act as tricksters of the awareness." As soon as Tetzcatlipoca finished his words, a piercing howl was heard in the cave. The awareness was aware that the coyote-dog that had come with the Quiet One was in the circle with us.

"Yes," Satan said. This science-religion they invented was a good trick at first. It almost took a turn toward awareness when that fellow said, 'I think, therefore I am.' But when the scientist-priests started using this new illusion to control people, the spiral took a turn toward more suffering. Very clever, those people. Now they had a foolproof way that had a trick. Not even my cousin Tetzcatlipoca and I could have thought of this thing they call objectivity. Biggest lie ever. Kind of makes me a little envious, if you all will indulge me, that I didn't come up with that one. Really, that didn't come from me. That was a total creation of the sense illusion that was being fueled by the so-called language of the gods. Now that was even a better one: numbers and mathematics. Again, indulge me in a little jealousy. I couldn't have come up with that one on my best day of trickery and lying. And mind you, with practice, I became very good at both, but I was outdone by the sense illusion that had emerged in the dreamtime of human beings."

"Can I say something?" I asked.

"Of course, anything," they all said through the awareness. "After all, we are here in this meeting to bridge the sense illusion with the awareness. Why do you think Tarrence has gone through the trouble of setting up this meeting? But we needed to give you some background information first."

"You have in part answered what I was asking. I was wondering where all this is going. Not that it isn't totally interesting—it really is. It's fascinating to hear all this. Also to know that Tarrence knows all of you and set this up; that's quite an honor," I said.

"Yes, Tarrence is in the awareness and is free from the mind illusion," they all remarked. "He's been working on this for some time—a long time when you take into account all the lifetimes he's put into it. This last one has been tough though. The two tricksters have given him real suffering to purify his senses."

"It's interesting that we're doing this here in the cave where my ancestor is shown in an execution for his ignorant behavior," I said.

"Yes. We're here for a reason," Tetzcatlipoca said in a serious tone. "There are places on the earth, which is just a part of the awareness, where there is a concentration of awareness. You would know this as power. This is a place of power and concentration; I guess you might say this is where the earth herself directed her awareness and worked on her liberation from suffering. Her suffering came from the ignorance of the brain illusion that was created by humans. Since the brain and body are just extensions of her and were completely intertwined with her awareness, it follows that this illusion had an effect on her. She tried a few times to teach them through lessons brought on by the awareness of the tricksters, but the ignorance persisted, even in these attempts at bringing balance in the awareness. And, as we said earlier, science became the ultimate ignorance. It was through this science that the final attempt at balance has been made possible. As you know, that happened not too far from here."

"You mean there's an actual place around here?" I asked.

"Yes, we can take a quick look-see if you want. Just so you will have a point of reference," Satan said.

"Let's go," they all said.

As soon as they said this, the awareness immediately shifted, and we were sitting on a hill covered with pines. Tarrence, Ms. Chavez, the Quiet One, and the coyote-dog were there also, sitting and looking into the distance. To my amazement, I noticed that Dr. Beerli was also sitting with them. All of the snakes had taken on anthropomorphic form, and they appeared as they had in artistic imagination for hundreds of years, except that they all had very dark skin and black hair.

I almost lost touch with the awareness. The sight was so overwhelming, it was hard to believe I was suddenly sitting with these folks in what is both real time and dreamtime concentration of awareness.

Tarrence spoke. "What you're seeing is necessary for your understanding, and that's all. There's no need for you to think this is any more real than anything else. Look around you, and try to understand where you are. You have been here many times in this life and in previous ones."

His voice was somber and had urgency to it. I looked around and saw a mesa covered with pines and aspens and surrounded by mountains. There was also a canyon to the right of me. The landscape started to become very familiar. But I was not completely sure this could be a place that I knew, even in the present awareness. As I was starting to doubt myself, I recalled that the canyon had a road going right by it in the present time. "This sure looks like Los Alamos," I said out loud.

"That's because that's where we are," Tarrence responded.

"I guess this must be the place that it had to lead to, eh? What does this mean though?" I asked.

"This is the place where the dreamers met in the dreamtime, like I was telling you earlier. All the history you learned in the cave is an important part to this whole thing. There was a critical ceremony done here twice in the dreamtime of the existence of human awareness. Those ceremonies continue to have a deep impact on all of the present awareness of the dream," Tarrence replied.

At this point, the only ones who remained with me were Tarrence, Ms. Chavez, the Quiet One, and the coyote-dog. We were in the center of the mesa, and there was a peculiar energy to the earth we were sitting on. All of a sudden the awareness became aware of several other people sitting in a circle. By today's standards, they were a primitive-looking bunch; at the same time they were obviously spiritual leaders of some kind. There was a man wearing what I recognized as ancient Aztec clothes, and a woman with red hair, painted blue face, and snakes tattooed on her forearms.

At another part of the circle, there were some African shamans, and in another section, some who looked like Mongolians and Asians. There were sixteen in all, eight men and eight women. They were chanting, and in the middle of the circle was a gourd that resembled the sphere I had seen on Tarrence's lap some time ago. It was very round and was painted with black, red, yellow, white, green, and blue swastikas moving in a clockwise direction.

I remembered then that the swastika—sometimes called the sun-wheel—was probably the oldest known symbol in the world. Except for the period when it was subverted by the Nazis, it had always been a sign of blessing and well-being.

Tarrence spoke. "This is the first ceremony that was held here several hundred years ago. This is a natural power spot, and that's why they came here. This is where they tried to balance the brain illusion that you heard about earlier. The illusion had become so destructive, these people here resorted to their own means to bring about balance. Unfortunately, their attempts emerged from the same brain illusion and not from the dreamtime awareness. Not to fault them—it's a tricky path. How do we know we're not following the brain illusion right now? It's only through the clarity that comes from silence that we can know, and we do know that we are within the absolute awareness and not simply on the relative side of things."

The circle of dreamers became very somber, and the gourd in the middle of the circle started to move by itself. The awareness of the gourd went around the circle of dreamers, stopped in front of each of them, and asked if they were willing to go ahead and place their intent into the gourd. As each one responded in the affirmative, the gourd then moved to the next one. The essence, or energy, within the gourd was making sure that the dreamers really wanted to enact such a cosmic karmic event and, in a manner of speaking, was contracting with the dreamers, one by one. The gourd would then provide them with the solutions to the world situation that they sought.

"The dreamers were caught by their own imperfections of insight, which they interpreted as the absolute awareness," Tarrence explained. "In reality, it was their egos inflated to such a degree that they were tricked into believing this was the absolute. It's so sad to see this happening. Such powerful and insightful people, and still they were tricked by the suffering—the suffering that was used as a trick by the brain illusion. In this manner they were able to justify selling their souls—"

"Yes, we know, the devil," interrupted someone who had been in the cave earlier.

I hadn't seen this entity emerge, and she/he left as soon as he/she finished the statement.

"See, this one is pretty tricky and never sleeps. That's how the circle of dreamers was seduced into the ceremony that you're seeing right now in the dreamtime," Tarrence said.

"This ceremony—the fact that it's being done here—that must mean something, huh? I mean, this is where the main plant for the Department of Energy's present-day laboratory is based, isn't it? This is starting to make a little sense," I said.

"Yes. Observe the ceremony."

Once the gourd had made it's way around the circle, it became luminescent and traveled counterclockwise six times. At the end of the sixth orbit, it went into the center of the circle and entered the earth. The circle of dreamers sat there for a while. I could tell by the looks on their faces they were concerned. Some of them didn't appear completely sure that this was a good thing.

"Too late though," Tarrence said. "The energy has traveled to all six cardinal points and has entered the earth at the seventh point, which is the center of the dreamtime. That gourd is still there, and it's still working its own kind of magic."

Then the land changed back to its present state. I could see a lot of buildings and modern streets going through the place we had just seen in its ancient form. Right where the center of the dreamer's circle had been was a larger building. I looked at Tarrence and asked, "What's this?"

"This is how it looks now. You've been through here many times. Right there in the center where the big building is…that's where they did it. They built it right there," he said in a serious tone.

"Built what?" I asked, though I already knew the answer.

"Of course you already know. That's where they built the bombs that were dropped on Japan. They were built right on top of the gourd that the dreamers left in the dreamtime. It was the dream's intent that they generated, that allowed them to go deep into the nature of matter and to release the energy they did. They were unconscious of it, but they all had their history with this place, just as you do."

"I recall that my grandfather used to own this land through a land grant or something. I remember how he used to farm around here somewhere." I was unsure of the exact place.

"Not 'somewhere.' It was right there," Tarrence said, pointing to the large building.

"You mean this is the very place? I thought it would be some remote part of the mountain where no one goes. I know that the government forced him out once they decided to build the bomb here."

Then the dreamtime changed the terrain once more to the way it was without the buildings. I could see clearly the way it looked before Los Alamos Laboratory was built. It had been a beautiful mesa, and I could see why my grandfather had loved this place. It was a perfect place to farm, and the pristine landscape had a sense of presence and awareness. It became apparent that in the Thirties this would be a secure place for people to hide and work on projects that required a high degree of security.

"After all, there was only one way in and one way out—that's why they chose this place," I said, half under my breath.

"No…. That's not why they chose it," Tarrence retorted.

"Why, then? Makes sense to me that they would want a secure area that's easy to protect from people snooping around."

"Let the dream show you. It's all in the emptiness of the dream," the Quiet One said.

The dream immediately changed to one in which the land was a farming place. I could see rows of beans and corn planted where the big building is today. There was a small hut where the people who worked the farm lived. There were cows, horses, and one mule grazing in a pasture close by.

A car drove up to the place—a 1930s vintage, as best I could tell—and stopped by the cornfield. Two men got out of the car and walked around. One was smoking a pipe, and the other was a military man of high rank. In retrospect, I know that he was General Groves. The one with the pipe was sniffing the air and breathing out smoke in all directions. He finally made his way to the center of the field and stood there smoking. All of a sudden, he smiled and called out to the military officer to join him.

"This is the place," he said, blowing smoke from his pipe straight into the ground.

"If you say so," replied the military person.

As I watched what was going on, I recognized the man with the pipe. I couldn't contain my excitement and blurted out, "That's Oppenheimer!"

"Yes, it is. You've seen him before also," Tarrence said.

"When? He's been dead a long time."

"You saw him in that very spot in the dreamtime," the Quiet One responded.

When he said this, I realized that the man with the pipe was one of the dreamers who had participated in the gourd ceremony earlier. I recalled that the military person was there also as one of the dreamers. At this point I lost my focus, and my logical mind kicked in again, wondering and doubting. "You can't tell me these were the same people. There's some sort of trick going on here," I said, frustrated.

"No tricks, just lifetimes of karma. All of us involved in this have had a part in the many lifetimes of karma that have gone into the history of this place...just like you and your great-great-grandpa," Tarrence answered.

"What's that all about? You're not going to tell me that was me, are you?" I asked.

"That's exactly what I'm telling you. Why do you think you're here in this very place? It's no accident that the dreamtime has brought you back to give you an opportunity to restore the balance—all of us have the chance to do that. We also have the chance to keep the imbalance going. It's really a matter of where our concentration is focused," Tarrence replied.

"So when you talk about karma and lifetimes, what specifically are you telling me?"

"I'm telling you that you are the one on the cave wall—you have been here. Karma is just cause and effect. You have the opportunity to plant seeds of harmony as you did in the past. What occurred here must change, and we have the opportunity to do so and to have an impact on the karmic dreamtime. What happened in this very place has been a threat to human rebirth ever since the original dreamers played around with that gourd," Tarrence said in a calm voice.

"Wasn't that just a gourd? It did look magical in the dream as it moved around. I could hear it rattling a bit. What was in it anyway?"

"It is never just a gourd, or 'just' anything, when you activate an object with concentration and intent. The gourd had the concentration of some very accomplished dreamers, and this gave it tremendous karmic potential. Inside the gourd were some hot stones. These stones were found not too far from here, and the dreamers knew that these were remarkable since they were always warm to the touch. Today they call these stones uranium. So you see—"

I interrupted. "You're not serious! You mean the dreamers were doing the ceremony with uranium even that long ago? This is interesting, but it's getting to be a bit much."

"So, you do see. There was the ceremony done by the dreamers in antiquity with the hot stones; then there was the ceremony done recently, again with the hot stones. Make no mistake about it, the ceremony was powerful both times, and a lot of human life has already been lost to the ceremony performed by the dreamers. Ironically, the dreamers were trying to put a stop to the suffering of the people due to the conquest and genocide. Instead they created more suffering and genocide. Concentration does not always come with discriminating wisdom, and intent is not always motivated by love and compassion," Tarrence remarked softly.

"Even with wisdom, there's always the coyoteing that occurs," said the Quiet One.

"Yes, there's always the chance that the ego gets involved, and you end up creating more suffering," Tarrence replied, as the dog looked up at me with what appeared to be a smile, which chilled me.

"So how did the government go about taking this land from my grandpa to create another ceremony, as you call it?" I asked.

"After those two men you saw in the dreamtime decided this was the place, it didn't take long. About a month after that, the army came and shot all of your grandpa's cattle and other animals. As you know, they told him and his family, including your dad, to get out due to national security. That was that. Nothing they could do.

"Something you need to know about your grandpa though. In his youth, he also dabbled with concentration and energy, not always to alleviate suffering. He practiced sorcery in the dreamtime, and he actually hurt a lot of people this way. It made sense that he lived right on top of the gourd, since it was in the lineage ever since you were here practicing the wrong type of concentration from the ego brain illusion," Tarrence said sternly.

I was beyond being surprised, and this new information was taken in stride. The whole time I had known my grandpa, he had been a prayerful and good man. Apparently during his youth, he had practiced ignorance, as Tarrence would say. As for lineage stuff and the destruction of the world being plotted either accidentally or on purpose on this very land, this was something that was interesting to me, and serious.

Maybe Tarrence was just making all this up in some type of hypnogogic, shamanic trick. On the other hand, what little I knew of karma, concentration, energy, and the historical facts about this place gave all of it a somber quality of truth. It had to be true. How else could this have happened? This whole idea of the atomic bomb was insane and had a diabolical sense to it from the get-go. It had to come from the depths of some twisted spiritual illusion and trick—some trick! So far, thousands have died for this trick of the brain illusion cloaked in scientific objectivity. Now there's a trick that puts an end to all sleight of hand, I thought.

I noticed that the dog was smiling at me again.

"What's up with that dog anyway?" I asked the Quiet One.

"He's just being; he's coyoteing. You see, he doesn't have a sense of self like we do. He's part of awareness being observed by awareness itself. He's not being like we are, just coyoteing. And through that arising of coyoteing, he or she is moving your insight toward the absolute," he said.

"Oh, sorry I asked," I replied, half-disgusted that I had no clue about what he had just said, realizing that he said something similar in the cave, except he added the insight part this time.

"I see that you're starting to get it," Tarrence said with his crooked smile.

"For some reason, I only know that this is true. Couldn't have been any other way. It would make no sense to think that some scientists came here to play with atoms simply because it was part of the scientific quest. That kind of randomness cannot be when it comes to something like this," I answered.

"'God does not play dice with the universe.' Einstein also said that," Tarrence said, laughing.

"So is the gourd still there?" I asked.

"Most certainly. Why do you think they're still here continuing the sorcery they call science? The science they do here is a direct descendant of alchemy, and alchemy was a deep spiritual practice, the practice of finding the philosopher's stone, which was God or the awareness itself. Once alchemy was discarded as just voodoo and science replaced it…well, that was the beginning of sorrows. See, science emerged from the brain illusion to disguise itself as the one that defined the awareness—as part of the trick of the brain illusion, of course. Science defined itself as the awareness and as the only way to the awareness. Everything else would become heresy unless subjected to the validation of the high priests of the new religion—science," Tarrence explained with an eloquence that surprised me.

"It was such a clever trick that even I am surprised at how good it has been," said the Quiet One. The dog was smiling again.

"The amazing part to me is that these dreamers were also susceptible to the illusion," I said. "You'd think that after having such a deep relationship to the dreamtime and awareness, they wouldn't have been sucked in to such an ignorant ceremony. They had to know what they were unleashing—they were too smart not to know."

"Yes and no…as everything else in the universe," Tarrence said. "They had a lot of knowledge, power, and even some wisdom. All this was clouded over by what was going on. All of the suffering, death, sickness, and losses clouded their vision with grief. Grief became something they held onto. They literally clung to it because it appeared justified and also the holy thing to do. It was the grief that gave birth to the anger and revenge that was plotted on this place. The justification—now, that was clever—you know, making it a holy and sacred thing. How could anyone oppose that or even question it? The illusion had a life of its own and was sprouting seeds and new life everywhere. Soon the illusion covered the knowledge and wisdom that had been attained, and it just turned to suffering. It's important that you are clear on this point: Nothing is worth clinging to, no matter how sacred or precious." Tarrence spoke dispassionately.

"What do we do now?" I asked.

"For now we're almost done with this part of the ceremony. Let's go over there and take a look-see," Tarrence replied. As soon as he said this, we were standing on the center spot in the dreamtime awareness. It was interesting that now Tarrence was also standing and had no need for the wheelchair. I felt uneasy standing on this spot where so much had happened and continues to happen. I couldn't help but wonder if all of this was just a symbolic metaphor, or if the gourd with the hot stones was really still there underneath the ground.

"It is," Tarrence replied, without being asked.

"Right here? Underneath where I'm standing?"

"Right where you put it in the first place," Tarrence replied, without showing any emotion.

"What do you mean 'where I put it?' I didn't put anything—"

Tarrence broke in. "Enough. You know you were here, and I'm trying to show you how to plant some different karma." His tone startled me. It sounded as if he'd lost patience and wanted to relay information without my getting in the way with analysis and doubt. Suddenly I remembered being there in the circle with the other dreamers, and I felt dizzy. My stomach became upset, and I threw up green bile.

I began pondering the implications of the actions that had taken place here. There has to be a way to end this and balance it out.

"There is," the Quiet One answered my thought.

"How?"

"Not so fast…. All in its right place," Tarrence responded.

"If I dig here, will I run into the gourd?" I asked.

"You'll run into that gourd when the time is right," Tarrence answered.

I could feel electric currents running through my body and could also feel the energy of the gourd moving all around us. By this time, my analytic mind just believed that what was happening was real and didn't try to invalidate the experience. The energy had been there for a long time, and not all of it was that of the energy placed there by the gourd.

Tarrence began to explain. "The vibrations you feel are coming from the origins of the dreamtime. It's the song of the dreamtime that was here from the beginning. That energy is pure and absolute; it's pure love and compassion. The mixing-up of the energy with the energy from the minds of the dreamers projected into that gourd—that's where the confusion in the dreamtime has been. This is the intention that became the cause for the effect.

"Karma is action through intention and is the cause of all suffering and freedom from suffering," Tarrence continued. "Since that time, dreamers have had to resort to all types of interpreting devices to understand the dreamtime, and only then can they understand even a little bit of it. You see, it's not because the awareness is cloudy. It's because of the cloudiness that has been placed on the awareness by the ignorant and attached intention of the brain illusion. Big implications, even though this happened a long time ago; in the dreamtime it happened right now and continues to happen every time there is a 'right now' in this moment."

The Quiet One took up the explanation. "You see, the sorcerers then, and then again in the Thirties and Forties when they were building the bomb, knew what they were doing. They were splitting the atom in search of the awareness itself, still thinking that they could then control the awareness. In splitting the atom, they were searching for the original spirit of God that the alchemists thought was trapped in matter—the lapis philosophorum, or the philosopher's stone.

"The interesting part of this is that the spirit the alchemists were looking for was the spirit of Sophia, or the female side of God," he continued. "I'm sure you're aware that this was lost or put away in western thought several thousand years ago, and the masculine energy has ruled with a total lack of harmony. The sorcerers are still looking for the spirit of God, except that in their ignorance, they only create destruction because of the lack of balance. All of this came in a dream, you know; the dream itself gave the sorcerers the key knowledge they needed to get into the center of creation itself. You do know about the dream Einstein had when he was riding on a beam of light. Well, it was no accident, even according to him, that he had this dream. Then Oppenheimer came here and smoked tobacco on this very spot where generations ago he was involved in the gourd ceremony. The original gourd later grew into the bigger gourd called "Fat Boy." It was hauled out the back way and dropped on our relatives in Japan. That was the culmination of the ugliest ceremony conjured up by the dreamers who had been trapped in a mind state of grief and anger."

I was impressed by the Quiet One's insights.

"Why is it significant that Oppenheimer was smoking tobacco?" I asked.

"Tobacco is the prayer and connection with the awareness," Tarrence said softly. "He was offering his prayer through the tobacco—back to the gourd with the hot stones inside the earth. You see, in what you call his unconscious mind, he had awareness that this was where he had been part of starting the ceremony in the dreamtime several lifetimes ago."

All of a sudden, my mind shifted to Carl. Carl would shit his pants if he heard this stuff. He would have me hospitalized and placed on heavy anti-psychotic medication. It's almost too far-out even for me, and I've been around this story for some time now. Why am I suddenly thinking about Carl? Maybe somehow he knows this is going on. Good ol' Carl. Why are you here in my thoughts?

"It's your doubting mind," Tarrence said matter-of-factly.

"What?"

"Carl represents that aspect of yourself that has been conditioned by the illusion; the analytic side that requires scientific evidence," Tarrence said. "In your thoughts this emerges in the image of Carl, because his whole life is like that—the totality of his life is to serve the illusion. It's really sad in a way, I guess, and then not really. He'll have plenty of chances in the present life or future lives to clear the smoke that the illusion has placed in front of his true nature—his own Buddha nature that is clear and will always be the awareness itself."

"So you're saying that everyone has this? Access to the awareness of the dreamtime, the original dreamtime awareness?"

"Not only do they have access, it's right there. Everyone *is* that awareness. It's just that fine veil that you call an ego, or self, that keeps people thinking they are separate and individual. So all that happened is not as profound as some would think. It's pure simplicity, really, and the smoke of the illusion becomes a thinner layer every time someone breaks through and becomes liberated. You see, no one gets liberated without liberating everyone else a little bit."

"Earlier we talked about how the illusion led to so much destruction," I said. "The ones who took the brunt of it from the ceremony, performed here by Oppenheimer and his gang of alchemical sorcerers, were the poor people from Japan. Why was that? I mean, it could have been anybody, but for some reason, it worked out that the Japanese were the ones who suffered the most from the ceremony performed here on my grandfather's bean patch. Guess it was my bean patch before that though, eh?"

"Now you're asking something very profound, and it has to do with the rules of dreamtime karma," said Ms. Chavez to my surprise, since she had been quiet for some time. "I guess you could call it the laws of karma, which are the laws of cause and effect within our layer of the awareness. The absolute awareness doesn't concern itself with all these things in the same way that we are concerned."

"So the laws of karma that were in play decided the Japanese would have to suffer from the ceremony of the gourd?" I asked. As soon as I asked, the place changed to the ceremony dream I had seen earlier. The dreamers were in their circle, and the gourd was moving around again. I could see a luminescence inside the gourd as it rattled from dreamer to dreamer. There were more dreamers now than the first time. Several of them got up and left when the gourd approached them. I realized that, even then, there were those who had not given in to the illusion brought on by grief and anger. As one of the dreamers got up, he made eye contact with me and smiled—a crooked smile.

"My God, Tarrence, that's you! I know that's you! That smile you couldn't hide from me in a thousand years. So, you left? You were not part of the ceremony, and you maintained your clarity. And Beerli and Ms. Chavez, you guys were there too, and you maintained your love and compassion!"

"Stay calm and quiet.... Yes, I did not go through with the ceremony. There is a price for everything," he whispered, as he gave his crooked smile.

Another dreamer left, and this one looked like an Asian elder, although it was hard to tell until I saw some of the markings on his sash. This gentleman joined Tarrence in the near distance, and they were talking in what appeared to be a very serious manner. After a while, the Asian elder bowed, Tarrence bowed, and the elder returned to the circle.

"Bet you want to know what we discussed, eh?" Tarrence asked.

"You know it. Looked like it was pretty important. You stayed, but he returned to the ceremony. That's peculiar."

"Not really," Ms. Chavez said. "You see, these two made a karmic deal—even then they were already bringing balance to the craziness brought on by the illusion that was a cloud of smoke in the minds of the others."

"Now wait a minute, easy with the smoke metaphors," the Quiet One interjected as the dog smiled at me.

"Why do you care about smoke metaphors anyway?" I asked.

"No reason," the Quiet One answered.

"Let me take you to the conversation," Ms. Chavez whispered. Again, as soon as she said this, my awareness was with Tarrence and the Asian gentleman.

"Are you sure you want to do this, Morehei?" Tarrence asked.

"I'm sure that it needs to be done. I'm not sure that I want to do anything," Morehei replied.

"You know both of our peoples will suffer because of this."

"Everyone will suffer because of this. We can't think of separateness at this time."

"Of course you're right, Morehei. There is no separateness in dreamtime karma. We'll give a chance at a balance in the awareness before the illusion makes it so cloudy that it will be almost impossible to have any clarity."

"What we do will insure that the balance of peace and silence will remain within the dreamtime awareness. It will cost—the cost of suffering upon suffering—like nothing ever seen before."

"Yes, there will be much pain—pain that will keep people in touch with the awareness," Tarrence agreed. "This type of pain will ensure that the illusion of the brain remains just that, an illusion. Pain will be the way to maintain concentration and oneness with the dreamtime awareness."

"Unfortunately, there is no other way out of this. They're proceeding with the ceremony, and the karmic seeds they're planting will emerge as an illuminating fire that will destroy the world itself. So we don't have a choice, really," Morehei answered.

As he finished his last statement, he and Tarrence reached into their bags, and each of them produced a small gourd. The two identical gourds were decorated very simply with black, red, yellow, white, green, and blue sun-wheels moving in a clockwise direction—the same pattern I'd seen before.

As they started to shake the gourds, a dim light appeared within the gourds. After a few moments of chanting and rattling, Morehei and Tarrence placed the gourds on the ground and put a circle around them, then sat and chanted a while longer. Then the two gourds became very bright and fused with each other, becoming one gourd.

"What's inside this gourd?" I asked.

"The small stones in this gourd are from the original dreamtime—the place from where all matter emerged. I think you'd call it the big bang—the stuff that was in the instant right before this," Ms. Chavez replied with authority.

"You can't be serious. How would anyone get these.... I mean, they can't possibly exist after the big bang."

"You're drifting back to the analytic mind of illusion, where not much is possible. That's the same trick that was played on you when you sat in that circle of dreamers," Ms. Chavez said sternly.

"What?" I blurted out.

"There, look at yourself in the gourd ceremony.... Why were you there? There can only be one answer: Ignorance. Ignorance had all of you in your pitiful brain illusion full of analysis and rationalizations as to why you needed to activate the ceremony that you activated."

Ms. Chavez's tone became gentle. "Now that illusion is all around you again, trying to distract you from what you know is absolute."

"I see. In the dreamtime, absolute dreamtime, all of this is simple and to the point. Therefore, the stones in the gourd just *are*. I see now."

Ms. Chavez smiled at me, and my attention went back to the two dreamers and the luminescent gourd with the creation stones inside. As they sang and chanted, the gourd started to move in a clockwise direction. Then it hit the ground and became seven gourds that looked like the original ones. These gourds flew into the air and landed on the four directions around the other ceremony that was being held. Four of the gourds went into the ground: west, north, east and south. Two gourds remained until the end of the ceremony, when the gourd with the firestones went into the ground. At this point, one of the two remaining gourds went up into the sky, and the other one followed the one that had gone into the center of the dreamer's ceremony. And then it became completely silent.

"I see. The balance has been there the whole time," I said softly.

"It always is. The absolute is always there. You don't have to go anywhere to find it; all you need to do is be quiet," Tarrence said.

"I know," I said with assurance.

"Tarrence and Morehei did something very powerful in their meeting. They activated the luminescence of the dreamtime that cuts through the smoke of illusion," the Quiet One said, as the dog gave me a big smile.

I was wondering about the dog. But instead of asking about him, I just smiled back, much to my own surprise. Carl would not only freak, he'd actually die if I told him about my returning the coyote-dog's smile, I thought.

"Yes, they started a karmic ceremony to balance the one that the other dreamers started. Both ceremonies had a tremendous price tag attached to them—suffering upon suffering," Ms. Chavez said.

"But it seems as if Tarrence and that Japanese guy made a deal to bring balance to all this—or at least it looked like they were doing something in that direction. With the gourds going in all directions and into the earth and sky," I said.

"Yes, there was a deal made. This is where it gets a bit tricky for most people to understand," Ms. Chavez continued to explain. "It's difficult because the brain illusion can only understand things in a framework of space and time. You see, what Tarrence and Morehei were committed to doing is to bring peace and balance—restore the silence. This can't be done unless something is given up to restore the balance. I guess, for a lack of a better word, there is a price. In reality, the price is basic energy—it takes energy to move energy, and energy needed to be moved in order to restore karmic balance."

"Pretty much like Christ paying a karmic price to restore balance," I said.

"Exactly. And what the dreamers did in the ceremony here both in antiquity and in modern times required an equal amount of energy to restore harmony. So Tarrence committed the suffering of a lot of Indian people to this—suffering is sacred and has a lot of energy. The suffering that our people have undergone for several generations is not without meaning. It's not wasted as would appear on the surface. This is a difficult thing for a lot of people to understand. All of the suffering through loss of land, families being torn apart, the alcoholism that you work with—all of it is part of the price that needed to be paid in order to heal the wound that was given to our mother, the earth, on this spot, and also to restore karmic harmony."

"Right within the pain is the medicine. Our Sufi relatives say that one should never be embittered at the amount of suffering one is entrusted with," the Quiet One said.

"True, this is how it is," Tarrence said calmly and assuredly. "Nature is in balance. It always is. Our awareness sometimes gets out of balance and harmony, and then we need to engage the natural process to get back into balance. That's why the dreamtime has given us ceremonies—so we can access the absolute awareness of the dream that was here in the beginning. Just like the original stones in the gourd that you just saw. Those stones are the awareness itself being manifested in form so that we can make sense of it in our relative awareness."

"I'm beginning to see. It's all one fabric interwoven throughout the dreamtime," I said, and was surprised at myself for saying this. The coyote-dog gave me a big smile. It was as if this dog understood the conversation. In retrospect, I have no doubt that the dog was comprehending and actually contributing to my understanding at that point.

"You were going to mention the role that Japanese dreamer had in all this. I have a feeling he made a significant contribution," I said.

"Significant, but very difficult for the relative awareness to understand," Ms. Chavez said.

"This one has to do with war and warrior tradition," the Quiet One said.

"You must understand that the warrior tradition is a way in which the absolute has tried to convey a way out to our relative awareness," Ms. Chavez taught in a kind voice. "It's a way to effectively stop the brain illusion with the confusion of war at the instant when the ego finds itself in between life and death. The natural processes of awareness then lead the person toward the absolute. All of it has a purpose, and the awareness itself is pure love and compassion…. That's why it has set up such a balance within the dreamtime, so that we can once more become part of the absolute dream."

"Warrior Gods have existed forever, all leading toward concentration and awareness itself," the Quiet One said.

"That's why Morehei became involved," Tarrence said. "He was—is—a dreamer of the warrior dreamtime. He came to the original meeting in order to help keep balance through the arts of war. The arts of war are very close to the awareness, since it's in the arts of war that our minds settle very quickly. In that instant of life and death, there is no room for any other thought, and there's a quick balance in the mind that approaches total concentration. Also, the rules of war are very useful in a ceremony like the one that was held here. That's part of the purpose of Morehei being here."

I became aware they were getting to the point but were a bit reluctant and wanted to prepare my analytic mind for what would come next. The realization of what they were taking me toward is one of the most difficult concepts I've ever had to deal with. It makes little sense to the ego that wants to hold on to logic. What follows is part of the illogical way of being that the awareness of the dreamtime has, which is distorted by the brain illusion. I've wondered about the nature of the brain illusion. If it's part of nature, why does it confuse the relative awareness of the absolute awareness itself?

In one of our talks, Tarrence alluded to this by explaining that, due to the needs of the earth-body, allowance is made for distortions of the awareness. Awareness is known through the earth via the sense stores of the body. There is a point in which all of the biological relative awareness of the cells themselves is taken into account by an overall prevailing body awareness. It is only through discipline and practice that these can align themselves with the absolute. Until this happens, then the crisscrossing of countless awarenesses is difficult to bring into balance out of the emerging ego awareness. The balancing act wouldn't be so difficult if the ego wasn't trapped in a space-time continuum. It's this very continuum that the ceremony transcends and allows for the relative awarenesses of the components that make up the person to harmonize with the absolute.

I realize this is not an easy idea for most, as it wasn't for me in the beginning of the teachings with Tarrence. One has to allow for an opening of his or her awareness to assimilate this without the layer of doubt; then the conditions for understanding will be present. Otherwise one has to go through all of the tricks and machinations of the brain illusion to arrive at the same point, except that will take much longer—several more lifetimes longer, according to Tarrence.

Tarrence knew there is a place where what we call 'physics' and the awareness are the same. He didn't lecture on this per se. Through the talks that we had, it became possible for me to acquire the realization that this is the same crossing. Awareness is the same at the particle level as it is in what we think is a unified awareness of brain through the evolutionary process. In reality, our biological awareness is simply the awareness of the earth herself as a living being. Since we are made completely from the earth herself, it follows even logically that the awareness we have must come from the particles that make the earth.

Taking this a step further, the earth is made of particles that were there forever in the absolute awareness. There is a point where the awareness within the particles is allowed awareness from the dreamtime awareness that is absolute. In order to understand this crossover, one must achieve absolute stillness and silence. Tarrence taught that the absolute manifests itself in the silence and the absence of all things and thoughts. Timelessness and spacelessness prevail, and in the emptiness, there is original awareness. This is most difficult, if not impossible, to convey in words.

Tarrence told me once, "If you can explain it, then that's not it," before he exploded in an uproar of laughter. Even with his body paralysis, the spasms almost threw him out of his chair.

My attention returned to the explanation of the ceremonies. "Well, now I'm ready to hear about how Morehei became involved," I said.

"OK, this is how it happened," Tarrence explained. "Morehei had seen the devastation through his awareness of the dream. He realized there was a lot of confusion because of the grief that was like a dark cloud over the awareness. He had seen this happen in other places and had been able to intervene before it got to the point that it did here. Morehei had a meeting with the dreamers in his part of the world. It was quite a meeting. All the dreamers from what is known as Asia and Europe were there. A couple of dreamers came from Australia, since they are still very much with the dreamtime awareness.

"In the meeting, it was decided that a great sacrifice had to be made in order to restore balance in the dreamtime karma. Already so much suffering had been forced on the people of what is known as Turtle Island. The screams and suffering were heard within the absolute dreamtime itself. Most of the dreamers from Turtle Island were also removed from the relative awareness, and their grief went with them into the original dream. So, as you can see, there was quite a mess that came out of what Cortez and his bandits started here. The smoke reflected on the relative mirrors of the interpreters of the dreamtime who were supposed to bring clarity blinded them. Instead, they were trapped by the brain illusion that became rigid through what they called theology. The only thing to do was to stop this at all costs—or so thought the dreamers who were caught in their grief.

"Morehei, coming from a warrior dreaming tradition, realized that the balance would occur only through an act of a selfless warrior," Tarrence continued. "He decided that he would offer the sacrifice of his people in order to restore the balance of the dreamer's ceremony. Are you with me?"

"I think I am. There is to be a karmic debt paid by Morehei in order to bring balance back into the relative dreamtime, and through that we can once more have access to the absolute," I responded.

"He's getting it," said the Quiet One, and the coyote-dog gave me a big smile.

"Morehei committed his people to pay the price for the ceremony, both ceremonies. That is, he said that they would balance out the equation with their suffering," Tarrence said. "Through that suffering, the awareness of love and compassion would be restored on the land called Turtle Island. Most of the dreamers were amazed at his courage, yet they couldn't help but try to go for the quick fix, as you have seen."

"So am I getting this right? He's committing the suffering of his people to restore balance? I think this is going into a place that will be difficult to understand," I said.

"It's the way it is," said the Quiet One.

"Yes. Morehei committed his people to balance out the ceremony," Tarrence said. "The balance could only occur through great sacrifice. The sacrifice was completed when the gourd and the power of the gourd were released on the Japanese people—"

I lost my calmness and interrupted Tarrence. "Are you saying that the bombs dropped on Nagasaki and Hiroshima were part of the karmic deal made here? This is unreal!" I screamed.

"Would you rather that the suffering upon the Japanese people be in vain, or just some random event?" asked the Quiet One.

"No, that's not it at all. It's almost like blaming the victim. This isn't working for me!" I was very upset.

"That's only because you don't understand the absolute power of suffering; you're caught in the relative," Ms. Chavez said. "The relative only clouds your awareness through the brain illusion. It's through this that the illusion perpetuates itself and keeps you helpless, even though you're a healer."

"It needs to be realized as a warrior awareness," said the Quiet One.

"What exactly is that supposed to mean? Who are you anyway?" I was frustrated.

"It means just that. That is, this can only be understood through the luminescent emptiness of the awareness. You're still trying to make sense of all this through your relative ego mind."

"And the second part? Who are you?" I asked again.

"Let's continue," Tarrence cut in.

"Yes, we must." Ms. Chavez said. "What has already been said is already having an impact on the dreamtime. We must continue. This ceremony is almost over." As she finished her statement, I realized we were back in the cave. My ancestor was still absent from the picture, and I looked around.

"Looking for yourself?" Tarrence asked with the crooked smile that by now I saw as his trademark.

"Ah, well, I guess. When you put it like that," I replied.

"There you are," the Quiet One said.

"As we were saying," Tarrence explained, "there are realms that go beyond what the ego awareness knows and is willing to entertain because of the space-time trap. What Morehei did was to reassure that the path toward the absolute would continue to be. You see, if he hadn't done this, none of us would be here. He also paved the way for the prophecy of Padmasambava to become realized; you know, the one where he talked about the Buddha coming or being in the land of the Redface."

"Meaning?"

"Sacrifice without awareness is meaningless and only brings more suffering. What Morehei did was offer awareness to the sacrifice of his people. There was no way the brain illusion would continue using the ceremonial gourd that by now you know was the bomb itself. In his warrior awareness, he ensured that this would stop in the time that it did. Even his warrior awareness and his willingness for suffering can't hold this from happening forever. Balance needs to be restored once and for all," Tarrence said with deep concern.

"So there's more that needs to happen? I thought this wasn't over, at least not when you look at how things are in the world presently," I said.

"The illusion is stronger than ever. People are not in tune or don't even believe that there is awareness. All they care about is going shopping," Ms. Chavez said.

"It's getting to be time," the Quiet One broke in.

"Yes. The ceremony needs to be concluded," Tarrence said. "We can't try to do everything at once. That would be giving in to the brain illusion that we need to fix things, when in reality, it's the nature of balance itself to become balanced. All to its own nature."

At this point the Quiet One passed some water to all of us. As we finished drinking, the Quiet One brought Tarrence's chair and helped him into it. He lifted Tarrence into the chair with a smooth motion and wheeled him out of the cave. Ms. Chavez and the coyote-dog followed. I followed too.

14

After the Ceremony

*O*utside the cave, the day was sunny and quiet. The smells of the early morning dawn were mixed with the juniper and piñon of the area. I heard the screech of a hawk and the singing of sparrows in the distance. I recalled the metaphor of hearing a sparrow take a drink on the other side of the mountain. That would require real silence, I thought to myself.

The Quiet One lifted Tarrence onto the seat of the truck, folded the chair, and placed it in the bed of the truck. Ms. Chavez made her way to the bed of the truck and sat down; I wondered why she just didn't get into my vehicle since I had space in the cab.

As they drove away, Tarrence made eye contact with me, gave me that crooked smile of his, and said, "Let it go, don't hold onto any of this, it'll just keep you stuck." Then the truck made its way up the path back to where we had arrived a few days earlier.

Coming out of the cave after four days was an experience I will never forget. Tarrence's last statement about letting go of the experience sounded a bit absurd, since this had been the most profound thing that had ever happened to me. Letting go was unthinkable, and I really didn't know what he meant by getting stuck. Years later, I came to realize that being in the moment means just that, and memories are mind states that really exist only in the moment as a memory generated in the brain.

Nothing to do now except to get back to life as usual. But that would never be possible again. Things already appeared different to my perception, and I couldn't undo the effects of the ceremony on my senses and awareness. At least now I have a notion of awareness.

Whom can I tell about this? Is there a need to process? Carl will try to have me committed and will probably send an army of mental-health types up here to round up Tarrence and his crew. Carl would really freak out the first time that coyote-dog smiled at him. That would be worth the price of a ticket.

I made my way to my truck and got in. There was an inner peace and balance that I had never known before. My mind wandered to the picture in the cave, and my last recollection was that my ancestor was missing from the picture. That must have been some sort of sleep-deprivation hallucination, I thought. There's no way that picture could just peel itself off the wall after being there for generations. Yeah, it's still there.

Is it? Only one way to find out.

My analytic mind was trying to reconnect with the linear world thought as I got out of the cab and made my way toward the cave opening. There's nothing wrong with my just checking this out. I'm sure the gang would understand this, I thought as I went in and reached for my little flashlight that I carried attached to my keys. I got close to the wall and shined the light at the petroglyph. What a shock to see that my memory was correct. The shaman being executed was no longer there!

What the hell is going on? I know I saw it before, and there's no way this can be a trick. I know what I saw, and I am not losing my mind. This dreamtime shit is getting out of hand, I thought, as my mind tried to make sense of the reality before me. I am definitely going to have to process this with all of them. I can't believe they just left as if nothing had happened. They just took off with no concern for what occurred. What's up with that? And they all seemed so peaceful and happy when they left. I'm going to find out who that Quiet One is; enough of the mystery bullshit. And that dog? Weird pup! These were some of the immediate thoughts that emerged as part of the mind states that were going through the space I was standing in.

There wasn't much left to do but leave. Since I had scientific pre- and post-data that something had occurred here, now it was time for analysis. It was amazing how quickly my logical mind was in the process of taking charge of making sense of the non-linear process that was still occurring. I could sense that there was a back-and-forth center of attention occurring, as my linear mind exchanged places with the awareness that was aware of even the linear mind. Awareness itself was watching the process, and yet there was no disintegration to it, as might be the case when someone depersonalizes. Instead of my knowing, it was the awareness that was aware of even knowing and cognitive processes, a very different way of being and impossible to convey in words.

After a few minutes, I was back in the truck, and as I moved it into gear, the sensation of movement was different. Again, it was the awareness that was aware. I wasn't operating from the usual ego-sensation processing system that I had been accustomed to all my life. This is interesting. I wonder how long this will last. I wonder if Tarrence and the others are like this all the time. They must be; that's why not much seems to bother them, and even being paralyzed isn't a big deal to Tarrence since he's in another reality. That's it, that was the first thing he told me, I recalled.

If there is just the awareness, then all else is simply happening and drifting away. It's as if there's no one there at any given time, since the thought that I identify at any moment is gone as soon as it starts. It's all conditioned. Conditions happen, and a consequence occurs. Is this that simple? It is. Why the big problem of attachment then, if this is just how it is? These were the thoughts emerging, and awareness was aware they were emerging.

Even though there were thoughts, there was also attention. I had never seen so much detail in the landscape far and near. The momentary experience I had a few weeks ago of seeing all the pine needles individually and collectively as a forest was there in the awareness as I was driving down the path away from the cave. My body was just part of the natural process occurring and perceiving. Everything else was awareness being aware. I was present in every moment. There was an underlying awareness and understanding to the process unfolding. Awareness was present in all the variations of light and shadow as these changed in rock crevices and trees. Clouds also had a keen awareness, and awareness had awareness of the awareness that was in the cloud itself.

Eventually I returned to the highway and made my way home. As I passed the turnoff to Dr. Beerli's place, I remembered seeing her just before the beginning of the ceremony of dreamers. I wondered whether she was really there; then I realized she was there in the dreamtime, and that was real enough. I'll have to visit her soon, I thought.

Farther down the road, I was aware of a turnoff that I'd seen many times. It simply said 'Zen Center.' I wondered what went on there and if this was real Zen, or just another New Age gimmick to get tourists to spend money. I thought I'd better check it out sometime, since I've done some Zazen practice and reading.

More cars appeared on the road as I approached town. Color was an intense presence in my mind, and I had never before experienced the very nature of color as I did at that moment. Red was red, green was green, and I could literally experience the essence of the color itself, and awareness was aware of this awareness.

When I got into town, I made the usual turns to get home. As I went up the street, I thought of getting a large mocha coffee at the Latte' Hey. What the hey? A coffee treat will be good as I re-enter this awareness, I thought.

I parked the truck and walked toward the door. The same homeless man was there, selling an underground newspaper. His expression was flat; no one could or would see him. I realized he might even be invisible to himself. For the first time ever in a situation like this, I looked at him, said hello, and asked how he was. He appeared to be shocked by this and didn't know how to respond.

Finally he said, "Good. How about a paper?"

I bought a paper and told him to keep the change, which was over three dollars. He appeared happy and went into the Latte' Hey ahead of me.

I sat at a small table and realized people were staring at me. I must be pretty funky after the past few days without a shower or change of clothes, I thought. They probably think I'm with the homeless guy.

The homeless guy picked up his order, and as he walked by my table, he said, "Go to the Zen Center." Then he left.

My mind reeled and wondered if the ceremony was still going on and if this was part of the dream that I was in all those days. Then I remembered what Tarrence had said of how it's all a dream. How did that guy know about the Zen thing though?

My thought was interrupted by a loud, "Wassup, my man! And look at you. Where have you been? Have you gone totally native or what?"

"Carl...how are you?" was all I could come up with after such a boisterous interruption.

"The real question is, how are you, my man—hey, what's going on?" he said as he stared at my face.

"Going on with what? What are you staring at?"

"Are you OK? You haven't looked in the mirror yet, or have you lost it? Your face is painted red, my man. I know this is the southwest, but hey, not even the local natives go this far. Please tell me this is some phase or prank. I don't want to think you've lost it," he said, as he got more serious.

"Oh, my face. I forgot. Guess I should have taken time to clean up, but I just came directly here to have a treat. Been through a lot the past few days," I said calmly.

"Don't tell me. You were up in the mountains with that crazy guy, what's his name...the paralyzed dude you told me about. This is getting serious, my man. You're losing your professional composure. What happened anyway? I could give you a medication 'script right now, my man. Tell you the truth, it really looks like you need it," Carl retorted.

"Carl...get off it. I'm OK. I just went through some stuff. Just because it wasn't western psychiatry doesn't mean you have to demean the experience by pathologizing it. That's what's wrong with our profession. Anything we don't understand, we assume is sick and we need to make it go away with drugs. The whole culture is doing that either on the streets or through the sorcery of psychiatry," I said with conviction.

"Whoa…whoa…whoa, my man." Carl was hurt. "You're talking gibberish now. You know that's not how I am. I've had training in cross-cultural work. You're out of line with those remarks, way out, my man."

"You see, Carl. You take a course in cross-cultural stuff and assume that now you know every culture because of the course," I expounded in a tone just above a whisper. "That is such an insult, truly an expression of White privilege. Are cultures other than western so transparent that you can see through all of them by taking a three-hour course? Who needs the medication, man? I think you're way out of touch, as is the whole profession."

"Where do you get off with all this? Come on, I'm just trying to help here. What happened anyway?"

"I was involved in a ceremony. If I told you the details you'd freak, so let's leave it at that," I replied.

"It must have been some ceremony. I've never heard you talk or look like this. Maybe sometime I can come up and meet this paralyzed dude."

"It's Tarrence…he has a name. He just happens to live in a body that does different things, that's all. Maybe you can come up sometime. You'll have to promise not to come off with this privileged attitude of yours though, and keep judgments to yourself. Although he'll know anyway."

"Are you saying he can read minds?"

"Yes, he can. Well, Carl, 'my man,' I need to get going so I can rejoin the world of the brain illusion." As soon as I said it, I was aware of the first time I heard this, and of the conversation of the snakes in the cave.

"Brain what? What the hell are you talking about? Illusion? Is this a Buddhist thing? You know I've studied Buddhism, so I know a little bit about the stuff," Carl said, stumbling over his words.

"Later, Carl. I gotta go—need to shower and wash my face. Too much Redface, if you catch my drift," I said and started toward the door.

"We have to finish this. I don't like your insinuations, my man. You know I'm not like that!" He was still hollering as I went out the door.

By the time I made my way to the truck, the homeless guy was nowhere in sight. Wonder who that was? And where did he go? That was part of the dreamtime, I guess. I'll have to check out the Zen thing sometime; the dream was pretty specific, I thought, and surprised myself at how sure I was. My questioning was becoming less and less when it came to the awareness of the dream.

I got to the house and listened to my messages. Dr. Beerli's was the fourth.

"Hello, calling to catch up. I'd like to meet with you when I'm in town day after tomorrow. That was amazing, wasn't it?"

Amazing? What was amazing? Not more riddles. No way can she know... oops, doubting the dream again, "my man," I thought.

I knew there was an interconnecting strand of something that was as real as anything in my experience so far in life. The interconnecting thread was subtle and stayed that way until I started paying attention to it. Once attention and awareness were focused on the interconnectedness, then it was everywhere. Not only was it everywhere, it became very obvious every time it manifested itself. There was a part of my psyche that still wanted a logical analysis every time that awareness was aware of the subtle process, but the analytic part was subsiding a lot faster than at the beginning of all this. Presently, the analytic emerging thoughts were more of a background noise than a real intrusion.

My meeting with Carl allowed me to see clearly into this; that is, his analytic thought process was predominant, and the awareness was part of the background noise that didn't get a chance to be in awareness. Therefore I felt Carl was a good person, but his training in the brain illusion had drowned any awareness within him. If he allowed himself the time to be aware, he would also start to get an understanding of a different nature.

This is the way it is for everyone, and it requires effort every moment, as it did on my part. I felt fortunate to have people like Tarrence in my life who accelerated the process. Tarrence would say, "It's karma, and fortune has nothing to do with it."

I returned Beerli's call to let her know it would be all right to meet day after tomorrow. She didn't say what this was about, and I decided just to go along with it, since that's the way it was going to be anyway. One thing was certain though: She had something pressing to talk about; I knew this from the serious tone in her voice.

The next day was ordinary. On the evening before our meeting I had a dream. In the dream I was back at the cave. My great-great-grandfather was sitting there as we had been in the ceremony. The peculiar thing about this dream is that he was wearing women's clothes, complete with jewelry, moccasins, and hair-do. His energy was different in the dream, and he smiled at me in manner that seemed friendly but could have been seductive. As he looked at me he said, "If we'd understood more about this, we might not have gotten into so much trouble."

When I woke up I was clearly aware of the dream, and I felt his or her presence with me throughout the morning. I wondered about its meaning, but I was sure that in my meeting with Beerli, some of it would be explained. So I decided to wait till later to get into it.

He must have been quite the character if what little I know of him is true. I wonder what he did most of the day? Perhaps he cut wood, maybe fetched water. In the meantime patients would come for help or advice. The life of an ancient shaman, that was something.

My mind meandered for a few minutes. The doorbell interrupted my thoughts. When I opened the door, Beerli was standing there, smiling.

"Good afternoon, and welcome. It's an honor having you here," I said and wondered where the honor thing came from, since I usually didn't say that to people.

"Thank you. It's nice being here. It was a nice drive, and the air is so clean. I had to make one stop on the way, but that's always pleasant. I stopped at the Zen Center and had a visit with the Abbot—nice man and very awake. He's from Japan, you know, and he's been here a few years. You must go there and meet him sometime," she said, still smiling.

"That's the second time in the past few days someone has said I should go there. I guess I should check it out sometime. Time is an issue, especially with the extra involvement with Tarrence and his crew. That's really taken a bite out of my schedule recently," I said, as we walked into my home office, where we could sit and sip coffee and tea that I'd prepared.

"Sounds like some synchronicity is going on in your life, yes?" she asked.

"Yeah," I responded in a teasing tone.

"I had the feeling you've been through a lot recently, and I just wanted to touch base with you," Beerli said kindly.

"You don't know the half of it. I was involved in an extensive and intensive ceremony thing with Tarrence and his crew. One morning I could have sworn that you were there."

"Perhaps I was," she said, laughing.

"Do you want to hear about all this?"

"Of course; that's why I'm here."

I went on to recount the events as well as I could—in abbreviated form so it wouldn't take four days to tell her what had occurred. She listened carefully as she sipped tea. Her eyes were focused on me, and I felt she was listening deeply, that she really understood what I was talking about. I didn't feel she needed any extra explanations, and I thought that she wasn't at all bothered by the story, quite the opposite of Carl. The validation she gave by her attention was something I really needed at this point, and she was a master at doing so. When I finished the story, she smiled.

"That's fantastic. I'm so glad some attention is being paid to the healing of the earth and what was done there at that place. The collective psyche has really given you a task, it sounds like, yes?" she said, reaching toward one of the muffins on the table.

As she did so, her sweater pulled over her forearm, and I noticed a tattoo of a snake, exactly like the tattoo I had seen on one of the dreamers at the original ceremony. She realized I'd seen the tattoo and proceeded to pull up her sleeve to show me the whole image. I was speechless.

Beerli smiled and didn't say anything for a few moments. Finally she broke the silence and said, "I told you there were a lot of synchronicities in your life, yes?"

"Yeah," I responded, just to keep the conversation going.

"You seem a bit confused about what is right in front of you. Empirical evidence is right in front of your eyes, and you still doubt? After everything you've seen? This is something that modern psychology is so blind to. They say they want evidence. When they get it, they don't want to believe it. I'm not saying you're this way. I'm just speaking about the field in general. You know this was Jung's struggle. He gave plenty of scientific evidence, yet he's still considered a quack by most, simply because it wasn't the evidence that supports what they want to hear," she said in a stern voice.

"I know. I live with it every day of my life. I have a friend who wants to put me on medication, and he doesn't know one-tenth of what I've been through recently. If he did, he'd have me committed, I'm sure. Anyway, you're one of the dreamers from the dreamtime ceremony, yeah?" I said, smiling.

"Yes, I was going to paint my face blue this morning, but I thought that might scare people on the road…." She laughed, then continued, "I was there and feel bad about being blinded by the grief and anger that all the dreamers were expressing. If it hadn't been for Tarrence and the Japanese fellow, we would be in real trouble now. You might even say that it would be hopeless. The awareness did not allow for total annihilation, and it's good that those two were there. Their courage will always be thought well of in the dreamtime. They committed a lot in their quest to undo the doing that we were involved in. That has always been within the dreamtime though."

"So, the deal they made was for real. I mean, I know it was real, but it really happened like that. It was a lot to take on, so much suffering."

"Suffering is not what you think. Suffering is sacred and a way of intervening with karma. It's the only way that karmic shifting can occur. A price must be paid; after all, it is cause and effect. Therefore, if a cause has been set in motion, then another cause can alter that cause, and the effect will be different than if just left alone," she explained.

"Kind of like the Christian idea of the Cross?"

"Absolutely. That was done in order to shift major karma, which had been set in motion by another ceremony in the dreamtime. The Crucifixion was a ceremony to change the effect. Of course, it's just like the Cross and the sacrifice made there. It took a tremendous amount of suffering to balance out the equation that had started out way in the beginning. But it wasn't original sin the way some people think," she added.

"Yes, it makes sense. It's just that the ego cringes at this sort of reality and wants to make everything sensible in a co-dependent way, it seems to me. The price paid in suffering, in order to bring balance back into the realm of awareness in the dreamtime, must be a small speck when seen from the perspective of the absolute awareness. Guess it's even beyond the collective unconscious, as the Jung people prefer to call it," I said to my surprise.

"Yes.... The collective unconscious is but a complex in the dreamtime, and many have been deceived into thinking that this is it. The Jungians seem to worship the collective unconscious, not realizing that this is only a small part of the dreamtime. Illusion is everywhere, and people are willing to pay attention to it and go toward it, even though it takes them into more suffering and yet more illusion."

"About the snakes?"

"Oh, yes, the snakes. I'm sure you know some of the history of the snakes. These are the symbol of an old European practice, according to history. In reality, the practice of the snake religion has been part of the dreamtime in every place on the planet, and it's only because of recent history that they have been associated with Druids and such. Snakes carry the awareness of the earth itself and therefore are still in touch with the original dreamtime as experienced by the earth herself.

"Why else would snakes be banned in Judeo-Christian religion? Even they knew that the snakes were knowledge, and that's why poor Eve is blamed for eating the fruit.... Well, you know the story. It was the earth awareness of the original dream that people were afraid of. Once the awareness is present, then it shatters through all the brainwashing that has been happening for a long time. And of course, then it gets polarized between men and women. At that time, men wanted to have the illusion of power, so they decided that the earth awareness of the original dream, via the serpent, was evil itself. My God—how does such delusion occur? I'm amazed that the awareness allows for such delusion to exist.... It does have a purpose in the final dream though," she added emphatically.

"And you were there early on? Sort of how I was there as my great-grandfather in the cave of the evil dreamers? Somehow we were there in another form but with the same energy?"

"Yes, we have been everywhere and been everyone. The energy exists aside from the body, and different aspects of the earth-body acquire the awareness that has been passed on by the occupant of the body. But you see, there is only one body, the earth-body, and it gets manifested in tiny pieces known as people, yet there is only the one awareness. It's this awareness in the one earth that gets passed on through what appears to be different people—part of the illusion of separateness. That has been the best trick yet. Separate from everything, even though we are obviously still part of the same earth.

"This brain we have is made of that earth," she continued, "but for some reason, the energy flowing through it gets confused if not focused. This becomes illusion, and when it's crystallized after many generations, then it's assumed to be the truth, with each succeeding generation only assuming that it is the awareness. It has to do with the four elements that make up everything. These basic elements are what make the earth and our own earth-body. Of course, the brain, being mostly water and fire, has a good representation of opposites, and perhaps in its development of awareness, these opposites have not been integrated by the mind-body. The elements are critical to all this, otherwise why else would these be the first words the Buddha uttered in the beginning of his *Middle Discourses*?"

Beerli taught this in a manner I had never seen before.

"So what now? You seem to have had a lot more practice at dealing with all this. Even with this knowledge, why haven't we done something before? Seems that Tarrence and his crew—I guess you're part of his crew, at least in the dreamtime—would have done something already," I said cautiously.

"All in good time. We were waiting for other dreamers like you. There are others who are still dreaming, and the ceremony at some point needs to involve all of the original power dreamers, like the Australians and New Zealanders, as well as some Africans. It doesn't mean we can't start. After all, the big gourd that the circle of sorcerers created—and in their insanity actually used on people—needs to be addressed soon.

"You know, there are still ceremonies being done at the lab in Los Alamos. They are still playing with power, and the sorcerer dreamers are still focusing their attention on causing more suffering. Why do you think Tarrence took you up there in such a hurry without the usual time of instruction and preparation? He knows that the balance needs to be restored before we really destroy our earth, and with it the original awareness that the original dream left with her. This would be tragic indeed."

"I have trouble seeing the big picture, I guess. Somehow I can't help but think, who cares if the whole thing blows up and it returns back to being just a massive rock with water, spinning around the sun. Who would miss it?" I said out of frustration. "I mean, why are we even necessary, and why is the illusion even an issue? Is there really a big picture, or is the illusion so tricky that we're being tricked into thinking there is something, when in reality it's all ego in the first place? Maybe it would be better to start from scratch and allow for things to purify and get rid of the sickness that we've brought on."

"That has happened already, and each time, the awareness has been allowed to remain within the earth itself. What has been done with this new ceremony is that the original awareness might be removed in a manner that none of us can understand at this point. True, the original awareness of the awareness cannot be destroyed, but it would be tragic if we had the chance to realize our place in this and missed it because of some crazy ego-focused bunch of dreamers who were too ignorant to understand that there is cause and effect. Of course, ultimate understanding is part of the ongoing process, and that is the gold at the end of the rainbow. We won't know until we get there, yes? Rest assured, it's there," she said, smiling.

"You're right. I really do believe that. It's just that at times it all seems senseless. But when I see the caring and compassion displayed by Tarrence, then I realize that he might already have the gold at the end of the rainbow...his loving way," I said, as if I had talked like this for a long time.

"There. That's it. Love. That is the stone. The alchemical stone, the lapis philosophorum, the female spirit of God trapped in matter or existing as awareness of matter. That was the treasure the alchemists were searching for. That is the essence of the original dreamtime: love and compassion. Simple enough, but it also takes the proper effort in order to attain the true realization and not the make-believe love and compassion that is so readily manufactured by illusion of the brain," Beerli replied.

"Yes. I appreciate your insights. That's exactly what was said at the ceremony. All you guys seem to know the same stuff."

"Of course there's only one kind of 'stuff,' and it's all interconnected. It's our ego that tricks us into thinking we're separate. A pretty good trick, and it keeps working."

Beerli looked at her watch. "Well, I must be going; I've already been here quite a while. You must go see Tarrence again soon. There is more that needs to be understood and worked with."

"I'll go up again in a few days. Again, thanks for the good talk." As I was about to open the door, I remembered and said, "Oops, I had a dream last night that I want to run by you, if you don't mind."

"Of course; I'd be glad to listen," Beerli responded cheerfully.

I related the dream about my ancestor dressed in women's clothes and what he had said about understanding all this.

Beerli pondered for a few minutes before saying anything. I could tell she was finding the right way of explaining her understanding of the dream to me. Finally she spoke. "It has to do with integration of anima and animus, to use the jargon. Plainly speaking, it has to do with integration or awareness and relationship with his or your inner male and female energy.

"Mind you, this has nothing to do with sex per se. It only gets played out in sex when there is no understanding of the energy. The apparition of your ancestor and what he said speaks to this. After the loss of the feminine— although it's never really lost; it gets repressed but still exists in the psyche— well, anyway, once the feminine energy was repressed in the overall collective unconscious, there were problems to be sure.

"You see, the female energy that was repressed by the male psyche developed a life of its own in the unconscious and therefore became empowered with shadow quality. This is because anything that is out of awareness is shadow and acquires a demonic potential to the ego and to things that the ego has an effect on. Just look at what the Spaniards did in this hemisphere. All undifferentiated male energy with repressed anima shadow driving it from the unconscious.

"Things here had not completely gone that way yet, but there was already a movement here to repress the matriarch, as can be seen by the very masculine energy that was being played out by the Aztecs in Mexico. In a sense, their masculine energy attracted the repressed female from Europe, and the relationship was not good. As you know, millions died because of this. You see, wounding seeks wounding. The wounded female energy was seeking to wound itself in the so-called New World.

"Well, I'm jabbering now. What your ancestor is referring to is that if the anima, or the female, would have remained as part of awareness, the imbalance probably would not have occurred and things would be very different now. It did occur, and the shamans were profoundly affected since they carry healing energy for the community. Their inner female energy created a deep anxiety within their ego, and instead of dealing with her and integrating her, they projected her onto human females—women. In acting out their power over women sexually, they also gave up their power and ability to heal. Therefore, they were open to the craziness that they enacted in the ceremony you saw in the dreamtime."

"I can see this for the men. How does this play out in women healers or women of power such as yourself?"

"Since we are the object of the projection, this activates our inner male. There was so much grief and anger, collective anger for many generations over the maltreatment we had received at the hands of the crazy undeveloped male psyche. Did you know, over nine million of us were killed for being so-called 'witches' in Europe alone? A total projection of the undeveloped female energy in the patriarchy that had taken over in the western psyche—my God, what an atrocity! And what a price paid by the women for healing the earth.

"Unfortunately, it was not all conscious, and since some of the suffering was repressed, it activated the devouring side of the female, which is very powerful, especially on the earth. I say that because the earth is female, with her own male spirit, just like us. As you can see, the grieving and shamed female psyche then was able to channel earth energy to defend itself, and this overwhelmed the men. Now the men defended themselves, and the cycle started spinning itself out of control.

"The final assault is on the earth energy itself, and this required the collective ceremony of the power dreamers, both male and female, as you saw. You see, once the cycle started spinning, they were overwhelmed with ignorance from the illusion, and they couldn't see beyond their pitiful egos, which were a mere fantasy of the illusion in the first place. The ego is twice removed in the unreal category," Beerli added, laughing.

"It really makes sense when you explain it like that. What's amazing is that the ego actually thinks that it can overtake its creator. How could anyone think he could either undo or create the earth awareness itself by using just a small component of the awareness and its origin? It's truly mind-boggling how ignorance can come into play in these things."

"Especially when ignorance is fueled by ego-inflation. The inflated ego has even less substance than the normal ego, and because of this it gets even more controlling and delusional." Beerli laughed again.

"In the dream, my ancestor appeared wearing both female and male clothes. Seems like there is some kind of image that alludes to his being homosexual. What can be made of this, other than maybe an integration going on?" I asked.

"Yes, the fact that he is wearing both sets of clothes is a clear indication from the psyche that there is a union of opposites. In olden times, people who could traverse across sexual barriers were seen as very special and had powers that others didn't have. They were known as 'those who come and go,' and they had more access to the spiritual realms. Since this image in your dream is unifying the opposite energies, that is, male and female, it appears this is something that you need to start integrating."

"What about what he says? The stuff about 'it wouldn't have been this way,' or something like that?"

"Precisely. If there had been a balanced integration of yin and yang, then there wouldn't have been the opposing forces creating such an imbalance. The balance with the earth energy would have remained, and there would not have been a need to even think of the ceremony that still threatens the survival of the earth itself. The earth would be wounded, of course, but she has healed before after crazy human beings lost their way," she continued.

"Interesting how all this gets played out in simple day-to-day things like the transference, and how many therapists and healers of all types have been caught in this duality to the point that it ruins lives. What about Jung and his problems with the male and female energy? After all, it's a known fact that he crossed the line with Toni Wolfe and others. I know it's a sore subject for present-day Jungians, but if we have to look at what went on at that place in Los Alamos, then this shouldn't be so difficult. Maybe we should sit down for a bit more," I suggested.

"Yes, a bit more," she said, still smiling, walking toward one of the soft chairs.

"It's true that Jung did cross the boundaries many times," she continued once we were seated again. "Later in life, he became aware of the earth energy that was propelling his organs, and he did realize that the energy was not used in the right way. Jung was a shaman without the circle or a tribe who could help him maintain his boundaries—much like the shaman in your dream. Once the cultural norms and controls aren't there, the shaman is at risk for all types of whims that the trickster throws out onto the path. Since the shaman does have power, it is so easy for him to become inflated and start operating from ego, which of course is the kiss of death. It's difficult to maintain selfless-ness in the midst of power. This is a teaching that is missing in many shamanic traditions, and it's something that would insulate them from ego possession.

"You see, if the ego is non-existent and it really doesn't exist—if it's just an illusion of reality—then there's nothing to trap the shaman. Jung understood this toward the end, and he did so intuitively. As you know, in his theories the ego is but a complex in the psyche that exists only at the whim of the collective unconscious, or the awareness as you have come to know it. By the way, did you look closely at all the sorcerers doing the ceremony?" she asked at the end of her explanation.

"Not very well, I guess…. Wait a minute; there was one. Yeah, a guy who looked like Jung as a young man. Oh, my God. Don't tell me he was there too! Shit, do you know what this means? I have a small idea. Man, there were all kinds of heavies there, eh? This is getting very interesting. What was he doing there anyway?" I rambled.

"Once you see the meaning of his work, then you can understand. He was involved in the ceremony, this is true. He realized very quickly that this had been a terrible mistake and a trick from the illusion. He tried to change his mind, but it was too late. Once the gourd had gone into the ground, it was done and sealed.

"Jung vowed to begin work to help in undoing what had been done. That's one of the reasons his work is based on the dreamtime—no accidents, you might say. Although he came back with his yin and yang a bit undifferentiated, he still was able to intuit the underlying causes of the problem with female and male energy. In his notions of anima and animus, he gives us the template whereby we can start avoiding some of the traps of the illusion. Of course there are others we might not even dream of."

"This is too much. Last year I was just minding my own business and now…. Carl would definitely have me committed and have all my credentials taken if he knew that I was believing all this," I half-whispered.

"Carl? Who is Carl? You don't mean Jung?" she asked.

"Oh, no. He's a colleague who believes that the answers to all of life lie in cognitive behavioral psychology. Anything that deviates from western models is seen as archaic and unethical since it hasn't been tested empirically; he worships at the altar of statistics."

"Yes. That is how the profession is going. But don't be too discouraged. Cognitive behavioral approaches are the beginning ways of looking at the mind. I like to see this as Buddha in disguise. You see, the illusion isn't the only one with tricks. The Buddha has all types of tricks up her sleeve too. So encourage Carl to study his cognitions. After all, what is the mind? It is what it thinks, no?" she said kindly.

She rose and started for the door again. "I really must leave now, and thanks so much for the good food and the wonderful conversation."

"Thank you for your insight and help in all this. It's good to have some validation from the profession. I guess I won't need it in time once I realize this is real and valid within its own right," I said as we walked toward the door.

After she left, my mind kept going from one thought to the next. The inter-connectedness of all this was pretty incredible, but then it made sense in view of all the basic teachings of most traditions. Most spiritual teachings talk about the interconnectedness and oneness of all things—this must be what they are talking about. I mean, how much more connected can you get? This whole thing happening the way it did, and all of it being a part of the dreamtime record so that it's always present, is always in the moment of happening.

Being at one with all is not something to strive for; it's the way things are. It's just that our relationship with illusion has made this so smoky we can't see it. It's through the silence that the smoke settles and we can see what has been there the whole time…. Wow, this is peace and the beautiful way that my cousins the Navajos talk about. Being able to be a part of the dreamtime and awareness in this manner is a great blessing.

As the evening approached, I thought about the work up in the mountains this week. I decided to go up early so I could stop at the Zen Center, since there seemed to be a push from all these interconnected events to go there. Nothing can surprise me anymore, I thought to myself.

15

Visit at the Zen Center

T he next evening I made preparations to go spend the night in the mountains. I traveled light, so it didn't take long. On the way out of town, I decided to stop at the Latte' Hey as it had become a tradition for me to get a double cappuccino and a goody to make the trip more enjoyable. Nothing was unusual at the Latte' Hey. The sounds of the cappuccino machine were reassuring, and the smell of freshly roasted coffee filled the air. The homeless guy wasn't there, and neither was Carl for once. I wondered where Carl was and what he was doing.

My thoughts went to what Dr. Beerli said about cognitive behavioral psychology. She's right; when you get to the crux of that system, what you find is the mind state, and you try to work with that. Yeah, tricky Buddha, I thought. Why not? Why should the Buddha be restricted to being this blunted affect, this sitting-all-the-time kind of person? Of course he could do whatever he wanted and have a full range of human stuff; just because he's enlightened doesn't mean he's dead.

I left the Latte' Hey, got into my truck, and made my way up the familiar road. The sky was cloudy, and thunderclouds appeared up ahead in the mountains. In the far distance, I could see bolts of lightning like you can only see in northern New Mexico. I recalled something my grandfather said about the sky relating to the earth, and lightning being the sky's way of waking her up so they could play and start creation. I wonder if this has to do with all that yin and yang stuff we'd been dealing with recently, I thought. Of course, it's just energy, creative energy, that's in balance. It's just the ego illusion that confuses it and has another creation for the same energy—that is, it creates suffering.

Soon I came to the turnoff for the Zen Center. There was a nice sign with some Japanese characters on it, and I assumed the characters also said 'Zen Center.' The road was gravel, and the land around the center well cared for. The juniper and piñon trees appeared to be placed in a special order. As I approached the center, I saw some local trees that had been shaped into Bonsai trees, which gave an added sense of peace with awareness to the place.

I parked and went up to the main door. There was no one. I went toward the back of the building, and there was more immaculate landscaping. A Zen rock garden was the most prominent part of the grounds in back, and there I saw what appeared to be some type of monk, with robes and a shaved head. Since I didn't know the etiquette surrounding these things, I decided to just mosey close to the garden and ask if I could talk to someone. I had no specifics. After all, I was here at the advice of the homeless guy and Beerli. As far as I knew, this was merely part of the whole dreamtime stuff that had completely engulfed my life for the past few months.

I approached the monk, who wasn't looking at me. Instead he was meticulously raking the garden. I waited till he had come around and finished a circular pass.

"Excuse me…. Is there someone I can talk to?" I asked.

"Yes, the Abbot is inside. Just ring the bell at the meditation hall, and he'll come talk to you," the monk said in a female voice, much to my surprise.

A woman monk—and such piercing, soft eyes, I thought to myself.

As I made my way indoors, I couldn't help but think that the monk raking the garden was a special person, and I had to admit she was attractive to me. She might be Tibetan, or she might be Native American; it's hard to tell sometimes, I thought. Guess there must be even more interconnectedness to all this.

Inside the building there was the feeling of emptiness, since there was very little decoration on the walls. The air smelled fresh, with a hint of some beautiful incense. I could hear falling water somewhere in the vicinity of the room I was in. The meditation hall was just a short way from where I was, and I walked softly without my shoes.

I looked inside. There was an old person sitting in the lotus position, and the feeling in the hall was peaceful. The feeling I had was similar to how I was around Tarrence. I rang the bell, and the monk bowed to the altar, got up, and turned to face me. I was shocked. It was Morehei from the dream ceremony!

His eyes can best be described as black fire. When Morehei looked at you, there was a piercing quality to his look, and his awareness was projected in that black fire that radiated from his eyes. He was short, and I guessed him to be in his mid-seventies. Despite his age, I had no doubt that he was a powerful man, physically and spiritually. I noticed a Japanese sword on the altar. A warrior just like before, I thought.

As he approached me, he bowed, and I followed with a bow also.

"Good day, and good to see that you have arrived finally," he said.

In my mind I thought, what does he mean, "finally," but then I realized that this is part of the dreamtime, and everything is interwoven.

"Yes, it's good to finally be here," I responded.

"Let's go into my room and have some tea," Morehei said kindly. By this time I was realizing that there was a major contradiction between the fire in his eyes and the kindness of his spirit. He was very soft and relaxed, and I felt unconditionally loved by this gentleman. We went into his room and sat on cushions on the floor. He proceeded to make the tea. All his movements were distinct, and he paid close attention to what he was doing.

"Making tea not to make tea but just to make it," he said. I wondered if there was going to be a whole new jargon and metaphor of being I had to understand, like it was with Tarrence and his crew.

"Yes, that's the best way," I responded, not knowing what else to say.

"You're right," he said with a soft smile, his eyes still fiery.

"I didn't know you were here till recently. I'd been going by this road for some months before noticing the sign on the turnoff."

"Attention is an important aspect to our life—the most important you might say. Many people don't notice much of what goes on in the day. Not even the fact that they are breathing."

Morehei handed me a small cup of green tea. Before he drank from his cup, he looked deeply into the tea and turned his cup four times in a clockwise direction. I did the same with my cup.

"I'm glad that you're here. There are always karmic reasons for everything. So you're here for a purpose that you might or might not be completely aware of," he said in a low voice.

"Well, I'm certain of that. I've been through some interesting events recently, and seeing you now makes me certain that my being here is part of the stuff that I've been involved in." I was still trying to fill in space with talk. He was silent for a few minutes, and I decided to go along with this and not say anything.

After the silence, he looked at me and said, "There is no time to waste. Most people think they have forever, not realizing the preciousness of time and the preciousness of their being here as a human being. Most of it is taken for granted. I'm aware of the work you've been doing. I've been visiting with Tarrence for some time now.... What am I saying? That's funny, I've been working with him for several lifetimes," he said and broke into deep laughter. "I know that you saw me at the recent ceremony, because I saw you and we made eye contact. All of the things that have transpired in the dreamtime from that ceremony have deep implications to all of us, and there have been some serious covenants made—especially by myself and Tarrence," he said with a somber look on his face.

"Yes, Tarrence has told me about that, and I actually saw when you two were talking in the ceremony. You were making the agreement to undo the ritual performed by the dreamers who had fallen into the illusion out of their desperate ignorance. So many people have suffered because of that ignorance, and it seems like it didn't have to be that way."

"There was or is no alternative. True karma can be changed if the price is paid, but at that time it was unavoidable. It cost the Native people of this hemisphere countless thousands, and many continue to suffer. It cost the people where I come from. So the price has been paid. There is no need to continue the suffering in this way, not unless we're tricked by ignorance and the brain illusion once more. That's why we must be so careful and use discriminating wisdom that can only emerge from the absolute awareness, the awareness that is aware of us right now," Morehei said.

"I've recently become aware of that awareness—somewhat—although it sort of eludes me most of the time. The only time I can really be in touch with it is when I'm in places like this, around people like you," I half-whispered. Since his attention was so close, there was hardly a need to speak out loud.

Just then, the bald nun or monk stood at the door and bowed. She just looked at him and walked away. My mind meandered. She is also quiet. Kind of the female counterpart to the Quiet One…. She didn't speak, yet she conveyed something to the old man. She's a pretty woman. Wonder why she became a nun?

"The mind has a tendency to wander?" Morehei asked.

"Oh…yes…it's just that I was wondering who that woman is."

"She's a nun. I've known her for a long time. She's also part of the dream that you saw and is working with all of the other awareness dreamers to change karma. Her practice has led her to high states of being in the awareness itself, and most of the time she is there," Morehei said as he motioned for us to get up and start walking. His steps were methodical, and he was present in everything he did.

We walked outside and looked at the plants and the landscape quietly. I didn't have a need to talk, and it seemed normal not to be talking all the time. There was communication going on even though no words were being exchanged. We walked away from the monastery and went into some arroyos and through sagebrush that grows in these parts. We stopped on a little knoll overlooking a bank on a deep arroyo. The signs of water carving the landscape were obvious.

I noticed movement on the bank about thirty yards away. As I focused on it, I saw one of the largest rattlesnakes I've ever seen slithering over the bank. The snake was aware of us, and I had the feeling that this was "the" rattlesnake, that is, the original one. The snake was about ten feet long and very wide. Its triangular head and piercing eyes appeared to miss nothing as it focused its attention on us. We just stood there looking at each other. Morehei stood completely still and appeared very peaceful, and I tried to do the same. Soon the snake moved on, and we kept walking.

Morehei broke the silence. "Some snake, huh?"

"Yes, it was like the original snake; it had so much presence," I replied.

"It was just rattlesnaking—it really wasn't a snake in the noun sense of things. That's why it had presence. Just as if you are simply—let's say, humaning—then there's no human being per se; only the rising and falling of humaning is what is left. Then there's no one there to take up space. It's a way to be silent and have peace within the awareness itself. To be any other way is to be caught up in Samsara," Morehei explained.

I had no doubt that what he said was true, and I actually understood it for an instant; then the realization drifted back to the being in the noun sense as I have been trained to think for many years.

"Samsara?"

"Yes, it's a term used for the illusion. Most beings spend all of their lives training their minds in Samsara. They get so good at it they believe Samsara is their true nature. It takes a lot of effort to undo this type of training over so many lifetimes," he explained.

"I've heard Tarrence say things to that effect."

"Ah yes, my good friend Tarrence. I must visit him soon."

Morehei started walking back toward the monastery. "It's been nice seeing you again," he said, and I understood that our visit was over.

"Thanks, it's been good to see you and also this place. I must be going now." I walked toward Ruby and opened the door.

"Give my best to my friend," he said as he bowed deeply.

"I will. Again, thanks for your kindness."

He turned around and walked away.

As I drove off, I started to wonder about what happened during the visit. I remembered that he caught me mentally wandering about. How could I help it? I thought. I mean, here is this old monk in the middle of the mountains in New Mexico, and I had seen him in a dream ceremony just a few days earlier. Not only that, the Bald Nun was very remarkable in that she paralleled the Quiet One. Then to top it off, there was the Great-Grandma of Rattlesnakes just *being*. How could I not try to figure this out?

There definitely was a conspiracy, as I mentioned earlier, but it was the type of conspiracy that defined the word itself. I was certainly breathing with, or sharing breath spirit with, the process itself, and the awareness was aware of the whole thing as it was unfolding. Unfolding from what? If it was unfolding, that meant it already existed in a folded form. Therefore the awareness already had awareness of the unfolded mystery, and as for things playing out, they were just that—playing out in the realm of our awareness. It was making sense in the manner that things make sense according to the explanation that Tarrence gave of the dreamtime. Wow, how did he know all this? I wondered.

I drove up the mountain to the clinic. My mind retained clarity, and I was "just seeing" as I drove on the familiar road. I could feel the road and could hear all of the sound vibrations being made by the contact of tire on pavement.

16

Day at the Clinic and Visit With Tarrence

*T*he day at the clinic went on in the usual fashion. Most of the patients I saw had family problems. Underlying many of the problems was a high incidence of alcoholism and drug abuse—not that I didn't know this before. I'm sure to most of the public, that isn't a major mystery unraveling.

However today the quality of the alcoholism and drug abuse appeared to have different dynamics. It was as if the problem itself, alcohol, was also recognizing me. There was a feeling that I was dealing with a conscious entity, aside from the patient who was struggling. One could speculate that this was some sort of depersonalization. Then again, after all that had taken place recently, maybe not.

Carl would definitely think so and would have me medicated instantly in order to stop the delusions.... Poor Carl, he'll learn someday. I was surprised by that thought.

After seeing the patients for the day, I decided to make a quick run to Tarrence's place just to say hello and see how things were going for him, since his physical health gave him problems at times. The road to his place was quiet, and today nothing was out of the ordinary. Thunderclouds were looming above, as is usual at this time of the day, and lightning could be seen in the distance.

Ruby didn't have any problem negotiating the rough roads, even though I had to shift into four-wheel drive halfway there. It sure is nice having the electric four-wheel drive on the fly, I thought to myself. Otherwise I'd have to get out and lock the hubs and get muddy. I felt a bit spoiled by technology. After all, people over the ages had walked this very road and never had the luxury to enjoy the ride.

Up ahead was Tarrence's place, and I made my way to the house. When I got close, I saw the Quiet One standing by the truck he usually drove.

I parked Ruby and got out. The Quiet One motioned me into his truck. What's going on? I wondered. There's no way I'm going to ask him though; otherwise he'll come up with some Zen Koan response that I'll have to mull over, and I still won't know what's going on.

As I sat on the passenger seat, the black coyote-dog jumped through the other door ahead of the Quiet One. The dog was happy to be in the truck, and was smiling and wagging his tail in a joyous fashion. The Quiet One got in and started the truck; then we started down the road.

After a mile or so, he made a turn I wasn't familiar with, but he continued over open turf with no constructed road. I could see some of the leftover houses and prayer places of the ancient ones about half a mile away. This is interesting, I thought. I wonder how come I've never come this way. Guess you'd have to know about this place beforehand. Wonder what this is about? Wonder who this Quiet One is anyway? Why is he so quiet? Seems to get along well with Tarrence—wonder if they're related? And this dog. What's up with this smiling coyote-looking mutt? The dog licked my face and smiled at me as if he understood my thoughts.

We went past the ceremonial circles and pits. The number of piñon and pine trees was increasing, so I knew we were going deeper into untouched forest. As the trees thickened, so did my curiosity, but I thought, I'll be damned if I'm going to give in and ask where we're going.

It was getting late in the day, and the truck was bouncing around quite a bit. The Quiet One started humming something I recalled from the cave ceremony. Pretty-sounding tune, although it does have a serious feel to it, I thought. We came to an open place among the piñon trees. It seemed to have been cleared on purpose, and the clearing was circular in shape.

The Quiet One got out of the truck and motioned for me to do the same. He was wearing women's moccasins and belt, and his hair was combed in traditional women's fashion. Wow, just like my grandpa in the dream. I should have noticed this sooner. What's going on? I thought.

The Quiet One started walking up a rocky path. I followed him until we got to a pile of rocks that seemed to have been placed there on purpose. He took some tobacco and sent it out in all six directions. He gave me the tobacco bag and motioned for me to do the same. Once we had finished this, he started removing the rocks from the pile. It didn't take long since the rocks were resting on a bed of latillas, or straight sticks used to support structures such as roofs and the like. I realized there was some sort of hole in the ground that was looking more and more like a grave. Earth smells emerged as we disturbed the earth that had been in place for a long time. I felt a little discomfort at this, but I figured the Quiet One was probably operating under instructions from Tarrence.

He started removing the latillas, and I helped. I was just mimicking him, and he didn't seem to mind. There was no eye contact between us, and he purposely appeared to be avoiding any communication—either verbal or non-verbal—with me. We finally removed all the latillas, and sure enough, we had uncovered a grave. When I looked into the hole, there was a bundle wrapped in very old leather. All kinds of disturbing thoughts were going through my mind. I really didn't want to do this, but like I said earlier, I was kind of getting used to this unpredictable dreamtime stuff.

The bundle had two pairs of leather straps tied to it, and it was obvious these were used to lower it into the ground. Although the bundle appeared old, it was well-preserved. No doubt the dryness had kept things from corroding and decomposing too much.

The Quiet One took two of the leather straps and handed me the other two. He motioned that we lift the bundle, and we did. By the time the bundle reached the top of the ground, I had no doubt there was a body inside, and I was feeling very uncomfortable by what appeared to be grave-robbing.

We lifted the bundle slowly, and I noticed the Quiet One had a very serene look on his face, as if he was in prayer. Still, I refrained from asking what was going on. I felt anxiety turn to panic when the Quiet One started unraveling the bundle. What the hell is he doing? I thought. This isn't right. I wish Tarrence were here. I for one would feel much better, and right now, I really should say something.

As he worked with the bundle, the Quiet One looked up at me and finally made eye contact, then nodded with a half-smile as if to reassure me. I hadn't realized how piercing his eyes were, since I had never really looked into them.

OK, I might as well help, I thought. I'm sure it took all he had to give me that look of reassurance, and I might as well go along with the trip. I came all the way up here, and the worst that can happen is that we get spooked by who-ever is wrapped up in these burial garments and such.

We proceeded with the unwrapping. Beneath the leather covering were layers of blankets. As we got to these, I sensed a feeling of familiarity with them. It was as if I had seen them before. How could I have? These blankets had been buried for God-only-knows how long.

We undid the blankets, and sure enough, there was a body, very dried up and shriveled, right in the middle of all the wrapping. In the rib-cage area were several arrows, some with a bit of the wood from the shaft still attached to them. The Quiet One grabbed the dried-up left hand of the dead one and pried it open. There in the middle of his hand was a medallion just like the one depicted in the cave drawing. It was a swirling sun-wheel with black, red, yellow, and white colors going in a circle, and blue and green surrounding those four colors.

I was aghast. It was clear this person we had uncovered was the same person depicted in the cave drawing, and I'm sure he was the one who appeared in the dream ceremony. I looked at the Quiet One, who was calm. He made eye contact with me again and motioned for me to pick up the medallion. I didn't want to, but I knew I had to. Once I picked it up, the Quiet One took one of the arrows out of the rib cage area and handed it to me, again looking me right in the eye. I took the arrow, and he proceeded to wrap the body up again.

Clearly, we had come to get these objects, but why was still a mystery to me. The medallion was a work of art. The design was one of several stones inlaid into yet another stone, and the work was exquisite. It felt familiar enough, but my mind was probably making too much of the situation.

It took us awhile to place things the way they were, and then we were back in the truck heading toward Tarrence's place. As soon as we started back, a huge black owl flew in front of the truck and landed on a nearby piñon tree, then looked directly at us.

I knew that the Quiet One noticed it, but he didn't say anything about it. He just gestured to it as if he knew it personally, and kept driving. It seemed as if the owl gestured back, but I don't really know, and the Quiet One wasn't about to explain this to me.

Here he goes through all this trouble to get me the medallion, and he won't say a word, I thought. What's up with this guy? He sure is peculiar, and I wish I knew who he is! And this dog of his…sorry-dogging, or coyoteing, or whatever the story is. Now this arrow and the medallion—what else? Why do I have them? Wait…. They can't really be serious—like what was said in the cave about that old guy being Great-Great-Grandpa. Not only that, but that the old man was really me? No way. That's too far-out even for all the open-mindedness I've attained.

When we pulled up in front of Tarrence's, I got out of the truck, but the Quiet One stayed with the engine running. As soon as I cleared the vehicle, he took off and left me standing there. I had never been here by myself at this dusk hour.

I went in and announced myself from the other room.

"Come in. Been expecting you. Did you get your stuff?" Tarrence asked, obviously knowing what I had been up to this afternoon.

"Yes," I said, showing him the objects and passing them toward him. "What do you mean, 'my stuff'?"

"No. I can't handle those. Those are for just you. And you know what I mean about 'your stuff.' Those belonged to you in another time. Don't tell me you didn't recognize the place or the blankets. It's time to start getting real here." Tarrence said this in a no-nonsense tone I had never heard him use before.

"Well, the guy who took me up there touched them. Why didn't you come anyway? It was a nice afternoon."

"There are certain things I cannot do, and things I shouldn't be around. Only certain special people can do what needed to be done this afternoon. Your driver is one of those people."

"What people? Who is that guy anyway? Why is he so quiet? Come on, Tarrence, I've shown good faith in all this. I need to know who he is," I said emphatically.

"You should have asked him," Tarrence said with a loud and deep laugh.

"OK, I get it. I still have to be kept in the dark about some stuff."

"Now, now, all in good time. He's a special dreamer. He's one who comes and goes. He's not even restricted by sexuality—he's not a man or a woman. And I know what you're thinking. He's not gay either. Because he's free, he can do things like disturb the dead, and it's OK. He has access to things that most of us don't, and he had to go help you retrieve your stuff. Although the arrow is hardly your stuff," he said, laughing deeply again.

"Special dreamer who comes and goes. OK, I'll bite, what is it?"

"Like in your dream the other night," Tarrence said.

"What dream?"

"The one with the person wearing men's and women's clothes. You see, the dream was showing you a most special person, a two-spirited person. The two-spirited person has access to all the realms, even across the male and female energy. Not everyone can do that—only those who have perfected the process through many lifetimes of understanding male, female, yin and yang kind of stuff. So are you happy now?" Tarrence said with his patented crooked smile.

"I guess. Thanks for the explanation. I had no idea about any of that."

"Now, you came for another reason. Sorry to have taken up most of your afternoon with the pursuit of old things and grave-robbing." This time he laughed so hard I thought he was going to bounce off the bed.

"Actually, yeah. The last couple of times I worked with people at the clinic, the drinkers, you know—well, I had the distinct feeling that something was watching or that there was something more to the addiction," I explained.

"Exactly what do you think alcoholism, or any addiction, is?"

I gave him the best textbook definition of addiction I had. I pulled out all the stops and let him know about the biochemical, psychological, family-dynamic, and every other aspect I knew about alcoholism and addiction. I gave a detailed explanation that I thought was nothing short of brilliant. When I finished, Tarrence laughed even harder. This threw me off guard since I thought my talk had been quite eloquent.

"What's so funny? I really don't see that I made any jokes about any of this," I complained. "What do you think it is then?"

"Medicine," he said in a serious tone.

"Medicine? You mean like for medicinal purposes?"

"No, as in medicine. As in Indian medicine. As in dreamtime medicine. Spirit, that's what I'm saying."

I was skeptical. "Can you explain a little more?"

"All of those drugs, alcohol, and all that, come from life itself, from the earth awareness. Since they come from the earth awareness, they have life and duality. All of those substances can be used for good or not. Your patients have activated the negative side of medicine, much like your great-ancestor with the medallion did. Once they activate the negative side of medicine, then there's a price to pay.

"You see, there's a contract between the medicine—alcohol or whatever— and the person taking it. It is its own ceremony. The person wants to have a different experience in the dream. The alcohol says OK, and the deal is made. Except that usually the person drinking is too ignorant to know that he or she has to make good with the deal. Once someone drinks it, then the spirit of alcohol waits for the time when it can take its due. Since it is spirit, it wants spirit in return. Therefore it takes someone's life. The whole time all this is done, the spirit is further disrespected by people treating it like an addiction or whatnot.

"This is for real, and you know the stats. How many thousands of our relatives has this medicine taken? This is part of the price for the action the dreamers did. In their ignorance and grief, they gave over many people and much suffering—much the same way present-day alcoholics do. They sell their own spirit for a brief spell in their grief and suffering, not realizing the long-term cause and effect they activate. But again, this was part of the deal," Tarrence said with sadness in his eyes.

"Deal?"

"Yeah, the deal made when the dreamers were planting their karmic seeds, just like you saw in the dream ceremony. I knew it was going to cost a lot. I just didn't realize how *much* suffering it would take to change the karma. My friend Morehei didn't either, but it needed to be done. Otherwise the whole thing would have been lost."

"Makes sense. I mean, the feeling I've been getting. It's real. I knew it was some sort of entity looking at me. I knew there was awareness. But I didn't realize the implications of all this. You're saying that all the suffering by our people, and all the dying through alcoholism, is for the purpose of changing the karma planted by the owl dreamers in the dream ceremony?"

"Yes. As you can see, our actions have profound implications. That's why the Buddha gave us such simple tools for living. If we followed those, then we wouldn't have to worry about all this. Also, the stuff that you know, you already knew. You need to start trusting that knowing," Tarrence said.

"So any ideas about how to deal with it?" I asked, knowing that he knew exactly what to do.

"Ceremony."

"Ceremony?" I parroted.

"Since the person activates the spirit of alcohol in a ceremony, then it makes sense that the spirit and the relationship with it must also be dealt with in ceremony. What you do—therapy—that's a ceremony. So you already have the makings of what to do. You just need to be honest with what you're doing. Have your patients enact a ceremony that changes the relationship with the spirit of alcohol. They must acknowledge it. They must talk to it. Once they talk to it, they establish a different relationship with it. Now they can make a deal with it. They can give it some other type of spiritual gift, like tobacco. Tobacco was put here by the awareness for just such things. The spirit of alcohol will take the offering since it's offered in a respectful manner, and the person's spirit will be safe within this new ceremony."

"Makes sense. I guess I could call it active imagination. The tobacco can be the transitional object.... Yeah, this can work," I said.

"Call it whatever you want. As long as you know that you're conducting a serious life-and-death ritual with your patient," Tarrence asserted sternly.

The Quiet One came and placed some food on the bed for Tarrence, then sat down.

"I'm sure you haven't eaten yet. Have some food," Tarrence said to me with a smile.

"You need to eat. I can grab—"

The Quiet One looked at me, and I knew to just stop and reach over and get some food.

"You must be a good cook," I said, smiling at the Quiet One.

He didn't say anything, just nodded at Tarrence and left. Tarrence ate some of the vegetables, drank some coffee, and relaxed.

"It's been really nice visiting you again," I said. "Although every time I come up, there's some new surprise. I guess they shouldn't be surprises anymore."

"No, they shouldn't. Actually, you should start knowing what to expect next."

"I'll do what I can. I've got to be going now," I said as I walked over to shake his hand.

"Thanks for coming." He reached out to me with his crumpled hand. "Take care of your stuff. It might come in handy," he said with a mischievous smile.

I went out, got into the truck, and started down the road. As usual, this had been another incredible visit, and I wondered how much more there could be to this. Where is all this going? I asked myself. It has to have a purpose. There's a reason all these people are popping out at this particular time. How can I anticipate? I guess that's what he wants me to do, but I can't just decide to do something, then "poof!" it happens. Oh well, just mind the road here, and see what lies ahead.

Right before I made the entry to the main dirt road leading to the highway, I saw a huge bird landing on a dried-up piñon tree. The bird, a huge owl, was looking in my direction. Must be one of the owl dreamers out for some sun and wanting to say hello, I thought to myself, and was surprised at how common this type of event had become. Carl would definitely think I'd lost it if he got a chance to see how I'm thinking these days. It would be something if he were to come up and see this for himself. Maybe in another lifetime, but then again, who knows? Probably that owl knows something, my mind rambled again, to my surprise.

I turned onto the main paved road and decided to go to the Buzzard's Beak for something to eat before I headed home. The Buzzard, as the locals called it, was a "down-home" type of backwoods "greasy spoon" that actually made some very good dishes. They had some wild-game specialties that were supplied by local hunters and poachers. They always had elk and venison on the menu, and I would stop by from time to time to have an elkburger. My thought on this was that elk meat was not contaminated with all of the hormones and additives that modern beef was loaded with. Also, I had been made aware that the way the animal is killed is important. Fear, anxiety, sadness can become part of your dinner through the meat you eat. Therefore, care has to be taken in these matters.

I made my way into the parking lot with the usual pickups and folks standing outside. By now they had seen me a few times, so there was "no never mind" made of my coming here.

Inside the Buzzard were families having a late dinner, and I got a booth in the corner where I wouldn't have to engage with anyone, since I was tired. Opposite and to the corner was the bathroom door, but it was situated in a manner that I wouldn't have to make eye contact with anyone going by. A perfect situation for a peaceful dinner after a tiring and very strange afternoon.

There wasn't much I could say to anyone about the events of the day. How can one describe the episode that can only be characterized as grave-robbing by most people? There was no rational way to explain that the Quiet One had special privileges in these matters. My hand went into the coat pocket where I'd put the medallion and the arrowhead.

Yep, still there, I thought.

What could this mean? I pondered. Do I take this reincarnation stuff literally, or is it just some type of awareness that needs to be accounted for? To take it literally would mean that I was in that body we dug up today at some point in the past. That would be complicated…. Or would it? More people in the world believe in reincarnation than not. That many people can't be wrong. Was I the shaman gone wrong? How did that happen? Is it important for me to know? Of course it is. I'm sure that's why Tarrence and the Quiet One orchestrated this whole thing.

My mind was in the process of deconstructing the day's events when out of nowhere I heard, "My man…wassup?" Immediately after that, I felt a slap to my back, as if a long-lost relative had found me. The interruption was like a Twilight Zone episode.

"Carl, what in the hell are you doing here? I can't believe it! What brings you to these parts? I'm blown away."

"Well, I called your office a few times just to check in on you, and they said you were up here and would be back this afternoon. I called your house with no answer; so I decided to come and check out the bush, as they say. I went to the clinic, but you weren't there either, so I looked around, hiked a bit, and was on my way home when I thought to grab a bite. My man, the venison is to die for," he said loudly, and I was embarrassed at being seen with this yuppie wearing penny loafers and all.

"Where are you sitting?" I asked.

"Oh, I'm done. I just had to go to the little boys' room; otherwise, my man, I would have missed you altogether. After coming all this way just to check out the situation—know what I'm sayin'?"

"Well, have a seat then, unless you're on your way?" I asked, hoping he was on his way, but knowing he would just take the seat.

"What have you been up to anyway? How come you don't keep me up to date anymore? Starting to think we ain't tight—like we're not homies or something," Carl said in his worst imitation of adolescent culture I had yet to witness.

"Just been busy with patients and with my own stuff. A lot of interesting things up here, and I'm finding the city a bit boring these days," I said softly.

"Have you seen that old dude recently? You know that old witchdoctor, or whatever he is?"

"Yes, Carl. I have seen Tarrence, and he isn't a witch or anything like that. Where are your manners anyway? He's a kind old gentleman who cares deeply for all humanity—"

"Chill, my man. Just making small talk. You know that I am Mr. Sensitivity when it comes to cultural stuff—I mean Dr. Sensitivity. Hey, who has more training in that than me? I go to every seminar; most of my continuing ed. courses are in that area. So chill, my man—

"Carl, you're very active tonight," I interrupted. "Why don't you just calm down a bit and lower your voice. You're starting to attract attention to us. Let folks enjoy their dinner," I said as the waitress came to take my order of elkburger and decaf.

When the waitress walked away, Carl became serious. "Actually I was up at the clinic where you work. They let me know you were with Tarrence, and they mentioned that you make house calls or meet with clients outside the office at times. I hate to be the one to lay this on you, but you know that is borderline ethical misconduct. You need to have boundaries. You've been trained better than that," Carl said sternly.

"You are kidding, of course. Different situations and different cultures require a different standard. It would be more unethical for me *not* to see people in different settings. That would mean some of the patients I see now wouldn't get seen at all. Since when has the profession given two shits what happens to the folks up in these mountains anyway? Where have they been for the past few decades, as people slowly die from problems that we know how to help with? How ethical is that? It might be ethical not to serve them, but it's also very immoral. Of course ethics has nothing to do with what's right or wrong. It's just a set of rules put together by a bunch of guys in some locker room in between rounds of golf and after they laugh at a few ethnic jokes," I said heatedly.

"Why do you always have to deteriorate into this place? What I'm talking about has nothing to do with anything except boundaries and standards that are there for your well-being as well as the patient's. That's all I'm trying to say, my man. No need for the defensiveness," Carl retorted.

"Come on, Carl," I said more calmly. "You know what an inadequate job our profession does with disenfranchised folks. The people up here have some of the highest incidence of behavioral problems, and all that's done year after year is to put Band-Aids on the arterial bleeding. I'm trying to find a way to be of help—better yet, to work with folks so they can help themselves. Tarrence is a natural helper, and what he's doing is beyond the individual. Tarrence is thinking collectively and on a wider scope."

"That Jungian term again. Where is your training? You know that the present standards are set by third-party payers, and the Jungian dream shit is nowhere on the billing forms. You have to play by the rules, or you're going to find yourself outside in the cold."

"If trying to help people 'where they're at' puts me out in the cold, so be it. I'd rather be out in the cold with a clear conscience than inside where it's warm, cozying with business people who are pretending to have the best interests of the community, while in fact they're just a bunch of money-grubbing jackals.

"It's about greed, Carl, and you know it. I know you know it, otherwise you wouldn't even be here. I mean, why are you really here? Something brought you here, and it wasn't just that you're worried about me. You're curious, and there's something in you that's afraid there might be something more to all this than simple, empirical, validated crap. There are other realities." I wished I hadn't said the last phrase. I recalled the first time I heard it, the first time I met Tarrence.

"What? What other realities. Now you come on; you know how I feel about mumbo-jumbo stuff. We're logical positivists, and we can only accept what science has shown to be true—well, you know, significant statistically anyway," Carl said with uncertainty in his voice.

"There are other ways of doing science and getting significance. People around these parts have been doing science for thousands of years. It's just that this other science derives from a different way of being in the life-world. Once colonialism came down, then all knowledge not coming from the colonizer was deemed invalid by our profession," I lectured.

"Here we go again—"

"Yes, here we go. When someone's way of knowing is invalidated by someone else, there's a serious violation of ethics, ethics set up by the United Nations."

"What? The UN? What does that have to do with anything?"

"'My man,' I'm surprised you haven't done your homework. Part of the UN charter states that if you impose a worldview on someone who doesn't come from that view, then you are guilty of ethnocide—sounds a tad more rugged than unethical I would say, eh, 'my man'?" I said with a grin.

As I moved to allow the waitress to put my plate down, I felt the arrowhead I had acquired that day poke me under my ribs. Somehow I knew this wasn't accidental, and I needed to back off from where I was taking the argument. Winning wasn't what this was about. Before I could think twice, I said, "Why don't you come up and meet Tarrence sometime?"

"Sounds like a great idea. Actually, truth be told, I've been more than curious about him. Would like to do that. Soon, I hope?" Carl said kindly.

"Soon," I said between bites of elkburger.

"That would help me understand some of what you're doing, and I won't have to aggravate you with all my stuff. Well, I think this is good. When can we do this?"

"How about next week when I come up. I can arrange for a time, and so can you. So, it's a plan, eh?"

"This sounds like it will be very interesting. Guess I should get on the road now. It's getting a bit late to be out in the country talking psychobabble," Carl said. He got up, then shook my hand before leaving.

I really started wondering what all this was about. I mean, what are the chances of running into Carl way out here; better yet, for him to want to come and meet Tarrence. This wasn't what I was thinking when I came to this place for dinner. Not after what happened today. I thought I deserved a little quiet time, and now—shit—Carl.

Well, everything else associated with this seems to be what needs to happen. I guess this is part of the whole trip and all this dreamtime stuff. I can't start judging now. Besides, I'm sure Tarrence has met with his fair share of Carls in his life. What pisses me off is that I know Tarrence is going to love him anyway and not see him the same way I see him. Carl deserves a good kick in the ass, and Tarrence is just going to shower him with kindness. It isn't right, but that's just how things are, I guess. Oh well, best be leaving here and head back into town.

As I moved, I heard the arrowhead and the medallion clink against each other. I reached into my pocket and felt them. It felt right.

I paid and got back on the road. As I drove down the mountain, there were a lot of process thoughts in my mind. The road had a different quality at night, and tonight was especially dark since there was a thick layer of clouds that shrouded what little bit of moonlight would have been available otherwise. Traffic was almost non-existent, which made traveling take on a feeling of loneliness.

I couldn't help but wonder what type of turn my life had taken and whether things could ever be the same again. Events of the day had left profound indentations in my psyche, and I hadn't integrated what had occurred. It would take some time to deal with this. After all, it isn't everyday you dig up your body from another lifetime and take some of your property back. I can't think of anyone in my experience who has talked about anything like this, and if they had, I would have been the first one to suggest serious mental help.

With this thought, I arrived at the summit of the mountain road where I would start descending into town. I could see the faint sparkling of the town lights in the far distance. I couldn't help wondering who all those people down there were, and what they might be doing at this time of night. I wondered if any of them ever thought about who they might have been in a previous lifetime. Probably not. Most of them are just trying to get by day to day without much time or energy left for anything else. No wonder a lot of them use the spirit of alcohol just to keep them going. The illusion has really gotten us all to a place of no place, and it's difficult to be aware of anything. Of course, awareness is aware of us not being aware.

During the next few days, my work went on in a very unremarkable manner. I did wonder how it would be to take Carl up to see Tarrence. By now, I wasn't worried about his embarrassing me with his ultra-empiricism. I knew Tarrence would be able to hold his own with the likes of Carl, and not much could shake up the old guy. After all, he'd seen almost everything in his life, even though he was stuck in that bed for most of it.

I even called Carl to make sure he hadn't changed his mind about going to see Tarrence.

Carl answered in his usual way. "No, my man, I am so ready to meet this old dude. Maybe we can do some real cross-cultural stuff—maybe even a research project. Hey, can you see it? What an article that would make: *Cognitive Behavioral Approaches Illuminating Shamanic Methods*—or something like that. Hey, this could be the beginning of something for a lot of people stuck in old superstitions. My man, I am ready."

I didn't say much; I figured, what's the use?

17

Tarrence's Visit with Carl

*I*n the meantime, I saw patients at the office in town. I wondered what would come of the "Carl-visit," as I was referring to it by now, and where my trepidation was coming from. In retrospect, I see that I was holding on to some protective idea of trying to make sure no one hurt Tarrence. Later when I asked him about this, he smiled with that crooked smile and reminded me that there is really no self to protect or to injure. Another part to this concern regarding the Carl-visit was that I wanted to have Tarrence to myself in some sort of narcissistic way, and of course this isn't a skillful way of being.

The next few days went by, and the time came when I had to meet Carl to make the trip up the mountain. He was waiting for me at the Latte' Hey just like we'd arranged. He had ordered my pastry and coffee just the way I like it, and this time it didn't bother me as much. I figured I had bigger fish to fry than to worry about Carl buying me breakfast. After the usual "my man" salutations, we proceeded to eat our meal. I noticed that Carl was remarkably quiet, which was a nice change.

"'My man,' you seem preoccupied this morning. You're being very, or shall I say remarkably, quiet," I said.

"I have stuff on my mind. I mean—I have never gone to see an old shaman—ever in my life," Carl responded haltingly.

"You're upset, eh? Why is that? I mean, just look at the data. Cognitive behaviorism would say that it's irrational for you to be afraid of something that's just a thought passing through. I mean, you're the Cartesian kind of guy." It felt good to rub it in.

"You're right. But you weren't there last night. I mean you were, but not really, I mean—oh shit—I don't know what I mean."

"Now you're not making sense. What in the cat hell are you talking about," I said, to lighten the mood.

"It was like for real. I mean it was real, but not really. I mean the dream. I don't even dream…except for last night. Shit, I don't need this interruption in my life. I don't like this, and I don't feel good about any of this. I feel like I shouldn't go up there today, like I need to process." Carl sounded worried.

I tried to comfort him with the latest psychological ideas on dreams. "You had a dream? Well, I thought in modern psychology all that's simply a biochemical process in the brain. So you shouldn't take it so seriously; that's all it was—you know, random firing of neurons in the brain. It's just the brain relaxing and resting from the day's activities. It's all a figment of the imagination, as they say."

"You'd be right, except, well, except that—no shit, really—except that I was there. Now don't think I'm bullshitting or losing it. I was really there. I have never done anything like this. I never want to do it again either." Carl whispered this as if the local mental-health van was waiting just outside the Latte' Hey to take him to an acute psychiatric ward.

"Well, what was it? There's probably a very logical explanation to all this. I mean, you at least believe in the Freudian wish-fulfillment stuff. Maybe it was an anxiety dream or something—maybe you had bad pizza for dinner," I said, hardly believing that I had taken on the western side as the devil's advocate in order to try and help Carl.

There is some dreamtime poetic justice, I thought to myself. I felt the arrowhead and the medallion in my jacket pocket and thought, these are real, and the implications are major for me anyway; after all, up till now, all this reincarnation stuff has been kind of theoretical. This is getting deep.

"OK, in the dream I saw this huge gourd," Carl said. "I mean, I was *in* the gourd for a little while. Inside the gourd were these little flashes of light. Then one of the flashes grew bigger, and it became the luminescent face of Albert Einstein. No shit, man, it was so real. Then this asshole, I mean Einstein, looks me right in the eye and says, 'You can.' I ask, 'Can what?' He answers, 'You can go faster, faster than light,' and then he smiles and says 'my man.'

"What's weird is that when he said it, I actually understood what he said. Then I saw some old guy with a crooked smile, and he said, 'This is what needs to be understood for balance to be restored.' Then I was back in my body, I mean the dream was over, well, you know. You must think I'm nuts. Whatever you do, I never said any of this. Shit, I can be diagnosed and drummed out of the profession." Carl looked around nervously.

"Crooked smile?" I mimicked Tarrence's crooked smile.

"It's not funny; that's exactly the kind of smile I saw. This shit is getting out of control," Carl responded gruffly.

"Come on, my man—just a little humor. You know what they say, humor is the best medicine, and it sounds like you need some medicine," I said, reaching into my pocket and handling the arrowhead and the medallion.

"I need to catch my breath is all. I'm interested in going up there and meeting this guy; after all I'm a scientist, and I know that if you can't weigh it or see it— well, you know what my man Hume said: 'Burn it,'" Carl said with renewed energy in the scientific method.

"I got you. Let's get on the trail. We have places to go and people to talk to."

I got up from the table and went to pay for breakfast. The thin blonde behind the counter was wearing an unusual shirt with a circle painted on it.

"How's things?" I asked her.

She looked at me and said, "Things are what you think, as in 'cogito ergo sum.'"

"What?"

"You'll see soon enough."

And with that, she focused on the next customer.

I thought this was a bit unusual but, relatively speaking, how could I think anything was strange in view of what was going on in my life at present?

The homeless guy was there again. He winked at me, and when Carl went by him, he said, "You can, my man."

Carl looked at me and said, "You asshole, you put him up to that. You're regressing to adolescence."

We got into the truck and started up the mountain. Carl was calm by now, and the scenery, air, and feeling of the different environment put us both at ease. Thunderclouds were forming as usual, and in the far distance lightning bolts could be seen—the type of lightning that splits apart and touches down in different places at the same time.

"Incredible. That's lightning like they do in the movies," Carl said.

"Nothing but the best for my man Carl. Putting on a light show for you. It's all electricity and stuff. Very scientific, you know. We figured you needed some nice gesture from the gods," I said in a teasing manner.

"Yeah, yeah, you just keep teasing. You really are different these days. You seem lighter, as if you're not worried about shit like you used to be," Carl said while looking off into the distance.

As we went by the turnoff to the Zen Center, he said, "You know, way back in my college days, I actually practiced Zen for a while. Went to some intensive retreats. Man, was it ever painful—at the time I thought it was useful. You know, young, searching, kind of a post-Sixties thing. Thank God, I found out where the real stuff is. Yeah, that was some time ago. Actually studied with some pretty highfalutin monks. Remember this one dude, just over here from

Japan—monster guy. Hit you with a stick just for the hell of it. Named Morehei or something like that." Carl was thinking out loud now.

I didn't want to say anything specific about what Carl had just mentioned. I realized he was up to the limit, getting his cosmic egg cracked. I figured his head would explode with any more material that didn't have a scientific metaphor from which to understand it. Instead, I just pretended to have a side interest in Zen and the thoughts he was expressing.

"I'm amazed, Carl. You and Zen…. Somehow that just doesn't seem to jibe at all. I can just see you sitting there and some guy smacking you with a stick. Not scientific at all—but wait, you could probably measure the direct effect of the stick hitting you and make a study out of it, eh? I mean, velocity, impact, subjective units of distress. My man, you were scientific even then," I said, trying to keep Carl interested and lightening the mood at the same time.

"Yeah, you got a point. I'm sure someone's done that by now. You know, a dissertation or something. Students take on just about anything to get their degrees."

"Just like we did. I mean, who gives a shit about comparing two groups of college freshmen on any given variable? Amazing that almost all we know about psychology is based on this type of so-called science—oops, there I go again. Sorry, Carl, just can't seem to help myself. You bring out my shadow I guess," I said, laughing.

"Make fun, go ahead. I guess to some extent you have a point. Not that I agree with you. I'm just being open-minded. After all, here we are in the country, going up to see God-knows-whom and for what reason. I must be losing my mind." Carl smiled back.

"Nah, you're not that lucky. Just getting the old proverbial cosmic egg shaken a bit. Nothing you can't handle though." I was surprised at the feeling of comradeship I felt with Carl at that moment.

"Guess you're right. If I lost my mind, then all would be taken care of, eh? Nice psychotropic meds, and the rest would be nirvana. Maybe not really. I guess folks who aren't in touch suffer quite a bit. I meant the ones who are totally gone though. Wonder what that's like? I mean to be totally gone?" Carl pondered.

"Must admit I'm surprised to see this side of you."

"Well, to tell you the truth, I haven't always been the way you see me these days. You know, you have to do certain things, and before you know it, you're way in it and kinda forget some other stuff. I guess being here, the dream is kind of like a breath of fresh air. I still believe in science though, so don't be getting any ideas. What do I say to this old dude anyway? Why am I here? Guess I should just enjoy the air."

"Well, Tarrence has told me that there are no accidents in the universe."

"Hey, wait a minute, Einstein also said that, didn't he? Yeah, he did. What is this? More mumbo jumbo, I suppose?"

"Guess you'll find out soon enough. We're almost to the turnoff to Tarrence's place. Just be normal. Don't go native or anything like that. Just relax. He's just a regular guy with some specific abilities and skills. People have their own way of doing things and their own experiences to base all that on. So chill," I said, as I turned onto the dirt road that would lead up to the house.

"This gets pretty basic real quick, eh? Man, we're just barely off the main road and here we are on some basic dirt road. My car wouldn't make it here. I would definitely bottom out if I brought the old Beemer on this stuff. It would be bleeding oil all over the place in no time." Carl rambled on about the road.

"Guess you might say it's symbolic or something. I mean we're not in a place where German science can thrive. You said it, the car would bottom out. Not that I'm saying science would bottom out or anything like that," I added.

"You just can't cut me any slack, huh, my man? Every chance you get, you got to dig a little. It's cool; I can hang, and I'm telling you science can hang also," Carl said, relaxed.

"Well, you think this road is something, we're going to turn off onto one that's even less developed pretty quick," I muttered.

"You are shittin' me. Less developed? There ain't no road as it is, my man," Carl said loudly, as we hit a bump and he bounced around.

"Not to worry. I'll just put Ruby in four by four. That's the most sacred number, you know—when you take four, four times. At least according to Jung. So we're doing the right thing," I said with a sheepish grin.

"How do you think of all this shit? And Ruby? You call your truck 'Ruby'? I've heard it all now. What have they done to you up here? You didn't used to think like this, my man."

"I thought it; I just wouldn't say it. Was afraid at what the man would do. You know, the shrink-man, the profession. If it ain't from the man, that is, the White man, it's wrong, ¿tu sabes? Just kidding, don't go off on me. Just stay cool. See up ahead? There's the house." I pointed it out.

"That's the house of this holy shaman? Man, that is a shack. That doesn't even qualify for HUD housing. It's falling apart. If it wasn't adobe, it would have fallen apart a long time ago. I've seen better houses at Chaco Canyon or Mesa Verde. How old is this dude anyway?" Carl said, bouncing up and down in the cab.

"Actually, Tarrence is one of the few remaining survivors from Mesa Verde," I teased.

"No kiddin'? Oh shit, you got me. Come on, man, don't mess with my head," Carl pleaded.

"Sorry, just couldn't resist the temptation. Just getting you ready for what lies ahead is all."

We pulled up to the house. I noticed that the Quiet One was there, or at least his truck was. I wondered silently what he was doing here, and hoped he didn't have any surprises up his sleeve like the last time. Carl just wouldn't be able to take too much more, at least not today.

"Let's go in and see how Tarrence is doing," I said.

We got out of the truck, and the coyote-dog came to greet us with his usual smile of joy. He was all over Carl, and Carl felt at ease with the dog.

"Interesting-looking mutt," Carl said.

"Yeah, he isn't really a mutt, but that's another story," I said as we entered and knocked on the inside door so as to announce our arrival.

"Come in. Welcome," I heard Tarrence say.

I went in, gave Tarrence a hug, and nodded toward the Quiet One. Carl came in after me, and as soon as he saw Tarrence, he turned right around and went back out.

I started to make excuses, but Tarrence just said, "Go help your friend; bring him in. You remember your first time meeting me. I guess I must be getting ugly in my old age." He burst into laughter.

The Quiet One smiled for the first time I was aware of. Well, thank God, he has some sense of humor, I thought, as I went after Carl. I found him leaning on a tree.

"What's wrong with you?" I asked in a judgmental tone.

"You won't believe it if I tell you. Remember the dream I told you about? Well, that guy was in the dream. I've never seen him before, and there he was in the dream. There's no logical explanation for this. What's going on. Am I losing it? Is this primary process? I can't do this." Carl was breathing hard.

"Calm down a bit. Just breathe, do your relaxation deep breathing. It'll be OK. It's just a transpersonal experience. It's very normal, nothing to worry about. This is what's called the dreamtime up here. Breathe, and come back in," I said, concerned. I was surprised at how much compassion I felt for Carl.

"OK, just give me a second. I just can't believe this shit. How does this happen? I know you're in on this, and it ain't funny. A guy could just keel over and die from this. And who is that dude in there with him? He's weird, I mean there's something odd about him—and this dog," he said, as the dog stood right in front of him, smiling. "What is it with him. Is he really smiling? Even the animals around here are into weird shit. My man, I will get to the bottom of this. Let's go. Sorry about the histrionics," Carl said with a half-smile as we proceeded up the broken stairs into the house.

Once we were back in the room, Tarrence sat up the best way he could in order to receive his new guest. The Quiet One was standing there in his usual fashion, not saying anything.

"Tarrence, this is Carl, I mean Dr. Jones. Carl, this is Tarrence, and this is the Quiet One," I said as Tarrence put out his twisted hand for Carl to shake. The Quiet One didn't move, and I was hoping he would tell us his name, since I referred to him only as 'the Quiet One,' but he didn't seem to mind.

"Good to see you again—I mean, good to meet you, Carl," Tarrence said, correcting himself mid-sentence. I knew that Tarrence knew about the dream, and probably a lot more that had to do with Carl, but I just allowed for things to unfold naturally, rather than offer process interpretations, which our profession is so fond of doing.

"Good to meet you also," was all Carl could muster.

"Have a seat, you guys; it's really nice having company. Been expecting you to come up and visit," Tarrence said, as we found chairs in the room.

I pulled up a chair close to the Quiet One. As I did, I noticed he was wearing the same moccasins that are traditionally worn by women. The way his hair was done in the back was also the way women traditionally wear their hair. He was dressed just as he was during our digging up the old shaman's body. I noted, but didn't say anything. I was integrating into my awareness that the Quiet One was a special person indeed, and he wasn't trapped by the usual identity crisis that most of us are caught in. That's why he could "come and go," as Tarrence put it during our last visit.

"So you also practice the art of soul healing?" Tarrence asked.

"Well, I wouldn't exactly call it that. I'm a psychologist with a medical background, so that would make me a psychiatrist," Carl answered, as if he were taking his board exams.

"That's what I said. Of course you'd have to translate the meaning from the Greek. You know 'psychologist' in Greek means 'study of the soul,'" Tarrence said.

"Wow, yeah, guess you're right," Carl replied.

"Study of soul, and you heal soul-suffering." Tarrence came back.

"What? Soul-suffering?" Carl muttered.

"You work with psychopathology, right? Again, from the Greek this is translated into soul-suffering. You are in a noble task. To work with the soul every day and to heal the soul is one of the very most important tasks of our time. The human soul is in deep suffering, as you know," Tarrence said.

"Well, I don't exactly do what you said. I mean, soul and those things are relegated to the churches or spiritual people." Carl seemed to have recovered somewhat. "I work as a cognitive behavioral psychologist and, at times, use medications to help people get rid of their symptoms."

"So you work with thoughts?" Tarrence asked immediately. I would have been surprised before, but not any more. This man was truly an enigma, and he flowed through different realms with a fluidity and ease that were unreal if you didn't know him.

"Thoughts, yes. You know about cognitive stuff?" Carl asked in a manner that could have been condescending, but was sincere instead.

"Yes. Thoughts. Cogito. Cogito ergo sum." Tarrence said in a scholarly voice.

My thoughts went to the cashier at the Latte' Hey who had said the same thing earlier in the day. There's no way she can know Tarrence, so this is some mysterious interconnection again. I shouldn't be so surprised at these events any more, I thought.

"I'm not sure. My Latin isn't what it should be," Carl answered.

"You know, Descartes and his splitting of the worlds or realms with his 'I think, therefore I am.' It was at this point that westerners departed from the psychology of oneness and separated themselves from the rest of Creation," Tarrence said, to Carl's obvious amazement and to mine also.

"I guess. As a psychologist, I haven't been trained too much in the classics, but yeah, Descartes's notion of subject and object is still in use," Carl mumbled.

"Not only in use, but it's the core of what science is about, no? After all, if there is no subject/object split, who's going to study whom or what? How can something observe itself and make assumptions without a reference point?" Tarrence asked.

"You have a point," Carl replied. "Most of the studies that I've been involved in have this duality. Actually we call people 'subjects.' Hadn't really thought of where that came from. We directly observe them and come up with answers to our questions about human behavior."

"Where is the soul in all this? After all, isn't that what the core of your identity is about? I mean psyche, soul, and the study of?" Tarrence asked kindly.

"Actually, well, truthfully, there is no soul in what we do. Like I said, for those who believe in that stuff, there are others who deal with it. We refer people to priests or whoever specializes in that area," Carl said, with a bit of a struggle in his voice.

"So you're basically saying that the person is compartmentalized still again?" Tarrence asked with concern.

"That's not the point. Our profession only works with certain aspects of the person. Our ethics do not allow us to do things we're not trained to do," Carl said confidently.

"I agree. I think the ethics of healers in all traditions prohibit this. Still, who makes the ethics for the behavior of the profession itself? Isn't it unethical or immoral for a professional body not to require the appropriate training for its healers? It is definitely unethical to misrepresent oneself—and it appears that psychology is misrepresenting by calling its practitioners students of the soul when they have nothing to do with soul. That's unethical anywhere, right? Even illegal in most states," Tarrence added with conviction.

"Your logic is correct. Never thought of it like this. It's very interesting," Carl said, giving me with a look that said "say something."

"Tarrence does have a point," I said. "Seems to me that a profession so stifled with ethics is that way simply because of a reaction formation. The very lack of soul makes it scream for itself. The soul wants to emerge from the repression that it's been in for several hundred years. Amazing how the soul's identity is still in the very name of what we do. Interesting stuff you guys are talking about."

"Aha," the Quiet One said, which told me that he was in agreement. It was the first time he'd acknowledged something I said in a positive manner.

"Going back to cognition." Tarrence decided to ease things and put Carl back into an area that was comfortable to him.

"Yeah? What about cognition?" Carl asked with relief in his voice.

"So you have your patients work with thoughts? With their minds, I guess you would say?" Tarrence asked.

"Kind of. Yeah. What cognitive behavioral people do is help people look at their irrational thoughts and try to replace them with rational ones—thoughts that are useful and helpful to their life," Carl responded confidently.

"That's a good thing. After all, that's what we are, our thoughts. We are what we think for the most part. At least until we're able to train the mind, as you say," Tarrence said kindly.

"Kinda. 'Train the mind'—that might be a bit much. We just help people become more rational in their thinking and behavior," Carl replied.

I knew Tarrence was going somewhere with this, but I didn't really know where. This was a very interesting exchange, and I wondered how come this had never happened in a setting like a university. After all, the meeting of the different worldviews was being discussed and analyzed by leaders in the field.

"Well. it's a work in progress, I guess," Carl said nervously. "No one really knows how the human mind works, and it's an ongoing study."

"No one in western psychology knows, maybe. You really can't say that *no one* knows how the mind works, because you don't know everyone, or you haven't asked everyone, right? So, forgive me, your statement that 'no one really knows the mind' could be considered irrational by definition. I don't mean to judge; we're just having a conversation," Tarrence answered.

"Wow. I didn't know I was going to get into this stuff," Carl whispered. "You have a sharp mind, sir. I need to process some of this."

Tarrence motioned to the Quiet One, who got up and went to the next room to brew some tea. He returned with four cups of tea for us. He served Carl first, and then me. Next he helped Tarrence sip his tea.

The Quiet One picked up his cup and looked deeply into it. He rotated his cup four times in a clockwise direction, then looked into the tea again. Then he very slowly brought the cup to his mouth, took a sip, and slowly placed the cup on the tray. His actions brought a complete and hypnotic stillness to the room.

Tarrence broke the silence. "Being in the moment is really the whole thing."

"Whole thing of what? You mean like a Zen thing?" Carl asked.

"I see you know about these things. Yes, exactly like a Zen thing," Tarrence answered.

The Quiet One took another sip of tea after doing the same ritual, and again there was silence in the room.

"When you think about it, that's really what you're trying to do with cognitive behavioral stuff," Tarrence continued. "You want your patients to change their thoughts, but first they have to become aware of them. The only way they can become aware of their thoughts is to create a silence in which they can let their thoughts be made aware by awareness itself. Then you have them replace unskillful thoughts with skillful ones. You actually don't have to go the second step. The nature of the mind is calmness and quiet. Once the mind is still, then you just are in the moment, which is really all there is. This truth has become such a difficult thing for modern people to allow; it's the nature of the brain illusion that keeps us thinking that everything we see with our eyes and senses is real."

"Now you're talking about illusion as in nothingness, right? I recall a lecture on this subject by that Zen monk way back when," Carl replied.

"Not quite. If you realize nothingness, then there is no illusion. Illusion, or Samsara, as my relatives from across the ocean called it, is the trickery of the sense functions that comes with being in a body. Of course I lost some of those sense functions some time back." Tarrence held up his crinkled hands and gave Carl his crooked smile.

"You are really something—you move from psychology to Buddhism to Latin and who-knows-what-else. You are something, sir," Carl said in a sincere, almost boy-like, tone.

"It really stems from being close to the center. There is only one center, one truth, or again, as my relatives say, one Dharma. The rest is fluff. We put a lot of extra stuff on the truth, and soon the truth is so veiled that all we see is the stuff projected by our own senses. In the silence the projections become quiet and, lo and behold, what is left all by itself is the truth. So simple," Tarrence said softly and kindly.

I could see a softness between Tarrence and Carl. A softness that I could never achieve with Carl. I realized the reason I had never achieved this was because I kept fighting with him, struggling with him. Here in this instant, I saw that Tarrence was simply loving him, and there was no way that Carl could not respond to that type of unconditional love.

"I guess we have a lot to learn, I mean, in our profession," Carl responded.

"It's all within you. The trick is to go out of the room that you're in—you're not trapped in there. No one is holding you hostage. It's OK to venture into the next room and see what's in there. There might be a whole different way of knowing and of understanding 'knowing' itself.

"I think your profession has been going in circles in the same room called science and has missed out on the richness of other ways of finding reality. In this process, many have been hurt. You see, it wouldn't matter what you do as far as staying in your own paradigm or whatnot. But if your actions, or lack of action, are causes or seeds of suffering, well, then it's important to try to find another way. Psychology has contributed to people's suffering many times. This happens a lot with people who might not necessarily come from the same room in which psychologists have been sipping wine for quite some time," Tarrence said kindly.

"Sounds like you're talking about cross-cultural stuff now. We're kind of becoming aware that one size doesn't fit all, but it's an ongoing struggle to find the right way," Carl admitted.

"It's difficult only as long as you refuse to go into the next room. Once you step into the next room, it's easy, isn't it." Tarrence looked at Carl as if to acknowledge that he was stepping into the next room.

"Guess so…. It's not bad. It's actually pretty interesting," Carl said with obvious pride in himself. He was no doubt wondering who this man was and where he got such knowledge about the world Carl was so enmeshed in. Carl's presuppositions about education and the way to obtain knowledge were being questioned, to say the least. It amazed me that when Tarrence made Carl question his worldview, it seemed OK; Carl wasn't compelled to be defensive. It seemed he was getting to like Tarrence and was wondering why he hadn't come up sooner.

"It's remarkable that none of us recognizes what our profession is about. I mean, the very root metaphor of soul. Never heard that in any of my classes, and perhaps we do a disservice to our students by not letting them know about these things," Carl said, apparently to his own surprise. "After all, the people whom we serve or treat are suffering from deep trauma, and most of them probably believe it's their soul that's suffering. When we treat their cognitions, well, we might be missing the mark. Not that we shouldn't treat cognition, but we should be able to work on the whole belief system."

"It's more than a belief system; it's really the way it is. Some things just are," Tarrence said casually.

Just then the Quiet One stood up decisively.

"Someone is coming up the road; he's probably expecting someone," Tarrence said with his crooked smile.

"I don't hear anyone," I said as I looked out the window.

"He has a way of hearing things far away," Tarrence said with the same grin.

"Well, I guess we should be going, since you're getting more company. Guess you're getting popular these days, eh?" I got up.

"Thanks for coming. And it's a deep honor and pleasure to meet you Dr.— I mean, Carl," Tarrence said, extending his crooked hand.

"The honor is all mine, and I really hope to see you again. This has been most informative," Carl said humbly.

"I need to have a word with you," Tarrence said to me, whispering so as not to make Carl feel left out.

"Carl, wait for me outside. I need to do something in here," I said to Carl as he went out the door.

"Well, that was something," I said. "You're amazing, Tarrence. Not only are you smart, but you're so nice about everything."

"Everyone has a spark of the sacred in them; there is Buddha in all of us. You must never forget this. Anyway, I need to let you know there's still one more dream ceremony that needs to be done. It's critical that we do it soon. I have only so many breaths left on this plane, and I need to do what I came here to do."

"I'll do what I can. I really believe that what you're doing is of great importance," I said, as I touched the medallion and the arrowhead in my pocket.

"You'll have to purify those objects," Tarrence, said nodding at my pocket.

"You amaze me. How do you know I have those objects with me?"

"They have life force in them. Anything with life force can be detected by another life force," Tarrence replied.

"OK. How do I go about this? I mean, purifying them?"

"They'll have to be purified by the time we do the next dream ceremony. That's critical. The old karma on the objects needs to be transformed. First, you'll take some cedar and smoke them off. Then you must take them way up in the mountains where there's a live spring—someplace where no one goes. It must be a pure place. Put the items in a basket and leave them in the spring for four days and four nights. The pure spring water will clean the old karma. Then you'll smoke them off with cedar again. Make a fire, and pass them through the fire four times in your hand—don't worry, it won't burn you.

"First, talk to the fire and let it know of your intention, then feed it some tobacco. The fire will know what you need and will then transform the karma in the objects. Is that clear to you?" Tarrence sounded so serious I knew this must be done in this exact manner.

"I'll do as you say. I'll get right on it. Is that it? Oh, how will I know when the dream ceremony is to take place?"

"You'll know," he answered with his crooked smile, in which I also detected a little sadness.

I went outside and saw the Quiet One standing by a truck that had just pulled in. I couldn't believe it—it was Morehei and the Bald Nun! The Quiet One and the Bald Nun obviously knew each other, since they hugged. I noticed that the Bald Nun was wearing men's traditional moccasins and men's clothes. Not that it's remarkable for women to wear men's apparel; it's just that there was a purpose and intent to the way she wore these clothes and carried herself today. Especially when seen opposite the Quiet One. The Quiet One and the Bald Nun balanced each other, but I didn't even pretend to know what this was about.

Morehei stepped out of the truck and bowed to me as he approached. He bowed to Carl and said, "It's nice seeing you again. I hope you've been keeping up with your Zazen." Carl seemed dumfounded and bowed mutely.

Morehei strode up the stairs, intent on his purpose. He went inside the house, and I watched through the window. He went into Tarrence's room and embraced him. These two obviously went way back—there was such joy between them when they saw each other.

My mind went back to the dream ceremony in which Tarrence and Morehei made the karmic deal and committed their respective peoples to pay for the karma of the dream ceremony that was taking place. I sure wish I could hear what those two are talking about, I said to myself. The Quiet One and the Bald Nun have gone off to talk by themselves, and I'm stuck with Carl. As soon as I thought this, I recalled what Tarrence had just said about everyone having a spark of the sacred. Suddenly I saw Carl in a totally different manner.

"Guess we should be getting on our way," I said to him.

"Yeah, there's some stuff I need to process."

"See you guys," I said to the Quiet One and the Bald Nun.

"Later," the Quiet One responded, while the Bald Nun merely bowed to us.

"They're a strange pair. I can't quite define it...but those two...there's something very peculiar about those two," Carl said pensively, not really knowing what to think.

"Yes, they're special people." I tried to explain the best I could. "They can 'come and go.' At least that's what Tarrence said. They have special abilities and aren't restricted by the usual identity as we know it."

"You mean they're gay?"

"Not really. Well, kind of.... You see, in traditional cultures there's male, female, gay, and then there's this other category that's allowed freedom to transcend sexual identity as we know it in the west. They're not stuck within an identity, and therefore have special spiritual abilities. I know it's complex when seen from the western side of things, but that's how it is."

I started to pull away from the house, but the Quiet One motioned for me to stop. He came to my side of the truck and said, "We need to go and purify the objects. I'll be helping you."

"OK, thanks. That's very kind of you," I replied. I knew something urgent was going on, but I really didn't know what. Here are these "heavy hitters" meeting at Tarrence's, I thought, and there's to be a fast turnaround on the objects, and then Tarrence seems to be in a rush to do the next dream ceremony. I wonder what's up? What did he mean by having only so many breaths left? Is this some sort of death-rebirth image, à la Carl Jung? Well, for now it's best to go along, and it's good that I don't have anything planned this weekend. I guess it wouldn't matter if I did.

"What's that all about?" Carl interrupted my thoughts.

"Oh, they want to do some ceremonial stuff, and they're inviting me to watch," I said, trying to appear casual about this.

"Seems to me there's a lot more going on than just some ceremony to watch. I can't believe that old man Morehei recognized me after all these years. He probably says that to everybody he meets...yeah...there's no way he could remember me. After all, the retreat I went to had a lot of other people, and it was a long time ago," Carl rambled.

"You never know about these old guys. They have a way of remembering stuff—even the minute details. Tarrence says that it comes from paying attention to the moment."

"Attention, yeah—but shit. To remember someone after twenty years? I must have changed some in that time." Still, Carl sounded unsure of himself.

"Maybe the outside changed. These guys focus on who we are, the essence of who we are. That's how they can remember stuff in a way that's kind of timeless," I said, as if I knew what I was talking about.

"Yeah, I remember from one of the Zen lectures. If you're in the moment, that's all there is, and it's easier to remember since you're really there. Most of the time we're not where we are. That's what they were talking about in those lectures. Shit, it took me twenty years to learn this?" Carl asked rhetorically.

"Better late than never. At least you're getting it. I know that some of the stuff Tarrence says to me goes right over my head until some time later. These old guys are something," I said as we bounced over the old road. I could see a truck coming up our way. As it approached, I saw Ms. Chavez and Dr. Beerli in the truck. They were obviously going up to meet with Tarrence and Morehei. Dr. Beerli waved and smiled as she went by.

"Wonder what all this to-do is about?"

"What?" Carl said.

"Oh, just thinking out loud." I didn't realize I had spoken out.

"Whoa! Would you look at that? Wow, I've never seen such a big one," Carl said, pointing to an owl standing on a half-dead piñon tree and looking right at us. "Shit, it's black! I didn't know they made them black. My man, this trip is a trip, ain't it?"

I looked right at the owl. His eyes looked remarkably familiar and had a sense of purpose in them.

"Yeah, they make them in all shades and colors up here. We try to please all the city folk any way we can." I tried to sound unconcerned. I reached for some tobacco in my pocket and put some of it out the window without Carl seeing, since I didn't want to give a lengthy explanation about the offering I was making to the spirit of the owl, or whoever that was.

I wondered what was going on at Tarrence's place about now. I was burning with curiosity as to the relationship between Tarrence and Morehei. Also, what was up with the two Quiet Ones? They seemed perfectly complementary to each other.

"I guess I'll find out when the time is right," I whispered, and as I did, I noticed that behind my sun visor was a green logbook, the type that government workers and military people use. I was sure that the Quiet One had put it there for me to find. I wanted to look at it but decided to wait.

"What? Find out what?" Carl asked.

"Oh, just muttering to myself," I responded off-handedly.

"Well, what a day it's been. That Tarrence dude is quite the renaissance man, ain't he? My man, he can go from cognitive psychology to Zen Buddhism without missing a beat. And his mind is so keen; he had me going on the dishonesty of our profession. Pretty tight argument if you ask me. How did I dream him before I met him? It was him, my man, and also, what about the Einstein image in the dream? Weird shit. What do you make of it? I mean, you've been hanging out here longer, and you might have some stuff on all this," Carl said cheerfully.

"Well, it's like Tarrence said once, except I can't remember the whole thing. Something about the dreamtime being the place from which all became what it is, and how in a way it's still like that. We're sort of complexes of the dream itself," I answered, as again I glanced up at the green government book clamped by the visor.

"Holy shit, now that's deep. Way deep. I read something about the Aborigines in Australia having some sort of dream trip going that sounds like that."

"Yeah, it's exactly like that. The interconnections of the psyche are pretty remarkable, especially once they're in your face, like the dream you had."

"Can't believe I'm going to say this, but I'm going to anyway. Just like what Jung said in his notion of the collective unconscious. Shit, I don't believe I'm talking like this. Not only that, it's starting to make sense, and that's the scary part. My man, tell me I'm not losing it—I know I'm not, but this is trippy shit! That dude Tarrence, heavy, my man, with a capital H," Carl rambled on.

"Now you can kind of see where I've been coming from lately. This is where you leave the cross out of the cross-cultural, and then it just is what it is, if you catch my drift. Glad to see that we can connect again, my man," I said as we approached town. "What do you say, get you a latte? Kind of get your archetypes into turbo?" I was still eyeing the green government book on the visor.

"I will even buy, my man. Latte' Hey, here we come!" Carl said in a jovial tone.

We arrived at the coffee shop and managed to get our usual table. The same crowd was there. Even the bits of conversation floating around were the same, and varied depending only on the time of the semester and the courses being taken. There were a lot of very serious people wanting to make sure everyone at their table knew how smart they were and how much information they had. I suppose me 'n' Carl fit the usual since we also talk about the same stuff every time we're in here, I thought.

"My man, why so serious? Tell me, what do you make of the Einstein in the dream?" Carl asked. I thought this would be a different conversation for once.

"Sorcery," I said, before I could catch myself.

"What? You are shittin' me? You think someone's messing with my head?"

"Sorry, just a slip. Freudian slip of some sort, you know; it happens, my man."

"No you don't. I know you meant something, and you ain't gettin' off that easy. Sorcery you said. What does that have to do with the Ein-man. Hey, he was just a scientist—genius—great and all that."

"Yeah, he was. Look at it, though. All science emerged out of old alchemical stuff, and the alchemists always had a mystical and spiritual component to what they were doing; it was conscious on their part. The only difference with modern scientists is that the mystical and spiritual is unconscious. Therefore it's in the shadow. And if it's in the shadow, then it can have a life of its own and you can't contain it. So I guess it's not proper sorcery, since most sorcerers can contain what they're doing and direct it in a manner that might or might not be good. That's what started the whole thing."

"What whole thing?"

"Well, you know. We drove close to it. All this science has snuck up on us and is threatening to destroy the whole planet. It was propelled heavily by Einstein's time in the dreamtime. He knew it, but by the time he tried to contain it, well, it was too late. Once the genie is out of the bottle, it won't go back in. But your dream sounds like what was said was important. What was it? Something about how you can move faster than light?"

"Yeah, that was it."

"Well, you were doing it in the dream. You saw Tarrence and Einstein at the same time in the dreamtime, so how can such distance in time be transcended unless you're going faster than light? Of course, the speed of light is just a metaphor. It doesn't care what the speed of light does. In the dreamtime, stuff is what it is, and it's our silly human egos that require formulas that really don't say diddly about anything. It just helps the ego illusion continue to feed itself on the unreal, and it continues to inflate on illusion. Illusion upon illusion. And this shit of how numbers are the language of the universe—please, what narcissism! Why in the hell would the universe talk such shit that don't mean nothin' except to an ego that has been fattened by the illusion of numbers, science, and shit in the first place?" I said emphatically. People were starting to look toward our table and listen. I realized I needed to tone it down.

"Whoa, you do have some stuff going. Tell me how you really feel." Carl was laughing at me.

"Sorry, I know I get carried away. Well, that's what I think of the dream, anyway, for whatever it's worth." My mind wandered to the green logbook in the truck. I wondered what was in it. Maybe some stuff about the next ceremony. Why does it look like a government book? Well, in due time, I guess all will show itself. Man, I'm starting to sound like Tarrence now. Best be getting out of here and back to the house.

"Let's get going. I have a lot to do in the next few days," I said.

"Yeah, let's. It's been real, or unreal—which is it? This has been a good and interesting day. When can we go up again?"

"Soon. There are some things I have to take care of first. We'll go in a few weeks. Tarrence took a liking to you, eh?" I said as we walked out.

Carl smiled. "Later," he said as we went our separate ways.

Visiting Tarrence was always interesting. Synchronicities abounded around him, and today was no exception. The whole 'cogito-ergo-sum' coincidence definitely was part of my recollection at that point. Must be some importance to the repetition of this, but it eluded me. I decided to let it go and not attach too much significance to anything—although everything appeared significant.

18

The Logbook

*O*nce I arrived home, I listened to messages and did some other housekeeping chores. The whole time I was doing this, my eyes kept wandering to the green logbook on the kitchen table. I wanted to see what was in it, but I didn't want to get interrupted by chores. Therefore I decided to discipline myself until I knew I had plenty of time to look at it.

When my chores were finished, I went to the table and picked up the logbook. I opened it to the thick paper that goes between the binding and the soft paper of the logbook itself. On the inside of the green binding was a citation or quote by Padmasambava, a Tibetan holy man, that reads, "*When iron horses travel on the road, and when iron birds fly in the sky, that is the time when the Buddha will be in the land of the Redface.*"

Then there was commentary by Tarrence. At least, since his name was on the bottom of the page, I assumed this was his journal. After the quote from Padmasambava, Tarrence wrote, "*Of course the Buddha has always been there as an awakened awareness, but then there will be a time when many in the land of the Redface will also become awakened and become free from the binding of the brain illusion or Samsara.*"

Since the date on this page was 1950, I realized that Tarrence had been studying these types of things for a long time. I wondered where he was when he wrote this and was hoping the next pages would reveal these details.

The first few entries were from the late Forties. Tarrence had been in the Army during World War II and had fought in the Pacific. There were accounts of his experiences on some of the islands, and some of the extreme difficulties that were encountered during those days. I discovered that Tarrence had been a sergeant in charge of a bunch of soldiers, and he distinguished himself in battle situations.

One night toward the end of the war, he had a dream in which he saw himself sitting still for a long time—probably predicting his years of being paralyzed, or so I thought. In another dream, Tarrence and an elderly Japanese man were singing while shaking two distinct gourds.

Tarrence had made it through the war and into occupied Japan. He felt very fortunate to be stationed in a village near Tokyo. In that village there lived a segment of people who still maintained some of the old traditional values. Tarrence wrote that many of the practices he was observing in his walks and travels had a familiarity with his own practices from early childhood. One of the places he visited was a Shinto shrine, where he observed people praying and giving offerings. Tarrence had written,

Since I knew about this, I decided to also make an offering. All I had on me were some cigarettes, so I felt that these spirits would appreciate tobacco. As soon as I left my offering, I felt as if the offering was acknowledged by some awareness, and this awareness was the same awareness that I had experienced when I was young, in the mountains of my homeland. It was as if the spirits that were here were acknowledging the spirits that traveled with me around my medicine pouch. I have no doubt that these spirits greeted each other warmly, and I felt as if I were home. As I was standing there in a prayerful attitude, someone came and stood by me. I felt like I knew this man. He half-smiled at me, and I at him. He told me his name was Morehei, and if I was interested, I should come to the place where his ancestors have worshipped for many generations. I agreed. I was really amazed at his lack of animosity at me for being who I was and for being part of the destruction that had been directed at his country and people.

I decided that I would stay here for a while even after the time would come for me to leave. There is something compelling me to stay, and at this time I don't know what it is. I know that my elders back home have taught me to listen to the inner voice, and I need to do that now. I think that this Morehei fellow might have something to do with it. So I decided to take the directions on the piece of paper he had given me and go find the place. I noticed that on the other side of the paper there was a short saying:

Awareness
Refined through suffering.
Transformation.

I thought the saying was interesting, and there was some truth in it that resounded deep in my being. He had mentioned that they met every day at this certain place, and I decided to go the following Saturday. I attended my usual duties until Saturday, then I took a jeep up to the place where Morehei had said they met. The place was out of town and up on the side of a mountain. The air felt clean, and there was a peculiar energy to this place. I noticed that there was a very simple structure, and there was smoke already flowing from an altar in front of the few people gathered here.

Morehei came to me right away and said, "Welcome home, my brother." I thought this was very kind, and I felt as if he meant "brother" in the real sense and was not simply being a kind religious person.

"Thank you for your kindness, brother," I said, as if I knew what I was saying.

"We visit with the mountain spirits here, and we work toward bringing peace and harmony to the world. We don't have much time left if we don't get this done, and I'm glad you are back to help," he said. When he said this, I wondered, "Back?" Back where? But I didn't question what was going on, especially since there were some very old people present. These old people looked and acted like medicine men and women from olden times.

"Where I come from, we do the same," I told him.

"I know," Morehei replied.

"Too bad that we had to be on opposite sides, and so much damage had to be done," I said in an apologetic tone.

"Do not concern yourself with this—karma is karma. This has all been planned and committed to a long time ago. The deal was made in another awareness, and many of us were there then," he said. I must admit that I was really lost at this point, and I didn't understand what Morehei was referring to. I had heard of old-time dreamers who could move through the realms, and I thought maybe that's what he meant.

"I know people who could do this in the dreamtime," I said.

"Ha! The dreamtime. That is the place where there is no time or space," Morehei answered with a smile.

At this time, there was some chanting, and the priests were all sitting in the lotus position. Morehei explained how they were chanting the Heart Sutra. This has become my inspiration over the years. The ceremony was simple, and it felt as if there was a real harmony between us all at the end.

When it was over, Morehei came toward me again and said, "It's important that you take some leave to spend four days with us in meditation at a very special place. The place is where the dream ceremony came full circle."

"What dream ceremony? Where?" I asked, unsure of myself.

"This will be explained as we go. It is important that you do this," Morehei answered.

"Say when. I have a lot of leave accumulated and might as well see the country."

I somehow felt sure that this trip was a good thing. Morehei then told me the days that we would go to this place. I trusted him and the rest of the folks here, since I grew up respecting spiritual leaders. These folks seemed to have medicine in their own way that was very similar to what I was used to. We parted and were to meet in two weeks to go to this still undisclosed place.

In the meantime, I was in communication with home, and I told some of my relatives about what I was doing. My grandpa wrote through my aunt, and he felt that this was good. He let me know that in his dreams he had seen that I was to work with the people I was around, and that their way was good. He let me know that he felt that through the suffering of the Japanese people, a lot of good could come for the healing of the world. Grandpa also mentioned something about how all of life, which is the universe itself, comes full circle. So I couldn't help but think that these old people must know each other in some way.

The two weeks went by rather quickly, and my leave was approved, as I expected. I made my way to the appointed place, which was where people went to meditate. I really don't know too much about this form of meditation, but it seems like some of the vision prayers that we do back home. I went in, and some monks at the door greeted me. They were very kind and let me know that Morehei would be with me shortly. Morehei appeared as promised, gave me the biggest smile, and asked me to follow him. He let me know that I would be traveling with them and not to worry about my vehicle. We got into several cars and took off. We made our way through many communities where the rebuilding was under way.

Traveling was mostly in a southwest direction as far as I could tell, but I wasn't too worried about where we were going. I thought this was interesting, and it was nice to be around people who weren't in the military but had a spiritual purpose. After several hours of travel, we arrived in a small place that was just an open field with a lot of trees and green mountains in the distance. Everyone had been very quiet during the trip, and I really didn't have any idea of what this was about.

I knew that we were close to Hiroshima and also to Nagasaki. The thought of being close to these places made me sad, uncomfortable, and angry—a mix of emotions. The monks were all still the same and appeared to be in good moods. I looked at Morehei, and he understood that I was having some difficulty with the trip.

"We are here," he said.

"Where?"

"Right in the middle of the end of the circle," he answered with a big smile.

"I really don't understand what you are saying. I'm not feeling very good either."

"It's probably some karmic feeling that you are in touch with. You will know soon. Have patience. It's best if you find out with your heart," he said kindly.

We walked for some time into some brush and trees. We came to a place where there was a shrine of some sort—I didn't know too much about the particulars. Also, this is my journal, and I wonder if anyone else but me will ever lay eyes on it.

"There is something that I have to say now. It's something that will require an open heart to understand. No need for guilt; just insight," Morehei finished.

"What?"

"When the bomb was dropped not too far from here, the order to drop the bomb was given in Navajo—you know, by the code talkers. Interesting that our relatives supplied the only code that we couldn't understand. Karma has a unique way of manifesting itself," Morehei said with a half-smile.

At this point in the logbook, I couldn't help but recall the deal that Morehei and Tarrence had made in the dreamtime ceremony. My mind boggled with the total interconnectedness of things. Even though I am not a Navajo, I am related through my Apache ancestry. Same people basically. Same language also, I thought to myself. Then I continued reading.

When we got to the place where the shrine was, there appeared to be an even older monk or priest from a nearby wooden house. He greeted all the travelers, and Morehei stayed close to me.

The old monk looked at me and said something to Morehei. Morehei explained that the old man was glad to see me again, and that it was a good thing that we were working toward peace and harmony. He let me know that it was good that someone with good intent who came from the start of the circle was here at the end of the circle, to try to balance out what was started by some who had been blinded by illusion. I didn't know what they were talking about.

Morehei said, "We are in the exact center from Hiroshima and Nagasaki. This is the very center of the two places where they dropped the gourds, or bombs, which were built in your home. I don't mean your country; I mean your home. You come from that place where the sorcerers gathered to do the ceremony that resulted in the two bombs."

When he said this, I was in such shock and shame that my legs felt weak. "Of course, the bombs were made just a short walk from where I grew up, but I didn't have anything to do with that. After all, it was the government that came and took over the land and did everything in secrecy," I defended myself.

"Yes, it's true what you say. Politically, that is how it happened. We are not interested in politics. We are interested in the laws of cause and effect—Karma. A lot has happened on that land over many lifetimes, and those actions and causes are closely linked with this land on which we stand," Morehei responded.

"You are talking about spiritual things that occurred a long time ago then? I'm not sure I follow, but somehow I believe that what you are saying is true," I said.

"These are heart truths. We are not here to blame or create guilt. Our sole purpose is to heal and restore balance—karmic balance. The actions we take now will have profound effects later, just like the actions taken by our ancestors had profound actions in the two cities opposite us. The screams and agony of our

people still fill the air around us. We must not allow that suffering to go to waste. That suffering must be put to a purpose, otherwise the karmic result will be more suffering. We must wake up from this ignorance. So don't spend any more time on guilt and feeling bad. We have already forgiven, even before all this happened— and so have you; you just don't remember yet," Morehei said.

After reciting the Heart Sutra four times, we all moved deeper into the trees. We came to a cave and entered it. There were sixteen of us in there, eight men and eight women. Inside the cave there was another altar, and the symbol on the altar was a circle divided into four equal parts. Each fourth was of a different color— black, red, yellow, and white; with blue bordering one half, and green the other. The design was such that it appeared as if the circle was moving like a sun-wheel. I recalled seeing this design in some of the ceremonies I had gone to in my youth. How could they have gotten the same design? It was amazing to see all this going on in such a faraway place.

"This is the symbol of the gourd put in the ground at your home when the dreamers did the original ceremony," Morehei explained.

"It looks very familiar."

"Of course it's familiar; you were there when this happened. It was another time, and in the dream you will be able to see it. Then you will know what your heart knows already," he said with compassion.

On reaching this point in Tarrence's logbook, I took out the medallion and the arrowhead. I looked at them for some time, and in my heart I knew there were deep implications in the meaning of these objects. I had no doubt that my karma was intricately woven with that of Tarrence and the people he was describing in the logbook.

There is no way I can transcribe the entire logbook here, but I'll draw from it enough to illustrate the parallel process that has been going on throughout human history. If not for these holy people helping karma in a non-political way, I'm certain this story couldn't be told, because there would be no one to tell it, and no one to tell it to.

I began reading Tarrence's words again.

I was instructed to sit with them and not to move. Incense was constantly burning, and I had no idea how long we were going to sit. What I recognized was that an hour went by and no one moved. Every so often, the people sitting there recited the Heart Sutra and still didn't move. I tried to do the same. I must tell you that by the first hour, the pain in my knees was unbearable; yet they sat. The pain in my back became unbearable; yet they sat. The pain in my mind became unbearable; yet they sat.

Two hours later, I was getting very angry with Morehei for sitting there with that sweet look on his face. You bastard, I thought, this is your way of making me pay for the war. Yet they sat. I went through moments of rage in my mind where I was glad we beat them in the war; yet they sat. The rage became murderous, mixed with the worst pain I have ever felt; yet they sat. I felt like I was dying—I wanted to die. I decided I was going to get up. I couldn't. Sonofabitch, I thought. Now I can't move. My mind was frozen in pain. That's all that there was, pain on top of pain. Pure physical pain becoming a pain of the mind—fear, anger, jealousy, and my ignorance—right in my face; yet they sat.

It wasn't till years later that I understood what was going on during the ceremony in Japan. We were involved in Metta, or loving-kindness meditation. Through the process of offering good wishes from the heart, a process of purification develops. The initial stages of the purification involve the letting go of many negative mind-states that have been ingrained over many lifetimes of unskillful actions and thoughts.

What appeared to be a day went by. All that there was, was pain. There was no "me" experiencing the pain. There was just pain with no body for an object. They sat. My awareness was aware that the pain was moving. There is no one with pain, there is just pain. I stopped wanting the pain to go away. I saw pain as just another sensation, like no pain. There was just awareness and awareness of awareness by the end of the second day. They sat, because we sit, then this became sitting, then there was just awareness. I sensed that there was an awareness that the body was in need of water in the worst way, and that became the focus of the awareness. There was nothing but thirst and the awareness of thirst, then there was just awareness—sitting. I couldn't help but think of the stories my grandpa told, of how the old people used to go out into the hills and sit in a circle. For four days without food or water they sat. Things were starting to come together for the awareness that I was being aware of having.

There was no more time, space, or anything. Pure awareness. Sometime during the last day or so, the oldest monk got up and came toward me. He lowered his forehead against mine. When he did so, he let out a loud screech, and I felt a surge of energy enter my being, and I saw myself in the middle of the universe. To my left, I could see the rings of Saturn, above me I could see the galaxies. I could see and be the whole universe. I was free from all that was bothering me.

In my awareness, I was able to see a time long ago by human time. I could see sixteen dreamers doing a ceremony close to where I grew up. I could see that the ceremony was enacting terrible suffering. I did not want to be part of this suffering. I saw Morehei and myself taking on suffering to balance out the ceremony. I saw the effects of the terrible ceremony and what destruction it brought to my relatives in Japan.

There was also a deep understanding that suffering was sacred and was part of the restoring balance for the illusion of ignorance that human beings had been in for so long. I knew that the people who suffered understood their suffering as soon as they transcended their physical being and gave their suffering willingly. The suffering became part of the relative mind that was merely being reflected by the luminescence of empty awareness. Peace, silence, and absolute stillness were all there was. It was so beautiful, beyond words. At this moment I understood the Heart Sutra.

I could see all of what I have been in many lifetimes, and I could see that Morehei and I have been close for many eons of years in human time. My heart filled to exploding, and I loved everything in the universe. I could see many holy people praying and meditating over millennia in order to restore balance and bring awakening to all beings. In the future, I could see the Buddha in Redface bringing awakening to my people, everyone being my people. I don't mean as a person, but as an energy in the part of the world known as the New World, or Turtle Island to older people. There were no separations between beings or things. Then I was aware of sitting again, and the ceremony was over. It has never been the same since.

We started to chant the Heart Sutra. After four times, the monks started to chant the Our Father, also four times. It was beyond words. It was as if Jesus Christ and the Buddha were there with us. When they were done with the Our Father, I felt compelled to sing a blessing song that I knew from my people. We sang it four times. Then there came a man and a woman. It was hard to tell who was the man and who was the woman. They performed the Tea Ceremony. It was so precise and in the moment, it transcended time and space. We drank tea. Then we ate a ceremonial portion of rice. Then it was over.

I had a chance to visit a bit with Morehei. "I find it interesting that you also chanted the 'Our Father,'" I said to him.

"Of course. Our brother Yeshua was with us at one time, and he still is in the dreamtime," he answered.

"Who?"

"That was his name. Yeshua. But the Greeks changed it to Jesus."

"You mean He was here?"

"He spent many years studying the Truth, or Dharma, in Asia. He had a very intensive meditation practice. His mind was very concentrated, and for many generations, we continue to practice the compassion that he became aware of. You know he was fully enlightened?" Morehei said.

"Interesting. Never thought about it, I guess."

"Where do you think he was from age fourteen to thirty? He had to be somewhere. And no one can achieve Samadhi and wisdom without proper practice and effort—just part of the karmic rules. It's natural law that cannot be any other way. Effort cause and effect," Morehei said matter-of-factly.

"This karmic stuff is interesting. So are there any other instances where there was a price paid in the dreamtime? What else could they have been thinking?"

"What they were thinking is the prophecy of Padmasambava—about the Buddha being in the land of the Redface. There has to be a path in which the Buddha is to walk into the land of the Redface, my friend. You see, at one time, we were all one family in the dream. In order to restore the family, the Buddha must be known in the land of the Redface—your home. Wisdom mind has worked this reunion in curious ways that can only be understood by Wisdom itself. Relative mind can only suffer at the thought that so much suffering had to happen because of the ignorance brought on by the illusion of the brain mind or small mind. The price has already been paid by the suffering of many of our people. Everyone is our people when you come down to it," Morehei replied with a knowing smile.

"I see. This is starting to make sense. Otherwise all of the suffering that happens would be a total waste. That would be meaningless; suffering with no use."

"Yes, my friend. You must quiet your mind in order to gain the clarity to understand. Silence of the mind is all-important. It leads to clarity and non-clinging," Morehei said a compassionate voice.

My friendship and practice with Morehei and his folks intensified. I became a regular meditator at the center the whole time I was there. Of course, there was the accident during that time also. It was during the fall—

There was a peculiar entry into the logbook that stood out at this point. Tarrence had written,

Suffering and the cessation of suffering. Four Noble Truths, this is the elephant's footprint into which all other footprints fit. Without this understanding, there is no freedom. Insight and true understanding of this teaching is the end of all teaching. Our people must try to recall this most basic yet deepest of all teachings.

This entry left me with a sense of urgency, and I knew beyond all knowing that this was true, although I didn't know why.

It was evident that Tarrence had intensive training in Japan. He was also completely aware of the purpose that he was involved in at present. The fact that Morehei was here was no longer a mystery. The two had been together for many lifetimes, and they were going about their business in an impeccable manner. I felt so fortunate to even know who they were…but I still wondered why my karma of being a terrible shaman had brought me to them.

Soon it would become obvious in light of the events that were about to transpire in my life.

19

Prelude to Ceremony

*A*fter having read some of the logbook, I had a more in-depth understanding of who this man Tarrence was. He was here for a purpose that went beyond ego-gratification, and his commitment to this purpose was impeccable. He was a true warrior, in the old sense of having conquered his own delusional self, and he was going through his present life in a way that was unselfish and compassionate. This doesn't mean that he was weak or co-dependent. More than once he stopped me in my tracks with his firm resolve, a resolve that sometimes went beyond what I wanted to hear.

I wondered what the upcoming cleansing of the objects would bring, but I knew that I wouldn't know until it was happening, and even then I wouldn't have the whole picture. Faith was my operating principle these days, and I was as sure of this as I had been of anything else in my life. After all, we all assume we know what's going on, even as we do simple things such as eating lunch. Most of the time we're not even present for this event. Therefore most of the time we're not even residing in our bodies, due to the machinations of our minds as they travel uncontrolled through one past or future event—never being where we are and the only place we will ever be: the present. Since I have tried to be in the present, I've noticed that my energy level is higher, and the old moods of fear and depression have not been as available to me. Guess this old-style cognitive Buddhism is being effective, I decided.

My mind went back to the day Carl and I left Tarrence. What were all those people convening about? I knew there was something brewing, and if they thought it was my business, they would tell me. I had thought of calling Dr. Beerli with the hope of gleaning information, but gave up on the idea since she would see right through it. No sooner had I given up on the idea than the phone rang. Dr. Beerli was on the line.

"Hello," she said. "Good to hear your voice."

"Thanks for calling. It's always nice to hear your voice too."

"Well, there's a reason I'm calling you."

"I'm certain of that," I answered.

"We had a meeting, as you know. The cleansing ceremony is more than just that. It's a very dangerous ceremony, dangerous to you. You might die or lose your mind—or of course you might come out OK." Beerli chuckled on the other end. I knew she meant what she said, despite her chuckle.

"Well, let me sit down. This is way more than I bargained for."

"Oh, no. This is exactly what you bargained for. This is not being thrown on you. You've made commitments in the dreamtime that must be followed. If you don't go through with it, which I'm sure is not an option for you anyway, there will be terrible consequences. You might die anyway," she said in a cold and serious tone. When she said this, I got nauseated and was speechless for a moment. Deep inside I knew this to be true.

"You're right. I'm going to do this. What do I need to do to prepare?"

"You already have done what you need. I need to explain some of the things we discussed. These are not popular things, and they have a profoundly serious nature to them. You see, when the dreamers did the ceremony in the dream-time, they did the ceremony to the earth herself. All healing ceremonies come from the earth, therefore most of the ceremonies done since then have been contaminated by the intent of the dreamers. That's one of the reasons there's so much sickness and suffering. Also, that's why so many of the healing cere-monies don't work—both in western and Indigenous ceremonies.

"Tarrence has been paying part of the price with his body," she continued. "Morehei and his people have paid dearly. So have Indigenous people all over the world, as well as people from the western tradition, who have been paying through the suffering of alienation. Women have also paid a dear price over the past few centuries. So you see, there's a lot at stake. Not that this is the only thing that needs to happen to bring balance. But this is what needs to happen now, in this part of the world. The earth has power points just like we do. Performing this ceremony is like applying acupuncture and re-energizing the earth's healing meridians, in the same way that we ourselves heal. The earth might want a life for this: yours."

"This is pretty intense! I don't even know how to respond," I said, extremely agitated. "I wish I would have just listened to Carl and minded my own busi-ness. Dying, what a concept. And I'm sure it won't be a nice death either. It will be full of fear, anguish, and God-only-knows-what. I really don't like this. I'm just a psychologist, a simple one at that. This is the kind of stuff your mentor would have been into; I mean Jung. Yeah, he lost his mind for a while in order to gain some insight, right? Well, he was a crazy Swiss guy, and I'm not. Why didn't he do this when he was over here visiting anyway? He went right by here."

"Yes, he was here. He did what he could, but all things to their own time. He was one of the dreamers who kept dreaming from the other side of the ocean. He was heartbroken when he heard how the dreamers had enacted the shadow side of the dream.

"But back to you. Explicit instructions will be given. In a nutshell, be mindful of the breath and of every moment. Do not let the monkey mind overwhelm you. Realize it's all illusion, no matter how real it looks. Even if you die, this will be a mere illusion," she explained.

Easy for her to say, I thought.

"You should not eat any meat for the remaining time till the ceremony," Beerli continued. "Watch your mind, and try not to engage with anger, ignorance, or fear. There will be purification before you go in. Tarrence and the others have worked out all the details in order to protect you as much as possible. Well, I need to go now."

With that, she ended the conversation and hung up.

You've got to be shitting me! I said to myself. She calls and dumps this heavy stuff on me, and then just goes? No, this isn't happening. As my mind wandered, I saw myself becoming angry, then immediately remembered her instructions. I also remembered Tarrence saying in his logbook something about "given the right conditions, anger will arise, but then it's just a mind state. It's no more solid than the clouds floating across the sky." This thought gave me peace and centered me for the time being.

After settling with a cup of tea, I spent some time going over clinical notes. I decided to go to bed early that evening, since I felt a deep fatigue coming over me.

I had a dream that night. In the dream, I was up in the mountains, kneeling next to a remarkably clear stream. I had the awareness that the water was alive but that it was contaminated. In the dream I prayed for the water. I felt deep sadness.

Tarrence appeared, sitting not too far from me. "This is what is. Water is life, and life has been contaminated at a very deep level. If it's not cleansed, everything will die. This water comes from the depths of the earth, and it has been touched by the gourds, both the old ones and the new ones. Water is used in all ceremonies. If you use water that has been touched by evil intent, purpose cannot remain clear, no matter how clear the water appears. The water spirit is sad." The dream ended, and I knew the upcoming ceremony was tied to all this.

A lot was going on, and it was difficult for me to make sense of it. The work I had been doing in the community indicated to me that there were a lot of problems, and those problems had been around for a long time. There were attempts from western and traditional systems of care to intervene, but many of the attempts seemed to fall short. Problems in the society also indicated there was a deep underlying force that kept people in their ongoing greed and ignorance. The levels of poverty, despair, mental illnesses, and chemical addiction continued, regardless of the money that governments threw at them. It didn't make sense to try to solve a problem that had a spiritual origin through political or economic interventions.

This must be one of the best tricks of the brain illusion: Take the toothache to the mechanic. It makes as much sense. The earth continues to be poisoned for the sake of profit, and in our ignorance we simply continue to be happy in the profit-making scheme. Somehow Tarrence and his crew have kept sight of what's energizing all of this, and they're willing to do something about it—must be some sort of sacred courage or something. How come they didn't jump on the bandwagon of making money? Must be the seeds of karma that were planted eons ago in another lifetime, I speculated.

The time for the ceremony was getting closer, and amazingly I was getting more relaxed and less fearful as the time approached. I was beginning to accept the idea of death, not just as an intellectual exercise, but also as a reality. Somehow I knew deep inside that I had done this before—dying, that is, although I had no recollection of the event. If I've done this before, maybe it won't be such a big deal, I decided. I suppose that right before I was born I had similar trepidations.

Beerli's serious tone about the possibility of dying in the ceremony really bothered me at first. Now I had a sense of purpose, and if through my death I could contribute in any way to the undoing of karma, well, this would in itself be the cause for future conditions, and who knows, maybe the next time around I could be a part of that too. Heaven knows I probably did some damage in the past.

I wonder what I did when I was the shaman depicted on the cave wall, I thought as I handled the medallion and the arrowhead. As I touched the edge of the arrowhead, my finger was cut. A drop of blood emerged. I thought about the teaching Tarrence had given me on how all of the karmic memories are imprinted in the blood. "The blood remembers."

Nevertheless, moments of agitation began to alternate with my sense of acceptance as I waited for the last few days to pass. I decided to pack some stuff and camp by Tarrence's place just to get this thing started. As I was packing, all my movements took on special importance. I was aware that this might be the last time I packed object by object; I was aware that this might be the last act of handling the socks, the sleeping bag, and so on. This gave my packing a peculiar attention, and my mind became joyous. My focus was intense, and my mind stopped being agitated. It just was in whatever there was in the moment. Death had served as an object of concentration as I had never known till that moment.

I placed my stuff in the truck with the same attention and drove off. I decided to get a last cappuccino and made my way to the Latte' Hey. Walking into the coffee shop, I was aware of my steps and of all of the colors on the door, walls, menu, tables, everything. The coffee smell was so clear, I thought I might not need to drink it to have the experience of it. And then—of course who would be there, and what would he say?

"My man!" I heard with such clarity, and there was Carl, sitting with milk foam on his face. I looked at him and felt only kindness and love. Actually, I was feeling this for everyone in the place, including myself. It was as if my heart was surrounding the place itself.

"My man, wassup?" I said, going along with his jargon.

"Just getting ready for the rest of the day."

"Me too, I guess. By the way Carl, what religious upbringing did you have?" I asked spontaneously.

"You won't believe it if I tell you...but, oh well. I've dabbled around in several from time to time. But—I grew up a strict Catholic, altar boy, the whole thing. Actually—and you're going to shit your pants—at one point I was considering the priesthood. Had the interview, some courses. My man, I'm telling you, I was on my way to being a man of the cloth," Carl said in a slightly embarrassed manner.

"That is something else. 'A man of the cloth'; black cloth at that," I replied, smiling.

"You look, well, you look different. What's going on? I know something is going on. When Tarrence had you stay a little longer with him the other day, don't think I didn't notice those things. He was planning something with you. I want to help, or be part of it. You know I'm there, whatever it is. I know that you're up to something. You're probably on your way up there right now, aren't you?" Carl went on. I was surprised at his intuition and his change of heart.

"You're right. I am going up there," I said, not wanting to reveal the purpose. I didn't even know the purpose, and I didn't want to frighten Carl with the details.

"What for? What are you and Tarrence up to? Also, those two people and the Japanese dude. Hey, the Carl-man knows something is shaking."

"There is stuff going down. I don't really understand all of it. I'm involved in some serious spiritual stuff that has been going on a long time—karma, cause and effect. Has to do with the land up there that my grandpa used to own, and all that has happened since. It's actually quite serious. This might be our last conversation, my man."

"What? Come on. What are you talking about?"

"There's going to be a ceremony, a very serious ceremony that will hopefully bring balance to the place and to the energy of the place. It's a long story, but I'm the one who has to go into the part of the ceremony where the balance was distorted. Has to do with past lifetime stuff. At any rate, it's dangerous."

I expected a lecture on logic from Carl. Instead, to my surprise he responded by saying, "That is heavy duty, my man. It's an important task though. Glad that Tarrence is helping you in this. I feel better knowing he'll be there guiding the whole thing. This is amazing stuff. Makes no sense, but I know this has to be. Somehow, for some reason, I really know this has to be."

"Carl, you're scaring me. I thought you would give me a Cartesian lecture on how this isn't scientific or ethical. You've come a long way, my man. What's up with that?"

"A lot has happened in the past week since the dream and the visit—I mean internally. It's not like things are different out here, but they don't seem like they used to. Also, last night I had this dream. Remember that black owl we saw on the way down from Tarrence's?"

I nodded.

"Well, it was there almost in my face. His eyes were incredible, and there was awareness, well, I can't describe it. There was—wait—it was like he knew, and I knew he knew. It was almost as if I were the owl and vice versa. I know this doesn't make any sense."

"It does make sense. This is that stuff I tried to talk about some time ago. The fact that we're not separate. Sounds like stuff is coming together for you." As I said this, I couldn't help but wonder who Carl was. After all, it seemed as if everyone involved in the dreamtime at this point was also involved in the dreamtime at some other time. It was as if we were all coming together for a purpose and had been together in a purpose before…several times at least.

"Well, this owl said, 'It needs to come together,' and I have no idea what he meant. When he said it, I knew exactly what he meant though. Now I know that I need to help, but I don't know how," Carl whispered, as if trying to keep this a secret.

I realized then that Carl needed to be involved at some level.

"Carl, I'll mention this to Tarrence if you want. I can't involve you in stuff I'm not too sure of myself. Sounds like you're involved already though."

"Yeah, I'd appreciate any info you can give me."

"I'll give you a buzz from my cell phone and let you know what's up."

"Maybe Tarrence will just tell me in a dream." Carl's grin caught me completely off guard.

"I'm supposed to be the intuitive unscientific guy here, and you're supposed to rely on science and all that," I laughed.

"Well, you know how the freshly born-again are," he responded jokingly.

"I've got to get going."

"Later, and keep me informed. The black-owl man is watching your back.... Can't believe I said that. Of course I'm joking."

"Later," I said as we left the Latte' Hey.

20

The Journey Begins

Driving up into the mountains during the early fall was always a treat for anyone. The scrub oaks were bright red. Aspens had a phosphorescent golden hue to them that always amazed me. Cottonwoods were bright yellow. The combination of the colors against the dark clouds that hovered over the mountains and the bright sun that managed to come through was more beautiful than I could ever recall. Yet it was so ordinary. I'm sure that for all of the trees and land, this is just what it is, I thought as I continued up the road. The colors are just colors, and the panorama is just another interplay of light and shadow as is the case everyday forever in these parts.

My thoughts turned to Carl and the black owl. Maybe it's coincidence; maybe it's really not about anything. Carl is a good guy deep inside, and he's simply getting into some things that don't have a scientific explanation. That could be why he's constellating the black-owl image. Initially, when things first emerge out of the psyche, they do have an evil potential, but so does everything. Intent is the key, just like with the owl dreamers and the gourd ceremony. The owl dreamers could have done the exact same ceremony with a different intent, and things would be really different now. Carl's intent is innocent at this time.

My mind became tangential and was brought back into fine focus when, on a distant piñon tree, I saw the black owl staring at me. He seemed to be letting me know that there was more than coincidence, and that somehow Carl was a player in this whole dreamtime drama.

What if the owl is bringing me a premonition of my own death? This thought sent a chill through me and interrupted the mindful place that I had been in. At that instant I could sense myself clinging onto life as I knew it. I didn't want to leave life any time soon. I took some tobacco out of a pouch I kept in my truck and let it sift through my hand as I went by the tree where the owl was. I nodded toward the owl, and to my amazement, the owl nodded back as if to acknowledge the tobacco offering.

Lightning struck nearby as I made the first turn off the main road. The lightning was so close I could smell its essence, a peculiar smell that can't be described. It can only be experienced. As Ruby moved up the road a little ways, a few drops of rain started to fall on the windshield. Earth smells were intense, and I wondered if they were this intense during the time one is in the grave. Of course not, because you're dead, I answered my own thought, and it brought a smile to my face.

I made the turn to the next road toward Tarrence's house, and I knew I would be there in a short while. My awareness was still keen, and I had the sense of being present in the surrounding world. I could see the house now, and there were no vehicles parked there. I was relieved since I wanted to spend some time alone with Tarrence. Even though the Quiet One didn't interfere, I wanted us to have some time by ourselves.

As Ruby pulled up to the house, I could see the individual straw that held the adobe together in the cracks where the mud plaster had long since been worn off. The house had its own peculiar feel, smell, and personality. I walked into the room where Tarrence usually stays. He was covered from head to toe in a sheet. My heart sank.

Oh my God, he must have died! I knew he wasn't feeling well, but I didn't know was this ill. Even as I was thinking this, Tarrence's curled hands reached out and pulled down the sheet, and he laughed like a little kid. It amazed me how he could joke about something like death, but he didn't seem to have any concern over it.

"Thought I'd come up early and just hang out until it's time," I told him.

"Good idea. Get away from all the distractions."

"OK if I just stay around? I brought my sleeping bag and all."

"Mi casa es su casa," Tarrence said in perfectly accented Spanish.

"I've been thinking a lot about all this."

"How's my friend Carl?" Tarrence interrupted.

"He's fine but a little bit worried about me and some of the stuff that he suspects might be going on. He's been dreaming a bit."

"The black owl been messing with him, eh? He *thinks* it's a black owl—he's just seeing, and he doesn't know it."

"I saw it too, the black owl. Just a while ago."

"The black coats, they're still trying to see everything. I wish they would see everything. Poor guys. They've caused so much suffering, needless too. They don't even know what to do with suffering. Waste, really."

"I'm not following exactly."

"I'm not against anyone's way, but I mean the church. Carl has been here with the church. It was through unforgiving people that the illusion was spread. They were as angry as the dreamers who were trying to get rid of them. You see, anger against anger, well, you figure it out. You don't need to be a rocket scientist to see how that adds up."

"You mean Carl was here as a Catholic priest in some other life? That's amazing! You know, he almost became a priest this time, too."

"What do you mean, 'almost'? He's a priest of a different religion now, actually the same religion. Once the church wasn't able to control the masses, then science was invented. Practitioners of science are priests of the new order— and sorcerers. Of course most of them have no idea what they really are doing. It remains unconscious, and this is where it becomes ignorance."

"In a way, we just continue doing what we were doing. Just a different flavor, I guess."

"You got it. Just like you. You were a priest of one sort, and now you're a priest of another sort. We're all trying, or at least I hope we're trying, to balance out past actions. It would be a waste to keep coming back and doing the same old thing, a terrible waste of precious human birth. We shouldn't take all this for granted. Time is too short to really understand and get a sense of the awareness that gives compassion for all sentient beings."

"So what does Carl have to do now? He's wondering about it and wants to contribute in any way he can. I told him I'd ask."

"For the time being, not much. There will be a time when he needs to take care of some things, and he'll be given help. For now, don't get distracted with what he needs to do; you have plenty on your own plate. I'm sure Beerli explained how serious this is. Have you seen your death?" Tarrence asked to my surprise.

"Well, been thinking about it, but not seen it."

"You will. What you will be doing is a selfless act. Giving your life is one of the highest forms of Metta. That is, loving-kindness. Metta is the ultimate medicine for what needs to be done in this ceremony."

"Metta. I read that word in the logbook. I guess it's an old Buddhist prayer or something?"

"Yes. The Buddha came up with it when his monks were full of fear and were being attacked by ghosts and spirits in the forest. He basically told the monks to send their attackers Metta, or blessings. This blessing is the only medicine that can transform ignorance. Sorcery is just ignorance, you know. What we will be doing is transforming ignorance or sorcery."

"I brought some food. Let me cook us something for supper. Is there anyone else coming?" I asked, so as to find out if the Quiet One would be here any time soon.

"No, just you and me. Supper would be good. It can be kind of like one of your last suppers while you're on this plane, eh?" Tarrence said, laughing.

I thought it remarkable that he was making jokes about my possible death. Still, I went along and pretended I thought there was humor in it. I prepared a simple meal of canned vegetables, bread, and tea. We ate together, and I had to assist Tarrence with his drink and much of his eating since he couldn't always handle the spoon.

"Beerli was explaining some stuff about the medicine. Something about how things have been contaminated for a long time. I gather that many of the altars are still that way," I started in again.

"It's unfortunate in a way, but fortunate also. I mean, the amount of power that can be released with the intent of ceremony. If there wasn't the potential for great harm, then there wouldn't be the potential for great good. Our ancestors all over the planet allowed for the illusion to cloud the clarity they once had. Power has that effect.

"A long time ago, power came from the heart. This kind of power requires constant nurturing. The nurturing that the heart requires is peace and silence. In the peace and silence is joy, which is the absolute ingredient for concentration, or a single-pointed mind. Nowadays power seeks a different song, or altar, and off you go. But that kind of power isn't balanced in the heart; it comes from a place that gives birth to the ego. Nothing wrong with ego; it's just part of nature like anything else. Trees turn green at the right time. Well, ego is also born at the right time when conditions are right, that's all. So, no need to condemn this poor product of nature called ego."

"It's from the ego then that the shamans of olden times decided to take matters into their own hands," I commented.

"Not to judge them, but yes, things were really terrible. People were dying from all types of sicknesses, and there was major devastation. All of this can be experienced either through the ego or through the wisdom of the heart. If you haven't prepared the heart through proper effort, well, then all you have is ego. And like I said, ego has a life of its own since it's part of nature. Ego does ego things. If ego isn't in touch with awareness or unconscious, then ego does very unskillful things known as evil."

"And the proper effort?"

"Proper effort has to do with being still. This is where the discipline that my brother Morehei and his tradition have kept going. They sit and sit and sit. What do you think I've been doing for the past thirty years in this bed?"

"Hadn't thought of it like that. I read some of your thoughts on this in your logbook. Interesting stuff. I can see where your being in this bed could be either a curse or a blessing. It must be a difficult way to achieve concentration though."

"Not really, not for me anyway. You see, the monks in Japan had prepared my mind. By the time the spirit of alcohol interfered with my physical body, my mind was fairly still. Otherwise I can see that it might have been quite a torment."

"Spirit of alcohol?"

"Yes, a drunk driver hit me. The spirit of alcohol controlled him. Alcohol was there at the ceremony, you know—the spiritual form was there. It continues to lurk about all of our communities. This is one of the spirits the shamans didn't count on releasing when they acted in their egotistical ignorance. Now we have all these programs, with millions of dollars, trying to help our folks, and to what avail? The spirit itself needs to be balanced. As you can see, there's a lot to be done. This is just a beginning."

It was remarkable that this conversation had a totally different quality from those we'd had before. Tarrence was being very direct and giving precise information. My feeling in the conversation was one in which I felt I was an equal and integral part of the task at hand. Tarrence still maintained his compassionate non-attachment; at the same time there was a sense of urgency to talk about these things. I had the distinct feeling that we would not have another intimate conversation like this one, but it was just a feeling.

"The shamans who enacted the ceremony a long time ago, couldn't they see ahead?" I asked. "I mean, they should have known their actions were creating a lot of problems for the future. They had access to that kind of power, didn't they?"

"Yes. They were powerful dreamers. There's that word again. Powerful. Any criminal with a gun has power though. Power that is not coming through the heart is ego power. This power can activate certain energies in the ego, which then can be utilized to perform healing tricks and other sorts of neat magical stuff. People really like this. The heart operates from quiet—total silence—and there are no tricks. The ego grows bored without tricks.

"You see, boredom is just lack of attention, and most egos haven't attained the type of discipline that keeps them still. Some famous psychologist also said this, about boredom and attention. The power of the heart is not its own. The heart simply opens and gets out of the way of the power of the absolute.

"This is quiet power," Tarrence continued in a barely audible whisper. "Mysterious power, power that is the dreamtime awareness itself. Some people call it God, the Buddha, Allah, Yahweh, all kinds of names. All the same concept. Quiet mysterious power that needs the silence of the heart to manifest itself."

"I guess I do want to see tricks. That's how we're wired. I can see where this could lead to problems. More tricks, bigger tricks, and so on."

"Yeah, like the last time you were in the cave. You saw some neat shit, huh? Especially the snake stuff. Well, that was necessary to get your attention. The important thing is whether you came out with understanding, the kind of understanding that is the essence of wisdom and compassion. This is the place where you can get caught when we go up this next time. Watch your mind for this kind of trap. Tricks are useful if they lead to wisdom. But at some point there will be no more tricks. They give a point of reference to the ego. That's all. The absolute has no tricks, no form, no sickness, no healing, no old age, and therefore no need to deal with any of these."

"I see. I've heard this, read this in your log. The Heart Sutra—beautiful." I was whispering too. My awareness was aware of an awareness that was aware of both of our awarenesses. This awareness went everywhere, and in that awareness, there was no judgment; there just was.

"Unfortunately, many of our Native traditional practitioners, or medicine people, don't know about this. They focus on power and leave out the heart—they like tricks. The tricks give them what they want in the way of material stuff. And it helps a lot of them get into the ladies' pants. Of course this is just ego interpreting the need for the soul to complete itself in its opposite. For men, it's a female soul; for women, a male. I'm sure Beerli already explained this to you. Fortunately, not all of them are this way and many of our medicine people are practicing the stillness of the heart."

"I've heard about this. I know that several of the medicine people across the country are in prison now for this type of thing. Sad, really, when you think about what you just said. It just keeps contaminating the altar with ego shit. That makes the altar just an extension of ego, I guess."

"Exactly. The medicine and the altar relate to you from where you are. It's an extension and a projection, the way most of them do it. You see, it's a very masculine energy. Undeveloped masculine energy gets involved and wants to 'do to' rather than to 'be part of.' When the heart is involved, then it's more of a non-being, which takes on a more female energy—yin and yang idea. The female energy removes it and allows for the awareness to intervene and move. But this is a bit much to ask from male providers, especially those who've been brainwashed by the energy of the black owl. They want to be the ones with the tricks. Ignorance is all it is."

"What about the medicine itself? Like the kind you gave me in the cave?"

"The medicine is innocent and in the heart. The medicine is so merciful, it allows for our intent to be carried out. The medicine is part of the dreamtime awareness and doesn't have the ignorance nature of the ego. Medicine is the essence of the four elements without the shadow side of nature, unless you unleash it with your intent. The reason I gave it to you back then was to facilitate the removal of your ego in that place. Otherwise you might have hurt yourself. The ego has a self-destructive awareness, in that it wants to remove itself but doesn't know how. The way it does this is through a crazy self-destructive mechanism that won't come out with any wisdom or any compassion—it's all self-serving.

"The medicine carried my intent and awareness when I gave it to you, and that's how the medicine related to you during the time that you were in the cave. Again, if the person giving the medicine is in a place of ego-ignorance, then the person taking the medicine has to change the relationship with the medicine. Not too many people know how to do this. Most people put their trust in the medicine people, not realizing they might be operating from ignorance. Hate to say it, but many of them are, and that's why there continues to be so much suffering."

"Like all the problems I see at the clinic," I said. "All the addiction, violence, dysfunction, and just pure crazy suffering. It's all emerging from this same place. No wonder it's such an impossible task to address the problems with simple health tactics. This is far deeper than the surface symptoms patients bring into the clinic."

"Yes," Tarrence answered. "Lately I hear stories of some of our providers doing ceremonies while under the influence of the same drugs that are killing our people. It doesn't matter if they do the drugs while in ceremony or not. All the behavior they engage in has a profound effect on the people, even bad eating habits. You can't separate the person from the altar. The altar is the person and vice versa. Some of our medicine people have forgotten this. They excuse themselves by saying they are 'just men.'

"Well, they aren't, and they do have responsibility to the altar on a twenty-four-hour-a-day basis. You cannot split the altar from the psyche. A lot of them have bought in to the whole Cartesian idea that you can separate subject and object. You can't do it. It's all one. To do otherwise is to bring on even more suffering and sickness to the community you're supposed to be healing. Serious stuff. I'm not picking on the men; it's just that the men are more vulnerable to this trap than our sisters. It's so obvious too. That's the sad part of the whole thing."

"It's kind of coming together," I said. "Why is the black-owl energy so intertwined with all this?"

"That's a long story. I'll give you the short of it though. You see, thousands of years ago, our relatives across the water used to be in harmony with the dreamtime and the earth. Their ways were those of the heart; they were energized by pure female energy and acted with pure masculine energy. Then the men, through the ego and ignorance, became jealous, decided to have a coup, and took over. Ever since then, for thousands of years, a lot of destructive energy has been discharged on women, and the whole culture is still dominated by men, starting with religion. The old tribal Semite guys suppressed the matriarch, and all the Judeo-Christian and Islamic religions that followed have been patterned after the undeveloped masculine dream.

"Once you remove the female, then you're operating on unbalanced male energy that doesn't have a mirror. Without the luminescent mirror of awareness, it's easy for ego-ignorance to inflate itself and believe that it has the absolute awareness. The entire fundamentalism in the world today is an off-shoot of this lack of relationship to the female soul. If it starts out in a negative direction, it can only keep going that way. All the data is there.

"In the entire history of the world, countless numbers people have been killed due to belief in these masculine energies. How can spiritual leaders advocate the destruction of our mother earth and our relatives and still be connected to the heart dream? They can't, so all they've been doing is practicing the worst kind of sorcery in the name of our Creator Dream. The black coats tried to do that here on Turtle Island, but the female energy remains strong.

"This might be the last chance to change all this. What we'll be doing will be a small start toward this change. There's a lot that needs to be done. A karmic shift can be started with the ceremony we'll be doing soon. It's all connected, and that's why Morehei, Beerli, Ms. Chavez, and the two Quiet Ones are involved."

I saw an opportunity to ask about the Quiet Ones. "Tarrence, this might be out of line—well, maybe not. But what about the Quiet Ones? Who are they? Why do they seem to cross-dress and not say a whole lot? What's up with them?"

Tarrence laughed for a while before speaking. "I was wondering when you were going to ask about those two. I won't go into too much detail; that would take a long time. You see, in the beginning of the creation of all in the dream-time, the two energies we've been talking about were one: female/male. The energies were intertwined and operated as one. Once the human form was attained, the ego nature differentiated the energy and made one or the other predominant in any situation. So men act more from the masculine, women from the feminine.

"Well, the awareness allowed for some very special people to carry both energies equally—some of them actually do it in a harmonious way. But like everything else, it takes effort to keep the harmony; otherwise the two energies are in opposition to each other, and there's conflict both within and without the person. You see a lot of this in the world today, where many two-spirited people have the potential but haven't opened their hearts—just like the ones who think they are 'one-spirit' people. Everyone is two-spirited, but the illusion through the power of religions has convinced people otherwise.

"The two you're talking about have done a lot of work with the heart and are very special. Special because they've opened the heart so that wisdom and compassion flow through the one-balanced, or harmonious, energy. Kind of like that symbol a lot of people wear. You know, the yin and yang in perfect harmony. There's a reason the symbol is popular; something within all of us is seeking that balance. The part of us that was intact before the dreamtime allowed us to have a form in which the nature of ego could emerge.

"The two Quiet Ones don't say a lot verbally. They don't have to. They speak from the heart. The heart, remember, can only reveal itself in silence and emptiness. When we talk, we fill up space, and it's usually from the brain that all this talk flows. There is a way to connect the heart to speech, but again, it takes practice. This is the reason that one of the five precepts given by the Buddha is 'right speech.' Being mindful of speech can lead to liberation of suffering. Those two know how to do this, but for now they need to help you from a place that is all heart. I hope this makes sense to you. They'll be helping you from this place during the time that you'll be in the ceremony. They're quite the pair, eh?"

"Yeah, they are. Are they trained to be who they are, or were they just born into it?"

"Yes to both questions. There are a lot of two-spirited people among us, but we've forgotten their role," Tarrence said softly. "We've learned how to look down on them. We've learned a lot of negative things from brothers of the order of the black owl. Traditionally the two-spirited ones carried the stories and songs. They're also allowed into places that most of us can't go, because they're special within the awareness. Now they're called 'gay,' and their lives are made so difficult that most of them never understand their role in the world. That's why there's so much left to do. What we're doing here is a small start to bring balance within the dreamtime awareness that we're in."

"There's so much to all this. Here I was doing this work with such a one-sided view of things. I can't believe that our profession can operate without understanding the essence of wisdom and compassion. We don't even try."

"Guess they don't think it's important," Tarrence said. "They can give drugs. Drugs are energy that blocks the heart and even the brain. I'm not saying all drugs are bad. Again we go back to intent. How many of your colleagues ever talk to the medicine they give their patients? They'd think I needed drugs if they heard me even suggest this!

"You see, all medicine is just that; it has awareness, dreamtime awareness, and needs to be related to in such a way. If conscious relating isn't done, then the unconscious or unknown part of the doctor's psyche is projected into the drug, and this is what the patient takes. Then the patient takes the craziness of the doctor, and of course the doctor feels better. This is part of the sorcery that has infected that altar also. Otherwise, why is 'doctor's error' one of the leading causes of death in hospitals? It ranks right up there with other illnesses.

"Disrespect for the spirit of medicine has its consequences," he continued. "There's a price for all this, and people are paying the price through suffering every second of the year. It's not right, and the medicine dreamtime awareness eventually can become so unbalanced that severe consequences can occur. This is partly what led to the first dream ceremony you saw in the cave.

"Of course the first one led to the second one, and now the world is on the brink of destruction. All because the medicine dreamtime awareness was not honored with conscious intent. Our shadow has been projected into medicine, which is the essence of the dream awareness, and we have taken on that projection through our own self-destructiveness. Just like I said earlier about the nature of ego and its selfish self-destructive nature. It's all there. My brother Morehei and I have been trying to figure this out for years, and we've come up with some notions. These notions or insights have emerged out of the silence of the heart."

"So all of it affects everything; just like the Buddhists say—interconnectedness."

"Yes, everything. This occurred simultaneously on the other side of the ocean. I won't give you all the details, but they had some power dreamers in the caves of Asklepius in ancient Greece. The main medicine was part of the dream. Eventually the illusion infected the altar of Asklepius, because the Asklepian practitioners were wounded healers. They became delusional and full of ego and started to practice ego medicine like the rest of the world. The Altar of Asklepius became desecrated through disregard. Healing energy has been abused all over, and all of us are paying with the ongoing inability to find balance in our personal and collective lives.

"I'm not saying all is lost. Yes, there is contamination and sorcery in the altars, and here's where we need discriminating wisdom. Since the altar is the heart of the earth, it is our heart also. If the medicine person, physician, or whoever is providing the healing, has an open heart, then the healing will come from this place. The fact that there are some healers who do this is the only thing that keeps the whole thing from completely falling apart. Healers who don't operate from their own egos do still exist, but they're very few and far between. That's why it's important that we work on opening up the heart. It's a difficult task."

"I had heard about some of the healings in ancient Greece. I didn't realize they were so closely related to the healings that medicine people were doing here on this side of the ocean. It's all the same thing; we just thought it was separate. No doubt the brain illusion again tricking and convincing the ego that we're separate."

"That's the ticket. That's the whole enchilada, 'my man.' You don't exist apart from anything else. Separateness has been the biggest illusion the ego nature has come up with. This Cartesian split has colonized the entire world, and that's why they can poison the local streams with nuclear waste—people thinking they can go to their homes in another state, and all is well. Ignorance at its best. Once they poison this little stream, they poison everything. So all has been touched by this illusion. Once the medicine dream awareness has been contaminated, all of it, including our mother, the earth, suffers. Time is short if balance isn't restored. We're going to give it a start, or try to. Hope it's not too late."

"I can see that. Amazingly, most of that contamination, or the worst part of it, had its start right here where they did the gourd ceremony. Who could've thought that just a few sorcerers during the war could have come up with so much suffering. The entire world is contaminated. I'm amazed that no one else sees this. I mean, it's so obvious."

"That's how strong the veil of the illusion is. All of this is right in front of our eyes, and we can't see it. At least there are a few of us who are willing to try to do something to turn it around. Remember that it's critical that we do not engage in anger—especially 'righteous' anger. This is the favorite trap of the illusion. Anger is anger. It fuels the veil, and before you know it, we're back in the same circle—performing sorcery in order to set things right. After all, the illusion feeds the ego to the point that the ego will assume it has absolute truth. We need to be careful of this.

"But now we need to stop all this jabbering. You have to get ready. In a couple of days we'll be doing the start-up for all this. By this I mean we'll be balancing ourselves in the very spot that needs healing the most. Relax, and keep watching your breath," Tarrence said in a manner that was polite, but also very determined.

This conversation was over.

"OK, just one last thing," I said. "I read something in your logbook about the four noble truths."

"Oh, yes. The truth is that life is in and of itself suffering. The reason that it's suffering is because we desire things, or desire that things be different. This is the hook that attaches us, and suffering is the natural result. It can be no other way. So staying with the idea, the most reasonable way out of this is to stop wanting things, and to stop wanting things to be different. In other words, be in the moment with what is.

"If you can do this and stop wanting to change what you can't change, then you're free from suffering. You must accept the fact that all is impermanent and in a constant state of flux. Also, never forget that the Buddha's teaching is very basic. He said 'I teach only one thing. That is, suffering and the end to suffering.' So you see, whatever you do, it creates either karmic seeds for suffering or karmic seeds for liberation. It can be no other way."

"That's it? It can't be that simple!"

"Simple, perhaps, but not easy. At least not until you do it. Of course there are different levels of suffering. For instance, the realization of impermanence causes suffering to the ego, kind of like what happened to you when you found out you were going to die. There are different levels to this, but this is the crux of it. Enough talk for now."

I walked around the surrounding area with no real purpose except to keep my mind quiet. Fantasies bombarded my mind, but I simply observed them. It became a very interesting pastime just to watch how the mind creates all sorts of images, thoughts, wants, and a whole universe of illusion, all within a few minutes of time—none of which had any substance.

After walking around for a couple of hours, I came back to the house. I checked in on Tarrence, who was reading. He invited me to set up my bed on the floor in his room. This will be something, I thought. Sleeping so close to Tarrence. I set up my sleeping bag and air mattress, lay down, and was asleep in a matter of five minutes.

That night my sleep was deep. I dreamt a man approached me, an unknown man. He came close and put his arms around me. When he left, I wondered who or what he was. I reached under my neck on the left side, since I felt he had left something there. I found a cluster of four black seeds.

I woke up very rested and saw that Tarrence was sitting on the bed in the only meditation position he could get into. I had no idea how long he had been that way, and I didn't know if I should move, out of concern that this might disturb him.

"Good morning," he said.

"Oh, good morning. I see that you're meditating."

"Proper effort. We must never forget to continue to train the mind to remain quiet."

"Yes, you're such a good role model, Tarrence. When I grow up, I want to have my mind trained like yours," I joked.

Laughing too, he replied, "It's already like that; there's nothing to train. You just have to be still enough so that you can see through the veil. The mind in its nature is already oneness and concentrated. That's the funny part of all this. There's nothing that needs to be accomplished. Well, you know all this."

"Tarrence, I had a dream where someone gave me a cluster of four black seeds."

"Good. Good sign and good dream. All possibilities emerge out of the darkness: four seeds, four directions. Yes, blessing from all of the Buddhas and intercessors from the four directions. Now, let's have some tea and toast."

"All right. I'll make some breakfast. Anything else need to be done?"

"One of the bags needs to be changed." He meant one of the bags that collected bodily waste and was always attached to him. I found a new bag and proceeded to change the one that was almost full.

"That's what we are—that's our body in transition. Those fluids were in the form of good food and drink just a few hours ago. Now it's waste, and some would consider it disgusting. A good lesson in letting go of the body. The waste will eventually become nourishment for new good food and drink," Tarrence commented.

"Got that right. I guess it all keeps going in a circle of some sort, eh?"

"It does. Some circles are bigger and take longer than others—like nuclear waste. I'm sure that the same holds for that kind of waste, but we don't have the time to wait for the circle to go fully around. Otherwise there would be no 'us' to be part of the circle."

"I get your meaning. Nuclear waste, yeah, some of it takes a million years to clean up. Guess that would be enough time to see the whole thing die."

"What's amazing is that even this thought didn't stop the sorcerers. That poor Einstein tried to write a letter to the world leaders appealing for a stop to the craziness, but he had already allowed for his dream to become part of the sorcery. He couldn't stuff the genie back into the bottle, or gourd, no matter how much he tried. Poor guy, he still kicks himself in the ass for not having a proper dream interpretation—you know, the one in which he was riding on a beam of light. Can't fault him though. Most people who've had such a dream go for the material interpretation rather than the spiritual. He was a great shaman, a power dreamer of the first order."

"You mean Einstein? For real?"

"Yeah, he's one of my dreamtime friends. You don't think he could have come up with all that just by manipulating numbers on a piece of paper, do you? He saw into the nature of reality and then came up with some bullshit numbers so it would make sense to other people. The man saw into the dreamtime, and the awareness revealed to him the nature of nature. It's funny that people attribute all this to the size of his brain. The brain illusion has no pride. He could have had a brain the size of a walnut, and he still would have seen through the nature of nature; he was a power dreamer."

"Was he at the gourd ceremony?"

"Oh, yes. He was ambivalent even then. The reason you probably didn't recognize him is because he was a woman at that time. He'd already glimpsed into the nature of nature, and even then he thought that by being part of the crew, he'd be able to impact the circle from within the circle. He knows better now."

I took time out of our conversation to make tea and toast. We ate and sipped. I was hoping for more Einstein stories, but Tarrence decided to talk about football and the San Francisco Forty-Niners instead. He knew all about the players and how they'd done the previous week. His ability to shift gears and keep me hanging was extraordinary and done with complete purpose. Every breath he took was accounted for. We talked about football for a while, and I was surprised by his use of the "my-man" jargon, as if to remind me of Carl. I really wanted to ask Tarrence about my role in all this, but I figured if he could be tangential so could I.

Then my curiosity got the better of me. "Tarrence, why me at this time? You know, I'm just minding my own business and all that. I'm sure there are other folks who could have been part of this ceremony."

Tarrence smiled and said, "I knew you were going to ask. Well, why not? Let me be specific. You have come into this life with a purpose. The fact that you carry different bloods makes you a good candidate. It's the blending in you that makes you the person to carry out this part of the ceremony. Most of the people here are from one tradition only, and because of that, they've had their script written for them from the beginning. But you've been marginalized from all sides, eh? The Indians pick on you because you're not full-blooded. The Whites don't accept you because you're not full-blooded. So you're kind of by yourself.

"'Full-blooded.' Isn't that a strange term?" he continued. "Of course you're full-blooded, otherwise you wouldn't be alive. Nevertheless, being marginalized sets you apart. It allows you to take risks, since you aren't contained by one group only and you're rejected by all. So you're the perfect candidate for this. It can't be any other way.

"The situation affects all people, and until everyone understands that there's only one group of people, we need to do it this way. I guess it's sort of an evolutionary process that's happening, but this ceremony needs to be done before people can realize these simple truths. And of course there's the most important reason: Karma. The body you're in is of the least importance. It's the awareness that you are that counts. There isn't time to wait. So is that a good explanation?"

"Now that you explain it, well, it makes sense. I've been wondering why I was here in the form I am. Somehow I thought that a so-called full-blooded Indian would be the one to do this. Guess we don't have to know everything."

"It's all about heart. If the heart isn't open, it doesn't matter what blooded-ness you have or don't have. This is about the release of the heart. After all, the Buddha wasn't a full-blooded American Indian, though he was an Indian of another kind."

After we finished our breakfast, I decided to take another walk. The cere-mony was to start tomorrow or tonight; I wasn't sure which. I was walking on a mesa about a mile and a half from the house when I saw the Quiet One's truck come up the road. Well, they're arriving for the party, I thought.

An hour or so later, I saw Ms. Chavez drive up, and I could see Dr. Beerli in the truck with her. Some time later, I saw Morehei and the Bald Nun pull up. Guess all the guests are here. Time to rock and roll. No sooner had I thought this, than I saw Carl's BMW making its way up the rough road. What the hell is he doing here? I wondered.

Now I knew this was more mysterious than I had ever thought it could be. As I was thinking about Carl, I felt a tugging around the ankle of my pants that scared the shit out of me. I turned around, and there was the coyote-dog smiling at me. Initially I felt like kicking him, but that melted away when I saw his friendly smile and obvious joy at coming up and successfully scaring me. This dog was like no other I knew, and his awareness was keen and purposeful. Coyote-Dog and I slowly strolled down to the house to see if there was anything I needed to do in advance for the ceremony. My mind was peaceful and quiet.

I arrived at the house and saw Carl there. He was dressed completely in black. My steps were very light, and I managed to sneak up and slap him on the back. "My man Carl, what brings you up here?"

"You wouldn't believe it. I had a dream in which Tarrence gave me explicit instructions that I had to be here at this time today. I must be going nuts. Imagine me doing something just because I dreamt it. I should take some of the medicine I prescribe. Man, this is getting weird. And what's with him having me dress in black? Weird, I repeat. I actually had to stop and buy a black shirt. But I'm here, and I guess this is an important event."

"Sounds like you're doing the right thing, my man. Don't worry; Tarrence and the folks have things under control. Anyone said anything?"

"No, everyone is sort of to themselves. They're all in the house.... I don't know what's going on, or what to do next."

"It'll be all right, Carl," was all I could think to say.

The Quiet One emerged from the house, dressed for the occasion. He was wearing some nice turquoise and silver on his wrists and neck, and his hair was done in a traditional female style. He motioned me inside the house, where I found the cast of power dreamers: Ms. Chavez, Beerli, Morehei, the Bald Nun, and of course, Tarrence. The Quiet One made sure that the coyote-dog also came into the house. Carl followed hesitantly.

Tarrence spoke. "It's time to go. We've waited a long time, in human time that is, to restore balance to this place. The gourd needs to be befriended; amends have to be made for the actions that all of us have taken in the past. Karma can be changed if we maintain our awareness and concentration on what is going on in the moment. I don't know when we'll have a chance to be all together like this again. I want to let you know that my heart is full of love for all of you and for our purpose here. Remember, it's the dreamtime and the awareness that we're all a part of that is actually allowing this to happen. Don't take anything personally; it's for greater healing that we do this."

The Quiet One approached me and asked, "Do you have the objects ready?"

I pulled the medallion and the arrowhead from my pocket and showed them to him. He handed me a red cloth with sage in it and let me know that I should wrap them in this. The Quiet One and the Bald Nun went to Tarrence's bed and started to move him into his wheelchair. Morehei and the others went outside. No one was saying anything, or even looking at me, except for the coyote-dog, and he just kept smiling. At one point I could have sworn he winked at me.

The atmosphere was heavy and serious when Tarrence was rolled to the porch. He motioned for all of us to come close to him. We gathered around solemnly.

Then Tarrence asked, "How many dreamers does it take to restore balance to a little gourd? At least sixteen, but the gourd has to want to be restored." He started laughing so hard that the Quiet One had to steady the wheelchair. Tarrence had just given a rendition of a popular therapist joke. Everybody laughed, mostly at Tarrence, because his hearty laughter was so contagious. Even the Quiet One managed to laugh, and of course the coyote-dog just kept smiling.

As they all got into their respective vehicles, I said to Carl, "You might as well get into Ruby. No way your car will make it to where we're going. All right, my man?"

Carl appeared apprehensive as he got into my truck.

"Relax, my man. Just because you're wearing all black doesn't mean you have to be like an up-tight priest."

"Come on. This is no time for joking."

"All the time is a good time for joking, my man. What would Hume say if he saw you now?

"Come on, just lighten up," Carl replied with a frightened look on his face.

"Lightening up," I answered.

"Yeah, OK. Just that I don't know what to expect. I only know that this is scary shit, and I should have never come up here in the first place. I should have just kept doing what I was doing. Matter of fact, today is my golf day. I could be strolling on the grass and not feeling all this crazy anxiety."

"But just look how boring that even sounds. Everything you do is predictable. The real stuff was invented by those who've gone where no one else has gone before." I replied, using the popular line from a science-fiction show.

"You're right. Those guys who took on new stuff were crazy. It's so much easier to stay in the paradigm. They give you rewards for that too, you know. Man, if my students saw me here.... I don't even want to think about the ethics board."

The lead truck stopped after it had rolled a few yards. The Quiet One came over to Ruby and said, "Tarrence wants to see you two."

We got out and walked to the truck where Tarrence was. He struggled to get his crooked right hand into a leather bag he held. He finally drew out an object, and upon looking closer, I saw that it was an elaborately carved crucifix.

He handed it to Carl and said, "This is yours. It has been yours. Make a relationship with this man here, Yeshua, also known as Jesus Christ. It's time for those who identify with him to start practicing his teachings. He's a good friend of mine. So this is the purpose of your being here. But now you need to go back home and let the rest of us continue with this part of our journey. Don't worry, it's all connected and you're not being left out of anything. Right now you just need to meditate and allow the awareness to reveal your role in all this. I'll give you a hint though. That is your cross, has been for a long time. Soon it will be revealed to you what needs to be done."

"I'm sorry for whatever I have consciously or unconsciously done."

"This is a good thing. There's a ceremony you'll do when the time is right." Tarrence pulled Carl's head close and kissed him on the forehead. Carl walked back to his car with tears in his eyes.

21

Full Circle

The Quiet One started the lead vehicle again. The roads had disappeared, and we were going toward the mesas in the direction the Quiet One had taken me to get the objects from my grave. The surroundings, the special effect of light and shadow, and the energy of the place put me in a serious contemplative mood.

The caravan climbed slowly and steadily. I could see Tarrence bouncing around the cab of the Quiet One's truck, and the Bald Nun holding on to him to keep him from bumping himself too much. From time to time he turned, and I noticed he was smiling. Morehei was riding with Beerli and Ms. Chavez. I looked in my rearview mirror, and there, sitting in the bed of my truck, was the coyote-dog, smiling at himself in the mirror. Some weird little dog, I thought.

We were getting close to the gravesite. I wondered if this was where the ceremony would take place. It was very close to the area where the government still had possession of my grandfather's land, and I knew that we couldn't trespass onto secure government property—at least not physically trespass.

Finally the Quiet One stopped, and so did the rest of us. The Quiet One and the Bald Nun got Tarrence into his chair, and we followed him.

This sure looked like the place where I'd gotten the medallion and the arrow. In the center of the cleared area was an opening in the ground that looked like a grave, except bigger. There were steps leading down the hole into the ground.

When we approached the opening, the Quiet One motioned for us to form a circle around it. Marking the respective cardinal directions were sticks with cloth bearing the same colors as the medallion. The blue was on a longer stick emerging from the entrance to the hole, and the green was on the part of the stick that touched the earth.

The Quiet One motioned for us to sit. Then he and the Bald Nun took out a couple of gourd containers. They proceeded to paint Tarrence's face with natural red paint. The Bald Nun painted his right side, and the Quiet One painted the left. By this time, Tarrence was in a meditative state, and his breathing was slow. Once Tarrence was painted, the two proceeded to go around the circle counterclockwise and paint the faces of all the dreamers. Then they descended into the opening in the ground.

Tarrence started to sing. After he sang four songs, Morehei chanted the Heart Sutra in Japanese and then in English. When he completed his chanting, Ms. Chavez sang four songs, then Beerli sang four songs in a language I didn't recognize.

My attention and awareness were quiet, and I felt peaceful. I could see in the near distance the grave we had uncovered recently. When I looked closely, I realized we were in the middle of a graveyard, an ancient graveyard. The thought of being in the center of a graveyard alarmed me for an instant, and then I returned to watching my breath, and awareness was being aware of itself.

Morehei was sitting in a full-lotus position, and his breath was perfectly synchronized with Tarrence's breath. Beerli and Ms. Chavez were sitting in half-lotus and were also in a state of meditation. Coyote-Dog sat facing the west, and looked right at me the whole time.

After perhaps a few hours, the Quiet One and the Bald Nun emerged from the hole in the ground, where they had been this whole time. Smoke was emerging from the hole. They walked toward me. The Quiet One gently took my left arm, the Bald Nun took my right arm, and they lifted me to my feet in the gentlest manner I've ever felt. Once I was on my feet, they walked me to the entrance of the hole. They let me stand in the smoke for a couple of minutes, then they motioned for me to walk down the steps as they followed.

The room was larger than I'd thought. In the west corner, water bubbled from a spring. Right above the spring was a gourd in which the water accumulated before being diverted out of the room by means of a clever design that appeared to be a canal or plumbing system that I was totally unfamiliar with.

They walked me toward the spring. When I got to it, the Quiet One motioned for me to take out my objects. I opened the red cloth and held it in both hands. Once the objects were exposed, the Bald Nun brought what appeared to be a grinding stone that had some burning sage and other herbs on it. She passed the objects through the smoke. She then took the arrowhead and gently bowed to the spring. Next, she very slowly placed the arrowhead on the gourd over the spring. Her last movement took at least five minutes. When she had finished, the Quiet One did the same thing with the medallion. They both remained kneeling for a few minutes.

They stood up, took me by the arms again, and led me to the middle of the cave, where they seated me on a pile of sage. I could hear Tarrence singing and Morehei chanting outside. I will never forget the sound in any lifetime. It will forever impact my awareness of the dreamtime.

Seeing some ancient paintings on the walls of the cave, I thought this must have been some very old ceremonial place, and I was sure I'd been here before. As if to verify this thought, the Bald Nun looked at me and nodded, and I heard the coyote-dog bark outside.

The Quiet One and the Bald Nun removed my shoes and proceeded to paint my hands and the bottom of my feet. The Bald Nun then went to her bag and took out a gourd. She brought it to me and uncapped it. To my surprise, she spoke. "This is medicine for your journey. Drink it; this will help you do what you need to do."

In a kind voice, the Quiet One also spoke. "Have a good journey, my relative. This will be a good start in restoring the balance. There isn't much time left if we don't do this. All of our ancestors are around you. God Bless You."

Then they got up and left the cave. The singing and chanting were still going on. Once the Quiet One and the Bald Nun were outside, they put a cover on the cave, which plunged it into dark silence.

Immediately my awareness became large, for lack of a better word and description. Even though it was completely dark and silent, I could perceive my surroundings in minute detail. Every pebble in the cave, the water bubbling from the spring, and the objects resting in the basket were all so clear, clearer than if I'd merely seen them with my usual eyesight.

With a shift in awareness, I could be outside where the others were still singing and chanting. There was a fluidity and ease of awareness being aware. The whole time there was the awareness of an awareness that was aware of awareness. These awarenesses seemed to know each other, and there was a complete harmony in the relationship. Suddenly I realized that all things are in a constant state of fluid change. All was empty. Awareness is empty; therefore there is nothing to change, and awareness is the only thing that remains transparent without the fluidity of all other perceived phenomena. Awareness became aware of the place where I was sitting. It was difficult to stay put and not go flying around in a peaceful state of awareness and oneness.

"Don't indulge the ego mind. What you think is awareness is just consciousness that is produced by the senses, all conditioned and empty. Stay with the breath. Wisdom and compassion will result," I heard Tarrence thinking.

This was amazing. Awareness was able to perceive thought, and Tarrence was able to talk to me without saying a word. I realized this is an area of awareness that we all go through as we move from our live body form to the dissolution of the body. Awareness went back to the breath and to the place where my body was. After sitting for some time in a meditative state, I experienced yet another level of awareness seeping through.

"Just be aware of it; don't do anything or try to understand it with your ego mind," were the instructions Tarrence gave at this point.

Awareness was aware of Morehei chanting the Heart Sutra.

Then I perceived a rattlesnake emerging from a hole in the ground at the east end of the cave. There was a shimmer of light over its head as it slithered toward me. "Hello again," the snake said.

I looked at it and wondered, "Again?"

"Don't tell me you already forgot. I'm the angel of light—Lucifer. The one you talked to not long ago. Come on, you remember." This conversation too was non-verbal; it was awareness being aware of dreamtime communication.

"Oh, yes. That time you identified yourself as Satan. The light over your head gave you a different look. Forgive my rudeness."

"Now that's one for the books; you're asking me for forgiveness. Well, we're starting off on the right foot, I can see."

"I guess that is a bit odd, when you consider how you're dealt with by most religions."

"All religions that are controlled by the brain illusion. None of them appreciate all that I've done. Ingrates. So, you're here to try to bring balance. Noble of you. Who do you think you are? I mean, that has been tried before, and look at how things are. Just as much suffering as ever—if not more."

"I'm not the one bringing balance. We're here to start to restore balance in this destructive gourd that was put here a long time ago by the power dreamers. That's all."

As I replied, Tarrence said, "Don't argue or try to prove any points with this one. You're not in a court of law, and there's no need to convince anyone of anything. Just be. Otherwise you'll spend the ceremony arguing, and nothing will be done. This must come from love and compassion, not from the best argument. If we need an argument, we'll defer to your inner Carl. He's good at it, and his Jesuit previous life will come in handy. But even he isn't here for that."

"I see," said the rattlesnake. "you're getting coaching. Very well. That Tarrence, he's really something. Where is this gourd anyway?"

"It's deep in the earth where the power dreamers placed it." I replied.

Now I perceived another snake emerging out of the hole.

"Here's my twin. My Meso-American counterpart from the New World. The noblest one, Quetzalcoatl, with all his beautiful feathers. The one whose heart became the morning star itself. What brings you to this dream?" Lucifer asked him.

"The same purpose that brings you, my relative. Aren't we here for a ceremony?" Quetzalcoatl answered.

"Don't tell me the others are coming also."

"As we speak. It wouldn't be right not to have us all here. This is an important event, the gourd ceremony and all. I just saw the gourd, and it's as beautiful and powerful as ever. Those dreamers were really something. They really gave it their all."

As Quetzalcoatl finished his statement, the third and fourth serpents emerged from the hole. Tetzcatlipoca was familiar to me, since he had a smoky luminescence about his head. Then Jesus Christ said a humble hello to me and to the others assembled in the cave.

"Twenty-two points, plus triple-word-score, plus fifty points for using all my letters. Game's over. I'm outta here," was the next statement that emerged from the awareness. Yet there was no one making the statement.

"Keep with the breath, don't get distracted. This is all wonderful and interesting, but stay with the breath. Do not get distracted," Tarrence spoke through the awareness of clairvoyance.

"Well, here we are again, all my relatives. It's good to be here on this occasion," Tetzcatlipoca said.

"Yes, my young brother. Here we are as our relatives attempt to bring balance to the dream. Most courageous, I think," Quetzalcoatl replied.

"A lot of dangerous sacrifice has already been made. Let's pray that this will bring balance so there won't be ongoing need for sacrifice. Enough is enough. We need to go on to something else," Jesus Christ said in a kind yet impatient tone.

"My big brother—always trying to bring the good. Remember that I too was the favored one for eternities of time. My interest in knowing was my crime. I'm accused of pride. How about this guy here, wanting to bring balance to this gourd business. Who in the hell does he think he is? Just because he has all his cronies up there singing and chanting. If that's not pride, then nothing is," Lucifer said scathingly.

I became aware of the shaman's presence, the one pictured on the cave wall. "Hello, good to see you again," I told him. "I don't know what to call you since you are me."

"So, you're purifying my stuff? Guess they got a bit contaminated during the time I was using them," he remarked, as he went close to the basket suspended in the spring water where the medallion and the arrowhead were. As he looked at the arrowhead, he said, "Ouch. That sure did hurt when it went in. Only for a little bit though. Then there was nothing for a while, and then back to the dream. I'm here to help with the gourd and to help with the balance. Balance cannot occur unless there's some sort of repentance. I'm here to repent and gain forgiveness from my relatives here. That will be a good start."

"Repenting is good and will bring healing to all that has been tarnished," Jesus said.

Tetzcatlipoca broke in, "Don't look at us. Every time there's some good thing to be done, looks are directed at us. People forget that we had a role to play in this whole thing. Without us, nothing would have come about. My brother, the beautiful plumed serpent, would not have known life itself without me. He didn't have to get so drunk that he lusted after his own sister though. All he did really was to get to know the female side of himself, which is where the beginning of his knowledge was. But his ego got in the way of his discerning mind, and he had to go jump in the fire. Even then, his heart became the morning star."

"You got that right. The whole process has slighted us," Lucifer said, allying himself with Tetzcatlipoca. "I made a deal with the awareness itself that I would help in this whole plan—then what? I get the bad end of the stick. My big brother there wouldn't have been able to do what he did, nor would there have been a need, might I add, if not for me. I even helped the awareness in that plan to torment Job. Poor old guy, never bothered anyone. I actually felt a little guilt over that. And still, yeah, our big brothers are the ones who are seen as the shining examples of goodness, while we're the ones who bring evil. We bring consciousness is all. We were the ones who brought knowledge to the dream."

"What's all this? Just so much talk! That's what got us into trouble in the first place," the shaman said.

"If nothing else, it's interesting. Awareness can be built on knowledge, which is full of compassion and love," Morehei communicated as he kept chanting the Heart Sutra.

"Complexes of your own unconscious. It's part of the shadow side of the personality. Maintain your center and awareness," Beerli let awareness know.

"Once you've gone through your inner world, then it will be time to make peace with the gourd and what it represents. You will go to it and help to heal the dream," Ms. Chavez said.

The Quiet One and the Bald Nun remained silent. Their silence maintained the balance between the male and female forces that might begin to act up with so much thinking. It seemed that in their silence they were and were not. They brought an emptiness that allowed for the ceremonial process to continue without my mind reacting to the extraordinary events—at least up till now.

I heard Tarrence's thoughts in awareness say, "This was the hook that got the dreamers in the first place. Their minds and their egos trying to figure it all out. Soon they thought it was their own egos that were causing the dream. They thought the dream was in them; they forgot they were in the dream."

Awareness became aware of Carl in his home praying rosaries. His mind had ceased to try to make sense of something that didn't lend itself to logical explanations. He was beginning to get in touch with the effects of the karma he had sown as a priest in antiquity and as the representative of a science that pays homage only to the brain illusion. Through a clairvoyance he had never experienced before, Carl was becoming aware of the suffering he had perpetrated as a priest in a past lifetime when he took part in the genocide of a people and their way of life.

"This is real. I'm glad to be a part of this ceremony to bring healing. Forgive us, God, for we know not what we do," he kept saying to himself as he held on to the crucifix Tarrence had given to him before the ceremony.

In the cave, Tetzcatlipoca spoke. "What's up with that priest anyway? What is he now? Yes, I know—a psychologist. What a bunch of bullshit. First they create the trauma, and now they pretend to try to help it. Shit, and we're the ones called the angels of darkness!"

"Amen to that, my Meso-American brother," Lucifer retorted.

I remained calm and centered. I'm sure, in retrospect, it was the connection I had with the other dreamers in the ceremony that helped me stay centered. It was as if we were one, and their attention to the moment was contagious. I couldn't have moved out of that state of mind if I'd wanted to, and it reminded me of something Tarrence had once said to me regarding the Sangha, or collective group. "It's important to be a part of a body of people who are in the same place of awareness."

"Don't judge so hastily," an unfamiliar voice addressed Lucifer and Tetzcatlipoca. "The illusion has been creating a different dream for a long time." To my surprise, a cobra had joined the other snakes.

"I know I'm not familiar around here," the cobra said. "I represent emptiness and nothingness. My image is the guardian of the one who came and went. Now, in the stillness of nothingness, there can be nothingness; out of nothingness will be everything.".

"Well said, my Asian relative. Couldn't have said it better myself. You sure have come a long way for this," Tetzcatlipoca replied.

"Keep your focus. Breathing is breathing itself," Tarrence maintained.

"Interesting," the shaman said. "What do we have here? Five serpents, each representing someone or something. This is what led to the confusion in the first place—too many choices."

"Represents awakening and a way to bring an end to suffering." Awareness was aware of Morehei's communication.

"It's time to move into the earth herself and make a peace offering to the gourd," Ms. Chavez announced.

"Time indeed. It's important that you do not go in as either male and female. Go in as emptiness," Beerli cautioned.

"What about all these beings here? All the serpents?" I asked.

"Keep your focus; watch the breath," Tarrence replied.

"How do I go into the earth?" I asked the general audience.

"Ask your grandpa. He knows about this, and that's why he's here," Ms. Chavez replied.

It was amazing that with all the personalities present, there was complete order and silence, even when someone was expressing himself or herself. There was a reverence and respect that is rare in most organized ceremonies. In addition, there was a feeling of urgency that awareness became aware of. It was time to ask my ancestor about traveling into the earth.

"Sir, Grandpa, Myself—I really don't know how to refer to you," I started.

"'Grandpa' is good for now," the shaman replied.

"You heard the instructions. I'm asking you to show me how to go into the earth and find the gourd."

"Then what?"

"Then the gourd will be balanced. Don't be difficult," Tarrence answered for me.

"This Tarrence has taken a real liking to you. I was just going to tease you a little is all. So let's go. You really have to let go. I know Tarrence has been telling you to do that for some time now. It's time to really put it to the test and let go—of everything. This means even your body and your mind. It's good practice anyway for when you die. So you see, you're getting more than your money's worth here. Dying-practice that's part of a package is a real luxury, and I know I didn't get that. I'm telling you, dying without knowing how to die is the worst thing, real scary shit," Grandpa said lightheartedly.

"Let go? OK, I'll just let it go then." As I said this, I felt my awareness become totally free of my body. Before this, my awareness was moving about but still had a body as a point of reference and perception. Now there was no point of perception—no eyes, ears, body, or thought. There was awareness and that was all, a free-roving and empty awareness that wasn't in any way subservient to perceiving.

"Pretty neat stuff, eh?" Grandpa said. "I bet you never felt this free before. Of course there are no feelings; what I mean is that you haven't realized this type of freedom. I guess you did—we did—you know, when you were I, but then you forgot when you came back. Can you remember now?"

"Yes, I remember." My awareness blended with my grandpa's awareness, and I had total recall of his memory as well as my own. I knew how to do all the things he knew how to do. He was no longer there in the form that I had perceived him. My awareness that had transcended space and time was again one with the awareness that I had once been my ancestor.

Blended with him, I now knew how to go into the earth. My awareness went to the hole from which the snakes had emerged. Awareness stood at the hole and began to twist itself in a counterclockwise direction, like a little whirlwind. This whirlwind of awareness made its way into the hole and into the earth. Every grain of sand, every piece of clay, every pebble and rock—they were all completely part of awareness. Awareness was aware of the different strata of earth layers that were made during the earth's evolution. I was aware of the skeletons of the dead ancestors that were buried all around the place where the ceremony was taking place. At the same time, I was aware of the people above the cave chanting and singing. This was wonderful, and I liked it.

"Keep your focus. Liking is a mind state. Right now you need emptiness, otherwise you'll be sucked up by other illusions of your mind," Morehei cautioned softly.

My body maintained its breathing rhythm, except that now my awareness of the breath was from a distance. I felt a closer affinity to the women in the ceremony. Perhaps this was due to the fact that the earth carries a female energy.

Awareness continued to spiral downward into the earth. At a certain point, I realized I was approaching the gourd. As I moved through the earth, I perceived a cave that was almost full of water from the underground water table or aquifer that supplied the area.

There in the middle of the cave was a smooth flat black stone. Sitting on the stone was a person whom I didn't recognize at first. Then I realized it was the man who had scouted the land on which to build the bomb. This was incredible! Yes, here I was encountering Oppenheimer himself in the middle of the earth. He seemed to be guarding the gourd.

"Why are you bothering this?" he asked.

"Bothering what? You mean the gourd?"

"You know exactly what I mean. This has been here ever since we put it here during the first ceremony. It doesn't need to be disturbed. Actually, it would be quite dangerous for you to tamper with it."

"Would it be any more dangerous than your tampering with the gourd that you put together here more recently? And you know exactly what I'm talking about! My God, what were you thinking?"

"You don't understand. It's science. This has nothing to do with right and wrong. We were solving equations, that's all. Trying to understand the essence of energy itself—in a way, getting to know God through understanding creation," he explained.

"What you guys did, under your direction, was to unleash the *destruction* of creation—the very opposite of what you're saying. You knew there was a chance that by igniting the gourd you could set the whole earth's atmosphere on fire—and you went ahead and set it off? I can't imagine what possessed you to do that! And you knew this was going to be used on people. This is evil intent, and you know it. This is why we're trying to balance the gourd that was placed here by you and the power dreamers many generations ago. I was with you, remember?"

He looked into my eyes and said, "I remember the eyes. You were there. Why are you doing this, then? You knew the purpose we had in the first place. You should leave this alone and allow things to progress. You're standing in the way of science. Science will figure this out; it always has. And the people who were hurt by it—well, you know the deal that was made. They took it upon themselves to be so noble. No one asked them to do that. It serves no purpose to judge me in this manner."

"My, my, don't we all use the same old lines," said Tetzcatlipoca, who had joined us from the world above. "These are old words, brother. Knowledge has nothing to do with any of this. Truth be told, you just wanted to play with the essence of reality itself. You didn't want to study creation or God. You wanted to *be* God."

"Yes, and we know what that brings," Lucifer added, as he or she had made its way into the underworld.

"You guys are all here, I see," Oppenheimer said. "Well, might as well have the whole gang. This person here wants to disturb the gourd, the intent that we put into the gourd, and bring about balance. He needs to be convinced that there are huge implications to tampering with an equation of this magnitude. Implications that far outweigh anything we've been able to figure out or even imagine with numbers."

"All was one, and before that, it was nothing," Tetzcatlipoca said. "That's the only mathematics you need to know. The Mayan dreamers knew this from time immemorial. Somehow they already knew that the numbers created by the brain illusion were really nothing. I guess you would call this the concept of zero. But you see, zero is just an arbitrary point on an imaginary line that only exists in the brain illusion. The nothing that the Mayan dreamers were talking about was the absolute nothing that is, within and without the brain illusion and within the dream itself. So, this is a bit different from what you and the other old guy with the frizzy hair were up to, eh? Although the frizzy-haired one, you know, brother Albert, had a sense of this, at least toward the end of his life. He knew this wasn't about numbers. He realized it was about the dream, since he got understanding from the dream itself."

"This is interesting—how different folks were getting to the same place but using different ways of relating to the dream," I said.

"The difference is in the point of reference," Beerli interjected. "Oppenheimer is coming from a masculine way of perceiving. This way is a ready-made trap for the brain illusion, because built right into it is the belief that this is the right way. Those who don't believe it's the right way get run over, including those who might perceive from a more feminine perspective. Of course this is a matter of human history. Look at what the masculine brain illusion did to the people of Turtle Island, and then look at what your mathematical model, that hides itself in the devil's objectivity, did to the Japanese people and is threatening to do to all life."

"Here we go again. Why does everything bad have to be of the devil? This is simply not fair," Lucifer said seriously and softly. "There's a point in which the illusion just propels itself, and I really don't have to do anything. So, come on, folks, a little mercy would be in order. Not to say just some common courtesy."

"He—she—has a point." Ms. Chavez spoke from where she was sitting in the ceremony above ground. "The masculine illusion fuels itself and doesn't need anyone to make it continue to go where it's going. Oppenheimer and his scientific objectivity were moving to create an illusion that would bring an end to all illusion itself. It's no accident that they named the place where they tested the gourd 'Trinity.'"

Jesus and Quetzalcoatl had been remarkably quiet, even though they had joined the others in this inner chamber far underneath the surface. Oppenheimer turned to them now.

"What do you two have to say on all this?"

"Our purpose here isn't to judge. Things are as they are. All things are good if they're from love and compassion. You know your motive and why you're here at this moment. You know the motive you had when you were at the first dream ceremony, at the beginning of the dream that brought awareness to the awareness. Love and compassion heal and complete all," Quetzalcoatl and Jesus said in unison.

As they were speaking, they took on a more human form. The human form then became two luminescent spheres. These two spheres then merged into one that gave a powerful and pure white luminescence.

"Well, it must be time for us also, brother," Lucifer said to Tetzcatlipoca. They went through the same transformation, and they too merged into one sphere that gave a powerful and pure white luminescence.

As I stood in wonder, Morehei's chanting cut in:

> "Avalokitesvara Bodhisattava doing deep Prajna Paramita clearly saw emptiness of all five conditions, thus completely relieving misfortune and pain. Oh Shariputra, form is no other than emptiness, emptiness no other than form. Form is exactly emptiness, emptiness exactly form. Sensation, conception discrimination, awareness are likewise like this. Oh Shariputra, all dharmas are forms of emptiness; not born, not destroyed, not stained, not pure, without loss, without gain. So in emptiness there is no form, no sensation, conception, discrimination, awareness; no eye, ear, nose, tongue, body, mind; no color, sound, smell, taste, touch, phenomena; no realm of sight, no realm of consciousness, no ignorance and no end to ignorance, no old age and death, and no end to old age and death, no suffering, no cause of suffering, no extinguishing, no path, no wisdom and no gain; no gain and the Bodhisattva lives Prajana Paramita. With no hindrance in the mind, no hindrance, therefore no fear. Far beyond deluded thought, this is Nirvana. All past, present, and future Buddhas live Prajna Paramita and therefore attain Anuttara Samyak Sambodhi. Therefore, know Prajna Paramita is the great mantra, the vivid mantra, the best mantra, the unsurpassable mantra. It completely clears all pain. This is the truth, not a lie. So set forth the Prajna Paramita mantra, set forth this mantra and say Gate! Gate! Paragate! Parasumgate! Bodhi Svaha! Prajna Heart Sutra."

As soon as he finished the Heart Sutra, my mind was empty, and awareness was aware of itself once again. Awareness was aware of the luminescent spheres that were in the cave, and these spheres were part of the same awareness that was aware of the awareness I had. The term "I" is simply a way to make the story work within the language that limits human awareness. When you are awareness, there is no "I," and the "I" becomes an ego construct for point of reference. Otherwise, there would be no story.

The two remaining spheres approached each other and slowly merged. Now there was just one luminescent sphere where there had once been four. There was a powerful awareness of love and compassion emanating from the sphere. There was neither good nor evil nor opposites of any kind within the unified sphere; there was only love and complete indescribable beauty.

Oppenheimer broke the silence. "This is most amazing! What's going on?"

"You should know," Tarrence spoke into the dream silence. "You've been witness to the solving of the ultimate equation. This is what you call singularity: The beginning and all that was when this dream began. All fantasy projection and all the illusions of what you think is solved in the simplest manner. Trinity, the Three-in-One, must become an equation where Four unite to make one. 'Trinity' is out of balance, just like the name you gave the place where you tested the gourd in Alamogordo, 'Fat Cottonwood.' And you made the gourd in Los Alamos, 'The Cottonwoods.' Very Sacred Tree. There is no equation however, there never was. All that has been, is; and there is no understanding needed. Just accept this gift of love."

Oppenheimer had tears in his eyes at this time, and I saw his heart become soft as he allowed the luminescence to embrace his heart.

He spoke softly. "This has no equation. There are no numbers except the ones we invent out of the opposition of our minds that have been deluded by the illusion. All is what it is, oneness and compassion. There is no good or bad, only our intent, which in the end also is nothing. It's true. Why couldn't we see it? We think God's language is 'numbers,' when in reality they're the limited projection of a few neurons in the brain. A brain which only operates when there is illusion and projection of itself. The brain believes the projection is what is real, when in reality it's just illusion being projected. My God, there is only projection of illusion upon yet more illusion. And we've been calling that 'truth.' The illusion of numbers validates the illusion, simply from which they come.

"Forgive us our trespasses as we forgive, lead us not into temptation, but deliver us from evil," Oppenheimer continued. "My God, it's been there the whole time. The answer, the whole answer to the whole delusion. We've prayed it thousands of times, and the whole time the illusion wouldn't let us see how clear and simple it is. It's the dream, the awareness and completion that aren't illusion. How did so many wise ones get duped?"

As Oppenheimer finished his thought, I noticed that Tarrence was dissolving in form and becoming a sphere, one that encompassed the colors of the medallion. As he did so, he turned clockwise into the earth and joined us in the inner cave. It was his essence. We were in clairvoyant communication, since all of us here were merely the essence of the dream we'd been in. Oppenheimer had left the cave.

Tarrence said, "His part is done. He came to help bring wholeness and forgiveness. Now it's time for you to go to the gourd and complete the purpose that we're here for. You must go deeper into the earth, where you will find it. All of the dreamers have dreamed this dream, and there remains only nothingness. There is no need for fear, since there is no fear in nothingness. You know how to proceed."

Somehow I did know how to proceed. I had the intent to go to the gourd, and as the intent emerged, I went deeper into the earth, to another cavern that had been there since the beginning of the dream.

Suspended in the middle of the cavern was the unmistakable gourd, just as I had seen it in the dreamtime ceremony at the cave of evil dreamers. The gourd was surrounded by all the colors of the medallion. Awareness did not have the same attitude toward the gourd that it had previously—or perhaps it was my perception that had changed. It's difficult to differentiate between awareness and perception, at least for the purpose of telling this story. There was neither evil nor goodness to the gourd—and yet surrounding the gourd was still the intent that was its driving force. Intent of the original dreamers was lingering as it had since the first instant they had placed it there. Awareness was aware that there was the fear, the anger, the guilt, and the ignorance of the illusion that had given the gourd its energy. The energy had built up over the centuries to the point that the new gourd had been built right above the same place where this original gourd was placed.

Awareness went inside the gourd, where there were some pebbles that now I recognized as the original material from which the creation that perception had invented emerged. There were sixteen small rocks, and all of them contained the original fire and heat that created the entire universe. Amazingly, the small rocks were still hot from the original awareness that had instilled the energy of fire into them.

Here I was in the middle of the gourd, and it felt completely harmless. I looked for Tarrence, but he wasn't with me anymore. Awareness realized that he knew it was up to me to continue with the ceremony. I had no doubt as to what to do next; all doubt had dissolved, since awareness was only aware of emptiness. I realized that the gourd had awareness, and that the ceremony had to continue with the gourd as a living entity.

"Good to see you again," I addressed it.

"Yes. I've been waiting for a long time. I was wondering if you would ever get here, but then, I always knew you would. You sure have taken the long road around though," the gourd replied.

"The first thing I want to do is ask forgiveness for our ignorance and the intent that we placed on you. We were angry and fearful—not to make excuses, but that's how the illusion worked itself out."

"As long as things come full circle—and they always do. The dreamtime cannot be any other way, always a circle: no beginning, no end. And forgiveness is always there; all you have to do is realize it. It's not something you go looking for."

"I'm beginning to realize that, about the circular nature of nature. Even the illusion is a circle that comes back to the beginning, which is the absolute itself."

"Speaking of circles, let me show you something."

Immediately I was in the place on the earth's surface where the dreamers had done the original ceremony and where the dreamers had dreamed the cremation of the earth by building a gourd with fire rocks—the atomic bomb. Awareness was aware of the building and the earth where the dreamers had implanted the gourd I had just been communicating with. Awareness was aware of the past and the future. I could see all of the sorcerers from olden times, as well as the modern sorcerers called scientists, mixing all types of intent with matter in order to release the voice of the awareness in a flash of destructive fire. All of their intent was clear to me as I watched them work. Intent that had greed, fear, and anger as the essence of it. It was the same energy that the original dreamers had placed on the gourd centuries before.

The place felt different now, since I had asked for forgiveness from the gourd. I had also prayed for the gourd and for the stones inside it, just as Tarrence had taught me in the past. Also, I was able to generate love toward the intent that was placed on the gourd by the dreamers, and this had neutralized the fear, anger, guilt, and ignorance. I realized the deep meaning of the Heart Sutra; without the five senses interfering in awareness there was emptiness. Still, intent from the senses had much power on the process of karma itself. Somehow, this was no longer so mysterious, although it's impossible to describe.

My awareness shifted back to my body, which was still sitting and breathing in the cave above. It was a strange experience to witness my relative awareness from the point of view of the absolute awareness that was aware now. I noticed that my relative awareness was focused on the Bald Nun, and that my body was very sexually aroused.

Tarrence interjected, "This is what I've been telling you about. When awareness comes in touch with the absolute, it wants to merge with the absolute. The brain and body illusion can only interpret this in one way, that is, to merge physically with someone—to have sex with that person. Then what? This is the end of the relationship with the absolute, since this causes suffering when done in the ceremonial context. This has been the downfall of many dreamers and healers, and it continues to be their downfall today.

"In every ceremony where there is power, there's the possibility of realizing the absolute, but one has to go through the illusion and understand how the illusion can create a false union with the absolute. This cost you your life once. This distraction leads to other distractions, and the ego becomes very full of itself. Just observe the arousal and gain insight into the nature of the mysterious conjunction with the absolute."

The Bald Nun looked at me and nodded her head in affirmation of Tarrence's words. My awareness moved from relative to absolute awareness that was aware of awareness and then back into the gourd.

"Close one," I heard Beerli whisper to Ms. Chavez.

"Keep going into the future," the gourd said.

It's peculiar, but I found myself simultaneously in the deep cavern and on the surface. Awareness went into the future. I saw Japanese people bringing some of the ruins that were left when the bombs were dropped on Hiroshima and Nagasaki. The ruins were then taken by peoples from all nations who built a shrine that looked just like the one Tarrence described in his logbook. The shrine rested on the exact spot where the dreamers had performed their ceremony both times. People from all tribes came to the shrine to meditate on the awareness and to bring balance to the place. What heals the gourd and balances the evil intent placed here by the dreamers is the intent from the awareness by the meditators at the shrine, as well as their love and compassion.

The gourd spoke again. "This is the ongoing balance. These are the third and fourth gourd ceremonies. Once these ceremonies are done, the balance will be restored to the earth awareness, and the dreamers will once again be in balance with the dream. This balance will allow all of those who are within the earth's perception to move into an awareness that will remove them from the illusion and eventually into the awareness of the absolute dream itself. You have seen it in the future and, as you know, time doesn't exist except in the illusion, so the ceremony of balance is at the beginning and the end of the circle."

Suddenly we were back in the cavern, and the cobra was present.

Morehei spoke in the clairvoyant space created. "The cobra represents the Buddha of compassion. It is only through compassion that this is possible. When I say Buddha, I mean it literally, as in awakening and not as a religion or theology."

The cobra approached the luminescent sphere that had joined us at this level and merged with it. "It's time to emerge," awareness said. As soon as awareness was aware of emerging, I saw my awareness move in a clockwise direction, and I moved through the levels of earth that I had been through on my way to the gourd. When I reached the cave where my body was, I had no sense of how much time had elapsed as far as the illusion was concerned. When I looked at the medallion and the arrowhead in the basket being washed by the spring, I saw that the gourd had joined them.

"It's time to go back in, into the body, that is," I heard the Bald Nun say, as I perceived her hands touching my arm. I felt the Quiet One touch my other arm, and they lifted me to my feet.

"You did a loving thing," the Quiet One said with deep kindness in his voice.

"Yes. Now it's time for the circle to complete itself in the field of space and time," the Bald Nun said.

I wasn't feeling well once I joined my body. The prevailing thought was to move back out where there was freedom, without aches, hunger, or thirst. Every part of my body seemed to hurt, and the pain was amplified by the fact that I had felt no pain for four days.

"Let's go pick up your sacred objects," the Bald Nun said, as she led me to the basket. After I picked up the basket, she led me to the surface, where the dreamers were still sitting in the same place and position.

I made my way to Tarrence, and he gave me his usual crooked smile. I hugged him, and he threw his curled hand around me and kissed me on the cheek. I hugged Ms. Chavez, Beerli, and Morehei.

"Well, we need to finish up here," Tarrence said.

Morehei appeared sad, and I felt sadness within my spirit on hearing these words.

There was a fire in the middle of the circle, and in the near distance, a freshly dug hole in the ground. The Quiet One brought a bucket of water and placed it next to the fire. The Bald Nun brought a basket with blue cornmeal and placed it next to the water.

Morehei, Ms. Chavez, and Beerli moved closer to the fire from all directions. The Quiet One wheeled Tarrence close to the circle. They all looked transformed and impeccable in their purpose. Each of the dreamers took water in a small ladle made out of a gourd with a bamboo handle. They methodically poured the water, four full ladles, into a pan that had been placed on the fire. The dreamers in turn took a pinch of the blue cornmeal and slowly made a circle with it. They presented the cornmeal to the six cardinal points, then slowly lowered it into the boiling water.

Ms. Chavez looked at me and asked me to come close. "Very slowly, pick up some of the cooked cornmeal and give it to Tarrence," she said. "Put it in his mouth for him to eat."

I picked up the cornmeal and presented it to the six cardinal points. I then put it into Tarrence's mouth, and he ate it. He asked me to give him the basket with the medallion, arrowhead, and gourd. He took the gourd and sang four songs. He smiled and handed me the basket with the objects. "Here. These are for you. Use them in a good way. Always remember, all is emptiness. Emptiness is everything. Cling to nothing." He gave me his crooked smile. When he did this, he took a deep breath. He didn't breathe again.

In the distance, the coyote-dog howled six times into the six cardinal directions, as if to accompany Tarrence's spirit into all things.

"The circle has come to the beginning and to the end," Morehei said.

"What do you mean?" I asked, though I knew the answer to this question.

"Tarrence is in the absolute dream, where he will remain now," Ms. Chavez said cheerfully. "His compassion brought him back this one last time just to complete the circle. He's finished with the illusion."

The Quiet One and the Bald Nun brought a wool blanket and wrapped Tarrence in it. They then brought a ceremonial deer hide and wrapped him in that. They carefully picked him up and took him to the freshly dug grave. We all helped to lower him, and we placed him in a sitting position. All that was exposed was his Red Face. The Bald Nun took a basket, and using a piece of rawhide, she tied the basket around his face. The last image of the Red Face I have is the crooked smile that remained there.

"Buddha in Red Face," Morehei said.

"The vision of Padmasambava has come full circle with the Buddha in Red Face," Beerli added somberly.

"Our brother has joined his brother. The Buddha in Yellow Face now can visit with the Buddha in Red Face," Ms. Chavez added.

"All male and female energies will have the compassion of the Buddha in Red Face," said the Quiet One, as he wiped a tear from his eye.

"All female and male energies will co-exist as they always have. Now the illusion will have less of a hold on these, because the awareness has absorbed the Buddha in Red Face," said the Bald Nun.

It was obviously my turn to say something, since I was back in linear time. I thought I ought to say something, but sadness was taking over my body. Then in awareness, I was aware of Tarrence saying "Stay with the breath; don't get distracted."

"I learned love and compassion from the Buddha in Red Face," was all I could say.

Epilogue

*T*his story is told as accurately as I can recall the events that happened in the dreamtime. It was told as it unfolded, and it has a life of its own. I was simply privileged by the forces of the dreamtime to be able to participate in this story—both as someone in the story and as the one telling the story.

Tarrence still comes and visits me in the dreamtime from time to time. He still has his crooked smile and never changes his mantra: "Don't get distracted; let it go; watch the breath."

I realize that the ceremony continues and that the balance has to continue through the building of the shrine where the destruction of the earth was plotted by the dreamers. It will happen; it has already happened in the dreamtime.

In Tarrence's logbook, I found some simple poems, one of which I will pass on as an ongoing blessing from Tarrence.

Yellow fluorescent leaves,
Beauty to the eye of awareness.
Death bringing yellow
Torment to the illusory mind.

Leaves budding ever so slowly,
Mind struggling with impatience.
Non-clinging,
Leaf emerges.

Sunflowers,
Bouncing in the breeze,
Sundancing.

First Snow,
Earth sleeps.
Dreaming of renewal
In spring.

Birth moment,
Same moment Death moment,
Birth, Death.
Impermanence

As I reflect on all that happened, I can only be grateful to the karma that allowed my relative awareness to blend with the Absolute during those days that I was in the ceremonial time. Many of the teachings Tarrence gave me are timeless and relevant to things that are going on in the world today. It is only through awareness, and loving kindness that emerges out of awareness, that we, as a complex of the dreamtime, will have any chance of achieving the wholeness that is already within us. The illusion of ego and self, which thrives on being attached to anger, jealousy, and greed, only serves to perpetuate suffering.

Awareness continues to be aware of being aware by the absolute awareness. Whenever *I* become aware of this, I always turn my awareness of gratitude to the incarnated Buddha in Red Face.

0-595-13898-5

Made in United States
Troutdale, OR
04/25/2025

30898666R00142